PAINTED SIN DUET

A TOUCH OF DARK, A TASTE LIKE SIN

LANA SKY

A TOUCH OF DARK

A Touch of Dark

A Touch of Dark By Lana Sky

Cover Design by Charity Chimni
Editing by Mickey Reed Editing
Formatting by Charity Chimni
Proofreading by Charity Chimni

ONE

he bigger they are, the harder they fall.

I hate that stupid saying, but sometimes it's the only one that fits—poetic justice, in a sense. My father used to be a monolithic figure in this city, a giant in his own right. But then he fell pretty damn hard, inspiring a million cliched headlines.

Ex-Judge Under Fire.

Racial Bias Suspected in Overturned Murder Conviction.

Today's doozy read: **Killer Vindicated?**

Some asshole brought a stack of the latest tabloids to the office and left them in the damn boardroom. To provoke me? Torment me? No matter the reason, any other day, I'd do the daughterly thing and burn them all.

Unfortunately, it's already pushing midnight, and I was able to sequester myself in my office only a few minutes ago. Locked behind the frosted glass door, the fake smile I've been sporting for hours falls flat.

Tonight, my father's drama has to take a backseat for once. What was that line he always spouted?

A man is only as strong as the cracks in his mask.

He loved uttering that one from the bench more than any other saying. As one of the harshest judges in the state, he excelled at peeling back the façades of those in his courtroom and revealing the monsters lurking underneath: Criminal. Liar. Sociopath.

Until now.

Overnight, he's gone from hero to hypocrite and his advice doesn't feel so warranted anymore. Some people wear masks for a fucking reason.

Mainly to hide behind.

Nerves creep down my spine as I finally feel along the wall for the light switch while looking everywhere but at my desk. Alone, I can't suppress what is so easy to hide around a room full of analysts hanging on my every word. None of them suspected what this day truly means to me—at least apart from the "I'm a workaholic" cliché.

How had Sharla from accounting put it? "You must be the only woman in the world who loves when stuffy meetings derail her birthday plans, Ms. Thorne. Like, seriously."

She had a point. The date on the calendar is an ominous reminder: I can't avoid my present forever.

Happy birthday to you.

That awful tune echoes in my mind as I face my desk and spot the beautiful gift someone left beside my computer monitor. A rectangular box wrapped in black paper and topped with an ebony bow.

I know that security footage or the guard downstairs will refute the suspicion that anyone came into my office while I was gone, but there is no erasing *his* presence. My nostrils flare, catching the familiar scent of sweat and cologne, and a grim sense of nostalgia washes over me.

Happy birthday to you.

I flatten my hand against my hip to stop from reaching for the phone. No. I don't need to call my therapist tonight. I'm a big girl. According to that fucking book she made me read, "mentally healthy" people can find the positive in any situation. Think happy thoughts and such.

Like, there will only be ten death threats waiting on my office voicemail once I gather the nerve to check. There's a positive. Score one for optimism.

You and your whole racist family can go fuck yourselves.

I hope you get raped like that Borgetta whore, you bitch.

I'm sure they'd love your daddy in prison.

The insults serve as a fitting soundtrack as I unwrap my present. Surprise. Like every year, I've received a bottle of vintage wine—but it's the thought that counts. Keeping in the spirit of optimism, I choke down my customary sip. Three years of receiving the same brand and I'll never get over the bitter taste. Or the name of the vintage, printed in red on a black label: *Enduring Tradition.*

I continue to sip as I run my fingers over the ebony business card the bottle came with—but I wait until my breathing steadies before flipping the card over. White font forms a simple message:

To another year. — Simon

My hand shakes as I pour more wine into a two-dollar mug scavenged from a drawer. It has a smiley face on the front, beneath the headline: *You're never lonely with a...*

I contort my mouth while eyeing my reflection in the floor-to-ceiling windows across from my desk. The woman staring back at me looks regal in her black Versace cocktail dress—a congratulatory present to myself that I now regret. The wine is worth more.

Adding insult to injury, I look exhausted despite the smile. Nothing like the beaming, prize-winning marketer gazing from the framed photo behind me. To be fair, she's a creation achievable only with the finest coating of makeup and tweaking in photoshop. Juliana Thorne is her name, and I barely know her.

A paragraph-long blurb on the company's website reveals all anyone needs to understand anyway. Selling lies is her one talent, and her résumé is the only interesting thing about her—that and her coveted last name.

Sighing, I set my mug aside. I've wasted enough time. Simon needs his answer after all.

I open another drawer and withdraw a blank postcard before grabbing a pen from the neat row beside my keyboard.

I'm fine. To prove it, I inhale deeply and drag the nib of a pen across the page. It only shakes twice. *To another year,* I write as neatly as I can.

With that, the celebration commences. I swipe my desk clean and tuck the postcard into the pocket of the black coat hanging on a hook behind my office door. Then I sling it over my arm and step out into the hallway that attaches my office to the main suite.

I'm the only one left behind, as per usual. The janitor already switched the lights off, saving me the trouble of having to lock up. So I toss my postcard, addressed only by name, into the outgoing mailbag and then take the elevator to the main lobby. Gus, the security guard, is lounging against his podium, flicking through a skin mag. He looks up at me and winks as I slip past him.

"Happy birthday, girlie," he says. Then he frowns. "Everything all right, Ms. Thorne?"

"Everything's fine."

"Good. I hope you aren't paying attention to the news, either. We all know that beaner got what he deserved. He killed that girl. Your father just had the guts to prosecute. It's not his fault he offed himself, is it?"

When I don't reply, he continues. "I mean, a man like your dad can't have an evil bone in his body, taking in a traumatized little girl out of the goodness of his heart—"

"Goodnight, Gus!" I force a smile before leaving the building, forsaking the heat for the frigid night air.

Outside, my grin falls flat as that mental tune starts up again, building in time with my surging heartbeat. There isn't enough room in my skull to care about my father's legal issues and the narrative being spun around him.

Happy birthday to you... Happy birthday to you.

I grit my teeth to refocus. A town car is already waiting for me out front. The driver appears by my side to usher me inside, and I'm left with only a blurred view of the city to distract me.

That and the chatter of a radio station coincidentally discussing the one topic that seems to be the talk of the town.

"That judge should be stripped of his title," a presenter says. "They only convicted the kid because he was an immigrant—"

"Not just any immigrant though," someone interrupts. "That 'kid' came from a family that isn't exactly innocent. Say what you will, but the Villas have their fingers in some shady stuff. Everyone knows it. But hell, if I wind up in a river tomorrow, we know why—"

"Could you turn that down?" I ask the driver, who complies.

But as silence falls, I quickly realize my mistake when my thoughts turn to what I know is waiting for me at the end of this short trip.

Simon always sends two presents. One goes to the office, which I'll have to open in a public setting. The second comes to my home address—which he manages to find despite how many hotels, motels, or high-rise condos I've rented, booked, or hidden in. The past three years, I've stopped trying to evade him and maintained the same sublet penthouse of a luxury hotel in the heart of downtown. It boasts the highest standard of security around, with cameras in all the halls and guards on twenty-four-hour patrols. I even paid extra for a private floor.

Regardless, like every year, I find a neatly wrapped box waiting before my door.

I stoop for it and unlock my door, knowing that, just like at my office, the guard down below will deny letting anyone up and a review of the cameras will show nothing. After so many years, the fear gripping my chest has become reflexive at this point.

Morbid tradition.

After stepping inside the suite, I cross the foyer and head straight for my bedroom, switching on every light I pass. The gift under my arm feels more familiar than the modern apartment with its open floorplan and gray color scheme. In a sick way, he became my fixture, Simon. No matter what, I could always count on him.

We will always play our game.

Tonight, I set the gift on the edge of my bed and fish a bottle of wine from under the mattress first. My toes curl shamefully. *Coward.* This brand is cheaper than the stuff he sent me and burns going down. I chug right from the bottle until my stomach aches and the world spins around me, a merry-go-round of monochrome. Only now do I sink to the floor and wrestle the gift onto my lap.

Happy, happy birthday.

He chose red wrapping paper, like always. *Her* favorite color. I run my fingers over the surface of it. Malicious intent lingers in the neatly folded corners and carefully applied pieces of tape. He selected the color of the bow, too. It's a deep, rich shade of purple. *My* favorite.

Details like that mattered to children the most. A favorite color, betrayed by a shirt or backpack, could spark a friendship over lunch with few words spoken. It was a craft you could hone to a T if you knew what to look for. The loner girl lurking around the edges, shuffling her brand-new shoes in the hopes they'd be noticed by someone. Anyone.

A good monster could prey on that weakness and turn anxiety into trust. I used to excel at it.

Enough reminiscing. A forced exhale can't ease the tension seizing my lungs as I unwind the ribbon and lift the lid.

Swaths of white tissue paper shield the objects inside. The first is a newspaper clipping. **Local Girl Missing** proclaims the headline. In the body of the article, the writer went straight to the point. *Seven-year-old Leslie Matoda disappeared shortly after four p.m. on October 28th…*

I stop reading. The article slips from my fingers and the wine bottle replaces it. Two hard pulls and the resulting dizziness almost erase the guilt searing a hole through my stomach. Almost. Squeezing my eyes shut can't block out the memories, however.

Naked trees formed a silent audience as he placed the knife to her throat.

"Now remember," he warned. "Simon says play…"

I gulp down more red liquid. Less clarity. Dizzy. Dizzier. It's no use. Terror crawls up my throat like bile until my mouth opens and only noise comes out. High-pitched and broken.

Damn it.

I'm *not* breaking. I'm practicing. My therapist is a fan of therapeutic screaming. "Try it into your pillow," she likes to suggest every other session. "I think you'll benefit from a cathartic release, Juliana."

Bullshit. Screaming couldn't help me then and it doesn't help me now. Not when smothered into my white duvet or muffled behind my hands. Crying doesn't, either. Or shouting.

It's only when I stumble into the bathroom and plow my fist into the mirror—sending glass shattering over the sink—that I finally feel something. Icy numbness followed by burning, stinging pain as drops of ruby-red moisture splatter my white color scheme.

But it's not punishment enough.

I slam my bleeding, aching hands onto the counters so hard they throb. Bruise. I kick dents into the cabinet doors and rip the gray shower curtain from the rail. It's still not enough.

It never is.

Neither is reentering my bedroom, yanking all the beautiful, expensive clothing from my closet, and tossing the pieces onto the floor. Or shoving my mattress from the frame. Breaking glass. Throwing objects. Smashing. Destroying. Obliterating.

I run out of steam near the foyer and only have enough energy left to topple the glass grandfather clock that guards the entrance to my suite. With a monstrous roar, it smashes to pieces, much like everything else in my life at the moment.

Happy birthday to me…

And many more.

TWO

J never get drunk. What in college was a fun quirk now feels like a curse. Or perhaps a biological defect inherited from my birth father. The man couldn't bother to remember my birthday, but he gave me a gift that keeps on giving: I can drink to my heart's content without ever blacking out. It helps that my stash of wine makes for a delicious diversion while providing no reprieve from the horrors I desperately seek escape from.

As Daddy would call it, *quite the conundrum.*

If only I weren't too much of a coward to move on to another vice. I'd give anything to finally utilize the prescription the new therapist wrote weeks ago, shoved inside my nightstand drawer. Maybe peace lurks within a different bottle? Bite-sized calm at a grand a pop?

As it stands now, I have nothing but five lamps in this room alone, turned to their highest settings, to combat the dark.

Thunderstorms worsen the onslaught of flashbacks. Like the storm I sense now, rumbling in the distance. The air is too still. Ebony clouds swirl along the horizon before the stillness breaks with a monstrous roar of thunder.

The taste of copper burned my tongue. I couldn't spit it out. He was behind me, prowling over the underbrush like a living shadow, impossible to outrun.

Guttural and low, his voice chased me. "Come out, come out, Juliana..."

Wait. A girlish bit of laughter doesn't belong in this memory. The images of the forest fade and I'm in my apartment again, gasping for air.

Despite this being a private, residential floor, the odd intruder isn't too uncommon. Most people wonder what it's like to live here in the Lariat Hotel, in the proverbial lap of luxury.

All they have to do is ask me and I'd tell them.

It's a charming, gilded prison.

The voices, one male and the other a giggling woman, draw me from my fetal position. I leave bloody streaks as I cling to the wall for balance and look out through the peephole. Two intruders wander the hall, both wearing cheaply made party clothes. I have toilet paper worth more than this girl's dress. Soft, bright pink, no expert tailoring in sight.

Her voice, breathy and high-pitched, sounds distorted through the door—but it's not Simon's, so I strain my ears to pick up every nuance. "I think we're lost." She giggles while leading her male friend by the hand. He keeps pulling on the sleeves of his oversized suit jacket but copies her manic, pixie grin.

"You just want to get back to that freak, don't you?" he teases. "Maybe we can get him to paint you like that. Naked and shit—"

"Knock it off!" She strikes him playfully on the shoulder, and they disappear down the corner, leaving laughter behind like breadcrumbs.

Freak? Painting? Naked?

The thread of a mystery entices me more than continuing my birthday celebrations. For now. Some Band-Aids and a pair of gloves disguise my bleeding cuts. For added armor, I slip my winter coat on and I've almost reassembled my façade.

Almost.

A glance in the mirror hanging near the door reveals the dreadful state of my makeup. God, I look awful, my eyeliner smeared and my lipstick faded. Sighing, I swipe it off and salvage what I can beneath a stern expression.

I never cry. I'm the woman who conquers the world with a frown and a mild shade of red lipstick. But bloodshot eyes give me away now. I see myself for what I really am: a fraud. A pretender. A goddamn murderer.

Stop it. I catch my bottom lip between my teeth and bite down hard enough to chase the thought away. Then I scramble for the door and enter the hall as thunder snarls. There's no sign of the couple, their trail of laughter now cold. I'm forced to chase their scent. Cheap perfume. Cloying cologne. I follow the smells to the set of elevators on the other end of the hall and take one down to the lobby.

I usually avoid this entrance. Guests and visitors alike flood in through glass doors at all hours. It's noisy and loud—kryptonite to my nerves. Tonight, the atmosphere feels even more electrified than usual. A glance ahead reveals why. A crowd swells beyond the lobby doors, held back by the hotel's security. Blurred faces jockey for space along the glass, illuminated by intermittent camera flashes. Reporters. For me? Daddy's house has been swarmed for months, but no one has bothered me yet.

My palms start to sweat, which irritates the open cuts, and breathing takes more focus. Ironically, there's a remedy for the anxiety nearby: the lobby bar directly to my left. Oh, the promise of more wine. Merlot makes for a tempting diversion, but something else catches my attention before I can claim a stool for myself.

Misery loves company, and I'm not the only one having a shitty night.

"How was I supposed to know?" a woman hisses into a cell phone. Hunched against the wall, she draws notice anyway, being tall, blond, and dressed to the nines in a black suit. Clutched in her free hand is a clipboard she's waving through the air like a shield against guilt.

"Look. I had no idea he'd be this pissed off. I saw the address on some documents in his studio and they had amazing rates and—" She purses her red lips. "No. It's too late to change it now. I think he's on his way. I have to go."

She hangs up and crosses the reception hall to stand near an archway that has a sign propped on an easel beside it. The real reason behind the sudden increase in publicity? The hotel sometimes hosts events open to the public. In fact, I've booked a few for clients of mine here and there. Book signings. Galas.

A Window into the Soul this advert reads, red font printed over a black backdrop. *Displaying the art of Sampson.* I'd recommend the design to my own clients: It's simple but bold enough to draw the eye to the artist's name.

Sampson. I've never heard of him, though I appear to be in the minority. People are waiting in a sizeable line to enter the ballroom, craning their necks for a glimpse through the doorway.

"Miss?" The woman with the clipboard watches me expectantly from the distance of a four-person gap. I've wandered into the line without realizing. "Do you have a ticket?"

I shake my head, and she nods.

"Don't worry. Sampson appreciates every guest, and we always offer vouchers at the door. I just need your name."

"Juliana Thorne," I say, stepping forward. "What exactly is this…"

My gaze cuts toward the doorway behind the woman and whatever else I meant to say dies in my throat. I'm vaguely aware that I'm still moving, drawn forward like a moth to a flame.

The portrait hanging from the wall ahead is a woman composed of ivory, lying contorted on a bed of blood-red roses, her eyes unseeing, her hands grasping at nothing. Etched with incredible care, she looks livelier than the person I see whenever I look in a mirror.

Woefully alive and yet painfully dead.

The artist didn't spare an ounce of detail. Every wayward hair, pimple, birthmark, and scar of his subject is on display in stark clarity.

"Incredible, isn't it?" someone exclaims beside me.

"W-what?" I blink as the rest of the world returns one jarring realization at a time. For starters, I'm standing in the back of the ballroom, nearly nose-to-nose with a painting hanging from the wall. A sheet of glass separates me from it and displays my reflection.

Wide-eyed. Mouth agape. Pupils dilated. Red lips that quirk into a frown. I've never seen this look on my face before. I take my time trying to pin down just what it might be but fail to come up with a single term.

"Here, you forgot to take this."

A glossy brochure makes its way into my hands courtesy of the blond woman who worked the door.

She catches me staring and winks. "I felt the same way the first time I saw one of his works. Enjoy." She scurries off, leaving me to survey the rest of the gallery alone.

Twenty women join the first, trapped in their own worlds of darkness and roses. Observed together, they rip me from the elegant setting, dragging me into each brutal scene. Flowers. Passion. Death. Those are the recurring themes.

I'm no art connoisseur, but I can recognize talent—and this artist oozes it in every brushstroke, along with a million other tiny details. Such as his indifference to his subjects. The cruel attention given to the fear lurking in those blank irises. The cold, twisted elegance of lifeless limbs.

Each portrait pulls me in before I'm swept along to the next. Far too soon, I find myself before the first painting again, unable to toe the respectful distance every other spectator keeps. Curiosity yanks me closer against my will, step by step.

Finally, I reach out with a trembling finger—

Commotion.

I turn and find a gaggle of people huddling together in the center of the ballroom, jockeying for a glimpse of someone: a man whose sheer presence urges people from his path. Literally. The crowd parts like the Red Sea.

"It's him," I see a woman mouth to her companion, wide-eyed.

Him. The lone unaffected figure, I presume. A man who takes my breath away—the same way walking outside, butt-ass naked in the dead of winter would.

Suddenly and lethally.

My father is—was—a judge, and I'm more than used to imposing men. We had politicians who controlled the livelihoods of the entire state over for breakfast. I lived in the mayoral mansion for three years. Summered with the governor's children.

Neither Daddy nor those in his orbit ever commanded a room as this man does. And for that, I count my blessings. Simon is terrifying enough to live in the shadow of—and he's just a shadow.

This man is darkness. He stands tall, wearing black almost from head to toe: a tailored suit that screams of old money and careful taste—and brawn. The ebony material strains over broad shoulders and muscular forearms.

Trailing my gaze upward, I expect a face worthy of the intrigue, but he's like one of these paintings: a mixture of handsome and strange. A stern jaw anchors what I can only assume are Romanesque features, mingled with a hint of the exotic, though a dark blindfold obscures most of them, hiding his eyes. It's tied neatly over the bulk of a black ponytail that reaches down to his shoulders.

Such a strange accessory, though it doesn't appear to hinder his confident stride.

"I can't believe it's him in the flesh," a woman nearby whispers. "He doesn't look like a kingpin."

Is he a celebrity of some kind? Or maybe the artist himself? I browse the brochure in my grip, but it only contains representations of the paintings, never their creator.

When I look up again, he's holding court in the back corner of the ballroom as men in black suits stand guard nearby, intimidating the crowd from coming too close. Beside the blindfolded man is the blond woman. Her gaze cuts in my direction as her lips move rapidly near his ear.

I turn back to the painting and try to shut the rest of the world out again. It's surprisingly easy to, the longer I stare. No need for pills or booze. Just soulless eyes formed from intricate strokes of paint.

The woman could be me in the right lighting. Therefore, she's the perfect canvas to project all my flaws onto. Alive, I bet she wore Versace and hated her birthday.

I bet she hated herself.

The longer I stare, the uncannier the resemblance seems. Am I seeing more of my reflection than the art? I brush my fingers against the glass, but I can't decipher what's paint and what's reflection.

"Do not touch, *por favor*." The deep voice accompanies the hand seizing my wrist without warning.

I shiver and whirl around. Then my brain stalls, spitting out a few disjointed thoughts before total malfunction. *Handsome. Dark. Up close.*

"The glass is fragile," the blindfold-wearing man warns. His voice is deeper than I expected by looking at him. Suave, grated tones fall like off-notes from a piano. Jarringly out of place.

"Sorry," I croak, wrenching my hand back. My heart races, surging beneath my skin. Strange. I press my fingers there, counting each frantic beat. Thump. Thump. Thump. "S-sorry," I repeat.

His jaw tightens in an elegant display of rippling muscle. "You need to leave."

"I…I'm sorry?" People are staring. Probably at me: openmouthed, my cheeks flaming. "I didn't mean—"

"I'll have my men escort you out." He nods, beckoning one of the stern-faced bouncers closer.

"W-wait."

Just leave, Juliana, a part of me urges. I have a birthday to conclude. Screams to smother. Dealing with some conceited prick should be an easy headache to tick off my to-do list. Or not.

"Are you the artist?" I ask.

At the sound of my voice, he grits his teeth. A silent denial? Or grudging acknowledgment?

"I…I'm interested in buying. I think."

"Are you even familiar with the artist's work?" A droll quality laces his tone. Amusement? No, something darker that makes me quiver in my heels before I can help it: hostility.

Another "admirer" of my family, perhaps? I bite my lip and resist the urge to kick myself for not taking Daddy's advice to hire a bodyguard. To be fair, my reasoning made sense at the time. Why pay for someone who would always prove ineffective against the real monster?

"Are you?"

My cheeks heat when I realize I still haven't answered him. "No," I say. "I've actually never heard of him until tonight."

"Oh?" He runs the edge of his thumb along his chin. I can't shake the feeling that the act draws attention to his face on purpose.

Again, I suspect he knows me as more than just a story from the tabloids. But I don't know him. "And your thoughts?"

The change in subject is enough to give me whiplash. "Well…" I return my attention to the painting. Nice would be the polite word—or something along those lines. Something to strike up a conversation around. Any other day, I'd know what to say. Tonight, I'm filter-less. "I think…I think it's terrible."

"Terrible?" The man laughs. "How so?"

"I…" I shrug, once again compelled toward honesty. "Not in a bad way."

"This isn't the place for you." His warm breath heats my earlobe and chills me to the core, making me jump. "I suggest you leave. Now."

"Why?" I counter, surprised by how irritated I sound. "If you recognize me from the news, I'm not drawing attention to myself."

"If?" he wonders, his tone dangerously soft. "Perhaps you've recognized me from the 'news'?"

"No." I feel like I've missed something. Maybe he is a celebrity—some pompous prick with his head so far up his ass that he can't stand not being recognized. "I think I'd remember you," I say.

A shadow flickers over the glass in front of me as I sense him looming over my position from behind. He smells strange up this close. My flared nostrils gobble up the scent but I can't place it.

"One would think *you* would."

I know he's gone without having to turn around, but the aftermath of his tone ricochets through me. I should do what he said: leave. But before I can take a step, my gaze returns to the painting and I'm riveted once more. It's as if the woman's dead stare perfectly sees through everything I try to hide and, unlike the rest of the world, she gives it to me straight.

You'll never fit in.

"Excuse me, miss."

The blond woman from the door yanks me from my reverie for the second time. She's lost her clipboard, clutching a stack of brochures in her hands instead.

"I'll leave in a minute," I insist.

"Oh, but I'm sorry. The gallery is closing." She gestures behind her. Sure enough, the crowd has dissipated. I'm the only guest remaining.

"Oh."

A tendril of anxiety gnaws away at the lining of my stomach. No, not yet. Five more minutes. Or maybe longer.

"How much is this one?" The question is out before I can reel it back in.

Impulsivity. It's one of the many traits my therapist urged me to work on. Acting on impulse led me to alcohol. Bad decisions. Oopsies. Mistakes.

"How much?" The woman blinks. "I-I'm not sure, but Mr. Sampson's work has sold in the tens of thousands before—"

"What about twenty?"

"I-I don't—"

"Fifty, then." I step closer to the painting, leaving her to decide on an answer, even as I reach into my pocket for my checkbook.

Odd. This painting makes for the first birthday present I've wanted in years. One dark enough to rival even Simon's grim offerings.

Happy birthday to me.

THREE

ome out, come out, Juliana…

I bolt upright, drenched in a cold sweat as my eyes fly open to my empty room, and the icy noose of fear loosens with the realization that I'm alone. It was just a bad dream, though Simon wasn't the nightmarish figure who chased me awake this time.

No. My pursuer sported a blindfold, his motives a mystery but his hatred more electric than the flashes of lightning greeting me from beyond my window.

An omen?

Or a reminder. Simon's days of gift giving aren't over yet. He always allows me twenty-four hours in between our games, but no more.

Usually, I'd spend that time stocking up on wine, but I'm forced to oversee the cleaning crew tasked with reassembling the shambles of my apartment first. They fix my bedframe and repair the damage to my closet, assembling the clothes in the correct color-coded order. One benefit of using the same company every year is that the workers know my preferences—but they never ask questions. I pay extra to ensure that.

I also order them to avoid the bathroom. For now, anyway.

Afterward, I catch up on a bit of work and find a message on my cell phone from Heyworth Thorne. *See you tonight, sweetie.*

Every year, he humors just one request, a truce of sorts: We forsake dinner on my actual birthday, but the night after, he insists.

How he loves to show me off. Perfect little Juliana: the traumatized brat he took in out of kindness and turned into an upstanding citizen. Presto! Like magic.

Love makes it easier to withstand the lying, but never the guilt. God, I wish I could be that person for him. The perfect daughter. I try. I've tried. But being her is like wearing a pretty dress. After a while, it itches. The material wears away at the seams. It tears.

Until it isn't so beautiful anymore.

Tonight, my disguise will be a black Vera Wang paired with something navy. Hmmm. I scour the glass display case along the back wall and hunt for a fitting necklace. The sapphire Daddy gave me a few years ago will do.

With my costume all picked out, I linger in the living room and watch the world waste away down below. The real estate agent referred to this view as "to die for." Maybe she's right. Three years spent where Simon can easily find me and one glance from the window makes the torment almost worth it.

I can watch people play out their lives from this height without them ever being the wiser. That woman walking her poodle has performed the same routine for two hundred and seventy-two days in a row. There are no calls from Simon to disrupt her charming façade. No. It's the scruffy man she lets creep into her house late at night when only the glow of passing traffic can illuminate him.

They do their song and dance day in and day out, but she never forgets to wear her pretty smile in the aftermath.

I practice mine in the reflection on the window. Wide, but not too wide.

I almost fool myself.

A sudden knock on the door interrupts my practice and a frown flutters across my lips, displacing my hard-earned expression. But then I remember.

Giddy. That's the only way to describe the bubbling sensation building in the pit of my stomach as I pad across the foyer and answer the door.

The blond woman from the gallery stands on the other end of it. She's exchanged the pantsuit for a gray skirt-and-blouse combo.

"Ms. Thorne?"

I nod, and she steps aside, revealing a man behind her pushing something long and square balanced on a utility cart.

"I took the liberty of accepting your bid on Mr. Sampson's behalf," the woman explains. "Were you still interested in the painting?"

"Yes." I lurch out of the way, allowing them inside.

Due to disposal limitations, the earlier cleaners left the glass shards of my grandfather clock in a bin near the door for later pickup, though I had them wipe the blood from the walls, at least. The woman eyes the mess before directing her attention to the empty wall adjacent to the floor-to-ceiling windows. Prime real-estate for a morbid portrait, apparently.

"Here?"

I agree and the worker snaps to attention. He removes a plastic covering, revealing the painting. When viewed in the overcast daylight filtering into the room, it looks grislier than it did last night. Ghostly and harrowing. I suck in an appreciative breath and write the fifty grand off as money well spent.

Once the painting is mounted, my one regret is not buying a matching frame for it. Encased only in a covering of protective glass, it looks far too delicate against my muted design scheme.

"Mr. Sampson appreciates your patronage," the woman says once I've signed the final document she shoved beneath my nose. "I'll let you in on a secret: He donates most of the proceeds to charity anyway. Though I have to say that not everyone appreciates his work."

"Oh?" I bite back the words that spring to my tongue. *No wonder.* If he treats every prospective buyer like he did me, I can imagine why.

"I'm surprised you haven't asked about him," she adds, an eyebrow raised. "No offense, but the few who do buy the paintings—and they all are mostly women—tend to use the sale as a foothold to pry. 'Are all the stories true?'" She mimics how I assume she thinks a socialite with thousands of dollars to spend on a painting sounds. "I will say I'm impressed. I think that's why I'm even here in the first place. He rarely offers a painting for sale, but hopefully he won't mind. At least you won't try to hound him for a date. To some women, he's more myth than reality now."

I picture the mysterious figure from last night and shrug. "I know what it's like to have people pry into my life. Sometimes, the intrigue is better than the reality."

"Fair enough," the woman says, but I can tell she's still bemused as I escort her out.

Alone, I finish another cup of coffee and find myself gazing at the painting, desperate to decipher the secrets lurking beneath every layer of paint.

Sampson. I've never heard of him—and in this city, anonymity only extends to those who don't matter at all or those who matter too much. Privacy is a commodity even I can't afford.

I'm tempted to look him up. Try my hand at Google. A part of me doesn't want to, however. Maybe that's the fun of it all. The allure. My first ever birthday present to myself in over twenty years and I don't even know who made it for me. Or why. Or what possessed him to blend death with flowers. Beauty with horror.

Or why he seems to despise me.

I'll never find out.

And unlike my dealings with Simon, I don't have to.

FOUR

a town car arrives for me at six on the dot. After cajoling the driver into taking the long route to the suburbs, I spend a majority of the ride silently rehearsing my lines in a compact mirror.

Hello, Daddy. Pause and smile. *I've been fine.* Blink. *You look wonderful, and so does Diane.* Flash an even bigger smile, and then the finale, uttered with a mischievous tilt of my head. *Will there be cake?*

It's the same script I've recited at every other birthday dinner, and he never demands more—only that I show up and let him have this one day. A handful of hours when we both can pretend that my past doesn't matter.

I owe him that much.

Determined to put on the best performance, I pour all my energy into arranging my flawless outfit and perfecting that easy, confident smile. I'm ready by the time the driver turns onto the long driveway leading to the secluded, astronomical-acre plot Daddy bought the moment he retired.

Squaring my shoulders, I exit the car and put my rehearsed steps into motion. Smile first. Confident walk. The moment I mount the first stone step leading to the door, it opens from the inside as if on cue.

And my stomach drops right to my stiletto heels.

Daddy is wearing that tired gray suit from his glory days and a pinched expression. No warm smile. No arms outstretched for our customary hug. Instead, he ushers me inside with a wave of his hand. "Welcome home, sweet pea."

I follow him uneasily. The house doesn't feel the same despite the cheery coat of yellow paint brightening the entryway. Something's wrong. A subtle tinge in the air renders everything out of place. Odd. Off. The feeling grows as we enter the private study—not the dining room down the hall, where I know everyone else is waiting, poised to shout "Surprise!" on sight.

Glimpsed from the side, my father's expression is as stern as it used to be when he was on the bench and nearly jumped out of his skin every time someone said "boo" to me.

"Juliana..." He sighs, and a telling sent wafts from his breath. Tobacco.

I raise an eyebrow. "Have you been smoking?"

"That doesn't matter." Concern weighs his weathered features down, exaggerating the wrinkles around his eyes and his mouth. He looks so old today.

Maybe I look older. I can't tell in the reflection staring back at me from the glass case displaying various legal paraphernalia. My face is transposed over one of his many awards. How fitting. I'm part woman. Part trophy.

"Juliana?"

"I'm fine—"

"You look tired." He smooths a wayward lock of hair away from my face. "Is it the storms?"

Storms. His subtle way of skirting around the dangerous topic we never mention directly: the past.

"We're in the middle of a particularly violent system according to the newscasters, sweet pea," he adds. "Maybe you should sleep here until it passes? Diane's kept the white noise machine you used to use, and there's spare Zofran in the medicine cabinet—"

"I'm fine," I lie. "They don't even bother me anymore."

"That's good…" His hand settles over my shoulder, imparting the comfort and vulnerability only he can.

Like always, I'm a child again around him. Heyworth Thorne, my hero. He saved me when I was only eight years old, from more than just a psychopath. He's tried his best to dust off my cracks and piece my broken mind together.

I smile hard to let him know that he has—force of habit.

But, this time, he doesn't smile back.

"There's something else, darling," he begins cautiously. "I know you won't agree, so I'll just come right out and say it. I want to put a guard on you. Full time. It's just for a little while and I'll ensure they stay out of sight."

"What?" My pretty little mask slips. Over twenty years of secrets. Have I blown the game already? "Why?"

I push past him and brace my hands on the desk to keep standing. Ice solidifies in my veins, choking the air from my lungs. I force in a breath and let it out. In. Out.

"I didn't mean to scare you." He closes the door to his office and comes to my side to dab at my dry eyes with a handkerchief. Another force of habit.

If we can't perform our charming father-daughter routine, we fall into the only other roles we know how to play. Protector and victim.

"It's just… There's a threat," he says. "Against me, but there's no reason to believe that this person won't attempt to target you."

"Target me?" I don't say the obvious: as if they haven't already. But the phrasing means he isn't referring to Simon. Someone new perhaps. "Who?" I ask, steeling myself for the answer.

These days, most of the city is out for Thorne blood. My gaze lands over the newspaper on his desk, and sure enough, emblazoned on the front page is a quote from a legal analyst on the Borgetta ruling: *Any man tasked with upholding the law should do his due diligence to ensure that no bias affects his ruling. In this case, the bias is clear: Mathias Villa was doomed for nothing more than the color of his skin.*

I stop reading, surprised to discover that it isn't the only topic to make the headlines. A glossy photo of the Lariat ballroom gleams beneath a row of text reading **Reclusive Artist Dazzles at First Public Showing.**

"Don't read that trash." Daddy snatches up the paper and tosses it into the wastebasket. Before I can question it, he forces a grin. "And let's not talk about the nitty details now. It's your special night. Did you enjoy yesterday?"

I nod. Strange. The motion doesn't feel like lying. "I did. I even bought myself a present."

"A present?" He cocks his head. "That does sound like a good day. What did you buy?"

"A painting." In some ways, I'm still riveted by the piece. Pale flesh intertwined with ruby red. Stark violence and beautiful irony.

Heyworth Thorne most likely wouldn't approve.

"A painting," he mutters while fiddling with his tie. He did the same thing the night his first wife died and he tried to explain to a fifteen-year-old me how accidental overdoses happened. "It's almost funny that you'd mention something like that…" He sighs again, more heavily this time.

I gently touch his shoulder. "Daddy?"

He's never looked *this* tired. This old. "Have you heard of someone named Damien Villa?"

"I don't think so." Though the name does ring a bell, I'm not sure why. No face comes to mind anyway.

"You should have," Daddy snaps, a hard note in his voice. "I told you: You need to be more attentive. Especially where that godforsaken place is concerned." He jerks his head in the general direction of the city and scoffs. "Damien Villa is the head of one of the cruelest crime syndicates on this side of the country. *La Muerte.*"

All I can do is feign interest while he watches me expectantly. "That sounds intimidating."

"Try murderous," he replies. "They work as the American arm for a Colombian cartel, though he's supposedly reformed. Some say his brother runs it still. He's a monster and a goddamn madman, but because he has enough money to throw around, he's making trouble for me where it matters."

"Are you okay?" It isn't like him to curse. Or glare so harshly that the vein in his forehead lurches against his skin. "Is he threatening you?"

"Ha! At least then I could do something about it," he snaps. "The bastard is too clever to do that, at least not outright. But…he's not above planting rumors. Some of them may even pertain to you, and if you hear anything—anything at all—you must promise to come to me first—"

"Why?" I take a step toward him, but he hunches his shoulders away from me. "Is this about…"

His sigh is unwilling confirmation. On principle, we've rarely broached the topic of the Borgetta murder case, but in the tumult of information spilling through the airwaves, I've heard enough to last a lifetime.

The details are foggy, but I remember the gist: a woman, Emily Borgetta, daughter of a prominent politician, was brutally raped and murdered by a man with ties to organized crime. Daddy threw the book at him: life served in the cruelest prison in the state. Ten years later, a lack of evidence allowed some appeals court to not only overturn his conviction, but declare him innocent—but a few weeks before the final decision went public, the man killed himself in prison. Now, everyone in the world is a legal analyst, the most ignorant of them claiming racial bias in the original judgment. Most spectators settle for calling my father incompetent. Or evil. Whichever looks better in a headline.

After he spent nearly a lifetime on the bench, this case has become a black stain on an otherwise glowing record—and it's killing him.

"I'm asking again: Did he threaten you?" Now doesn't feel like the right time to mention my own log of menacing voicemails. "We could always go public. Do a news conference."

"No." Daddy clenches his fists so hard that his knuckles whiten. "Oh, he wouldn't give me the satisfaction. That sick bastard—" He cuts himself off and meets my gaze directly. "He's dangerous, Juliana. Especially now. And as for a news conference… I haven't told you before, but I've decided to run again, despite these disgusting allegations. I'm announcing it officially at a press conference soon, and I want you to be there. I need you to be there."

I digest the news in silence and wind up observing my hands. They shake. Flattening them against the desk's surface can't disguise it.

After five long years, it's fitting that Heyworth Thorne would choose now, of all times, to jump back into the fray and defend his name. The dread knotting in my stomach is more selfish than anything. Whenever he campaigns, his surveillance of me becomes obsessive. Not that increased patrols have ever stopped Simon before.

But no. It's more than that. An uneasy Daddy means more questions. More covert calls to my therapist to ensure I'm complying with my sessions. The return of his surprise visits to my apartment to discreetly check that I don't have wine stockpiled in the fridge.

He loves me.

He loves his reputation more.

"Don't worry, Daddy," I say, sweetly uttering my expected line. "I'll be fine."

"I'm still getting you a bodyguard." His hardened expression warns I won't be able to change his mind with a bat of my eyelashes. "You won't even know he's there. So don't hold too big of a grudge, eh?" He props my chin against the pad of his thumb and contorts his lips into what passes for a smile. "Now what do you say we get this evening started right? Diane made your cake."

I nod, and we exit his office. It's only on our way through the foyer that I remember what sparked the morbid turn in our conversation in the first place.

"Damien Villa," I start as Daddy waves off someone peeking around the corner who quickly scurries out of sight. "What does he have to do with painting?"

"He owns a gallery," Daddy says, slowing his steps. We're close enough to the dining room to hear the muffled commotion coming from within. Eight people I suspect. The same mixture of family, friends, and neighbors who attend every year. "The police suspect it's how he launders a majority of his money. He's used the prestige and other so-called legitimate business ventures to amass enough political sway to pressure my old donors."

"Why?" I ask. "What does he have against you?"

"Don't worry about him." Daddy takes my hand and gives it an impatient tug. "I'll tell you another day, sweet pea. For now, how about we make this night something to remember?"

I recognize the tremor in his voice. He's pleading, and the scared, desperate little girl I used to be rears her ugly head.

Keeping him happy means smiling on cue.

Maintaining the façade.

Being perfect, darling, wonderful Juliana.

"Sure, Daddy." I beam and step around him, my script at the ready. "You look wonderful, by the way. And you said Diane made cake? Oh, how considerate."

At last, he returns my grin with one of his own, and arm in arm, we enter the dining room to shouts of "Surprise!" The biggest one of all being how my smile doesn't slip once, even as my mental clock continuously tracks the passage of time.

Tick. Tock.

FIVE

I'd kill someone with my bare hands for a glass of wine. Just one. From the good, cheap bottle tucked behind my headboard, preferably. Daddy wouldn't approve, but hell, I've earned his love tonight.

Like the best daughter, I simpered and charmed and had the most "wonderful" not-birthday birthday dinner in existence.

But I'm not ready to receive my next gift.

Lost in my thoughts, I didn't have the sense to request that the driver take the usual detour, so we've arrived at the Lariat way too soon.

Too early.

Simon prefers for me to stumble across his presents rather than lie in wait. A glance at my watch draws a sigh from my lips. Way too early. There's at least an hour to kill.

As I step out onto the curb, I consider the bar. It beckons me from beyond a glittering row of windows. Oh, the promise of salty, stale, expensive wine.

On my way into the lobby I notice that the poster advertising the art of Sampson is still there. A steady line of people streams in and out at the discretion of the blond woman with her trademark clipboard.

She spots me from across the lobby and smiles. "Couldn't stay away?"

Maybe not. The distraction promised by wine isn't as appealing as the cruel honesty of death and floral arrangements, apparently. I'm slipping into the crowd of eager voyeurs before I know it. An unseen figure presses another brochure into my hands, but nothing holds my attention for long—apart from the maze of canvases.

Sampson likes his subjects nude. And it seems he never paints the same woman twice. They all stare from various angles, wide-eyed and contorted in some grotesque pose. Despite the myriad of differences, one feature always appears in every single portrait: pink lips, slightly parted. A knowing, petulant pout.

As if every muse relished her master's attention, right down to the final stroke.

"I thought I'd find you here."

I recognize the crisp voice of the blond woman. I turn to face her, realizing that, once again, I'm left staring long after the thick of the crowd has dissipated.

"I don't do this often," she says before I can apologize, "and I must say that Sampson isn't very fond of humoring admirers. But, as his manager, I'll take the liberty of schmoozing anyone willing to buy. I'm Carla, by the way."

She presses something against my palm. A business card, black and sleek with a glossy finish. Déjà vu strikes like a lance and I nearly drop it. It's so similar to Simon's calling card...

This font, however, is industrial silver. The address printed on one side is presumably Sampson's base of operations.

"I can't guarantee a meeting in person," the woman warns. "But I won't exactly turn you away if you'd like to look at his more… obscure collection."

"Oh?"

Her mischievous wink ignites my curiosity. What pieces might a man like this deem too distasteful for the public eye? My chest tightens at the thought. From disgust? Or anticipation? I'm not in a hurry to decide.

Instead, I finger the card's glossy front before slipping it inside my pocket. If I call a town car now, it would be roughly a ten-minute trip, delaying my opening of Simon's gift just a little longer.

But would the delay be worth it?

I can't settle on an answer during the short trip back to the lobby. The usual crush of people has dispersed, leaving just a few tenants and visitors milling about. This time of year, everyone wears some variation of a heavy coat, disguising the bulk of their features. Could one of them be Simon concealing my present beneath the winter layers?

I'd never know. He prefers to haunt me from afar, always watching. It's his elusiveness that makes him so terrifying, especially back then…

"Are you okay, miss?" A hand brushes my shoulder, belonging to a security guard.

I nod and have no choice but to enter the elevator to keep up the façade.

I'm okay.

At least I am during the silent ride to my floor. Then the elevator doors part and my ruse slips once I find an empty hall, no wayward visitors in sight.

No distraction.

Slow, heavy steps carry me to my door. My palms sweat inside their gloves, which aggravates the healing scrapes. I shake them firmly in a vain attempt to dispel the nervous energy. When that fails, I lie to myself. *You're ready.*

Or not.

As I round the corner, my eyes fixate on the glossy numbers on my door first before roving downward…

And settle on my gray welcome mat.

Five seconds of searching pass before I finally accept that it's empty.

My stomach churns, wrestling with the remains of overly sweet cake and non-alcoholic champagne. How I hate surprises. For the first time in years, Simon's late. Either that or he's settled on a new spot to leave my first gift of the night. Inside? I take my time fishing my keys from my pocket, but the door budges at the slightest touch, already opened a hairline crack.

I shove my hand into my pocket for my cell phone, but I can't explain what makes me push the door open wider without calling 911. Yet.

The light switch lurks just beyond my reach, but I don't flip it. I have a visitor, it seems, who prefers the darkness over the typical introduction: his scent gives him away. Spicy. Masculine. Wrong.

Daddy doesn't smell like this.

Neither do the doormen or usual security guards.

Neither does Simon.

My new intruder's cologne itches like pepper among an amalgam of different scents: shaving cream, rich liquor, and the faintest hint of sweat.

I should call the police, anything but call out, "Who are you?"

"*Buenas noches.*" The raspy baritone is the most alarming attribute of all. It reaches out to me from the living room, carrying a thick accent. "Do come in. Don't mind the intrusion—and I wouldn't call the police if I were you." The warning comes as my thumb twitches against my phone's touchscreen. "They tend to be so easy to corrupt."

"There…there are armed guards downstairs," I croak.

His answering laugh is a slap to the face. "Again," he continues, "easily bought off, Ms. Thorne. Even your father's reputation can only go so far. Come in. Have a seat. I merely want to talk. This shouldn't take long."

His mention of my father triggers a cold suspicion. Perhaps his warning wasn't for nothing. I'm in the living room before I know it, rounding the leather chaise to find a man sitting on it. Alarmingly massive, he transforms the spacious room into a claustrophobic prison. Yellow lights from nearby buildings give vague definition to his frame: a strong jawline veiled by the shadow of long, black hair neatly tied back into a ponytail. The outline of a blindfold, worn even now, stands out in stark contrast to his skin.

I should have recognized him from his voice alone. The man from the gallery.

And suddenly so much makes sense.

"Are you... You're Damien Villa," I rasp. My stab in the dark lands more accurately than I'd like. Another bit of laughter is my reward, decidedly colder than before.

"Ah, *perdóname*," he murmurs. "The innocent daughter of Judge Thorne turns out to be not so innocent after all. And I was inclined to give you the benefit of the doubt, Juliana."

"What do you want?" I take a step back, aware of the fact that the door is still open behind me.

"To talk," he says.

"Talk? You mean use me to threaten Heyworth Thorne? Go ahead. You can try. Then get the hell out." My callous laugh rings hollow. I sound weak, not brave. Tired and pathetic. "I'm sick of you goddamn people wanting to hold him accountable for one goddamn mistake—"

"Ah, *perdóname*, but you misunderstand." His voice contains the same qualities as lightning. Biting. Stinging. Raw. "My current visit has nothing to do with your father, Juliana. This is about an entirely personal matter."

Personal?

"The painting you bought," he continues before I can question. "I ask that you return it. That wasn't meant for you."

My painting. I crane my neck and spot the rough outline of my new possession. The morbid hues feed off what little light there is, creating a ghoulish effect: glowing, dead eyes staring directly into mine.

"I bought it," I say. Though the reminder might be for myself more than him. I bought it. I own it. Mine.

"Oh, but that was a mistake," Damien murmurs with chilling insistence. "On your part. It was never for sale, especially not to the likes of you. Return it to me and I shall overlook this…insult."

"Insult?" I cross the room, observing the painting in all its gory, disturbing detail. The artist's intentions elude me still—cloaked in layers of color and shades of mystery. "How could what I think insult you? Unless…you're Sampson." It's not a question. In a way, I'm stating something I probably already knew.

A madman isn't content to just let his show be displayed unseen. No. He must watch the people watching. He must gauge the full effect. Terror and disgust form the icing on his masterpiece, and he doesn't feel complete without a taste of it.

"The painting belongs to me," he says, evading the subject of his identity. "I'll make the arrangements to have it returned—"

"No. It's mine." I look back at him to watch my words register. "You can't have it."

"Oh?" He stares ahead through the fabric of his blindfold, seemingly transfixed by the view beyond my windows. "Should I take something of yours, then, as retribution?"

My body jolts at the sound of his voice, reacting without permission. Daddy had a pit bull once. Danger was his name. Every now and again, while dozing peacefully by the fireplace, Danger would suddenly startle awake and bark at the shadows. Daddy would shout at him to quiet down, but the beast only settled when whatever unseen threat he'd sensed diminished.

My nerves feel like that now. Humming with awareness of an ominous presence my eyes refuse to register.

"Are you threatening me?" I manage to ask.

"Negotiating," he retorts. "Despite whatever you think of me…I won't have my art used as a pawn, if you please."

"What I think?" Laughing, I shake my head. "I don't even know you."

"But I know *you*, and I know your family. Tell me: Did you enjoy strolling into my exhibition, aware of all eyes on you?"

He's implying something, though I'm not sure what. Something obscene, I think. Cruel.

"I live here," I point out. "Why shouldn't I attend an event held in my fucking lobby? And why hate me?" I add before he can get a word in edgewise. "I am not my father."

"Ah… But you think like him. So entitled to that which was never yours to claim."

Few men could speak the way he does and pack quite the same punch. A criminal, Daddy said. Funny, because this man sounds like a judge, someone accustomed to handing down punishments for any perceived snub.

"I'll return your money in full, of course."

"Keep it." Knowing that its supposed creator now sits behind me, I perceive the portrait from a different angle.

The woman's slight, desperate pout makes more sense. Paired with the unmistakable attractiveness of Damien, her final fate feels all the more tragic.

"So is it true that you use these to launder money?" I sound so disappointed. Though what a stupid question. Of course the art is a gimmick. "Do you?"

Silence lingers between us, forcing me to come up with my own answers. I always did my research when it came to the people in my orbits. Clients. Friends. Possible dates. I learned the hard way that it's better to suspect someone's potential motives from the outset—not that it's hard. The average person tends to fit into the same few categories like a book, easily judged within a few short minutes of conversation. Thriller. Boring contemporary. Paltry mystery. Tabloid.

Dangerous or not, Damien is no different from the egos and corporate giants I decipher for a living.

"How much do you pay them, your models?" I wonder, employing my usual trick of rapid-fire questioning. "Do you sleep with them? Do you photograph them first? How do you get them to look like that—"

"Do you think this is a game?"

Oh. I cross my arms to guard against his tone. So he doesn't want to play. Fair enough. I'll have to take a page from Daddy's book and judge him off his cover alone.

My eyes narrow, seeking out what little detail I can in the dark. I expect to find him brooding—most artists are. Instead, he's pensive. His voice betrays the impatience his body does not. He's all smooth lines and lean muscle, reminding me of a predator benevolent enough to hiss in warning before pouncing for the kill.

"Not a game," I concede. "As I said, the painting is mine. You can't have it."

"Oh?" That word again. So simple. So subtle. His voice is like music, containing more subtext in the underlying melody than the actual lyrics. "I would ask you to reconsider, Ms. Thorne."

"I'll think about it."

"And perhaps I'll *think* about returning something of yours."

My throat goes dry as I process his tone. Then I remember.

Ice washes over me with an intensity I've never felt in my entire life. Not all those years ago in the forest. Not moments ago when I found an intruder in my home.

For the first time ever…I forgot. Simon. His game.

I forgot.

"W-was there something on my doorstep?" Even I can hear the tremor in my voice.

And like a shark sensing a single drop of blood, he cocks his head. "*Sí*. There was… A bit old for dolls, aren't you?"

No.

As I watch, he withdraws something from his pocket and my heart twinges in recognition: a porcelain doll with carefully coiffed blond hair.

"Sammy," I whisper, horrified. "Give it to me!" I reach for it but stop short, inches away, as his posture shifts.

"Should I?" He's running his fingers through the doll's hair, disrupting her neat coif. Simon always took care to style it the same way. Like she did.

"Give it back." My breaths quicken, shallow and ineffective. The doll's face is visible from here, illuminated by a strip of neon-yellow light. Glassy eyes. Painted grin. Rosy, red cheeks. It's a replica, but one so damn close to the real thing…

"You can have her if you want," Leslie pleaded, grasping at my hands. "Just don't be mad at me."

No! I fight the memory back with bared teeth. "Give it back—"

He lifts the doll by her tiny waist, and I lunge forward. At the last second, he pulls her out of my reach, testing just how much I want it. Enough that a ripping sound echoes as I clench her tiny body in my fist and try to tug her free.

But he's too strong. Without warning, he stands, shrugging me off as easily as a gnat. "Sammy," he murmurs, a chuckle lacing his tone. "It even has a name?"

The color drains from my cheeks. She does. We have a ritual, Simon and I. His favorite tool of torture is my own memory. Samantha. She was Leslie's favorite character to spin our games of house around. Such a perfect doll, ten times more expensive than anything I could ever afford.

Sammy, beautiful Sammy, was the source behind our only fight ever.

Sammy, stupid Sammy, was the reason Leslie died.

"*Please*," I rasp, knowing I could never overpower him. "Give it back."

"I will. When you return what is mine." He turns while manipulating something in his free hand. Slender, thin. Long. It extends as I watch: a white cane he taps against the floor.

"I'll show myself out," he says at the exact moment I utter, "You're blind?"

"Have a wonderful night, Ms. Thorne." He starts for my door, using the cane for guidance.

So the eye covering isn't for dramatic effect. Yet I'm unconvinced he isn't putting on an act. He moves too confidently, every motion smooth and assured. Almost like he learned the layout of my apartment down to the slight right angle one must turn to enter the foyer and approach the still open door.

"Pleasant dreams," he tells me as he crosses the threshold.

It's only when he's gone that I remember how to move. I slam the door in his wake and engage the lock. I'm not afraid. *Liar*, my body claims. Muscle and bone go limp in defiance and I'm forced to brace my weight against my palms to catch my breath.

Tap. Tap. The tap of his cane forms a morbid tune that tracks the departure of Damien.

Eventually, the sound trails off and I'm alone again.

With Simon? It's his time to shine, after all. Day two. Sammy was the second present. Dread solidifies in my stomach; I know where I'll find the third.

I push from the door and sway to regain my balance. It's like I'm transported back all those years ago. Locked in the dark, forced to feel my way through touch. Forward, using the wall as a guide. To the left. Down a little more. Right. The floor beneath me switches to smooth tile, and I feel along the wall for the light switch.

Harsh iridescence plunges everything into stark relief. The white walls I never bothered to paint. The pristine countertops still stained with blood. The broken mirror displaying fractured pieces of a hundred different Julianas.

I had the workers skip this room for a reason.

Simon still hasn't grown tired of this hiding place. My present waits in plain sight, lying across the sink basin. A single rose, snow-white. A red ribbon encircles the stalk, choking it. The allusion is less obvious than Sammy, but it's memorable nonetheless. A white woolen hat kept brown curls warm paired with a long scarf in a bloody shade of red. *Her* red.

I'll humor Simon tonight. I don't run screaming from the room or crawl to my stash of wine. My exhausted body deposits me there, right beside the door, and I sit and stare. I won't remember fully—not yet.

There is still one more puzzle piece to be delivered.

One more day to play the game.

He'll win in the end. He always does.

And in a year, we'll play again.

SIX

*I*t's one of those mornings that pounces, going right for the jugular, ushering in another day of toeing that invisible boundary between hunter and hunted. Simon claims nightfall. It's only fair. I'll have to leave my suite before sundown and return after, just in time to open my final present.

Finding a diversion shouldn't be such a hard task.

I could take Daddy up on his offer and visit more often. Let him see how happy and wonderful I am. He doesn't have to worry, no siree.

Or…

I can crawl on my hands and knees into my bedroom and drink Moscato straight from the bottle. Imbibed with liquid courage, I manage to stand using my bedframe as a crutch and stumble into my closet.

Without bothering to shower, I peel off my stale birthday dress and pull on a black sweater and pants—but I can't shake the feeling that something is missing as I enter the kitchen. While the coffee maker runs, I lean against the counter and tap my foot. Eventually, my fingers join in, abusing the granite like a makeshift piano. I can't put a name to the sensation building in my veins. It's almost like I hear a clock counting down the hours to some unknown event. *Tick. Tock.*

My coffee starts to pour. The steady drip of liquid into the pot feeds the building suspense like a match over a flame.

Drip.

Drop.

A knock on the door echoes to silence as the last few dregs of coffee anticlimactically drip down to join the majority steaming in the pot.

"Who is it?" I call to no response.

Strange. I don't get visitors. Not ones who come announced through the front door without the aid of a shadowy reputation or stealth to hide behind. Damien? I swallow hard and reluctantly leave the caffeine behind.

A glance through the peephole reveals the face of a stranger. Not Simon. Certainly not Damien. This man is younger, with closely cropped brown curls and a wary smile.

"Delivery for Juliana Thorne," he declares, offering up a potted plant when I crack the door.

The flowers, branching from twisted stems, are small and white. More delicate than Simon's symbolic rose, and nothing like the carnations Daddy sends.

"They're beautiful." I start to finger a wayward petal.

"I wouldn't do that if I were you," the courier warns. "This stuff is oleander. Really toxic. Here—" He juggles the plant on one hand and withdraws an envelope from his pocket with the other.

My name is written on it. I accept both and the man disappears before I can voice a single question.

Not that I have to. Flowers and mystique seem to be the calling cards of one artist in particular.

Though I must give the man credit. He knows his floral arrangements. Oleander blends in beautifully with the muted colors of my kitchen. White over gray and poison over granite make a splendid combination. Who knew?

I pour myself a mug of coffee and take my time peeling the envelope open bit by bit. Inside, I find a black card almost entirely covered in painted versions of my deadly, white flowers. Running my fingers over the designs barely convinces me they aren't real, each one lavished with detail. I can still smell the fresh acrylic. Still see the deliberate, careful strokes of the artist lurking within every line and streak of ivory. Inside the card is a simple message written in a stark, uniformed script.

Sammy and I hope you reconsider—D.

Of all the emotions to feel, intrigue shouldn't be one of them. Did the blind man write his own threatening message?

My racing heartbeat distracts me from pondering the answer. It hammers away at my eardrums. *Thump. Thump.* Rough parchment and dried paint brush my fingertips as they continue to stroke the tiny flowers. Despite the courier's warning, I'm afraid the artificial oleander might pack the most potent punch. Its tiny vines and leaves invade my thoughts, planting dangerous ideas. Like the memory of the card in my pocket and the address of a certain artist's gallery. Images of doll-like eyes and porcelain skin. Red. Roses. Death.

And my actual doll he stole.

Simon's time is nearing, but two additional cups of coffee don't ease the transition of time. Minutes linger, and I'm left without a distraction. Alone in an ocean of idleness without a paddle.

Writing. I could try that. But when I finally fish a pen from a kitchen drawer, my first impulse isn't to jot down notes for a new campaign. It's a name. I write it out in black ink, arranging the letters over a napkin. *Damien. Thank you for the flowers,* I start to pen. Halfway through, I stop and toss the makeshift note into the trash.

I return to my bedroom, standing upright this time. The woman I spot in the full-length mirror near my bed looks like a perfect representation of confidence. Cool exterior. Watering, bloodshot eyes...

Shit. I rub them on my sleeve and turn my attention to my extensive wardrobe. Oleander. I can't get the pure color of it out of my head, though I only have one ensemble in the same lethal shade. A dress bought for some unremarkable occasion and promptly shoved to the back of my closet. I extract it out by the hanger and eye it warily. It's a simple sheath dress with a plunging neckline. Far too daring.

Out of morbid curiosity, I try it on, and I'm unsettled by the results. My hair spills across the scalloped top like blood, unseemly against such a blinding shade of white. Surround me with flowers and I could be one of Sampson's paintings.

Dress me in blue and I'd be the perfect doll for Simon.

Seal my eyes shut with glue and I'd be Leslie.

The thought forces me to remember my third present. I find it in the bathroom, lying on a bed of glass shards. I gingerly remove the ribbon and wrap it around my wrist: a glowing reminder. The rose, I tuck behind my ear.

My reflection greets me from the destroyed mirror, but I don't recognize the person I find. Someone stupid enough to visit one monster in her spare time before another comes calling.

I grab my coat from the hall closet and find the business card inside the pocket. A minute-long call is all it takes to have my usual town car service send a driver around. Ten minutes later, I'm stepping out from the shelter of the Lariat and heading across town.

Damien likes his privacy. His haunt is a tall building near the waterfront. Dark brick and sleek glass form an impressive structure that I assume is privately owned when I reach the entrance and find both glass doors locked. There's no sign. Merely an intercom affixed on the outside wall. When I press the button marked *call*, a gruff voice comes from the speaker, laced with static.

"What do you want?"

That's a damn good question.

"Name?"

I jump as the voice comes from the speaker again. Clearing my throat, I answer, "J-Juliana Thorne."

Silence. I'm left standing there with my thumb poised over the silver button while the rest of my body is angled toward the car. I should leave. I will. My hand falls just as an electric buzz comes from the door, followed by the click of a lock disengaging.

"Come in." The speaker crackles. "Take the elevator to the third floor."

With one last glance at the car waiting behind me, I enter the building, fighting a sense of trepidation with every step. It's surprisingly clinical for the lair of a madman. The entrance opens onto a small hallway, which branches off in two directions. One leads to a dead end, while the other stops before a set of silver elevator doors.

I strike the button for the third—and topmost—floor, and seconds later, the doors part, revealing another hallway, this one carpeted in a dark shade of gray and lined with black walls. The only illumination is cast by lit sconces glowing a dim, fiery orange.

How melancholic. Did he decorate with the intention to intimidate in mind?

It's only as my heels sink into the plush flooring that I remember his blindness. *Supposed* blindness. I close my eyes, imagining how this view might "appear" to someone like him. Even behind my eyelids, the muted color scheme makes the darkness feel heavier. Thicker. My skin heats when I near a sconce. I pass it, the world cools again. Hot. Cold. The dueling sensations go to war over my flesh with every step I take. My fingers graze the smooth surface of the wall, only to suddenly meet air. A doorway?

I open my eyes.

Damien likes his workspace dark. Few lights illuminate what the daylight filtering in through sparse windows doesn't. Wooden floors pick up my footsteps and broadcast them loudly to the man at work in the center of the room, hunched over a wooden table.

Behind him, arched windows display swaths of the waterfront and little else. The room itself is massive, with vaulted ceilings that amplify the slightest disturbance. Like my thready breathing and his heavy sigh.

Though he's wearing jeans, there's nothing at all casual conveyed by the ensemble. Tension enhances the muscle revealed by the short sleeves of his gray shirt. Every piece is tailored to perfection, impressive even from this distance. The man treats his body like his art, no stitch placed without intent.

"You came." He pushes back from the table and inclines his head in my direction. "Though I expected you to contact me by other means. I shall have to remind Carla as to the importance of my privacy."

My heart lurches. Charming Carla. Have I unknowingly gotten her into trouble?

"I insisted," I lie, disguising it behind a forced laugh. *Haha.* "She thought I'd appreciate your art."

"Now that is interesting," Damien muses. He strokes his thumb along his chin. The fingers of that hand are black at the tips. From sketching, judging from the materials spread out before him. He's working on a large piece of paper using only sticks of charcoal placed at strategic positions. "I've never questioned Carla's judgment before."

He's unreadable behind the blindfold, and his neutral tone obscures whether he means the statement as a threat. Left to decipher him blindly, my nerves dance with indecision. To tense or not? Fight or flight?

I settle on neither. For now.

"Anyway," he continues, waving his hand through the air before grabbing a piece of charcoal with it. "All that matters is you've changed your mind. I'll make the arrangements to return my painting and you may have your doll—"

"No. I haven't changed my mind... What are you doing?" I draw closer to him when I shouldn't.

He started sketching again while he spoke, and the rough contours catch my eye. A woman. She's outstretched over white paper, her limbs formed of inky black. Unseeing eyes stare out as her lips contort around a final, gasping breath.

"It's beautiful." The words spill from me without permission, but in my head, they aren't quite a compliment. Beautiful. Ugly. Grotesque. "How can you—"

"Don't touch." He grabs my wrist before I even register reaching out. How? He tugs when I try to snatch the limb away, tightening his grip. "Beautiful," he says tacitly. "I thought you said it was *terrible*."

I twist my wrist to no avail. He's too strong. The pads of his fingers capture sinew and bone beneath them and press just hard enough to sting.

"Let me go—"

"What are you wearing?" He cocks his head as if sensing something that I can't, his nostrils flared.

"Get off!" I tug my arm again. "Let go."

"*Perdóname.* What are you wearing?"

Snark is my first instinct. "A dress," I spit out.

"And?" Impatience seeps from him like the poison from my oleander. Invisible. Deceptive. Like he's hunting for something.

"And…" I look down at my feet. "Heels."

He frowns, still unsatisfied with my answer. "And?"

"And nothing." Then I remember my newest gift. Swallowing hard, I add, "And…a rose in my hair."

He lets me go and his hand drifts toward a piece of charcoal before he flattens it against the table instead. "I take it that you appreciated my gift."

He laughs and the deep, guttural rumble robs me of my senses for a brief moment. I blink. He and the rest of the room disappear. Reappears. Disappears.

With my eyes still closed, I utter my reply. "Very much so."

A sound catches in his throat. *Ah.* Not quite a laugh. He's amused. He's annoyed. "*Por favor.* Tell me, what color is your dress, Juliana?"

"Why?" Trying to decipher him triggers a dull throbbing in my temples.

The discomfort isn't because of the question itself, however. It's how he asked it. Politely. Curiously.

"Black," I finally admit.

Another partial laugh is my reward. "A lie."

I glance at him sharply. "How can you tell?" Maybe he isn't so blind after all.

His gaze isn't on me, but focused straight ahead, toward the light coming in from one of the windows. "I know."

"Well, then you should also know that I've decided to keep the painting." Have I? Only now do I feel like examining my reasons for coming here in the first place. To evade Simon, possibly. To thank Mr. Villa for his thoughtful gift. To hide. To concede. To refuse. "You can burn the doll."

"I'm very sorry to hear that, Ms. Thorne." His tone dips an octave deeper than before. Picking up a thinner stick of charcoal, he continues to sketch, adding detail to an outstretched hand. There goes at least one mystery: He *has* to see. There's no other way he could be so precise. "I trust you can show yourself out."

Squaring my shoulders, I turn to do just that—but I've barely gone a step before he calls out, "By the way, Juliana. You sound different in white."

"How did you…" My footsteps falter, my heart clenching painfully. "Fine," I croak rather than accuse him of lying out loud. "You want your painting back? Let's make a fair trade, then. You give me something I want. I give you what you want."

"Your doll isn't sufficient enough?" he counters.

"It's already served its purpose." I think of Simon and shudder. He couldn't have planned a more memorable way to present his Sammy replica than this—held hostage by a newer monster. "So do you want to trade or not?"

"Trade. Information, perhaps? Like that of your father and his reputable donors and the careful, gilded cage he's built around you that you can't even see?"

"No," I say hoarsely. "Don't you dare talk about him—"

"Then what?" He's still sketching when I turn around, his posture angled toward the drawing, conveying complete disinterest in me. "What could the daughter of Heyworth Thorne want from me?" he wonders.

My answer escapes in a rush. "I…I want you to paint me."

Do I? The veracity of the answering pinch in my stomach surprises me. Yes.

"Paint you?" He sounds too soft. Like I suggested he stick a brush up his ass rather than use one.

I'm flashed back to last night. What was that word he used? Insult.

"If you even can," I add, returning to the table one halting step at a time. "For all I know, it could be a ruse, just like your so-called blindness. Dad—Judge Thorne told me that you really use them to—"

"I'm sure he told you plenty of things about me," he says dismissively. "I could tell you more about him."

The implied threat has the effect of shutting me up.

"So the woman who calls my art terrible wants me to paint her. Would this piece hang in your father's office, I wonder? A gift for when he runs again for mayor?"

"How did you know that?" The second I reply, I recognize his statement for the bait it was.

"Only a man as conceited as your father would demand more power rather than reflect on his past misuse of it," he smugly retorts. "And only his daughter would desire what she considers terrible."

I attempt to shrug off the venom in his tone but wind up flinching. His accent can cut like a whip when he wants it to. "There are worse things to be called than that."

"Oh?"

"Yes."

Like perfect.

The drawing he's working on now is anything but. It's goddamn terrible. Beautiful lines. Cruel, honest mortality.

"*Por qué?*" He drops the stick of charcoal and it makes a stray line in the wrong place, marring the woman's detailed torso. Then it rolls off the table and hits the floor, continuing toward me. "And how should I paint you?"

I can imagine the answer he expects: prettily.

"Like them," I say instead—and there is no need to elaborate. I want him to paint me naked. Dead. Honest.

This time, Damien doesn't reply. His fingers fan out in front of him, trapping the sketch beneath them. Then they curl, crumpling the drawing into a ball, which he tosses onto the floor.

"Explain," he says, invoking that harsh, commanding tone.

My lips part, words spilling out on cue. "How do you see them?" I'm closer to the table before I realize it, bending to snatch the discarded sketch. Despite how protective he seems to be of his art, he doesn't warn me away. "How do you pose them?"

Another question goes unanswered as I unfurl the drawing and observe it up close.

"Come here."

My eyes cut to him sharply. *No,* every nerve in my body warns. He's got them on red alert, humming with nervous energy. "W-why?"

He raises his hand and crooks one beckoning finger. "Come."

"No," I say. *Liar.* I'm already inching closer to the opposite end of the table.

A blur of motion is all I register before my chin is in his grip. Startlingly warm fingertips tilt it expertly while five more come to graze the side of my jaw.

I suck in a breath. He has the softest hands I've ever felt. Like velvet. Hands that must wear gloves to perform any menial tasks. Hands that could only commit the most sterile of murders.

Dangerous, sinful hands.

"You want me to paint you?" His breath fans my cheeks, unbearably warm.

"Yes…" For some reason, I don't shy from his touch. I let him examine me. There's more to the manipulation of his fingers than a desire to intimidate. They capture the curve of my face. The swell of my cheek. My hairline.

Finally, he sits back and opens a drawer concealed on his end of the table. From it, he fishes out a fresh sheet of paper, and with the thinnest strip of charcoal, he makes a few soft lines. Gradually, a woman's face takes shape. It's round, her features average. Some might call her attractive if it weren't for her exaggeratedly wide eyes and pursed lips.

Recognition hits in a slow-burning realization. It's me.

Then again, she isn't me.

There's fear in her eyes, more apparent the more of her he reveals in lines of black. She's thin—too thin—standing tall. Her hands are outstretched, grasping at the air in front of her. Unlike his other creations, she's fully dressed in a simple, white sheath dress.

I'm tempted to accuse him of feigning blindness again—but the details are vague enough to be guesses. Besides, it's the woman's expression upon which he lavished the most insulting attention. Her dour, terse frown could only be described as…lost.

Or terrified.

"Is this meant to scare me?" My voice rasps. I find myself licking my lips and swallowing hard to ease a sudden dryness in my throat. I've been standing here, watching him longer than I've realized. The angle of light coming in through the window is sharper, dimmer, and my ankles throb, confined in my heels.

"Scare?" With a sigh, Damien finishes off the last stroke. Then he lifts the drawing and offers it to me.

I scoff. That caricature looks nothing like the woman I strive to be. She's pathetic. Weak. She's the person I want to drown in a bottle of wine. "That's the best you can do?"

As I reach for it, Damien withdraws the page just beyond my range. "Uh-huh." He nods once, indicating my body, I presume. Namely what I'm still clutching in my fist. "Exchange."

I consider tossing both scraps of paper into the trash. I should.

In the end, I let the discarded drawing fall onto the table within his reach, and he lets me pull the fresh drawing from his grip.

"Do you feel that was a fair trade?" he asks, while I retreat toward the light of the nearest window and observe his distorted creation up close. She's not me—despite how uncannily familiar her nose is.

She's not.

"I expended the energy to create both drafts," he continues. "You stole one without permission and yet bartered it for another. So…" From the corner of my eye, his silhouette flickers. "Is this a fair trade?"

Ignoring him, I sweep my gaze along the drawing again. Then I tear it in half and let both pieces fall. "There," I tell him, unnerved by how patiently he's sitting, no emotion revealed whatsoever. "Now they're both unwanted. Besides, I thought artists like a challenge. That looks nothing like me."

"Is that so?" He stands swiftly, catching me off guard. He must have had the cane propped against the table, because it's in his hand now. It extends, tapping the floor before him, and he advances on me far more quickly than he should be able to.

Instinct seizes control of my feet, propelling me backward. Back…back. Until I hit a wall and can't go any farther. I'm forced to watch as he approaches, but I'm offered no warning when he touches me this time. Bold and sure, his fingers graze the side of my throat, tracing the pulse thrumming there.

"I'm not so sure of that…" His mouth tilts downward, his thumb pressing harder.

"W-what are you doing?" I avert my gaze to the opposite wall— but I don't move. For some insane reason, I endure the second appraisal, and this time, he extends his search.

Down my throat, following the midline of my collarbone. A ragged gasp escapes my lips as unfamiliar heat creeps through the satin over my rib cage. Too low. Then even lower, down to my hips. He keeps the contact featherlight. Barely noticeable.

Yet inescapable.

Finally, he steps back, and his cane retracts, able to be slipped inside his pocket.

"I would not question my sight if I were you, Ms. Thorne," he declares, the corner of his mouth quirked. He's amused once again.

"With all due respect, Mr. Villa, I don't feel like arguing sight accuracy with a blind man."

"And you shouldn't," he bites back. "How frustrating it must be to have your sight and yet not be able to see things as they are."

"What's that supposed to mean?"

He laughs and shakes his head. "I do not think you'd understand."

Before I can voice a comeback, he reaches for me. Two quick fingers capture the rose behind my ear and yank it free.

"Stop!" My trembling fingers swipe at nothing.

He's too quick. His free hand crushes the bloom, molesting the petals. In pale clumps, they litter the floor, finally followed by the discarded stem.

"Roses are not your flower," he declares.

"Oh? And oleander is?" The bravery I hope my voice carries falls flat. My gaze won't leave Simon's mutilated flower. My reminder. Coherent thoughts scatter like those broken petals. I'm clenching my fingers, aching to shove the remains together and somehow make it whole again. "I'm leaving—"

"Do you want to know why I paint my subjects nude?" he wonders suddenly.

"Considering that you supposedly 'see' through touch, I can imagine why."

Rich laughter echoes in the wake of my irritation. He deploys the reaction the same way someone else might a narrowed gaze or terse expression: as a warning.

"People hide behind layers," he explains. "The more you remove, the more of the real person is revealed underneath. For instance, the loss of a single rose can strip a woman bare in ways she doesn't realize."

"Is that so?" I cross my arms over my chest. "Frankly, Mr. Villa, this conversation is becoming inappropriate—"

"You want me to paint you," he says over me. "And yet, *frankly,* Ms. Thorne, there is nothing about you worth painting. I capture people. Not their masks, and you have crafted a rather elaborate one if I may say."

"E-excuse me?" No one talks to me like this. I can't remember the last time a man even raised his voice to me other than the recent voicemails. It's a benefit of living in a cage of glass, steel, and concrete. Money creates an imaginary world with padded edges and gossamer chains.

The rules are simple: ignore and pretend.

"I've changed my mind," I say, turning on my heel. "You can have your damn painting *and* the doll. Have a good day, Mr. Villa—"

"Strip." The command comes so softly that I had to have imagined it. A cruel joke played by a twisted mind?

But no.

The air feels heavier and my cheeks are on fire. Wounded pride won't let me move without first choking out a question. "What did you say?"

"I told you to strip," he replies, his voice eerily calm. Almost taunting. "Unless you're afraid of the person you're hiding beneath that priceless designer frock."

"Afraid?" I force my own bit of carefree laughter, but the notes ring hollow. "So you're a sexual deviant as well as a hack—"

"I'll say this once," he interjects. "You can insult me all you want, but never my art."

My spine stiffens at the subtle shift in his tone. A shout wouldn't carry the same level of malice. No. He's honed intimidation into an art form.

"Now, I'd like for you to leave. *Adiós.*"

My heels rock against the floor, but I don't budge. Instead, I watch myself from the window's surface. Proud, perfect Juliana.

He's a liar. If only he weren't a better one than I am.

My fingers sweep along my hip, gathering my skirt between them. I move slowly, registering the cold air with every inch of fabric I wind up my torso. When the material clears my head, I let it fall with a resounding thud. At the same time, my gaze goes to Damien. I want him to blush. Or leer in the chilling revelation that he isn't blind. Anything but sigh.

With the aid of his cane, he returns to the table and sits. He snatches another sheath of paper from the drawer while his free hand beckons sharply. "Come here."

"W-why?" Anxiety surges beneath my skin, whipping my nerves into a frenzy. What the hell am I doing? Standing half-naked before a stranger, for one. Of all the things to consume my attention, it shouldn't be his disinterest.

"I'll ask you one more time to come here." He sounds like he's scolding a naughty child and considering withholding a toy.

"What are you going to do?" Regardless of my unease, I come to the opposite end of the table, and he nods to the expansive surface before him.

"Lie down."

A refusal springs to my lips but dies before I can voice it. Turning my back to him, I perch myself on the edge of the table and shift my weight so that he's on my left. Inch by inch, I lower myself backward until the chilled wood bites into my skin.

"Don't relax," he warns as his hand settles over my outstretched wrist. His fingers give the flesh an examining brush. "I want you to feel."

The request haunts me as my gaze flickers up to the shadowed ceiling. These days, I don't have time to feel. I project— confidence, fearlessness, perfection.

Who am I without that so-called priceless frock crumpled on the floor?

I doubt a blind psychopath can tell me.

"What are you doing?" I croak as his touch continues up my arm, encroaching on my collarbone.

He says nothing. Every now and again, I hear the telltale hiss of charcoal scraping parchment, but I'm not brave enough to check his progress for myself.

Instead, my eyes drift shut as if of their own accord. Darkness and silence are the only tools I have to decipher the events taking place around me. Electricity humming. Artificial heat blasting. Hot, smooth skin exploring my own.

It should feel worse. I can't escape the thought. Having him touch me should feel worse than it does. If only there weren't a discernible method to his madness. He touches me where he must, gleaning what secrets my flesh contains before moving on to another area. Scratch, scratch goes the stick of charcoal, tracking his progress.

My arms. Shoulders. Hands.

My breasts…

"W-wait!" I can't smother a cry when he cups one with his palm. "Don't—"

"Leave, or stay," he warns, his palm stilling.

My heart races, threatening to hammer right out of my chest. Somehow, I manage to lie still, and he continues his study of me.

He's not slow and deliberate with this part of my anatomy, however. One pass is all he makes before moving on. You've sketched one set of breasts, I guess you've sketched them all.

It's my hips that consume the most attention.

"You have scars," he says, unable to disguise a note of curiosity. "From what?"

None of your business. The words don't come out, and he continues his groping without waiting for a response.

When his touch finally withdraws, the sounds of sketching pick up in earnest. Bold, sure strokes. Smaller, light dashes.

I let my mind wander, trying to envision what he comes up with. All I can picture is a shapeless mass of shadow. Somehow, I know when he's finished without him having to say a word. My eyes open slowly, and I roll away from him, crossing my arms over my chest.

Pitch-black windows give a vague inkling of how much time has passed. Hours at least.

When I finally look over my shoulder at him, his hands are braced flat against the table and the tips of his fingers are blacker than ever. He touched me like that, tainted with the stain. I'm dotted in more fingerprints than the actual paper—like a canvas.

"Well?" He gestures to the finished drawing, his head cocked as if listening for my reaction, and I'm painfully aware of my rapid, shallow breaths.

I look down, biting my tongue. He made this sketch larger than the last. It consumes nearly the entire page: the result of shading and smeared charcoal.

The woman staring up at me is an enigma. I don't recognize her. Or maybe I don't want to. She's more like a specter: someone I catch only glimpses of before I banish her with red lipstick and my custom wardrobe.

Someone I hide. Scorn. Shun.

But she gets her revenge now. Damien's sought her out and pushed her presence right in my face.

"I request that we end this visit now, Ms. Thorne," he says, rising to his feet. After extending his cane, he heads for the door, steadier than I feel. "Keep the scrap paper, but forget this address. Best regards to your father. I'm sure it will be quite the media spectacle when he announces his return to politics."

He's gone through the doorway before I fully register the intent of his words. *Definitely* a threat that time.

What's more alarming is my reaction. I'm not trembling when I finally place my feet on the floor and pull on my discarded dress.

I fully intend to leave the drawing, and I make it all the way to the elevator doors, wandering a hallway devoid of Damien. My finger strikes the button. The elevator arrives.

But the doors close without me inside.

There's no one there to witness my return to that lone table. Upon retrieving the sketch, I fold it carefully, tucking it against my palm.

Maybe I'll throw it away.

Or maybe I'll keep it for Simon.

No matter how many gifts he's sent and no matter how many years he's haunted me, he's never seen this woman.

SEVEN

*J*escape Damien's lair only to reenter a neon jungle that doesn't appear to have missed me any. Or so I think. I'm shocked to find a town car waiting patiently near the curb— the result of an overzealous driver? Or Damien himself? I don't ask, though when I climb into the back seat, the clock on the dashboard proclaims it's after midnight.

Then I remember. Panic racks my spine, though it could be pity. Or terror. Poor Simon. For the first time in twenty years, I've stood him up.

Worse than that: I've forgotten all about him…*again.*

Were I in my right mind, I would urge the driver to rush home, hoping to make amends with my deranged torturer before time ran out.

I'm too tired now. My eyelids flutter, weighed down by hours of tension. I've never felt so worn. So apathetic.

As the driver pulls before the Lariat on cue, I watch it loom above me in all its glory. "Never mind," I hear myself say without reaching for the door. "I think I'll stay at the Harrison tonight."

It's a less prestigious hotel on the other end of the city. One favored by the riff-raff, some might say. A place someone like me would rarely deign to stay at.

And the one place where Simon won't look for me now.

P

*M*onday is a workday. There's no sheltering from it beneath thin sheets or a worn duvet. Sluggish with dread, I drag myself from my suite at the Harrison and return to my apartment just as dawn kisses the horizon. I round the corner near my suite with my hands already outstretched, prepared to face my punishment.

Only to find my doormat empty.

My throat tightens, constricting what little oxygen I manage to breathe in. It's a bad sign—the first of many. My final present of the year isn't waiting for me on the kitchen counter beside my potted oleander. Neither is it on the glass coffee table in the living room.

Bitter apprehension suffocates the remaining air from my chest as I start toward my bedroom. It's raining out. Icy drops speckle the windows, the view beyond them. The world below becomes a blurred kaleidoscope of motion and noise, like a merry-go-round on warp speed. My apartment, however, is frozen in time, and I can't escape the insane feeling that everything, down to my white carpet, is watching me.

Waiting for something.

The door to my bedroom is cracked, just how I left it. However, the maid came while I was gone. She made my bed and tidied the closet, leaving her trademark card behind. No signs of Simon here.

Not even in the bathroom. Inside it, all I find are broken glass and dried blood.

I flinch as muffled notes of piano music begin to play. "Moonlight Sonata." I follow the melody back into the living room and find my cell phone, clinging to the last cell of battery life. I cringe at the time I find flickering on the screen. Late. So late. My boss is the one calling, but I don't answer.

If I shower now, I can make it to the office in less than twenty minutes. Wishful thinking, as it turns out. It takes more soap than usual to make me feel clean. Naked and dripping with moisture, I attempt my makeup.

First, a blood-red lip, like usual. Poreless foundation. Powder, powder.

Wrong. Lining my eyes with kohl doesn't chase the redness in them away. Beads of liquid seep from behind them, ruining my attempts to create a fearless smoky eye. I try again. Again.

Damn it.

In the end, I settle for washing my face and slicking my hair into a bun. My outfit of choice is a black pantsuit that takes forever to button. I'm still fastening the last one as I hunt for my heels to the soundtrack of my incessant ringtone. Note to self: Lay off the Beethoven. I've never realized how fucking pretentious it sounds before.

Because I'm never late.

The grim thought chases me out onto the street, where I find my town car waiting as expected. However, rush hour traffic foils my timeline. I'm racing into my department forty minutes later to hushed gossip and startled expressions. Someone offers up a nervous hello as I rush into my office, but I don't have the energy to return the greeting.

Focus. I shake my head to clear it and brace my hands over my lap. It's Monday. A new day. One when Simon's game is almost over and I'm free for 363 more until next year rolls around.

Freedom.

The hope plays around my mind as I shuffle from meeting to meeting, working on assignment after assignment. I even stay late, stretching my shift into a twelve-hour day despite how my temples throb and my eyes burn after hours of computer strain. Gradually, the office empties until I'm the only one left behind.

Only now do I slip on my coat and head for the elevators. When I reach the lobby, my lips contort into my trademark smile, ready to wish Gus goodnight. But I round the corner near the main entrance only to find his podium empty, a lady's magazine lying on top. My stomach churns; I've stopped without realizing it. Slowly, I force myself to take a step and shake off the unease racing down my spine. He most likely ran to the bathroom.

Regardless, uncertainty builds with every step I take toward the main doors. Roughly ten feet of space separate me from them. My car is waiting; out front, I spot the ruby glow of taillights. I won't take another detour tonight, to a madman's dwelling or otherwise. I'll go home. I'll be a good girl.

I'll wait my turn. Simon's game isn't over yet.

But this time...I think he sent someone to play with me. Their footsteps are softer, echoing mine. Thwack. Thump. Thwack.

"H-hello?" I call out.

The figure casting the shadow flickering along the wall up ahead is too tall to be Gus. Too slender.

Too fast.

I run, pumping my arms, reaching for the door—but something slams into me before my fingertips graze the glass. I land on my knees, tasting blood, and a split second is all I have to react. *Run!*

There's a side exit directly across from Gus's desk. I lunge for it, but sudden tension on my hair locks me in place as a cry rips from my lips.

"Don't move," someone breathes into my ear, their voice harsh.

And I'm transported twenty years into the past.

EIGHT

*We were playing, a code word for competing. Dolls,
toys, clothes—the quality mattered more than the
game. Mine was a neighbor's hand-me-down, about ten years out of
production. I'd done my best to brush out her gnarled, brown hair
and arrange her faded, navy dress, but it was no use. Everyone else
had the latest plastic creations. Once again, I had to play on the
outskirts, designated the "trailer trash" character in this dolly
neighborhood.*

*"Then I'm trailer trash too," Leslie declared, shooting me a smile that
displayed her two front teeth. She thought she was coming to my
rescue, like always, but therein lay the rub.*

*No one would ever mistake her designer doll for anything less than
one spit out by the finest boutique.*

*Her doll never dwelled in a house that doubled as a meth lab. Leslie
never had to trade her for cigarettes stolen from her parents' stash or
spend hours scraping old grime off her with a toothbrush.*

*"It's late," one of the other girls declared. She began to pack up her
toys, signaling to the other girls to do the same.*

*Once again, I had put my skills as a social leper to good use. As
always, Leslie was the only one who stayed behind. She helped me
stow my ratty selection of dolls and accessories into my backpack—*

but like any good friendless pariah, I spurred her attempts to make nice.

"I'm walking home," I told her, preemptively rebuking our customary ride home in her dad's car. "I'm not some stupid, spoiled brat like you!"

Rather than get upset, Leslie simply blinked in that slow, understanding way of hers. Then she gathered up her sparkly bookbag and nodded. "I'll walk too."

The only flaw in my boast was that I had no idea how to walk home. I'd always taken the bus before Leslie's friendship. But even back then, I refused to lose face. So I picked a direction away from the school and started walking while Leslie followed.

We lived close to each other, ironically enough. She was in the brand-new development just outside of town, while I was in the trailer park behind it.

Both areas required a ten-minute trek on a lonely stretch of road that climbed into the hills. What Leslie didn't know was that even my neglectful parents never let me walk home alone. I'd done my best to disguise my unease, marching with my chin jutting into the air.

But bravery couldn't save us from a stranger's predatory intent. We heard him first: heavy footsteps and intermittent whistling. I still remember the tune, the one from the opening of a popular Saturday morning cartoon. It teased us from beyond a border of trees. Louder. Softer.

Until it sounded as though it were being hummed directly into my ear.

And there was no escape.

ain drags me back to the present as something scrapes the flesh of my throat. Something sharp. Thin.

"Don't move," a man growls into my ear between pants. He doesn't sound like Simon—the only shred of comfort I can find. He isn't my monster, and I'm not the same little girl I was twenty years ago. "…want to die…stop—"

Scream! It's the first lesson taught in every self-defense class I've ever taken. Scream. Flail. Fight.

I kick out with my legs and brace my hands against the floor of the lobby, crawling forward, but agony explodes between my shoulder blades, driving the air from my lungs. The stench of body odor betrays just what is pinning me down: my attacker himself.

He's heavy, easily dragging me back. I feel that icy scrape again against my shoulder, biting deeper the more I struggle. A weapon.

Don't look back, a part of me warns. *Run!*

I make myself deadweight, throwing my body against the floor, and his grip loosens enough for me to ram my elbow back, striking something solid. Then I'm stumbling to my feet, racing for the main entrance. I grab a handle and tug, but it doesn't budge. Neither does the other. Shit! They're both locked—only Gus has the key.

Don't panic.

Move.

There!

The side entrance draws my notice again and I lurch toward it, desperate to ignore the shuffling sounds behind me. Air trickles in and out of my lungs as my few options flash across my mind. I'll never outrun him.

So I let myself trip and go down hard. He rushes over, and I roll onto my back. I catch only a glimpse of an unfamiliar face beneath the shadow of a black hoodie. He's tall. Young.

He doesn't even see the kick coming, aimed squarely between his legs. Groaning, he doubles over, and I lunge to the door. It opens, depositing me into a narrow alley beside the office. Blindly, I race past an overflowing dumpster in a frantic race to the street. A lack of noise warns that there's no one behind me.

Yet.

Surging traffic and the distant howling of sirens disguise most sounds, however. I won't hear him until it's too late. Lost in this sea of people, no one would ever notice me scream if he does catch up. They push past me, specters locked into their eternal routines, oblivious to me.

My shoulder throbs. My bottom lip is on fire, bitten in the scuffle. A limping gait carries me to the main street, but I keep going, right past the idling car. The driver is a shadow perched behind the steering wheel, waiting. Watching.

He could be Simon.

Hell, the man marching toward me carrying a briefcase could be Simon. Or the driver honking as he speeds by. Even the figure shoving me aside with an impatient shrug of his shoulder.

He's everywhere.

Air seeps from my lungs, impossible to contain, but somehow, I keep walking. Staggering. Running.

I've never learned my lesson after all these years: I can't escape him. The shadows converge on me as strangers stare. Their attention burns like spotlights, illuminating my path no matter where I go. How fast I run.

To where exactly? I don't know. Not until I'm pounding on a set of glass doors while my hand paws at the silver button of an intercom. A voice laced with static says something from the speaker. Demands something. I should reply. Be collected. Be polite.

But I can't seem to stop banging my fist on the door. A substance paints the glass with every blow. It's dark, appearing almost purple until a passing car's headlights ignite the color, revealing what it is: a bright-red liquid.

Bzzz! The door jolts against my palm, suddenly unlocked. No explanation comes from the speaker, and I don't wait for one. I'm in the elevator before I know it, tracking something over the floor that glints like a morbid breadcrumb trail. The doors close, locking me inside, but I just stare at the buttons, unsure of which one to pick.

Tick. Tock.

Simon's still watching. I can even hear him now, humming into my ear. *Dada, da dum…*

Ding! The elevator rises without me having struck a button. On the second floor, the doors open, revealing a trio of strange men who start inside before they notice me there. Shock alights their stern expressions, and one of them reaches for his breast pocket, his eyes narrowed.

"What in the hell?"

I lunge through the space between them and find myself in another hallway resembling the one above. This one branches into several rooms. The first I pass is narrow, darkened, empty. Light spills from another doorway up ahead. Voices drift out.

Deep. Masculine. Accented.

"I've warned you," a man says, his voice chillingly familiar. "Stay out of it. Understood?"

"Why?" Someone scoffs. "Don't you trust me?"

"I don't," the first man replies. "You're sloppy, Mateo, and I'd rather not see you in prison. Have patience. I will handle this."

"You say that as though I enjoy having to beg you for help on my goddamn hands and knees. But you promised me retribution for Mathias. Remember him? Our brother—"

"Stop." The warning isn't directed at me though I freeze paces from the doorway. "It seems as though Julio needs more training."

Damien stands in the center of a room decorated in muted shades. Black leather armchairs form a circle around an industrial-gray coffee table. Steel-gray walls and wooden floors feed the shadows gathered in the corners. Only the light cast from a hanging fixture combats the darkness.

But even it is no match for Damien. The blindfold reduces his expression to nothing more than a stern frown. Emotions seep from him regardless, painting the air like canvas. Alarm. Anger. Confusion?

"Juliana Thorne," he says coldly. "What a surprise. I'm afraid we'll have to cut this discussion short, Mateo." He inclines his head to a man I only notice now.

Tall like he is, but with a thinner face and shorter hair. He eyes me coldly, his upper lip drawing back from his teeth.

"*Gracías*, brother," he snarls. "I can see that you've *handled* this, all right."

"Leave." Damien's tone may be level, but only a fool would challenge it.

His companion draws himself to his full height, squaring his shoulders. On his way out, he slams into me. Hard. I stagger against the wall and slide to the floor. The room blurs, becoming muted colors and harsh shadow. It's a nightmarish painting dominated by one unmoving figure.

"Breathe!" he growls, his voice cutting deep.

I am, aren't I? I can't *stop* breathing. Gasping down air. Choking it back out. Faster. Faster.

Thwack! Stinging pain flares through my cheek and I flinch in shock as frayed nerves reset and register the sudden nearness of an imposing figure.

"I apologize." He slowly withdraws his hand, his frown stern.

It's almost funny how I feel his slap more than anything else. My fingers race to the throbbing skin, tracing the abuse.

"I don't typically humor unannounced visitors." An unsettling mixture of politeness and malice color Damien's tone as expertly as the charcoal he shades his drawings with. "So what brings you here tonight, Juliana Thorne—"

"My birthday's over." The words fall flat. Broken. Then I'm laughing, forced to draw my knees to my chest as the sound racks me to my core.

He says nothing when I finally trail off, waiting. Expectant.

"It's over. It should be over," I blurt out in a rush. "But twenty years. Twenty years. I never missed a night before. Not one."

"What should be over?"

I flinch. The sharp note of curiosity in his tone shouldn't be there —and he's too hard to read without a gaze to search. I'm the one rendered blind against him.

"Nothing," I croak. Just a shadow. Just a nightmare. Just... "My birthday."

If he's confused by the conflicting statements, I can't tell. And his silence only makes it worse.

"I...fell. At work," I add. "The door was locked. It wasn't supposed to be locked. I fell and..." I'm rambling.

He permits it, aptly listening to every word. Pretending to, anyway. No one ever listens. My therapist just reflects to me what I should feel. Daddy only ever hears what he wants. The world demands pretty, shiny words and adjectives to describe whatever petty bullshit they hope to sell. Darkness isn't appealing. It can't be wrapped with a bow and sold with a smile.

So I lied.

Until now.

NINE

*W*ords spill from me like blood—ironic since I'm still bleeding. My shoulder throbs. Salt and copper itch my nostrils, but every truth ripped from my soul stings ten times worse. Maybe because none of it makes any damn sense. I've been playing the world's oldest game of Simon Says for so long, I don't even know where to begin.

Eight-year-old Juliana did her best when rambling to the first responding officer. *"He made us play..."*

I'm less coherent now.

"Three days," I croak. "I just have to play along for three days."

I'm still laughing. Louder. Harsher. Tears mix in, thickening my voice. My chest heaves, but in this moment, I can't smother my cries behind my trembling fingers or in the sleeves of my coat.

I'm sobbing.

And Damien observes it all in his own callous way.

"Don't move."

I jump when he takes a step, but I'm not his target. Without the aid of his cane, he enters the hall, but I remain hunched on the floor, watching the unfamiliar room from behind the border of my knees.

Little decoration obscures its intended use. There isn't even a television or a stereo system. Just black leather furniture and a cold air of business that lingers long after any other inhabitant has left.

One fact is obvious: I interrupted something. How rude of me—but how strange of *him* to let it happen. There were times when even Daddy would send me away while he had company. The mayor's time was expensive after all, what with campaign contributions to schmooze and donors to win over. He'd visit me in the morning, of course, usually with some small token of affection and a reminder to smile!

He would certainly never lower a crystal flute of wine before my nose and urge me to drink.

"Small sips," Damien warns. "This is a vintage Romanée-Conti. Some consider it…overwhelming."

"Th-thank you." My cheeks heat as I accept the glass. The wine swirling inside might as well be liquid gold; I recognize the brand, a bottle of which sells for around thirty thousand dollars —and that's for a recent run. Ironically, I taste nothing as I drain the glass in one sip.

If he's irritated by the disobedience, he hides it well as I set the glass aside.

"Why are you here?"

"I…" I breathe in deeply and exhale. "I don't know."

I should've called Daddy. Or gone home and waited for another morbid reminder from Simon. Instead, I crawled to the lair of an artist whose soft hands disguise more than they should.

I ran to a madman. He stands tall, shrouded by shadow and light, holding his own glass of wine, which he has yet to sip from.

Instead, he sets the glass on the coffee table with no difficulty. He must have the layout memorized.

"You're bleeding." His nostrils flare, his frown more pronounced.

"Oh…" I clutch at my arm. "It's a scratch. I-I fell." The lie rings hollow as I finally look at my shoulder.

A long gash slices through the fabric of my designer coat, revealing my torn blouse underneath and a swath of red. The bastard had a knife, I assume as tears flood my eyes. Simon's favorite toy. At least the wound doesn't feel too deep.

"Here."

I blink and find a white strip of fabric dangling from an outstretched hand. Woodenly, I press it against the worst of the bleeding.

"I'm fine," I lie again. The wine has put everything back into perspective, and a new fear blossoms in the spaces of my psyche Simon doesn't infect. It's too close in here. Too quiet with just me and him. I brace my free hand against the floor and start to stand.

"Since you are here, we might as well discuss your previous proposal, Ms. Thorne," Damien announces while I use the wall as an anchor to climb to my feet.

"My…what?"

"Painting you," he says as though art is the most natural topic in the world to move on to after blood. "We can discuss my methods and decide whether or not you agree to my terms. How does dinner sound?"

"You're serious?" My eyebrows rise, my voice still hoarse.

It would help if he laughed. Something to prove he was taunting me outright. Anything other than his cool, unreadable persona.

"Yes," he says. "Dinner. Somewhere public."

"Dinner." I'm a parrot, echoing him in a detached monotone. "Now?"

"Of course." Unperturbed, he nods. "Unless you've changed your mind."

Pain in my fingertips makes me glance down. I've been subconsciously wringing them together, scraping my nails against sore, raw flesh. "I…I don't… I'm a mess."

"There's a bathroom down the hall," he interjects. "First door to the left."

I should scoff at the callous suggestion. Instead, I move on autopilot, following his instructions until I find myself locked inside a surprisingly spacious bathroom. The color scheme leaves little to be desired: dark tile flooring and more gray walls. His choice? Or perhaps the result of a lazy interior designer taking advantage of a blind client. Even before the thought finishes forming, I doubt it's true. Damien is a man few could manipulate.

So the decoration is his choice, then. Perhaps he likes his guests to feel a sample of what he might. A disorienting lack of color. Dizzying monochrome. Little definition to speak of.

It requires me to close my eyes and *feel* to discern anything at all from the stark surroundings. Sleek fixtures and smooth surfaces. Harsh, violent water pressure that easily rinses the blood from my hands. Dim lighting allows me to look at myself in the mirror and not cringe at what I see. If I squint, I can almost find my old self looking back. Perfect Juliana. Forgiving shadows obscure what brighter light wouldn't.

My breathing hitches as the taste of copper burns my tongue. The flesh of my throat aches with the memory of roughly ground fingers from an unknown assailant and the knife he placed there.

I *feel*, and there isn't enough wine within reach to make it all better.

If Mr. Villa has a reservation to uphold, then I make him blow it. I linger, desperately trying to rebuild my shattered façade. Each time, I fail. Try again. Fail harder. Tears mix with cold sweat, coating my cheeks until I can't discern one from the other.

With a sigh, I give up and slip into the hall.

"Ms. Thorne?" He's still waiting for me in that small sitting room and inclines his head as I approach. "Change your mind?"

I finger the sleeves of my coat, sensing the heat his body throws off even from across the room. "It's late. Most places are closed by now anyway."

He shrugs. "It's of no concern. I have a special agreement with the management of this particular establishment. Shall we?"

I can't ignore the expertly concealed dare.

Are you brave enough, Juliana?

I'm not. Ignoring his hand, I step toward the door and clear my throat. "I should go."

"By all means." What sounds polite on the surface holds more depth than his art and I'm instantly on edge. A deaf man could discern the sarcasm in his voice.

I nearly laugh out loud. How could I be so stupid? "And let me guess, the paparazzi are already waiting outside, courtesy of an anonymous tip? Or are they waiting at this so-called restaurant?"

"I assure all of my guests complete discretion and privacy." The statement could be interpreted in so many ways. Some harmless. Others not so much.

"Oh really?"

"You're more than welcome to see for yourself." He's behind me now, his breath on my neck, his footsteps soft against the hard floor. Damn near imperceptible. "Shall we?"

He pushes past me with enviable grace and extends his cane before him. His arm is slightly cocked, perfect for slipping a hand through should I give a damn about propriety.

Spurring the gesture, I follow him to the elevators and through the opening doors. Locked inside with him, I hold my breath until we reach the first floor. He must have called a car when I was in the bathroom, because there is one waiting for us, idling alongside the curb.

I don't know what I expect as we exit the building. Should I grab the door for him? My hand flutters toward the handle, but it's already in his grip. I see that someone wiped away my blood at least.

"After you, Ms. Thorne." He steps back, letting me pass. Then he proceeds to lead the way to the car.

As we approach, the driver circles around to open the door to the back seat. I wait until the man beside me enters first and retracts his cane. It's not too late to run and thumb my nose up at his offer. My body aches. I'm still bleeding.

I'm still terrified.

And he knows it. He leaves little space on the seat for me to claim, confident I'll bolt. When I finally lower myself beside him, I can't deny a sick satisfaction at the confused quirking of his jaw, but his heat creeping through my clothing quickly smothers the triumph.

"May I?" His palm extends toward me, facing upright. "Your arm," he clarifies when I flinch.

My lips part, but in the end, I say nothing and shove his bloodied handkerchief into his hand. He touches my wrist, ghosting higher toward my shoulder. He doesn't discover the wound right away, and he gently probes the flesh beneath his thumb until a hiss escapes my lips.

"You fell?" He sounds skeptical, but I grit my teeth against a retort. "Your coat, *por favor*," he prompts, his voice tighter than I've heard it yet.

My first impulse is to resist as he peels my jacket back—but I am the idiot who got into the car with him in the first place, and I can't be seen in public bleeding and broken.

My fingers shake as I tug at my collar, but he assists me, revealing the thin blouse I didn't intend to be seen in when I threw it on this morning. Knowing he's blind doesn't ease my nerves one damn bit.

It's too close in here. I'm painfully aware of every brush of his unnervingly soft fingertips grazing the rent edges of my blouse.

"Take your arm out of the sleeve."

I turn to the window, disguising how my cheeks flush. At least he sounds more efficient than predatory.

"Fine." I bite my lip and undo the first four buttons, providing enough slack for him to slide the damaged sleeve down my shoulder.

"It isn't deep," he says. How he can tell as much from touch alone? I don't bother asking. "You shouldn't need sutures.

Though..."

I wince as he runs his finger directly over the wound, heedless of the blood that coats it.

"This was made with a knife. You were assaulted."

Hearing him say it makes it all too damn real.

"I'm fine." I shrug him off and attempt to snatch the handkerchief back, but he pulls it out of my reach.

"I'm sure you are aware that your father has plenty of enemies. I should take you home. Or at least call the police—"

"Or you can let me out right here and leave me alone."

He pauses as if mulling it over. But the doors remain locked—I'm sure I heard the driver engage them. Tension fills the air, feeding off the inescapable fact that he holds all the control.

"I've humored your valiant attempts to appear unaffected, Ms. Thorne," he says, proving as much. "Don't assume that you can lie to me. Even without my sight, I know that you're trembling. That you came to me so hysterical my doorman broke protocol to let you in."

Hysterical? I grit my teeth. "I'm fine—"

"I know that you were sobbing," he continues over me. "And I played your game by not mentioning it before, but I know you're crying even now."

Damn him. I impulsively swipe at my eyes. They're burning. Wet. Because I'm tired. I barely slept last night. The long work hours have strained my vision and triggered a pulsing headache. That's why.

"You said you *fell*." He voices the statement with a sudden concern that chafes against my already sore pride. "And yet you didn't call your father or the police—"

"I didn't come here for the third degree," I snap.

"*Sí*. So why did you come, then?"

I glare out the window in lieu of answering right away. Blurred buildings pass by in a blend of color. We're somewhere uptown, I assume, hopefully near enough to the Lariat that I could walk to it. My fingers twitch toward the door handle, but something keeps me from grabbing it.

Making a scene now would be both cathartic and utterly stupid.

Not that he'd allow you to embarrass him. The thought comes from someplace deep, impossible to suppress. When I finally let my hand fall, it isn't out of fear. It isn't.

"Are you going to paint me or not?" I demand, changing the subject when the silence becomes unbearable. "I can pay you, of course."

"I don't do it for money." His voice dips down to that unsettling octave. Once again, he's defensive. "And, as I said, we'll discuss my terms and you can decide whether or not you will agree to them. Shall we?"

Huh? Startled, I glance out the window behind him. We've stopped. A high-rise towers above, formed of silver accents and polished glass. The restaurant he mentioned must be inside it. I start for the door, desperate to escape the tension—only to remember that my blouse is undone and I'm wearing one sleeve of my coat. I scramble to assemble myself while Damien patiently waits.

"Take your time, Ms. Thorne," he says, his head cocked, his ears bared to catch my rapid breathing.

He and the driver must have a routine worked out. The other man exits the vehicle first but comes to my end. As I rush out, I turn and find Damien using his cane to maneuver around the car. A part of me wants him to trip. Stumble. Anything to prove that he's human and not infallible.

As if to spite me, he mounts the curb without a hitch.

"Shall we, Ms. Thorne?" He starts for the building's entrance, utilizing his cane. Near the doors, he pauses. "After you…"

I stalk inside with my head held high, expecting one of the quaint, expensive haunts Daddy would drag me to. Places with gilded wallpapers and employees who bend over backward in the hopes of earning a tip to supplement an income that doesn't come close to the cost of a chef's special.

Instead, I find subdued colors and a hushed silence that instantly mutes the noise from the street. The lobby is sparsely decorated but in a way that leaves no doubt in one's mind as to the caliber of humans who frequent this establishment.

Filthy, decadently rich.

"This way." Damien heads forward, using his cane to test the path before him.

A beaming woman in black silk stands behind a silver podium and automatically recognizes my host. "Mr. Villa," she says warmly. "A private room for two, as requested."

It strikes me that the decor looks as though it were ripped right from his studio. Dark walls and polished wood floors illuminated by dim lighting designed to make any visitor feel more disoriented than…

Well, than a blind man.

TEN

A man could bring his enemy here. Or his lover.

It's too intimate. Dark walls form an elegant, if claustrophobic, prison. In lieu of a table and chairs, a leather chaise dominates one wall placed behind a low table—making for a vastly different layout from any restaurant I've frequented.

The only decoration is a row of black curtains shielding one half of the room. All in all, I'm reminded of a private box in a theater and my mind hums with terrifying possibilities. Few things could entertain a man like Damien—and every potential scenario sets my already frayed nerves on fire.

"My usual wine," he requests of the server before seating himself at one end of the chaise. "Anything for my guest?"

I bite my lip to keep from asking for the same. "Water," I choke out. There. Now to keep up the air of being unaffected.

A cursory glance of the room reveals few places to sit without being near him. A spot at the far end of the couch offers the most distance.

"So, you can guarantee the discretion of this place?" I take pains to sound skeptical while gauging his reaction. Damn. Not even a wince. "Unless this was your plan all along? Manipulate me into ruining my father's career?" It sounds so damn obvious when said out loud. "Have a nice night, Mr. Villa—"

"I promised you discretion, did I not?" His face is as stoic as ever, but his hands are clenched at his sides. Once again, I've insulted him. "You can leave," he adds coldly, jerking his chin toward the door. "Or you can join me. The show is about to begin."

Show?

As if on cue, the black curtains part to reveal a sheet of glass behind them: a window.

Confused, I lower myself onto the couch. I assumed the word choice was a taunt, but now? "What is this?"

The main event, apparently. This room overlooks a larger area presumably meant to serve as a stage. Rather than an audience or gallery, rows of mirrors reflect the scene unfolding a good ten feet down below.

"We can't be seen," Damien informs me. "And trust me when I say that no one here gives a damn about your father."

I can guess why. Fixated on the view, I moisten my lips with my tongue and try to steady my breathing. It's rapid and shallow. Am I disgusted? Maybe.

Down below unfolds a scene my father would never expose me to.

Strapped to a black pole is a woman wearing only a leather collar around her neck and nothing else. Her breasts are bared, her body taut with anticipation as a man paces before her, barefoot over black flooring. He's naked as well, sporting a long, black strip of material in one hand. It lashes at the air with every step he takes. A whip.

"What in the hell?" I scramble to my feet, unable to tear my gaze away. There's something primal about the scene. Naked flesh and taut muscle moving fluidly with nothing to disguise it. No protection. No masks. "What is this?"

"Expression," Damien says calmly. "If you are offended, I can arrange for you to be safely returned home—"

"So this is where you get your inspiration from?" I make that word as nasty as I can, oddly satisfied when his jaw clenches. I've broken through that collected exterior. But I have enough sense to regret it as he inclines his head in my direction.

"Not everything is pretty colors to appease your vanity, Ms. Thorne."

"Oh?" I swallow hard and fight to make my voice as haughty and bitchy as I possibly can. "I guess that's how every sick freak tries to justify it—"

"Never call me that." He doesn't have to specify what. *Freak.*

I take another step away from him, toward the door. "Then what should I call you?"

"I suggest you ask yourself the same question. You're offended. Why?"

I scoff. "Because this is disgusting!"

"Why?"

"B-because..." I break off, sensing the trap before he can spring it.

Clever bastard. Once again, he's trying to manipulate me into saying the one thing he seems eager to hear: There's no way in hell I could ever understand him or his fucking art.

"You told me to enjoy the show? But how can you?" I make a show of glancing around the room only to realize that the display is more for my benefit than his. Still, it proves my point. "There isn't exactly a play-by-play."

"Ah." He sits back, suddenly at ease. His fingers form a steeple beneath his chin. "I brought you here for a reason, Ms. Thorne. Put your unique appreciation for the unusual to good use. Narrate." He clips the word between his teeth, an unmistakable dare. A terrifying threat.

"You're disgusting."

He shrugs in a gallant display of indifference. "And you see less than I do. We can agree on those assessments of each other, at least." *And I have you pegged.* The insult stings without him having to voice it aloud. *Spoiled little rich girl.* I could never understand such a twisted, edgy artist.

"They're fucking," I snarl, starting for the exit. "Even blind, you shouldn't need that explained to you—"

"That's not what I asked." His voice cuts the air, harsher than the whip lashing the naked woman, stopping me in my tracks. "I told you to describe it. What you see, as you see it."

"Like how?" I look over my shoulder and feel my cheeks flame. "Naked man. Mounting naked woman. Using his penis to—"

"No." He strikes the leather seat with the flat of his hand. Hard.

I jolt to attention, hating the gasp that trickles from my lips.

"Don't tell me what they're doing. Tell me what you *see.*"

"I see…" My gaze returns to the glass. The woman's face is upturned, her eyes wide and unfocused. My heart surges, picking up on her alarm. "She…she's afraid." Before my mind can even travel down a dark road, something in her parted lips catches my attention.

"Why?" Damien wonders, almost as if sensing the same thing I do.

"Because…this is stupid." I turn away, only to be faced with a monster, hunched forward, demanding an answer. His unforgiving snarl offers no escape.

"Why?"

"Stop." I clench my jaw. "I'm not doing this."

"If you lack the ability to articulate a simple, physical act, Ms. Thorne, then by all means. Leave."

And go where?

I was almost murdered tonight. The fact sinks in only now, while two people screw behind me and a madman orders me to play his twisted game of show and tell. I could have died, and no one would be the wiser. Not Daddy. Not the police. Just silence and Simon.

"You have no idea what I've been through."

"Then tell me."

I hate how his voice softens, still cold but less harsh. He's harder to rebuff like this. Harder to ignore.

"Tell you what? How I *feel*?" I spit his word out like it's the naughtiest of expletives. "Right now, I feel like a tool. I *feel* like I'm an idiot for humoring you for this long to be honest."

He says nothing. Waiting. Expecting. He knows I'll run.

Two deliberate steps carry me away from the window as I intend to do just that. Freedom is within reach. So I can't explain why I turn back to the couple again.

The man took the woman off the pole. He has her on her hands and knees, facing our direction. His hand rises and lowers in sharp succession, bringing the whip across her lower back. Something in my stomach twists, like a knot tightening with every blow.

"She's in pain." The voice doesn't sound like me. Broken and monotone; the drone of a sleepwalker in the midst of a nightmare. "But…"

"But what does she feel?" Damien is impatient in his prompting this time.

"She…likes it." I hate the assessment even as it leaves my mouth. "Her mouth is open," I find myself saying, almost to justify the reaction to myself. "She winces when struck, but she's licking her lips. She's not pulling away from him."

If anything, her hips arch into every blow. When the man pauses his assault to swipe a hand through her hair, she shivers into the contact.

"She enjoys it, but she's still afraid."

"Why?" Every quietly uttered question reminds me that I'm not alone. He's there, listening, sensing.

"Because she likes it too much." The man starts to strike her again. With every lash, her entire body quakes, and her teeth capture her lower lip. I recognize the look, admittedly in a different context. "She can't move away. Even if she wants to."

"Oh?" His voice is even softer. "And how can you tell that?"

How? The same way I can look at his paintings and know that, despite the rumors, they aren't part of some money-making scheme.

"Because it's written on her face."

A rush of cool air alludes to the door opening and a woman walks in, balancing a bottle of wine on a tray and two glasses. Without batting an eyelash, she sets the tray down on the table before the couch and pours from a bottle that I assume is twice as expensive as whatever he served me earlier.

When she leaves, I don't wait for Damien's say so to snatch one of the glasses for myself, and then I return to the window, bracing my free palm flat against the glass. My outstretched fingers form a frame, the man and woman trapped between them. Tiny puppets enacting a sick fantasy for the other people no doubt watching them from other private rooms.

"Do you bring all of your subjects here?" I ask the man behind me.

"No." The word lands harshly. "I seek different things from different people."

"And what do you seek from me?"

I already know the answer. Nothing. He merely wants me to stop pretending that I could ever see anything in his art beyond the surface. I'm a superficial bitch—how dare I believe otherwise.

"Tell me what you see," he commands rather than answer my question. "Describe it."

"He's kissing her."

I never stopped watching them. There's no rhyme or reason to their act. No rehearsed movements or enticing grins given to their audience. It's just them, locked in a room, forced to confront their darkest desires.

"He doesn't want to," I add as the man rams his tongue between the blond's lips. "He wants more, but he's holding back for her. To reassure her."

"Of what?" Damien wonders.

"That…" I shy away from voicing more. This is wrong. My eyes dart to the door, but in the process, I catch sight of the man on the couch, his posture rigid, his attention focused solely on me. Reluctantly, I mutter, "That he'll only ever give her what she wants."

"And what does she want?" His question lands more ominously than it should. I'm his pawn being maneuvered like a piece on a gameboard. Checkmate. He seeks surrender.

As for the woman? She wants…

"Freedom," I whisper.

She is on her back now, being herded against the pole, which provides enough stability for her to climb to her feet. The man watches, his whip at the ready. Without warning, he lashes out, striking her across the hips. She leans into the wicked caress, her eyes fixated on her partner, swollen. Begging.

My breath fogs the glass the longer I watch. In all honesty, I've never witnessed something like this before. Sex in its rawest, truest form. No lights. No cameras. Just lust and inhibition.

And Damien.

"My terms," he says as the couple finally collapses against each other, panting and spent. The curtains draw together, obscuring our view until I'm faced with pure darkness. "I require discretion."

"Of course." I grit my teeth, feeling my lips contort into a sneer. "Because the first thing I want to do is tell my father that I'm consorting with you. He warned me that you're a liar," I add, merely to twist the knife. "And a criminal."

And dangerous.

"Our sessions will consist of one per week for a month, an hour each," he continues without missing a beat. "I prefer to meet at night in my studio." He pauses as if to gauge how well I'm following the rapid-fire requests. When I say nothing, he continues. "I also require that my subjects abide by my request during that time."

"And what request would that be?" I face him, curious despite myself. Could this request hold the secret behind his model's morbid poses?

"You submit to me during the allotted time. Fully. I do what I want with you and you do not question."

I can't even pretend that I'm not curious. "In what way?"

He shrugs. "You will be paralyzed during our sessions. A simple drug related to succinylcholine but modified for recreational use. This synthetic version allows you to feel, breathe, and maintain your consciousness, but you will not be able to move."

I'm not familiar with the drug, but I recognize a dangerous scenario when I hear it. This one has all the makings of some sick joke, but he isn't laughing.

"I'll be like this for an hour?"

A slight tilt to his mouth makes heat flood my stomach. "Give or take. It doesn't last long in the body."

"And people actually agree to this?"

"I would understand if you declined." *As you should.* For the first time, I can clearly sense what he doesn't say out loud. *Refuse. Admit it: You can't handle this.*

Of course I can't. But my lips won't move to voice that out loud. I find myself picking imaginary lint off my jacket. "And you say that your subjects let you do anything. Like what?"

His jaw tightens in a way that can only be described as challenging. "Anything I deem necessary."

"Touching?"

"*Sí.*" He leans back against the chaise. "I would need to 'see' my subject."

"How well would you need to see them?" The skin on my neck prickles at the thought. I'm suddenly aware of just how thin this blouse is. Paper fucking thin.

"Thoroughly."

My face is hot. I should take comfort in the fact that he can't see —but I don't. He's aware of each breath escaping my lungs, quickening with every insinuation. A smart woman would be polite. Play coy and avoid mentioning the one subject he seems impatient for me to broach.

"Sex," I say, jumping in headfirst. "Do you sleep with your subjects?"

"Some of them."

"Oh?" I shuffle my heels against the floor in a futile effort to regain my balance. "While they're paralyzed?" I'm picturing it before I can stop myself. Perhaps that's how he gets his sick fix: incapacitating his partners in some twisted bid for control.

But he laughs. "I heed my partner's preference, Ms. Thorne."

"Well, I'm not sleeping with you."

"I wouldn't expect you to." He laughs again, deeper than before. Not to reassure me, but to warn. Sex with me is the last thing on his mind. "Think of it as a research method, one only employed when necessary. I try to give my subjects whatever they need to draw out the emotions I seek."

It's a nice way of putting his perversion—I have to give him that. "And what do you 'seek' from me?"

"Nothing." He shrugs. "Frankly, my painting you would only be to relieve your curiosity. Nothing more."

"Oh?" This time, I recognize the bait for what it is, though it doesn't ease the sting of his trap.

"There's nothing about you that I feel is worth uncovering."

Bingo. I do my best to grit my teeth and let the insult fly by. A normal woman might respond by tossing wine in the bastard's face and catching a car home. I'm low on the wine part. Retaliation is my sole motivation for stalking to the table and refilling my glass.

Before I can aim any of the liquid at him, I take a sip. Then another. "Is that so?" I rasp once half the glass is gone. "Try me."

"You live alone."

"Clever. As if you couldn't tell that much when you broke into my apartment."

"You enjoy living alone. At the same time, you hate it." He pauses pointedly as if to say, *Am I right?*

He's not. But I take another sip rather than humor him with a response.

"You're not comfortable with sex. I'll go so far as to presume that you don't date often, certainly not recently. I'd assume you were a virgin, but most women with your upbringing feel the need to rebel at least once or twice sexually."

Bastard.

"Ah, I guess you employ this party trick with all your guests?" I snap in between sips of wine. Sip. Sip. Sip. My hand shakes, sloshing some down the front of my blouse, but I can't even muster up the energy to curse. He's doing that thing again, talking to me in a way that no one else would dare.

"Your color of preference is black," he continues.

"Strange assumption for a blind man to make." I'm cringing at my rudeness. Whatever. The smug set to his jaw only reinforces my determination to hold my own. He's asking for it. "Unless this is really an act you put on—"

"Black is neutral," Damien says over me. "Imposing. People who wear black are less prone to being approached. Few people will inquire about a black dress versus one in a bright, intriguing shade of pink. In short, it's safe."

His tone implies just what he thinks of that: pathetic.

"So, I guess that makes you an expert on fashion?" I chase the question with another deep sip. My skin still feels hot. Odd. Wine never affects me like this. "What color am I wearing now then, Mr. Villa?"

He cocks his head as if listening for the answer. "Mostly black," he says. "A hint of white."

I cross my arms over my chest. Fucking liar. "So you *aren't* blind—"

"As I said: It's easy to tell when most people wear black," he reiterates. "Think of it as a certain…way of walking. Of talking."

"And the white?" I croak, fingering the collar of my blouse. It's funny. I don't even remember owning it, but sure enough, I found it in my closet, a shade purer than my dress. "I thought you said black was my only color?"

"Preference," he corrects. "And my guess is that…you were distracted."

"Distracted?" The memories of this morning are a blur, minus one inescapable truth. I was thinking of Simon. "What else?" I demand, taking a step toward him and the final sip of my wine. "Tell me, oh wise Mr. Villa."

"You're sheltered. Your father goes to great lengths to ensure that." He laughs darkly, in a way that implies far too much familiarity with that subject. "I wonder if you even know half of the extent."

"Sheltered." The glass slips from my grip. *Ping!* A million shards of glass crunch underfoot. A bit like my pride. "You don't know a damn thing about me."

"Oh?" he murmurs, turning my own haughty phrase against me. "You're sheltered but not innocent. You've suffered," he adds before I can prove him wrong. "And yet you believe that pain gives you license to keep suffering."

"Screw you!" My hand flies out, gathering speed, and the palm strikes his cheek. *Thwack!* I stagger back, clutching the stinging limb to my side. I shouldn't feel the guilt slicing through my chest so keenly. The world shouldn't be spinning…

"I let you do that once," Damien murmurs. His face blurs in and out of focus, distorted by the blindfold. There's only shadow where his eyes should be. "I won't let it happen twice."

It's more than a warning. The weight of promised violence wraps around my neck like a noose, weighing me down until I hit the floor on my hands and knees.

My head throbs. The room splits in half, and suddenly, there are two of everything. Two tables. Two bottles of wine. Two mysterious, angry blind men sensing my motions through every sloppy sound I make.

"You're drunk," he declares on the cusp of a sigh.

"Liar," I croak, watching the light play over the floor. "I don't get drunk."

"Get up." He's in front of me, standing with his hand outstretched. From this angle, he's more imposing than he should be. A hulking monolith of a man.

I don't know why I reach for him this time, interlacing my fingers with his. He yanks me upright, but the world pitches beneath me, impossible to balance upon. My legs fold, but something catches me by the waist before I can fall. Something strong. Firm. Warm.

"I've got you." The voice sinks into my skin, resonating in my bones to spite me.

My palms flatten against the firm planes of his chest, and I push back but my legs buckle, making one thing clear: It's either him or the floor. Instinctively, my grip tightens over his forearms, rousing tightly coiled muscle that flexes beneath my fingers. God, he's *strong*—another realization that catches me off guard.

"Come." His breath fans my throat. "Sit."

He angles my body toward the couch and I can't stop the descent. Boneless, I land on the cushions width-ways, staring up at him.

"You drugged me." My words slur together, even as I know that my accusation isn't true. A drug would make me feel better, but I just feel numb.

"I warned you that the drink is stronger than what you're used to." The confidence with which he makes that assumption drenches me in foreboding.

"You don't know a damn thing about me."

"Don't I?" He cocks his head.

I shiver, bracing my hands against unyielding leather. He seems different from this angle. Bigger. To use his word, *imposing*.

"I know that every year on which just so happens to be your birthday, someone sends you the exact bottle of vintage Romanée Conti that I've served you, but you never drink more than a few sips."

Shock grips my chest like a ruthless fist, squeezing the air from it. "You've been watching me." More than just watching. Peering into that black box that arrives every year to know the bottle. Unless he could decipher wine brands through touch alone, he had to have someone read him the label. "You're sick."

"I'm thorough, Ms. Thorne," he corrects without a shred of guilt or shame. "Know thy enemy."

"Enemy? So, you spied on me because you hate my father?"

But why tell me this now? Fear of the answer solidifies in my stomach and creeps up the back of my throat like bile. There has to be a reason.

"I always do my research, Ms. Thorne," he says. "I know you. I've watched you, as have so many others in your life."

Watched. Something about how he utters that word makes me roll onto my side and attempt to sit upright. I fail, smacking my head off the armrest as my ineffective limbs refuse to support my weight. "How? Why?"

"Curiosity. I want to be near enough to sense your reaction the day that all of your father's lies come crashing down around you." With that, he straightens his posture and elegantly extends his cane. "I'll have a car sent for you," he says as he starts for the door, tapping out a path.

"Wait!" I flail again in a desperate attempt to stand. Dizziness. The next second, my head is between my knees and my stomach is heaving.

I hear silence. Then footsteps coming closer. Closer...as the world spins faster and faster.

ELEVEN

I've never been hungover in my life, but I recognize the nauseating punishment my body enacts. College rumors don't do it justice; sobriety returns with a vengeance. Too exhausted to move, I just suck in air through my nose and attempt to decipher my surroundings.

I'm on my bed, I think. There is no mistaking the rasp of my custom sheets and the firmness of my mattress. How I got here. Well…

Those details are fuzzy. Alarmed, I blink my eyes open to make out the familiar comforts of my room. Gray daylight streams in through the window. Too bright. I groan and roll onto my side to escape it. Then I hear them.

Footsteps, soft and slow, approaching the bed. I jerk my focus toward the sound and spot him lingering just beyond my reach, dressed impeccably in a mixture of gray and black. In one hand, he's holding my favorite white mug. Steam wafts from the top and my nostrils wrinkle. Coffee.

"I recommend small sips," he says and sets the mug on my bedside table.

The resulting sound echoes like a gunshot, drawing a groan from my lips. My brain feels like a bowling ball bouncing off a skull made of tissue paper.

"What...what are you doing here?" Uh-oh. Something flakes off my chin as I speak. Dried. Crusty. I fight to lift my hand from the bed and swipe at my mouth with a trembling finger. Vomit.

"You were in no state to be left alone." He sounds disgusted by that fact and I shudder at what else I might have done to earn such a reaction. Not that I need to worry. Damien seems more than willing to tell me. "I didn't touch you more than necessary," he adds, a chilling preface.

I glance down and find my blouse partially undone. Someone wedged a damp cloth beneath the sleeve over my injured shoulder. My pants are still on, but my heels aren't. *Oh God.* The dried vomit takes on a different meaning.

"This is breaking and entering," I rasp. I try to sit up only to wind up on my back. The world won't stop spinning.

"It would be," Damien admits. "If you didn't invite me in."

Even drunk, I doubt I'd be so stupid. Rather than challenge him, I state the obvious. "Well, you can leave now."

He doesn't so much as flinch at the vitriol I spit his way. Instead, he reaches out, his fingers outstretched. I stiffen, choking on the air, but he grabs something from the nightstand near my bed. A handkerchief, one of his.

"Here." He drags the cloth against my cheek without warning. Without permission.

Sputtering, I cringe out of his reach. "Did you forget you're supposed to be blind?" I croak, eyeing his blindfold for any concealed slits.

"I can hear your breathing," he explains, letting the cloth fall onto the sheets. Sighing, he stands back and inclines his head toward the bedframe. "And I was listening from the other room. You haven't shifted much from the position I left you in."

Listening? Just how long has he been here, lurking outside my bedroom? I swallow hard and grasp the end of a sheet, dragging it over me as if the thin material can protect against his perception.

"Is that how you get by?" I wonder, annoyed that I sound more curious than mocking. "Remembering people's body positions?"

He tilts his head. "Well, I do paint the human body for a living. At least that's how the saying goes, isn't it?"

"Because you *don't* paint the human body for a living," I finish for him. Daddy used another word to describe his true profession. "You're a *criminal.*"

"Drink the coffee slowly," he tells me while withdrawing an object from the pocket of his slacks: the cane. Each delicate tap echoes as he heads for the door.

"Wait." Why I stop him, I don't know. His jaw clenches amid the snapping of teeth as he pauses near the doorway. "You said something last night." My heart squeezes as my brain sluggishly attempts to remember. What was it? "Something about my birthday," I add, fumbling with the words as they race from my mouth. "The wine. You knew. How?"

A simple shrugging of his shoulders and Damien becomes unreadable. "I don't remember anything of the sort, Ms. Thorne. Enjoy the rest of your day—"

"Wait." I manage to haul myself upright, using the pillow as a crutch. The words on the tip of my tongue don't leave it easily, almost as if every cell in my body resists the notion I stupidly propose. "So...so, when do we start?"

"Excuse me?" God, he sounds even more unnerving when he's confused. His voice dips an octave and his accent sharpens, honing every word into crisp syllables.

"When do we start?" I try to sound casual and fail. It would help if I didn't feel like roadkill. Or if this man weren't lying to me, withholding secrets about my own damn life.

I'll get to that, eventually. Until then...

"Painting me," I say, forging on. "I remember your terms." They were crystal clear: paralyzed by a drug, naked, and helpless at his mercy.

"And you agree to them?"

Do I? The ominous tingle running down my spine says no.

"If I *did*," I begin before he can say anything cutting, "when would we start?"

"This isn't a game."

I flinch. He's using that whip-like voice again, and my hungover brain struggles to impress upon me one key detail: He's a stranger in my house, able to navigate it with uncanny ease, especially for a blind man. He looks far too comfortable, lording over my master bedroom, which suddenly feels like a closet. I should be calling Daddy. The police. Anyone.

Not pushing his buttons, morbidly eager to learn more. He claims to know me, but I don't even have that luxury.

"I'm not playing." My voice almost sounds stable enough to back that statement. "So were you lying when you offered your services, or were you serious?"

I'm shivering. Only now am I aware of how my teeth are chattering. My blouse feels like tissue paper, ineffective against how my nipples have stiffened. Biology is betraying me in the worst possible way. Gritting my teeth, I drag the sheet farther over me.

He notices. The corner of his mouth twitches as if he's aware of everything I desperately seek to hide. The resulting expression isn't quite a smile or a frown. It's more terrifying than either.

It's curious.

"Yes or no," he demands, squaring his stance until he dominates my doorway and there's no way past him. I'm trapped. Physically. Figuratively. "I don't play with possibilities."

Suddenly, my lips feel dry enough that I run my tongue across them. Dehydrated flesh grates on the moist surface like sandpaper. Unfortunately, the pain doesn't reboot my common sense.

"Yes," I blurt as my stomach flips. "I'll do it. So, when do we start?"

"I should let you recover from last night," he says as if the idea just occurred to him.

As if I'm that fragile. That weak.

"No." I shift my weight and place my feet on the floor. "How about tonight?"

And this time, I'll corner him with questions he can't refuse. I'll get to the bottom of Damien. Even if…

My mind shies away from the train of thought. *Even if it kills me.*

"Hmm?" I prod when he doesn't answer. His jaw is tight again, his head still cocked like a predator avidly tracking his prey. Have I stumped the cool, collected Mr. Villa?

I suck in a breath when he nods. Apparently not.

"I'll consider it."

"C-consider it?"

He turns on his heel and exits my room without explanation, navigating toward what sounds like the foyer. "Have a good day, Ms. Thorne. Drink the coffee." He pauses, allowing the command to linger on the air. "I'll be in touch to inform you whether or not I'll humor your request."

"Humor?"

I hear the door open and close. By the time I manage to climb to my feet and stagger into the living room, he's gone. I race to the peephole and peer into the hall just in time to catch his silhouette flicker around the corner.

"Bastard," I hiss.

But as my voice echoes around me, I remember…

I'm alone again. With no one to stand between me and Simon. With no one there to see how my breathing becomes rapid and my body trembles. There's no time to regret the action. I already have the door open and I'm stumbling into the hall.

"Wait." I round the corner and find him standing before the elevator. A hiss of annoyance catches on the air. Yet he maintains the perfect poise of a gentleman.

"Can I help you, Ms. Thorne?"

"Why not just do it now and get it over with?"

He frowns at the suggestion. "I have other arrangements, and frankly, considering how much you drank, the alcohol is most likely still in your system. Mixing that with the drug I use can have dangerous side effects."

Fair enough. I take a step back and the elevator car arrives with a musical chime. I'm wringing my fingers together as he steps inside and feels along the wall panel for the ground floor button. It's the most convincing show of blindness from him yet. A minor hint of weakness. As the thought crosses my mind he nods, setting my body alight.

"Keep your phone close, Ms. Thorne. When I'm ready for you, I'll call. *Adiós*."

The elevator doors slide neatly shut, closing him off. And suddenly my chest deflates as I exhale the breath I wasn't even aware of holding.

TWELVE

*D*amien can go to hell. One where he's forced to have *all* his senses to better contemplate his eternal suffering.

When I return to my room, I sample his coffee out of spite and almost spit it right back out. Damn. It's perfect, made exactly to my daily preference.

Too exact. Almost as if he's stood over my shoulder and watched me brew it for the past ten years, tweaking my habit to an art form. I take only one more sip before I toss the rest down the sink. Then I cross to my painting and observe it in the growing daylight despite how time stubbornly marches on. I'm late again. Or I would be if I were to go into the office.

Even the thought of returning now makes goosebumps prickle on the back of my neck. Not entirely because of what happened—but because of what hasn't.

No one's called reporting a break-in.

No police have asked about my attack.

The fact that someone could invade a public building in one of the busiest cities in the world without so much as a video popping up on social media is...

Chilling. Only Simon could pull it off—or someone far worse.

Rather than speculate, I call the building and confirm that Gus is alive and well at least.

"He had to leave early last night," the security supervisor explains. "Bad Chinese food."

Unease gnaws at my nerves as I linger in my apartment, sensing the flickering shadows from the corner of my eye. Every noise from the hall has me jumping, and my mind races with possibilities. Simon? Or Damien?

Which monster would I prefer? That's the true question and I hate that I can't answer it. My thoughts are too jagged to untangle.

In the hopes of finding some semblance of peace, I shed my rumpled clothing and climb into the shower of the guest bathroom, where everything is pristine and unbroken. God, I hate the woman watching me from the mirror. It's angled so that I have a clear view of myself, even while underneath the spray. Pale. Thin. Wide-eyed and haunted.

My right shoulder is bruised around the cut, which looks much worse when viewed from a distance. My lower lip is bitten, and even Damien couldn't clean up the worst of the vomit.

I'm disgusting, more grotesque than one of Sampson's paintings. All I need is a bed of blood-red roses to complete the aesthetic.

For now, my only accessory is the white towel I wrap around myself as I return to my bedroom and eye my closet critically. Every single item repels me. There's too much black. Too much tailored perfection. I spot a crumpled mass of wrapping paper and ribbon in the wastebasket near the foot of my bed and stiffen. How long has it been since I've worn that shade of purple?

My wardrobe doesn't contain the color at all. Maybe not since that day, all those years ago when I was dressed from head to toe in the shade. The best clothing Goodwill and Walmart could supply.

I wince. Bitter nostalgia strikes like an invisible fist to my stomach. I inhale raggedly and find something else to focus on. Like Damien. I left his sketch of me in the living room.

Still dripping wet and wearing only my towel, I head toward it. I'll rip it up this time and toss it into the trash, where it belongs.

Wait. My footsteps falter near the mouth of the hall before I even register my nostrils flaring. A faint, almost floral taint. Cologne? His scent announces his presence without my having to see him there, sitting on my couch, his posture imposingly erect.

"W-what are you doing here?" I mean to sound indignant. Not curious.

"Good evening." Damien inclines his head without facing me directly, almost as if he's riveted by the view from my window.

It's already late in the day. Indigo twilight washes over the horizon as a storm rages on. Thunder rumbles ominously. Lightning flashes. Funny. I didn't notice either until now.

"You weren't near your phone." His low tone perfectly mimics the muffled sounds of the storm.

He's wearing black again, the hypocrite—a suit tailored to perfection, crowned by a blood-red tie. Rather than the white cane, a real one made of carved wood leans against his knee. The handle of it is silver, shaped into the visage of a roaring lion.

"I wasn't?" I ask innocently. "I've been busy today."

"You haven't left this apartment." He sounds too damn sure of that, as if daring me to make the next leap in logic.

"Oh? And how would you know that?" I clutch my towel so tightly that my knuckles whiten. Things came back to me while I was in the shower. Memories I shied away from exploring in full, each one far too vivid to be from a nightmare. "Because you've been following me, haven't you? You knew what kind of wine I'd gotten. No one knows that—"

"I know everything about you," he says amid another foreboding strike of lightning. "Like the fact that you haven't expressed an interest in art a day in your life. That you manipulate lives for a living. That you and your father are one and the same."

"What the hell is that supposed to mean?"

He shifts in my direction and, God...I can feel his gaze piercing through me when it shouldn't.

"It means, if you want to play this game, I'll let you. To use your turn of phrase, let's get this over with." He lifts something clenched in his fist. A pen? No, it's too wide. Another flash of lightning illuminates the liquid inside and the long, thin tip encased in a plastic lid. A syringe. "I'll let you get a taste of what it's like to be truly helpless."

As if I don't already know how that feels. The storm building in intensity around us only compounds that fact. God, I just pray I won't panic, not around him. "Get out."

"*Sí.* As you wish." He rises to his feet, reaching for his cane. "Burn whatever information of mine Carla gave you. And you can keep the damn painting. I won't contact you again—"

"How long have you been watching me?" I blurt.

A denial should be his first instinct. Not a rich bark of laughter that resonates through my core, deeper than another roar of thunder. Strange. I should be having flashbacks about now.

Vomit-inducing memories. Damien shouldn't be the one anchor tethering me to the present.

"Do you really want to know?"

"I… Do you stalk all of your potential subjects?" I counter.

"As I told you before, you are not a subject. *They* all concealed something worth learning."

Apparently, I don't.

"So, how does the injection work?" My throat goes dry as I eye the syringe still tucked into his free hand. The liquid catches what little light there is, giving off a faint shimmer. "You said it lasts for an hour."

"Typically. But one may perceive even a minute of being immobilized as an eternity."

He's not even being clever with the threats anymore. They spring from him like knives, conveying the one thing he seems hesitant to say directly. *You can't handle this.*

"So why do it?" I ask. "Someone doesn't have to be frozen for you to touch them."

He laughs again and the hairs on the back of my neck stand on end.

"If you have to ask, then you don't really understand my art as you claim to, *sí?*"

His words have me eyeing my painting again. Oh. As implied, the answer is in plain sight. There was no physical reason for his method. No, his motives are purely psychological. Every stroke captured the model's desperation. Her fear.

"Shouldn't you do this in your studio?" I ask. He doesn't have a briefcase with him, or canvas, or any other supplies.

"No," he says, his face illuminated by another flash of lightning. Thunder crashes, and the light in the room grows dimmer, swallowed by roving storm clouds.

I stiffen, ready for the fear. Visions of the forest. Simon. Anything but him.

Damien won't be banished so easily. He remains, tilting his syringe for my benefit. "This is merely for you to get a taste of just what you're requesting. I don't tailor my methods for anyone."

"And I'm not asking you to." Though why is that, exactly? I couldn't say.

My toes curl into the carpet as if to hinder every slow, careful step I take toward him. I stop just beyond his reach. If he comes for me, I can react. Or so I tell myself. "How do I know you won't kill me?"

"You don't." His voice falls flat.

"Fine, then." I tilt my chin and desperately try to combat the tremor in my voice. "What if you rape me while I'm like this?"

"Oh, but it wouldn't be rape, would it? In case you've forgotten my terms, you submit to me for however long you're under the drug's influence."

He sounds too damn smug. As if he's well aware of my pounding heartbeat. He wants to scare me—and he has.

"So…I'd have to trust you," I say, much more for my benefit than to score a reaction from him. But that word. It makes his upper lip pull back from his teeth.

"You'd *submit*."

"And everyone does this?" I shouldn't sound so hollow. So calm. Not when I can barely coax any air to go into my lungs.

He says nothing, letting me piece the answer together on my own. I'm not sure how long we stand there in silence before he finally taps the tip of his cane against the floor. "Goodnight, Ms. Thorne—"

"So we'll do it here, then?" I inch toward the couch. That strip of expensive leather and padding has never seemed so menacing. Damien's presence can turn everyday objects into new and unusual weapons of torture. I've walked this path a million times and never felt this sharp, aching thrill. "Or the bed?"

But I'm already sitting down, painfully aware of him behind me. He has yet to move away from the door. Maybe he won't. A sharp hiss is my only warning that once again I've foiled his expectations. For good or bad?

I'll worry about the answer later.

Minutes trickle by. Far too long. I'm freezing, still wearing only my towel. I should change. I start to rise and nearly jump out of my skin as a sharp thud shatters the silence, too close to be thunder.

"Sit," Damien commands.

From the corner of my eye, I see him lift his cane, the source of the sound. My legs fold like lawn chairs, depositing me right back down.

"S-should I get dressed?" I ask him.

"No." Slow, steady footsteps bring him to me.

I sense him, even before his hand settles over the back of the couch, searching. He swipes along the rim until he reaches my shoulder. With deliberate familiarity, he circles his fingers around the ridge of muscle and bone.

"It will be an intramuscular injection," he says. Warning me? "There will be some initial discomfort. Then numbness. You'll be able to breathe, but speaking will be difficult and I recommend against it. Do you have any medication allergies?"

I shake my head.

"Fine, then." He sounds resigned, more to his choice than my own. "Sit still. After this, I'll accept no change of heart. Do you agree to my terms?"

I should mull over the question, creating a dramatic silence worthy of the coward he thinks me to be. Mainly, I should cower and shiver beneath his touch. Not glisten with sweat I know he can feel.

"I agree," I say, copying his formal language. "I agree to your terms—" My voice ends in a hiss. Unseen, he must have injected me, right into the muscle of my upper arm.

"Discomfort" was an understatement. Burning fire consumes the muscle and spreads. I can feel it trickling into my bloodstream. My fingertips sear. My legs. My chest.

"It will take at least ten minutes for the full effect," Damien explains.

I hear a noise that sounds like his cane being propped against the back of the couch. Knuckles cracking next. Fabric rustling. His coat being shed, I realize as he circles around to face me.

He cocks his head, listening. I'm starting to recognize how he compensates for the loss of his vision—he's attentive. Calculating.

"S-should I lie down?" My voice comes out a scarce whisper, though I doubt the drug has taken effect this quickly. The sight of him has its own paralyzing effect. He's here, enforcing his presence in a way even Simon never has. I taste his flavor on my tongue and I'm not sure whether to spit him out or…

"It's up to you," he says, reinforcing his indifference to this entire situation. Poor man. I've confounded him—even though he's the one who broke into my home and put the choice before me in the first place.

My arm is starting to throb, so I decide to lie flat on my back with the site of the injection toward the open end of the couch. I've barely settled against the leather when I catch his frown.

"Remove the towel."

I can't silence my gasp. "H-how did you know?" Ignoring the fact that I mentioned getting dressed, I could be wearing pajamas for all he knew. No. Towel is far too specific. Just how long has he been here?

"You were in the shower," he says, only extending my curiosity. "You then went into the bedroom, but you didn't enter your closet. I didn't hear hangers being moved. Or drawers being opened. You take at least ten minutes to dress normally, but you were out in three."

He recited such a methodical list for a reason. To inflict the most terror. And he has.

My eyes go to the door. I can still move my limbs. Long enough to get help? I brace one foot against the floor, preparing to stand.

"How long have you been watching me? How? Do you always come into my house while I'm—"

"You should conserve your energy, Ms. Thorne. We're already at two minutes."

"Then admit it," I hiss through gritted teeth. "How long have you been stalking me?"

"I think a better question is: Who *else* might be watching you, Juliana Thorne?"

I flinch at the insinuation. He knows of the wine, but is he aware of who sent it and why? Does he know about Simon?

"As for why, it's simple: Because I can. I've had a window into your life you couldn't realize in your nightmares."

My fingers clutch the couch on either side of me, readying for the moment I decide to run. Which is exactly what he wants me to do. He's goading me on purpose. Scaring me. I should damn well take the hint. I shouldn't question.

"If I'm so uninteresting to you, then why waste your precious time and resources following my *boring*, predictable life?"

He frowns. "I'll tell you why: Heyworth Thorne."

"My father?"

"*Sí*. Don't sound so surprised, Juliana. I'm sure you've gotten enough reminders this week alone as to why someone might have a grudge against your father. Why *I* might…"

Ah. A not-so-subtle insinuation that he's spied on me in my office as well. "So you know about the messages I've gotten. Friends of yours?"

He chuckles. "I prefer to send more…direct messages, Ms. Thorne." His fingers flex at his sides, drawing my attention. I see a sudden image of him hunched over a sheet of paper, channeling his rage into vivid sketches.

"What do you have against my father?" I'm merely stalling now.

I'm not as naïve as Mr. Villa appears to think, and the recent news coverage merely exposed an open secret: Daddy isn't as perfect as he pretends to be. Neither is his judgment.

"Did he convict you of too many traffic violations or something?"

"Too many traffic violations…" He laughs again, more deeply than before. The sound serves as a chilling foil to another crack of thunder, louder than all those before it. "You should really read a newspaper article, Ms. Thorne. It's right there in black and white."

Ah, but wasn't he the one who spelled it out for me? I'm sheltered. Innocent. A fucking pathetic coward. Daddy has his own demons to deal with, and I've been more than willing to let him battle them alone.

"Enlighten me, then," I demand. Forming the words takes more effort than it should. The clock on the wall reveals why. Seven minutes.

"No." He crosses to me like a snake, sensing out my position through motion and sound. His hand reaches out, his fingers searching until they find my chin. "I'll let you think about it, Juliana." He tilts my head back and my limp muscles are no match. I can't even raise a finger against him. "I'll let you play with every dark scenario that might flit around that simple mind of yours. You worried that I might kill you. Rape you. But do you know what I *really* want to do to you?" He leans in close, his breath hot on my skin.

My throat refuses to form words. Even a gasp. All I can do is stare.

"I'm going to let you sit here in the fucking dark. Alone." He drags his thumb in a cruel imitation of a caress as terror locks me in a vise-grip. "Do you know the real reason why I stayed with you last night? You *begged* me to. Nothing terrifies you more than silence. The darkness. The emptiness…"

He's lying. I cling to that hope, even as the repressed memories from last night flutter to the surface. Thrashing on sweat-soaked sheets, seeing Simon in the shadows. Grasping someone's hand so tightly that I could sense the bones and ridges that made up their fingers. Touching skin so soft that I could tear it. Croaking a single word over and over. *Stay. Stay. Stay. Stay.*

My eyes blink rapidly—the only physical act I have control over.

"Enjoy your night, Ms. Thorne." He steps back, silhouetted by the storm raging behind him, and moves beyond my line of sight.

"D-don't…" I have to shove the word off my tongue, my chest heaving with the effort.

He'll leave anyway. I wait for the sound of the door slamming shut. For the silence that's become the soundtrack of my adult life.

I wait.

And he lingers, lurking just beyond the reach of my peripheral vision. Air trickles in and out of paper-thin lungs. The clock tells me why; it's beyond ten minutes. My muscles and nerves have become deaf to any command my brain issues. I can't even turn my head. Only my ears aid in sensing just where he is. Paces from the couch. Maybe in that exact spot where the carpet turns to the tile of the kitchen. From there, and with his height, he'll have the perfect view of me. Sprawled upright, trapped beneath the towel. Without my fingers to support it, the terrycloth rides dangerously low. And yet…

It's not my body he seems to be after.

My heart lurches as his footsteps return, drawing closer. At first, I fear he'll stay where I can't see him. But no. He enters my line of sight, sans his cane…and I shouldn't be relieved. Not given the way he looks. Jaw clenched. Furrowed lines around the edges of his blindfold.

Panting. The sound comes from me, clashing with the muted sounds of rain and thunder. It picks up, feathering into breathless gasps as he advances step by step. He hunts me through the act alone, his head cocked, his posture rigid.

I nearly jump out of my skin when his finger brushes my cheek. He wasn't lying. I feel everything. The softness of his skin. The faintest slickness of sweat, even though I'm freezing. He traces a path to my mouth and hovers his thumb over my parted lips, sensing how they quiver.

His other hand comes slowly, almost reluctantly, to seek out my forearm. Then my collarbone. Finally, he finds the edge of my towel and sinks his fingers into the material. He tugs it away and my lips flutter open around a gasp.

Helpless like this, I have no comparison to any other moment in my life. Simon made me feel small and cornered, like a mouse, always running on a wheel that would never move. Damien, in this moment, makes me feel like…

Prey. Only he's a disinterested predator. I'm more helpless before him than I've ever been around any other monster—even the one who tried to kill me. Yet he controls how much of me he wants to see. My lips at the moment. Then the tender, bony ridge of my rib cage where my heartbeat can be felt the most.

Watching him stand over me is too damn surreal. So I force my eyes shut and listen, copying how he must sense me. I'm nowhere near as warm as he is, and my hands aren't halfway as soft.

My pulse quickens, and I can almost visualize the sound pulsating through his fingertips, giving me away. Touch feels far more penetrating than sight ever could. He can feel what my facial expression wouldn't reveal. My fear. Terror. Curiosity?

The other women, the ones so intriguing that he rendered them motionless to decipher their secrets. I bet he explored them far more intimately than he does me. Good. I should count my blessings. Thank God he isn't interested in peering too deeply beneath my shell.

Wrong. His main goal seems to be to circumvent my expectations at every turn. The hand he has on my chest curls, cupping more flesh, kneading it just to the point of roughness. To hear me scream. As easily as he deciphers me, I'm finding that I can do the same to him. He wants me to protest, so I make a concerted effort to say nothing.

I don't gasp. I don't whimper. I don't even breathe.

I simply feel, locked inside my own body. Now seems like the wrong moment to realize that he's the first man to ever touch me like this. Really touch me. Naked flesh beneath roaming fingers. Should I feel robbed of some precious moment? My future lover has been beaten to this intimate discovery. He'll have to be content with whatever Damien leaves untouched.

Which will be nothing.

Something in the air changes. Thunder surges as if feeding off the emotion conveyed in the thumb he wedges between my lips to pry them apart. Determination. Morbid curiosity. How far can he push me?

Another searching path of his hand down my chest conjures up the answer I don't want to face. Too far. He's closer, his footsteps landing in menacing tandem. I hear his breath catch on a resigned sigh. He'll play this stupid game I've set in motion. He'll play to win. The hand on my chin curls, cupping my face fully, tilting it back

"Are your eyes open? I'm assuming they aren't," he says, employing that uncanny knowledge of me to unsettling effect. "You always run when you're frightened. Cower." His thumb strokes upward, stopping short of my eyelid. "Open them."

He's right. Playing the role of a frightened mouse is the role I play the best. I've grown accustomed to fear's bitter sting. How it grapples for control from my limbs and paralyzes me more than this drug ever could. I should feel it now, the icy tendrils of terror. Hell, I welcome it.

But he's wrong.

I keep my eyes shut, feeding off the tension building in his fingertips. He senses my disobedience without ever having to see it.

"Remember your word, Juliana Thorne," he warns, issuing another callous stroke to my cheek. "I know honor is a murky concept in your family, but you promised your submission. Open. Your. Eyes."

Another crack of thunder reinforces the malice in his tone. But I keep myself blind. For the first time in my life, it isn't because I'm afraid of what I'll see. I know the sight awaiting me: a stern-faced villain bolstered by crackling lightning and distracting shadows. Deciphering him through touch is ten times more disorienting. There are no snap judgments I can make. Just slow deliberation based off the sparks ignited in my skin wherever his touch roams.

Daddy's method won't help me here. Damien requires a new form of deduction. Like the fact that even when he boldly grazes his hand over my breast there's no real malice in it. The thumb braced between my teeth reveals more. It stiffens, capturing the gasp choked from my throat. At first, he presses harder, relishing the perceived triumph. Not even a second later, he withdraws the pressure.

"Apparently, you still believe this to be a game."

I've never known such a thick, impenetrable silence before. Even the weather seems to pause its assault, riveted by the man whose anger bastes my skin with every breath. Another harsh stroke along my chin tilts my face toward the palm of his hand. With no control, I'm at his mercy. He could toy with me like a rag doll, or worse. But no, Damien's style is more psychological than anything.

"I think you've been alone too long, Juliana," he tells me, his voice grated. I suspect he knows damn well just how long it's been. "A good, wholesome woman such as yourself shouldn't be reacting to me."

Apparently, he doesn't know me as well as he thinks. I've never been good, always pretending. Wholesome is a term that best applies to the extent of my lies. Whole. Consuming.

"Are you that desperate for..." He trails off, letting my imagination run wild to fill in the gap.

His attention drifts lower, more slowly than before. Spreading fingers and dull nails perform their search with more intent. Friction sparks. Fire follows. Locked in place, my muscles can't even shudder beneath the violation. I've never wanted to recoil so badly in my life. I've never been so attuned to my body's reaction to anything. Not Simon. Not anyone.

"Open your eyes, Juliana." He's closer. His words strike my lower jaw like fire.

My ears pick up the slight ambiance they normally wouldn't. The crunch of fabric conformed to a muscular body. The creaking of my floor. Rain lashing glass. The high-pitched, breathy noises coming from my throat.

He must crouch to his knees, crushing the carpet beneath his bulk. The leather hisses, presumably brushed by the fabric of his shirt. Those hot fingers drift lower…

"Open your eyes."

It should be impossible for him to know that I haven't. Almost as impossible as it should be for me to sense the hard swallow he takes. A low sound nips at the air. Thunder? No. It's too deep. Too masculine. Too damn close.

His dominant hand has never left my face. His thumb performs a near constant stroking, up and down. Down and up. Quicker each time, the next brush more menacing than the last. Gritted teeth create an ominous warning amid the backdrop of yet another flash of lightning. This one so bright that I can see it, brilliant silver against my eyelids.

"Open." His voice rumbles against my ear. His thumb flicks my cheek, while his other hand becomes even bolder.

"N-no…" Only God knows how I manage to rasp out the word. I'm still paralyzed. Speaking feels like trying to scream with an iron weight pressing down on my chest. But he makes it possible. So confident that he knows me so damn well. "Want… to…feel…"

He laughs. Such a terrible, violent sound. My toes would curl if they could. Instead, my mouth waters and I know he can sense the moisture against his thumb. It returns to its position between my lips, testing what little control I still have over my jaw.

"Feel?" His touch moves lower.

More sparks. More fire—no, *explosions* set off beneath my skin.

"I can make you feel a million things, Juliana Thorne," he promises. Dark things. Awful things. His hand slides between my legs, giving me a mere taste of what his threat conveys.

And I choke on it.

Too much. Too much heat ripping through me. Too little control of my body. All I can do is breathe in and out. Noisily. Pained. His thumb is a rigid anchor and my tongue seeks it out, desperate to retaliate in some way.

"Open your eyes. Though perhaps I should do the honors, figuratively speaking?" He drags my legs apart as he speaks.

While I'm blinded, the sensations of slick leather and silken fingers resonate tenfold. Cool air assaults heated flesh. I suck in a breath. Too sensitive. My eyelids flutter. Make it stop.

Never have this end.

"Your father is a man of contradiction," Damien grits out. Something brushes my earlobe, imparting a tendril of alarm. Moist. Soft. His lips? His mouth, lowered so close that I feel every lash of his tongue as he speaks. "In public, he pretends to be the beacon of justice, but in private? He hides and obfuscates whatever he can. He's had all of his past records erased. Wiped clean. Did you know that? Not the good cases of course, but the others... Now, be the good little girl you are for everyone else and open. Your father could order you to jump off a fucking cliff and you would, wouldn't you?"

Probably.

The heart-stopping fall would be preferable to this; at least I'd know what to expect. I'd see the bottom in advance. I'd never have the chance to regret my decision for very long.

But this…

Lightning strikes. Thunder rumbles, and all the while, Damien breathes his hate into my skin. There's no clear line of sight to the end of my fall. I could be suspended for ages. Or hit the ground without warning.

"Open."

I don't bother denying him out loud. *I can't.* His thumb twists inside my mouth until the nail grazes my tongue. Boom! Flash! He's created his own storm inside me.

"I don't particularly care to molest you, Ms. Thorne." He almost sounds convincing. If only his accent didn't wrap around that little word—*molest*—and strangle it beyond recognition.

I know the word he substituted it for. Destroy.

I don't particularly care to destroy you, Ms. Thorne. But I will.

The hand between my legs twitches in warning as his voice straddles that guttural octave. "Open your goddamn eyes."

"N-no—"

Inferno. He must have anticipated my response, because silken fingers cup me without hesitation. Ruthlessly. My thoughts scatter at the contact. Total shutdown. What little air I have in my lungs escapes in a rush. Every nerve I possess overloads and then comes back online, one after the other. Sensation first. Then the parts of my brain capable of interpreting it. Heat. Fire. Sweltering. Raw. Skin. Soft. Everywhere, everywhere, *everywhere.*

Motion rustles near my earlobe as he murmurs something unintelligible. *Open.* I register a ragged inhale. Sharp exhale. Then he growls, "*Mierda.* What game are you playing?"

As if I'm the one who wields the control. I wish I were. I'd push him off. Run away. I'd cower and hide like he wants me to.

"Open," he snarls.

But the darkness is addicting. Beneath its veil, I can interpret more of him than ever before. He's closer, leaning his weight toward my position. What must be his torso brushes the tips of my knees, not quite forcing its way between them. But almost. Heat fans my neck in tandem with his breathing. Harsh. Slowed. He's grappling for calm, something I doubt I'll ever find again.

"For the last time…open your eyes."

I don't. He retaliates.

Only the power of my imagination allows me a vague inclination of what he does next: slide a finger inside me. My frozen muscles don't offer him any slack. He has to force it. I have to feel it. Friction—bitter, searing friction. Tightness. Closeness. A feeling beyond fire or inferno. A nuclear blast.

A strangled cry crawls up my throat, but I barely hear myself beneath his grunted exclamation.

"*Qué mierda!*"

Doused. He pulls back so suddenly that that's what it feels like: being drenched in ice water and left to freeze.

His mouth remains near my ear, however, his thumb trembling against my tongue. "You're a virgin."

He sounds incredulous. He sounds…furious?

I don't know whether to lie or admit the truth. So I say nothing. But he wins. The breadth of his confusion feels far too great to experience through feel alone. I have to open my eyes and see his clenched, disgusted expression for myself.

He's closer than I thought, hunched against me, his hand still between my legs, his face almost parallel to mine. There's no avoiding the path my eyes take. Even blindfolded, his features form a beautiful silhouette in the dark—but make a terrifying contrast when lightning flashes.

"Are you?" he demands. Another searching thrust of his thumb fractures my attention. Can't focus. "Too tight," he grates, speaking more to himself than me. "Have to be."

I bite my tongue and he draws back, rising to his feet. The loss of his heat deals a harsher blow than it should. Cold air cruelly replaces him as he starts to pace. One of his hands tears through his hair. The same one he had inside me. The nails on it assault his scalp, ripping strands of ebony hair from his neat ponytail. In place of *me*.

I'm the real target of his rage. To prove it, his head swivels in my direction and I sense his focus on my fingers. Looking down, I see why. They're flexing against the leather, straining for leverage as the hand on the clock inches minutes past an hour.

But I'm a long way from moving. If anything, the slight tease of freedom is a million times worse. I'm not so helpless, but still at his mercy. Still vulnerable to the threat he voiced. *I'll leave you here in the dark.*

"D-don't. P-please!" The plea scrapes my throat as he stalks past the couch, beyond my sight. With my eyes wide open, it's harder to assume what he's doing. Wood drags across carpet. Fabric swishes through the air. Footsteps angrily approach my door. "W-wait—"

"Once upon a time, you were left alone in the dark." There's what could be mistaken for pity in his voice. Almost—and it unnerves me like nothing else. "Afraid. Abandoned. In so many ways, you will always be that little girl."

The door opens. Slams shut. Rain hammers against my windows, drowning out my rapid breathing.

Shadows loom across the floor. He must have disabled my automatic lights somehow, because they don't come on no matter how my fingers flutter. I'm frozen. For one minute. Two minutes...

There's no bluffing on his part. I'm swallowed by the silence. The loneliness. It circles me like a predator, waiting for the right moment to strike. It comes as lightning illuminates the sky and thunder reverberates through the very foundation of my building. Panic.

Bit by bit—cell by fucking cell—movement returns.

But all I can do is scream and remember.

Simon says...

THIRTEEN

ou're never lonely with a...

"Smile so hard and you might hurt yourself!" Sharla from accounting makes the assessment as she drops a stack of documents onto my desk.

My mouth practically waters at the prospect of more work. These will take hours, if not days to review. Less time to think. When I swipe my hand longingly over the pages, the perky blond raises an eyebrow.

"You must be having the best day ever. You haven't stopped smiling since you came in."

She's right. I haven't. My mouth aches with the effort it takes to maintain my flawless expression. I'm happy, all right. So damn happy.

"Thank you." I beam wider as Sharla saunters off and closes the door of my office behind her.

The moment she's gone, I lift a mug from the corner of my desk and drain it in one go. The liquid running down my throat isn't coffee—the one risk in my façade I'm willing to take. As they have since the moment I woke up, memories from last night play tauntingly across the inside of my skull and only alcohol can counter them. *This* sinister brand, to be exact.

Maybe I'm as much of a masochist as I am a coward. The bitter taste serves as a harsh reminder of just what Damien is capable of. Stalking. Drugging. Abandoning.

It took two hours after he left for me to regain control of my limbs and crawl into my bedroom. I only had enough strength left to switch on every damn light before a pounding headache drove me beneath the blankets and into a dreamless sleep—a quick Google search revealed a headache could be a potential side effect of succinylcholine. So that was that. He hadn't poisoned me at least, and somehow, I woke up in time to hobble into my closet and get dressed for work.

But something else he said makes me compile another search, and the results are more puzzling. Legal cases have never interested me before—not even my father's before he took the bench. A cursory search reveals a few of his landmark cases as a defense attorney, but little else.

Erased, Damien said. In fact, the only thing even remotely out of place is a single headline from over twenty-one years ago reading **"All Charges Dropped Against Child Murder Suspect."** My father was briefly mentioned as the defense attorney, but the police apparently had no solid evidence and the suspect was never named. Nothing nefarious in that. Still, the topic of murder makes me shudder. Could that case be why Heyworth Thorne picked me, of all children, to adopt? Misplaced guilt?

Perhaps Damien thinks that fact might shock me. Oh no, my father didn't happen across me by chance, but he sought me out because my case paralleled another he'd worked on. How evil.

But the bastard is a liar. And he's ruthless. There were some lines even Simon hadn't crossed. I asked my questions last night, but this morning brought my answers: Damien is more than just creepily intuitive.

After fishing out the bottle of wine hidden under my desk, I fill my mug to the brim and down half of it before focusing my attention on the small object beside my computer keyboard. It's black and square-shaped, and it resembles an earpiece one might use for telephone calls.

Or spying.

I found it tucked discreetly near the bulb of my desk lamp this morning. I didn't have to look hard—it was almost as if whoever had placed it there *wanted* me to find it. For all I know, there could be more. Or a camera watching me from some unseen corner.

If so, I give my audience a damn good show. I smile until my jaw feels liable to fracture from the stress. I comb through my work at record speed. I even deign to join the others for drinks after.

Anything to ignore the persistent reminders of last night. My throbbing arm. My worn, broken fingernails. The slight ache between my legs…

Stop. No fear. No flashbacks. He won't win again. Determined, I keep on smiling. At the bar, I buy a round of drinks for everyone and take the first shot to come my way, pushing the thoughts back.

When the last tab is finally paid, I enter a town car alone and direct the driver toward the Harrison Hotel rather than the Lariat. I book my usual suite and toy with the idea of buying a bottle of wine from the downstairs bar. Something cheap enough to make a rich bastard choke.

Somewhere during the trip down the hallway, I lose my nerve and enter my room painfully sober. Groaning, I strip my coat, leaving it by the door. Then I switch the light on and head straight for the bed, intending to sink beneath the covers and into oblivion.

A shadow catches my eye at the exact moment an ominous scent floods my nostrils: *roses.* My footsteps falter, forcing me to clutch the wall for balance. I'm just paces from the door, but escape feels miles away.

"Wait," my intruder commands. He stands near a massive window with his back to me.

I tense. He's dressed in black, accented with gray tonight. Like always, the blindfold is tied neatly over the ridge of a black ponytail. In any other circumstance, I might consider him appealing.

As it stands now, I can't read the bastard at all.

Daddy's tried-and-true method fails me thoroughly where Damien is concerned. The man wears no mask. There's nothing to judge. Just plenty to hate.

"Get the hell out." I'll beat him to the punch. My fingers swipe at the door but tremble too badly to grip the handle. I knot them into fists and inhale. *Get a hold of yourself.* "Now," I huff between ragged breaths, "before I call the police—"

"I'd like to suggest that we renegotiate our previous agreement." He's too calm. Even though I know he can hear me pawing at the door again.

Yes. I get it open. All I have to do is throw myself over the threshold and run.

"If you're still willing to agree to my terms, that is."

"Your what?" I snap. How dare he keep talking as though this were a normal meeting. A normal day. As if we were normal goddamn people.

"My terms."

"Terms?" I parrot him while looking over my shoulder. "Did they include leaving me incapacitated?"

And alone. In the dark. Something he himself mocked me for fearing. Not that it matters. He can play silly mind games all he wants—just as long as he keeps his toys to himself.

"By the way, I found one of your little spies." I expect him to at least flinch in some semblance of guilt. The bastard doesn't even sigh. "Right. You called me boring, but how interesting must *your* life be if you decide to listen to mine every fucking day, huh?"

Oh, because he *has* been listening.

"Please close the door, Ms. Thorne. Then we can discuss why I'm here." He doesn't sound so suave anymore. The catch in his voice prompts a manic surge in my heartbeat—but out of fear or triumph?

My, my, it looks like I've annoyed the unflappable Mr. Villa.

Good.

"I don't think so." I pull the door open wider. "I want everyone in this whole damn building to hear. Come for me and I'm screaming." Which will be quite the feat considering I'm barely speaking louder than a whisper. "Now, get out—"

"I wanted to…apologize."

I tense, waiting for the laugh. The cruel punchline. The mocking taunt. Panic sweeps through my veins when seconds pass without him performing either act.

"Most men send flowers to do that," I croak. "They don't break into people's private rooms. Though, with your affinity for destroying things, maybe you should stick to mangling rose petals. By the way, I looked into my father's record as you suggested."

He inclines his head. "Oh?"

"Congratulations. I've learned that he's a good man who's done his best to right his past mistakes. Anything else? Any more nasty hints you want to drop? No? Then get the hell out—"

"You sound healthy enough. The drug can sometimes cause lasting fatigue. You've recovered?"

He's doing it again. Displaying that terrible knack of humanity like a switchblade, shoving it discreetly where it can penetrate the deepest. He doesn't *really* care. Despite the way his head tilts, putting his ear in the prime position to catch my reaction: gritted teeth and rapid breaths.

"I recovered, all right. I had plenty of time while I was *crawling* to my room alone, in the dark, to reflect upon why I should listen to my father the next time he warns me about a dangerous, psychopathic—"

"And here I was, assuming that you had such a wonderful day." He cocks his head with devastating candor, his voice ice cold. So much for playing contrite. "Whatever happened to your smile?"

Bastard. Finding his little toy was one thing. Hearing him parrot such casual banter from my daily life is another entirely. I'm shaking, and this time, I have no trouble stepping into the hall.

"Goodnight, Mr. Villa," I spit out without looking back. "Enjoy the view. And from now on, you can take your so-called apology and shove it up your ass."

Such a callous statement would demand a slow, collected walk to go with it. Any other night I'd try, but I can't reach the elevator fast enough. Once outside, I chase down a cab—but rather than the Lariat, I have the driver take me to the one place I instinctively know Damien won't dare venture.

I go home to Heyworth Thorne.

And I intend to tell him everything.

FOURTEEN

I open my eyes to a perfect bedroom ripped from the pages of a home and garden magazine. One of those glossy editions featuring rooms resembling a dollhouse setup more than anything people actually live in. This dollhouse family loves their pastels: lemon-yellow walls reflect the bright sunlight streaming in through a bay window.

Tucked beneath a matching duvet, I barely slept. Though not for lack of trying.

My cage was carefully prepared in advance, courtesy of Diane, Daddy's second wife. I recognize her handiwork; she must have come into the room last night, fished an ornate box from the antique wardrobe in the corner and withdrew enough nightlights to fill every single outlet. Then she switched on the white noise machine hidden behind a potted fern to block out any hint of an approaching thunderstorm.

She even left clothing out for me: jeans and a simple blouse— both black and unassuming. After getting dressed, I make a show of yawning as I descend the steps to an audience of one.

"It's not like you to pop in so late, sweet pea."

Daddy stands in the doorway of the kitchen, sipping coffee from a mug while wearing his trademark grin. Ours mirror each other, in fact: pearly white and perfectly straight. But he strays from the script; his eyes narrow and give me an anxious sweep.

"Is everything all right?" He doesn't require a drug to see through my defenses.

"Everything's fine," I lie, straight-faced. "It's just... I wanted to check up on you."

"Oh, really?" He sighs. "I may be getting on in years, darling, but I'm not oblivious. Now, don't lie to me. You saw the news last night, didn't you?"

I say nothing as my heart hammers away in my chest.

"I don't want you to worry," he continues. "The police will find out who is behind these horrendous crimes. The perpetrator won't get away."

The sarcasm in his tone makes me suspect that he has an idea of who that perpetrator might be. "You think Damien Villa is behind this?"

"Not him directly," he admits without an ounce of hesitation. "His family perhaps. His brother. They're dangerous, Juliana. But I don't want to discuss this now. Come, I bet you're starving."

He inclines his head for me to follow him into the kitchen, where a steaming plate of breakfast is already waiting for me, courtesy of his chef, Craig. Daddy takes the seat beside me and fishes a cigar from his pocket.

I glance at the clock. "Isn't it a little too early for that?"

Rather than answer me, he takes a puff of the cigar and inhales the smoke so deeply that he coughs.

I make a show of fussing over him, patting his back. "Daddy, you know this isn't good for you—"

"I increased the guard duty I have on you, at least until the conference," he admits, in between two more puffs. "I told them to give you your space, but they're alert. Have you noticed a difference at all?"

Difference? Yes, I have. Primarily, a deranged lunatic strolling into my home like he owns it.

"Y-yes." By some miracle, I keep my flawless smile intact. "I've felt safer."

"Good. Good." Daddy sighs. Apparently, I'm not the only one exhausted by these past few days.

"What's wrong?"

When I shift closer to him, he slaps his hand over the newspaper lying nearby. I only catch a glimpse of the headline before he rolls it up and tosses it aside: **Borgetta Prosecutor Found Dead of Suspected Suicide.**

I reach for my untouched mug of coffee and gulp a mouthful of liquid to disguise the shudder ripping through me. Another murder. Could Damien or his family truly be behind it?

I don't know and that terrifies me.

"How are the campaign preparations going?" I ask, desperate to change the subject. Looking at Daddy's tortured expression, I realize I've stepped on a landmine instead.

"Slow," he replies. "It seems my prior donors have been discouraged from continuing their contributions."

He doesn't have to say why: because of Damien.

The man isn't done "discouraging" me, either. My cell phone rang once in the early hours of the morning, displaying a message from an unknown number. I deleted it without bothering to listen—I have no proof the call came from him—but it fit his MO.

He merely wanted to reinforce his presence and drill one fact into my skull: He can always find me.

"Juliana?" Daddy covers my hand with his. "Are you all right?"

"Fine." I widen my smile only to belatedly remember the topic at hand. "I'm so sorry, Daddy. Discouraged... What do you mean?"

"Intimidated." He scowls into his mug. "It seems the bastard is determined to thwart my campaign before it can even begin."

A preemptive strike. Like nipping a wayward rose in the bud—or poisoning a potential threat with oleander. Swift and malicious with an unmistakable artistic flair. The man truly is a sadist.

"But why?" I swallow hard, hating the hoarseness in my voice. "Why is he doing this?"

"Oh..." He shakes his head, but I don't miss how his eyes cut to the discarded newspaper and back. "It's this damn mess with the Borgetta case. What happened to his brother was unfortunate but—"

"His b-brother?" Coffee sprays from my mouth, splattering the table. I cough to disguise my shock. Then I snatch up a napkin and dab at what I can reach. "I-I mean...oh, now I understand."

Of course. How could I be so fucking stupid? Damien's brother was at the center of the case my father tried, and all of his cruel taunts make sense now: *I watched you. Know thy enemy. You're just like your father...*

"They're all criminals, that family. I don't give a damn what anyone says. The other brother, Mateo, has been rumored to belong to a Columbian cartel, and Damien pretends to be above it, but he's a part of it too."

Daddy's never sounded like this before. Callous. A sneer contorts his features; he's a stranger. A heartbeat later, he squeezes my hand and chortles, his charming self in the blink of an eye. "But I don't want you to worry about this, sweet pea. Enjoy your breakfast—"

"Daddy, can I ask you something?" The question is out before I can even process it.

"Anything, darling."

"Why are some of your past cases struck from the record?" It should sound so harmless in hindsight. So harmless and innocent that my father nearly jumps out of his skin.

"Juliana…" His tone hardens in a way I've rarely heard. He spoke to criminals like this, seen only in clips of his glory days sometimes plastered over the news in conjunction with the current headlines. "Were you looking for a case in particular?"

"No," I admit. Only now I wonder if I should be. If Damien was more than planting suspicions in my skull for the hell of it. "I was just curious. Looking for examples of all of the good you've done to help combat the press."

"Old cases get cleared from the records all of the time," he says. "I'll leave you to your breakfast."

He leaves, taking his cigar with him. Presumably to return to his office and fume.

The moment he's gone, I grab the newspaper he left behind and read it surreptitiously from under the table. As expected, the headlining story contains even more scandal.

The man who prosecuted the Borgetta murder case ten years ago —a man with emergent ethical complaints related to evidence tampering—was found dead of a gunshot wound to the head last night. Self-inflicted, according to the police.

Daddy's sudden interest in my security makes sense now. He's afraid.

Though maybe he should be. I run my fingers along my shoulder, struck by a sudden realization: Simon isn't the only monster bold enough to hunt me these days. Could I be the star of the next grisly headline? My stomach churns and breakfast becomes an afterthought.

If Damien Villa is behind these murders, it wouldn't be much of a leap. Given the morbid nature of his art, there's no telling where a man like him would draw the line from paralyzed subjects to lifeless victims. Murder could run in the Villa family. Though how would I know. I never had siblings—the closest thing I might compare that affection to is my friendship with Leslie.

And I'm still suffering the consequences of failing her.

How far might someone go for their brother?

While I haven't read too much into the case overturning the Borgetta conviction, I'm inclined to believe my father's judgment.

After all, some display their darkest impulses for the world to see.

Like Damien's art…

I shiver, recalling how illustrated, hollow eyes held me captive. In the model's painted gaze, I found terror, fear, passion, life. Those elusive traits a certain artist claimed I didn't possess.

Just how long has he been watching me to know as much? I left his bug in my office drawer—a rather stupid hiding place in retrospect—but something warns me there are more. In the boardroom? In the hallway? The lobby? I name every location I can while avoiding the most obvious target.

The thought of Damien listening in on my private moments is enough to drive me upstairs, into the shower. I turn the water as hot as it can go and scrub my skin raw. Then I redress in Diane's borrowed clothing, sequester myself in the guest bedroom, and do the one act that Simon, after all these years, never made me do. I call the office and I take a week off work, citing the drama around my father's overturned cases.

"I just need a few days," I lie.

When I return downstairs and join my father in the great room, I intend to announce my desire to spend the rest of the week. As Daddy angrily flips through the channels to avoid the news stations, the words are poised on the tip of my tongue. *You need me here.*

Try as I might, I can't spit them out. Seven days is more than twice what Simon ever took from me at one time. I've already conceded my life to one dangerous man. Psychopath or not, there is no way in hell I'll surrender more of myself to another.

Emboldened, I tell Daddy goodbye and have his driver return me to town. On the way there, I call the management of the Lariat and demand my suite be searched upon my arrival. For good measure, I request an armed escort.

Two can play the surveillance game.

Flanked by a guard twenty minutes later, I feel confident enough to face Damien head-on. Once I reach my door, I boldly swipe my keycard and step inside. Only to suffocate.

Roses.

Exotic masculinity.

Intimidation.

My nostrils flare, catching every scent before my other senses even register the danger.

"Wait, miss!" The guard grabs my shoulder, making me trip over the threshold. He mutters something I don't hear.

I'm too busy hallucinating. Somehow, I manage to choke out a statement of my own. "What in the hell?"

I step farther into the foyer without waiting for an answer. My eyes blink, unwilling to register the scene before them.

Someone drenched my gray color scheme in a bloody shade of red. It's everywhere. Rose petals, to be exact. Hundreds coat the floor in a haphazard spread. Menacing enough on their own, the mutilated buds are merely the icing on the cake of unease my tormentor sought to deliver.

I don't realize that I've circled around to my coffee table until I'm standing before it, a trail of crushed petals in my wake.

There, lying on the exact spot where I was the other night, is a square object wrapped neatly in crimson paper. A black bow gives it a wicked finish. Anticipation and sweat slick my palms, and it's suddenly impossible to breathe.

"Miss?"

I look over and find the security guard watching me from the mouth of the foyer, his lips pursed.

He has a radio pressed to his ear and static issues from it. "My manager is pulling the camera footage now. Should we call the police?"

"No." God, I don't know why that word leaves my mouth. Or why my gaze won't leave the box. A foolish thought crosses my mind before I can quash it. How might Damien's gift differ from Simon's?

There's no mistaking who delivered this parcel for me. I smell him, tainting the air. Cologne. Mocking smugness.

I know as surely as I know my own name that he's overseeing this very moment. Waiting.

"I...I overreacted," I say, my voice rasping. "This came from a friend. You can go."

"Are you sure?" The security guard looks torn between the floral massacre and his crackling radio. "If you want to file a police report, it should be done as soon as—"

"I'm fine." I force a grin to prove it and nod toward the door. "Thank you. I'll contact the manager if I need anything else."

The moment the door closes after him, my posture deflates. Damn Damien. I almost wish he'd sent me something truly awful to put Simon to shame. Something I could march down to the police station or leak to the tabloids—possibly turning part of the vicious tide against Heyworth Thorne. *Something* to counter the sickly-sweet perfume of dying roses and prove once and for all that this gesture is a threat.

Or I could leave. Daddy wouldn't question too much if I returned home now with my tail between my legs. He'd prefer having me underfoot, always protected.

I'm still torn between the two possibilities when I finally cradle the present in my hands. It's lighter than expected. I undo the bow and strip the wrapping paper to reveal a wooden box with silver fixtures. After making sure no brooding madman is lurking in the shadows, I sit and lift the lid.

Inside, on a bed of red silk, rests a small sketch reinforced on a wooden base. I hate the gasp drawn from my throat when I recognize the woman staring up at me. At first glance, it's a chilling rendition: someone with features similar to my own, frozen in a mask of terror. A second glance, however, reveals something far worse.

The artist was skilled enough to depict everything down to the moisture glistening on her lips. The sweat slicking her skin. Her wide eyes and her bare chest heaving with bated breath. How her exposed throat almost demands raking teeth and violence. Destruction. *Lust.*

Poor woman, whoever she is. Damien violated her in charcoal and ivory.

In disgust, I flip the damned thing over and set it aside. Only to reach for it again and observe every line more closely.

I'm not sure how much time has passed when I finally notice the folded slip of paper lying in the box beneath where the sketch was. The message scribbled on it reads more like a command than a contrite request: *I assume this apology suffices. My studio. Tonight.*

A sound tears from my throat, startling me. Laughter? It's been so damn long since I've heard the real thing. No polite, restrained *hahaha.* I'm doubled over, clutching at my stomach as uncontrollable giggling reduces me to a quivering mess with streaming, watery eyes.

When I regain my composure, I rip up his stupid note and sprinkle its remains over the carpet of petals. Then I enter my bedroom, intending to pack. Return to Daddy. Damn Damien to Hell.

But the bastard didn't content himself with violating just one room of my suite. His scent conveys a haunting warning before I notice the lit lamp on my nightstand. Someone left an object resting against its metallic base. Small. Black. Shaped like an earpiece.

That son of a bitch. Judging from the faint layer of dust on the device, it's been hidden, out of sight, for a while. Months, perhaps. Maybe even longer. I have no doubt that every bit of data and moment of vulnerability collected was used to create the profile of this vain, boring, materialistic woman he claims I am.

Tears prickle behind my eyes, and I choke down a desperate gulp of air. *Breathe.* He won't win tonight—I can't let him win. Without thinking through the consequences, I snatch up the device and bring it to my mouth.

"Enjoying the show?" I croak into it, hating how broken I sound. Fuck Damien. In fact… "You asked me if I was a virgin? Why? Is that how you get off? Manipulating women into bed? Does your blind-man act not earn enough pity on its own?"

Low blow, Thorne. I've never spoken to anyone like this before. Anyone. A thrill runs down my spine, feeding my resolve. Excitement, rather than shame.

"Sadly for you, I'd rather have sex with my doorman. Someone who doesn't need to paralyze his women to feel in control."

I break off, panting. For all intents and purposes, I'm shouting to myself. As far as I know, he could have severed this line. But no. A psychopath would never cut off communication with his victim first. He's listening, and I intend to give him a damn good show.

"Frankly, I'm disappointed, Mr. Villa." I creep toward my bed and mount the edge of the mattress. Unease flickers through my belly, but I ignore it. I've played by the rules of politeness for so damn long. He's pushed me to the brink.

"I thought you'd be better with your hands. Should I give you a demonstration, you sick bastard?" I turn, lying back on the mattress. My fingers flutter hesitantly before roving down my hip and finding the clasp of my jeans. "Listen and learn, Mr. Villa. You wanted something interesting to spy on, didn't you? Well, here's a sample of what you'll never hear in person."

I flick the bug aside without bothering to see where it lands. Somewhere close. Then I eye the ceiling and focus on...

I don't know. My hand seems to move on its own. It slides between my skin and the fabric of my underwear, finding the spot he assaulted that night. Damn it. The flesh feels different. Stimulated. Slightly sore. Because he's a bumbling, sloppy idiot— not because of the effects of the drug, rendering my body immobile against him.

It has no trouble at all reacting to me. One stroke of my finger along my entrance and I suck in a breath. I rarely have time for self-indulgence. Simon was always watching. Maybe he still is. I swallow hard and start to pull my hand away. But my finger crooks as if it has a mind of its own, stroking again. Faster. Harder.

Another, softer sound tears from my lips. A gasp. *There.* That's enough. Damien doesn't deserve any more of my debasement to entertain him. But even the thought of his name makes my chest tighten. It takes more effort to force air into my lungs. Because I hate him. Not because my traitorous body remembers what it felt like. His breath on my ear. His voice, hoarse and constrained— unsteady for once. *Are you a virgin?*

Why the hell did he care?

More importantly, why the hell can't I stop hearing him ask me that damn question?

Virginity. Virgin. Virginal. My hips arch against the bed. My touch becomes bolder, every finger desperate to recreate the friction he had. Almost. Almost… *Yes.* Sparks prickle as my finger flicks. I drive my teeth into my lower lip to smother the sound crawling up my throat. A groan rips from me, loud despite the attempt. He'll hear that and there's no taking it back.

Good. He can mock me all he wants. Sell the tape to the tabloids, even. But that will never erase the fact that he's listening. Right now, the artist is forced to bear my own form of art.

I stop thinking and let my body take what it wants. Rapid strokes. Deliberate motions. More. More. More

But I don't feel the fire until my brain follows suit, displaying images without permission. Thick, soft fingers. A masculine voice reverberating through my skin. His taste on my tongue.

Hate must be the world's best aphrodisiac. My skin burns, overheated. Every breath doesn't feel sufficient. My eyes squeeze shut. Fingers curl.

There.

I only have the sense of mind to roll onto my stomach and smother whatever sounds I make into my duvet before everything inside me catches fire. Fuck Damien. I hate him. I swear I can hear him goading me on without an ounce of shame. *Don't tell me what you see, Ms. Thorne. Tell me what you feel.*

Empty. And stupid. And…lonely.

Boneless, I lie flat on my bed as my final cries echo back at me. The silken material of my duvet did a poor job of muffling them. Every word is clear. Make that a name ringing out as I pant and remove my hand from between my legs.

I give myself only a second to recover. Then I roll from the bed and hunt for the bug. I carry the damn thing into the bathroom, held between two fingers like a dirty piece of underwear. Damien's voyeuristic show ends with a splash as I drop the device into the toilet and flush it. After watching it disappear, I climb into the shower and scrub myself clean for the second time today.

Dripping wet, I crawl into bed without bothering to towel off. Before closing my eyes, I turn on every single lamp I own, flooding the entire suite with light.

And only now can I find some semblance of sleep.

Fitful, nightmare-ridden sleep, haunted by a man more terrifying than Simon.

Simon forced me to play his games.

I never initiated a round on my own.

FIFTEEN

hree days. That's how long I last alone, locked inside my suite without even work to distract me. Each one ends with me having to field a phone call from Daddy. Odd. Before, his customary checkups came weekly, disguised behind the pretense of casual conversation.

Tonight, he's far blunter. "I don't want you going out alone without calling for an escort."

I can tell from the background noise that he has the news on. A crisp-sounding reporter drones on about the latest headlines, but they're too faint to make out. I take a stab in the dark and guess. The Borgetta case.

"What happened?" I ask. Yesterday, he questioned me about my habits. Why wasn't I at work? Who knew that I had a detail following me? Why had I taken almost a minute to answer my phone?

"Nothing," he says too quickly. "They're calling for a storm tonight, so I just think you should stay in. I have to go. Have a wonderful evening, darling."

A wonderful evening. I'd laugh if the current state of my day weren't so pathetic. Without a television to use as a distraction, I lugged my old laptop from the recesses of my storage closet and spent the past twelve hours attempting to do work on the ancient dinosaur. For all I know, Damien bugged it as well. Just in case, I type FUCK YOU into a blank document, hoping whatever spying software he uses allows him to catch it. As my computer sluggishly attaches my finished files to my email, I open the browser and find myself hovering the mouse over the search bar.

The first news site I venture onto reveals an inkling of why Daddy's so on edge—and not just because of Damien. A witness in the Borgetta case was reported missing by his family and found dead hours later. No leads.

Not only that, but the article links to one with a headline that catches my notice: **The Curious Case of the Villa Family—and Their Money.**

According to the author, Damien immigrated to the US in his late teens with two younger brothers, Mateo and Mathias. Twenty years later, he's amassed a small fortune, but the circumstances surrounding his finances remain murky at best, and rumors of crime have dodged the family for decades—the worst of which was solidified when his youngest brother Mathias was convicted of Emily Borgetta's murder.

And my father was the judge who all but sentenced him to death.

I shouldn't pry anymore. Besides, Daddy told me all I needed to know of Damien. The key takeaway being: *madman.* I exit the browser only to find myself on the same page seconds later.

My, my. The topic of Damien certainly triggers an avalanche of search results. Thousands, actually. Dominating the top of the list are articles headlining his art and alter ego Sampson. Apparently, he doesn't go out of his way to hide that part of himself.

Most of the articles read as though they were written by sycophants who've never met the man in person, so different from the few cynical pieces regarding his family. *Artist captures the morbid honesty with dangerous charm.* That earns a snort from me. I've found more charm in a cactus than I could ever find in Damien.

Regardless, I keep clicking, determined to hunt down anything sordid. Bingo. He was at the center of a scandal once, which nearly tanked his investment business and dragged his name through the mud: the Borgetta murder.

Despite the fallout, he put the bulk of his fortune into his brother's defense fund as recently as this year. Each appeal brought new disturbing faces to light: potential evidence tampering, rumors of corruption in the prosecutor's office, and racial bias. In fact, the overturned conviction came almost entirely from Damien's dedication.

But it wasn't enough to save Mathias.

No wonder he hates my father.

I close my laptop and eye the view from my window while digesting the new information. So Daddy may have blurred a few of the facts. Why? I sigh rather than come up with an answer.

Gradually, darkness falls across the horizon, but I can't muster the strength to turn my lights on just yet. It's easier to face myself in the dark. How disgusting am I?

Not enough, apparently. Three days later and Damien has yet to respond to my parting gift. Not that he should. Screw him.

But that's the punchline, isn't it, a part of me taunts. *You want to.*

I don't. Despite everything, I barely even thought of him. During the day…

At night, my fingers took on a life of their own as my brain played a distorted slideshow of the night he drugged me. Over.

And over. And over. Like a waking nightmare. One that left me gasping, and writhing, and flushing with a mixture of shame and guilt.

Fuck Damien. I almost want him to show up unannounced. It would give me a chance to play my final card. To see the look on his face when I call my father—

Speak of the devil.

There's someone at my door. The handle jiggles, sounding impossibly loud in the silence. I swallow hard and slip from the couch while flicking through possible culprits. It could be a security guard or one of the men Daddy put on my detail finally deigning to show his face.

Or…

Someone determined to get in *without* announcing their presence. Without knocking, they try the handle again. Roughly. After the stunt with the roses, I had the hotel change the locks. I can't shake the feeling that my visitor is caught off guard by that fact. They try the handle again. Again.

Only now am I aware of how late it is, past the hour when I'd usually be asleep. The perfect time for someone to slip in unannounced. Simon?

Air leaves my lungs in a rush. Before I can fully process my plan of action, I'm bounding into my bedroom on the tips of my toes. My phone is on my nightstand and I grab it, scrolling through my numbers. Daddy. The police. Someone. My trembling fingers can't seem to settle on a contact.

"Th-this isn't funny." I know he can't hear me. I threw the bug away.

Calling the police is a better course of action. I raise my phone to my mouth only to jump when a sound ricochets from the foyer. *Bang*! A sterner thud. Not merely a test of my handle, but a deliberate tug on it.

"If this is your idea of a joke…" I swallow the thought as my footsteps back me toward my closet. I'm a child again, drawn to obvious hiding places.

Hide. Run. Don't breathe.

The police never believed me then. They rarely do now. Good monsters know how to hide in the dark. How to master it.

"Stop," I tell the shadows as another thud reverberates from the hallway. "You win."

Bang!

Terror robs me of the ability to speak. My chest heaves as I stand against the closet door, clutching a heel I don't even remember grabbing from my floor. I brandish it in a shaking fist. Waiting… Waiting…

Finally, my tormentor grows bored and calls to me by name. "Open the door, Juliana."

God, it's like my body reboots at the sound of that accent. Then anger jolts me into action. I march into the foyer, and I don't bother to look through the peephole before throwing the door open. I can smell him.

Sure enough, he swallows the doorway, blocking the light from the hall. An enigma of black cotton and gray satin.

"You fucking bastard. How dare you—"

"Step aside!" He brusquely shoves me from his path as he says something else over his shoulder. Snarled words I don't understand. Spanish?

It's only when another man pushes past me that I realize who he's speaking to. Dressed in black and built like a bear, this newer man switches my lights on and prowls my suite with a hound-like intensity. I swear I hear him sniffing the air.

Denied my anger, I can only question, "What is this?"

His jaw clenched, Damien says nothing, leaving me to decipher what's happening on my own. They're searching for something. Someone. He's far too tense. Worried? If this is his way of apologizing, I'm not convinced.

After a few minutes, the brawny man reappears from down the hall. "*Claro.*"

"Good," Damien replies. I'm not sure I've ever heard his voice so hard. His accent crackles like lightning over thunder. "Return to the lobby and survey the crowd. Report back if you see anything out of place. If not, take up a post on this floor. Somewhere discreet."

The man heads for the door. "*Sí.*"

The moment he's gone, I whirl on the remaining intruder. My palms connect with his chest and I shove hard. He barely even flinches. Fine. I settle for slapping him instead. I've barely connected with his cheek before my wrist is captured in his grip.

"You're hysterical." He sounds as if he's trying to convince himself of that fact in order to maintain his composure. The last time I slapped him, he issued a warning. *I won't let it happen again.*

"*I'm* hysterical?" My voice echoes back to me. A stranger's. "You sick, fucking—"

"Whatever you experienced just now, I was not behind it." The certainty in his tone robs me of rage before I'm ready.

"Liar." I try hitting him again, but I miss. The world spins and I wind up clutching his forearm instead. Too tightly.

When he loosens his grip on my wrist, I expect him to shove me off. He finds my shoulder instead and loops his fingers around the sleeve of my T-shirt, keeping me upright.

"Trust me, Ms. Thorne. When I come for you, I won't have to break down your door."

I want him to be lying. Which makes no damn sense. He shouldn't be preferable to any other monster hunting me. Desperate to prove it, I latch onto the one thing his sudden arrival has made clear.

"How many bugs do you have hidden in my room?" My lips nearly graze his chest with every motion. He's too close. But he displays no intention to back away.

"Three. The one by your bed was the clearest, however."

"Well, I hope you enjoyed your final show," I tell him through gritted teeth.

He says nothing. *Oh?* I rake my gaze upward and find his expression…pinched? Unnaturally stiff jawline. Furrowed brow. He listened to my private show, all right.

And I should feel disgusted by that. Horribly violated.

Not…curious.

"Let go of me."

He does, but for some reason, my hand still grips him tightly.

"I want you to get the hell out—"

Darkness. Without warning, the lights shut off. A second later, lightning flashes.

And I'm miles away.

Are you afraid of the dark, Juliana? Think they'll find you soon?

Let's play another game.

"What's wrong?"

That voice was too deep. Not Simon. I blink, panting as I interpret my surroundings. Dark…but warm. No trees. I'm in my apartment again, but the man with me now shouldn't sound so damn concerned. And I shouldn't be clinging to him like a frightened child. I make a concerted effort to loosen my grip, but his hand remains on my shoulder, imparting just enough pressure to steady me.

"Power's out." I intend to sound unaffected. Not breathless. Blackouts were always the worst trigger. Sudden. Unexpected. After a summer of violent storms, Daddy had to buy a backup generator just to keep me—

"The outage must be a result of the storm," Damien replies smoothly. "There is a generator."

As if the building heeds his request, the power whirls back to life. My collection of lights would usually inspire relief. Not alarm. Apart from a voyeuristic asshole listening in, no one ever sees me like this. Panting. Eyes watering. Shaking.

"You should leave now," I croak, my obligatory rebuff. I don't sense any indication from him that he intends to. Yet, anyway.

Apparently, Damien has something he wants to say. I decide to beat him to the punch.

"Is that how you spy on me?" I'm eyeing the device attached to his left ear, barely noticeable against his dark hair. Only after a second do I realize he can't interpret the gesture. "With what's in your ear?"

He boldly fingers the device and lifts his shoulders in the semblance of a shrug. "I have a direct feed at another location." Smart man for not saying where. "This helps to supplement what I prefer to call oppositional research."

"Bullshit." Something about how he said "direct feed" makes me swallow hard. "You mean you have a dedicated room where you go to *spy* on me?"

The boring life of Juliana Thorne in HD surround sound, perhaps? Who's the dull one now?

"It's only recently that I've taken to keeping a more…consistent vigilance," he admits.

Consistent. My lungs promptly deflate of air. "Oh?" I wonder innocently, aware of how a muscle in his arm jerks beneath my touch. "How recently? As recently as three days ago?" I should leave it at that, but my lips won't stop moving. "When I gave you a taste of what you'll never, ever have?"

Bingo. He can't hide how his throat lurches, but an answering flutter in my chest alarms me far more. I flex my palm, intending to push away from him.

"Well, now that you mention it…" His fingers seize my chin, tilting it. At the same time, he lowers his face, bringing his mouth near my ear as if he memorized the distance. Close enough for his breath to fan my earlobe with every grated word. "It *was* as recently as three days ago," he concedes, "when you fingered yourself to the tune of my name. Or pretended to, perhaps…"

My cheeks flame. No one makes everyday words sound as vulgar as he does. *Fingered.* My own twitch against him. The last part of that statement, however, has my mouth contorting into a frown.

"Pretended?"

He can't see what I'm doing—I know that. Regardless, his nostrils flare anyway as if seeking every trace of the fingertips I parade beneath his nose.

"I definitely wasn't pretending." Only belatedly do I realize that statement could encompass everything. *To the tune of my name.* "About the f-fingering part."

"Oh?"

I shouldn't be able to track that shadow that falls across his features, even with the blindfold. He's dangerously easy to read in this moment. Tense. Waiting for something. A cue to leave, I think. And, God, I should give it to him. Get the hell out—but he's the one who started this game, and I can't resist taking one final cheap shot.

"Oh *yes.*"

He tenses even before I hover my thumb over his lips. They're surprisingly pink. Soft. The slightest pressure is all it takes to make an indentation—and have him sharply inhale.

"If only you knew." I draw my hand away, fully intending to kick him out. I don't expect him to cup my face in retaliation, his thumb expertly finding my own mouth. I inhale raggedly, waiting.

He should leave it at that: a sleazy tit-for-tat. He shouldn't lean closer. I'm rendered motionless even though I have plenty of warning to turn my face. Run. Move. Something.

His mouth finds mine easily, separated only by the width of his thumb. "Oh, I would like to know," he breathes against my parted lips. "I'd *very much* like to know why you panted my name."

He sounds angry. Insulted. Intrigued.

Enough. I shove against him. At the same time, he lowers his hand and covers the distance between us.

Preemptively, I call his bluff. "You wouldn't dare—"

Our lips meet. Stiffen. Deepen their contact.

It's not a kiss. Even as his tongue swipes my mouth open and invades without warning. It's a battle of wits.

And I'm woefully unmatched.

He shouldn't taste sweet. Like cognac mixed with something fruity. Poisonous fruit. He rams his flavor into me like he's forcing me to swallow every illicit drop. He shouldn't feel so damn soft. My body shouldn't catch fire.

I shouldn't extend this.

He slides his hand around to the back of my throat, holding me captive as he steps in closer, using his height advantage as a weapon to knock me off-balance. My hands fly to his shoulders, clutching at the fabric of his suit jacket. Another searing taste of him unnerves me, deeper than the first. Another.

"S-stop." I break away and find myself stumbling in the direction of my room.

He follows me, eerily steady.

"Get out," I snap.

"Is that what you really want?"

Yes. My tongue struggles to push the word out as thunder rumbles ominously.

Days ago, I could face the threat of a simple storm alone without pacing before the row of windows in my living room or anxiously watching the clouds approach. I'd dread the thunder, but wine was my only defense—I had nothing to compare the loneliness to.

Now, when the first few drops of rain speckle the glass, there's no bottle within reach. Lightning flickers closer with every strike, heralding the terror of my past.

The woods.

Leslie.

His voice twisted its way through my skull.

Simon says…

"Juliana."

I whirl around, heart in my throat. "What?"

"You're afraid." He cocks his head, drawing attention to my current state. How I stand. How I breathe. How my gait wavers with every step I take over the carpet. "You're uneasy…" His posture stiffens and I imagine him listening for intruders in the shadows. When his search turns up nothing, he frowns. "Tell me why."

My teeth skewer my lower lip, trapping a frustrated hiss. I'm tearing my fingers through my hair like a madwoman. When lightning strikes, I jump.

"Fine." Teeth gritted, I turn from the window and find him seated, his posture erect. "Storms tend to usher bad men into my life." What I intend to be a cruel jab falls flat. I'm the one who winds up flinching.

"Bad men." He parrots the phrase emotionlessly. "Explain."

I force out a breath and turn on my heel. I'm treading the same path he was earlier. A ruthless trek from one corner of my living room to the other. My bare toes tingle as if sensing the steps he took, large and purposeful. *Ugh.* I shake my head to clear the thought. No use. The tingle spreads up my legs and I'm walking faster.

"I know you dug into my past," I say over my shoulder. "Don't pretend like you don't know."

"I'm aware of what happened to you as a child," he admits, phrasing the words with subtle care. "You were attacked in the woods by an unknown assailant. Your young friend was killed in front of you and you weren't found until over forty-eight hours later, on the verge of death. The murderer was never caught and some insensitive reporters sensationally suspected that you, an eight-year-old girl, may have been the culprit all along. Jealousy, they claimed."

I stare from the window, seeking refuge in the howling storm. I don't know why his knowledge shocks me so much. Of course he's done his research. Still. When most people discover my past, out come the kid gloves and coddling. Few would dare confront me about it in clinical, stark terms.

Fewer care to listen.

"I am aware of the published accounts, anyway," he adds. "I assume thunderstorms make you relive it."

I swallow hard. "Yes." God, I sound so damn pathetic. *He* does this to me. "It stormed that night…"

"When it happened?"

Forest. Cold. The memories threaten to unfold, but I bite them back. "How did you know someone was breaking in?"

"Intuition."

My eyes widen. "Are you magic in addition to blind—"

"You're stalling," he interjects. "What is it about the storms that makes you so afraid?"

My eyebrows furrow. "Desperate for a new emotion to paint, Mr. Villa?"

"No."

I shrug off the genuine curiosity in his tone. "They—" Lightning flickers across the horizon, and I lick my lips with a nervous flit of my tongue. "They make me feel…alone."

Alone.

Trapped.

Helpless.

Hopeless.

Lost.

"It was storming when you went missing," he deduces.

"Yes." Lightning flashes again and my apartment fades.

Gnarled trees loomed overhead, obscuring an indigo sky. Simon was watching. Hunting. Prowling.

Come out, come out, Juliana.

Cologne. My nostrils flare, chasing that scent, even as terror knots in my stomach. The more I breathe him in, the faster the forest recedes. Thunder bellows, rattling the walls, but I'm still here.

"When we went missing—when *I* went missing…my parents were too high and too drunk to notice for two damn days. I was hiding in a ditch in a hillside and I didn't move for so long my legs had grown numb. I couldn't even walk. A jogger found me, but they thought I was—" I break off, frowning, before I realize why.

Three-and-a-half whole sentences without interruption or a kind voice urging me to state how I "feel." A world record. He doesn't even press for the juicy details. What did he do to you? What did you see? Was he even real?

I almost wish he would. Or that I was brave enough to seek out a bottle of wine instead of him. Even alcohol can't loosen my tongue this much.

"Do you know what that's like? Hearing the world rage around you, bellowing and howling and knowing you're all alone. Your name isn't the one being shouted. No one can hear you screaming…"

I've said too much. My face feels strange. I reach up and find that my cheeks are wet.

"Is that when you received the scars on your hip?"

I glance at him sharply. He must have read my file. I can imagine how the crisp report described it: *Juliana, age eight, found with a seven-inch laceration on left thigh.* Has he known the answer all along and merely feigned his confusion before? Looking at him, I can't tell. He's fully focused on me, his head inclined, listening. Just listening.

"Y-yes." My fingers drift to my hip, tracing the old scar over the fabric of my pajama pants.

"And, afterward, you were adopted by Heyworth Thorne."

It's like he's feeding me lines from a fairytale I know by heart, skeptical but patient.

"Yes." I return to my view of the city and flatten my palms against the glass, framing the world outstretched below me. "You may think he's a racist, or incompetent, or whatever, but he saved my life. He saved me. I used to dream of what it would be like to live outside of the trailer park, you know? Never in a million years could I envision a place like this. A life like this."

"Did you know what he did before becoming a judge?"

"A defense attorney," I say. "It's why he accepted the appointment to the bench in the first place. He was tired of defending criminals. He wanted to put them away."

"And he told you this?" Damien wonders. I don't like his tone; it's too damn soft. "Interesting."

I sigh in lieu of dissecting his motives and watch my breath fog the glass. The silvery cloud obscures a nearby building, transforming it into a mass of yellow dots and inky darkness.

"Even now, I hate the rain," I murmur, the icing on my sordid little tale. "I really do."

"I've always enjoyed it," the man behind me confesses. He sounds too casual. As if sitting on my couch, discussing the weather is the most natural act in the world. As if this—us—is natural. "I used to enjoy watching the sky light up and feeling the moisture on my skin."

His use of past tense sticks out. I glance at him again, focusing on the blindfold. "And now?"

"I enjoy listening to it." His lips twitch into something not quite a smile, but not a frown, either. Wistful. "Someone told me once that every lash of thunder and drop of rain plays like music. A unique song only heard in that exact moment. Fleeting and never to be experienced by anyone again."

"That's quite a deep musing coming from a psychopath," I blurt. Surprisingly, he doesn't bite back. "Are you a musician as well?"

"No." He shakes his head. "Without my sight, I will never see a finished piece of my artwork. But, as you are aware, my hearing is quite intact. Not a second would go by without my hearing the flaws in any piece I created. Therefore, I'd create nothing."

So, he's a perfectionist *and* an accomplished stalker.

"Do you miss it? Seeing."

"No," he says without an ounce of hesitation. "I don't."

"Because you can hear just fine," I say pointedly. "In fact…"

I barge through my bedroom door and switch the light on. Three days have reduced my bed to a crumpled mass of sheets. My closet door is partially open with clothes thrown haphazardly on the floor of it. I look back and find Damien paused near the threshold, frowning as his foot warily taps my discarded heel.

Without thinking, I cross to him and kick the shoe from his path. Why? I have no damn idea.

"Where?" I demand, glancing around the room. "Where are the rest of your little toys?"

If I were a psychopath, where would I hide my secret listening devices? The drapes? Behind the potted plant in the corner? I make a show of loudly checking both places but come up short.

"Where?" I demand while marching toward him. "Maybe I'll even let you keep one. Poor man. I'd hate to deny you of your sole entertainment—"

"Ah, but I don't want to hear a recording of you moaning, Ms. Thorne."

My breath catches. He sounds too damn...heated. "Oh?" I croak. "Fine, then. Tell me where the other bugs are."

"No." He easily swats away the request and takes a step closer, homing in on my position. "But I'd much rather hear you moan in person."

I blink. *Breathe.* He's taunting me. "As if."

He takes another step and I'm frozen in place. Deliberately, he reaches for me, stroking his fingers along the side of my cheek. Then he cups the side of it. Deep down, I know that he's giving me all the time in the world to run. I don't. Not even when his lips claim mine once again.

I shiver as he tugs me forward. His tongue rims my mouth, a teasing request for entrance.

"S-stop," I croak without pulling away. I inhale his laugh directly.

"Do you really want me to?"

Yes. I want him to stop. But like a true madman, he doesn't give me the chance to demand it. His fingers trace my throat in a fiery caress, traveling down to my collar. Lower...lower still. My nipples sharpen in tense anticipation as he skims the cotton of my shirt. Pressing hard enough to sense but nowhere near hard enough to really feel. My mind plays a devious game of remembering how he felt after he'd drugged me. Raw heat over paralyzed muscles. I'm anything but frozen now.

My chest flutters. My toes sink into the carpet beneath them, desperate for leverage.

"You should leave, Mr. Villa," I breathe, hating how fragile my voice sounds in comparison to the muted storm raging outside.

He doesn't.

He steps forward, jarring my precarious balance. I assume he miscalculated my position for once—but no. He moves again, deliberately ramming his chest into mine, hard enough to jar back. Back. Back. My knees strike the base of my bed. Another firm nudge from him urges me onto it.

I stare up at him, panting. No matter how hard I try, I can't find enough air to command him to stop. And he knows too much—from the layout of my room, apparently, down to just how my body would fall when shoved onto my bed from this position. One of his hands captures my upper thigh and nothing in the world could prepare me for the cruel mixture of sensations jolting through my body. Fire. Ice. Slowly, his other hand finds my opposite thigh. He tugs, and my legs part, opening enough space for him to step in between.

"I suggest," he starts, his voice alarmingly thick. Guttural. "I suggest you…assist me, here. I'd rather not crush you."

I shudder at the word. *Crush*. And also what I know he left out. *Yet*.

When he nudges my hip, I'm reminded of his request. Assist him.

"To do what?" I've never heard this quality to my voice before. Husky. Like Sharla from accounting whenever Dave from research walks by her desk. Funny. I always thought Dave wasn't her type—but now I know.

Now, I know what it feels like to lie to yourself. It's hell. It's heroin.

In a breathtaking display of balance, he braces one knee against the mattress. I have to bite my lower lip as he uses my own thigh for reference to know where to place his limb, grinding against my flesh.

My hands fly out, finding his hips. An appreciative sound catches in my throat; the man is pure muscle. Coiled ridges of it flex beneath my touch as he braces one hand beside my hip. The other lands near my head, fisting in the sheets, and he's above me. My breaths fan his throat, disrupting the strands of hair framing his face.

"What are you doing?" I ask once I remember how to speak.

"Negotiating."

Thunder rumbles. Our lips meet again. Teeth. Biting. Tasting. Grinding—

Through the thin fabric of my pajamas, I feel the unmissable rasp of tailored fabric, heat, and…sin. I break away with a gasp. "Get…out—"

"The sheets."

From the corner of my eye, I see him raise a handful in his clenched fist. His nostrils flare inches from the fabric. His expression hardens.

"You didn't wash the sheets." His knuckles whiten, ivory over black silk. Shamelessly, he brings his fist to his nose again and inhales more deeply. A muscle in his jaw jumps, and I feel his chest expand, nearing mine.

He looks tenser than I've seen him. Poor Damien. My toes curl at the thought of just what he's seeking from my bedsheets. Or why he can't seem to let go of his fistful.

"We will make an exchange," he proposes, his voice composed once again, deep and suave. My inner thighs quiver as his lips part and a thick, red tongue traces the bottom one. "I'll give you the location of the remaining devices…"

"Good," I croak even as alarm bells go off inside my mind. This feels far too simple.

"And you…" His fingers find my lips as though magnetized to them. A newer scent blends in with his usual mix of aromas, and I almost miss his next words. "For every location, you give me something."

"Like what?" I muster up the courage to ask.

"A reward." His thumb grazes that dangerous sliver of space between my lips, imparting a million disturbing insinuations. "Something I can't capture with a mere recording."

"Y-you recorded me?" An image pops into my head of him locked in one of his cavernous rooms, replaying those sick, twisted tapes over and over again. "Why?"

From this angle, I have a perfect view of his twitching throat. Hard swallow after hard swallow. He doesn't say.

"And if I refuse?" I wonder as if that's really in question. I am going to. I will. "What? You'll sell your little recordings to the tabloids, hmm?"

"No." His upper lip curls back from his teeth at the mere suggestion. "I don't sell from my private collection."

Instantly, the heat in my belly cools. "Just how many recordings of women do you hoard?" I press my palm against his chest to push him off. "Goodnight, Mr. Villa—"

He shifts his weight to block my path. Trapped. His mouth grazes my ear from this angle and I feel the jolt down to my toes. Too damn close for comfort.

"What is your price?"

"I don't have one." I apply more pressure to his chest, but the bastard doesn't budge.

"Oh?" His voice deepens, heightening his accent. "I'll tell you the location of one of the devices in exchange for...a taste of what I'll never have." One shift of his weight and he has me pinned. Helpless. Limp. Breathless.

"What are you—"

Black. Darkness. Thunder.

Every light cuts off, plunging my room in shadow.

And I'm in the forest. Lost. Trapped.

"Let's play a game," he murmured, pointing from me to Leslie with the tip of a knife. "Eeny, Meeny, Miny, Moe or rock-paper-scissors..."

"Juliana."

The rough voice doesn't belong, combating Simon's slithering drawl. I cling to it, clawing my way to reality bit by bit. I see darkness. No forest. Lightning. A flash of my room. A shadow, reaching for me.

"Focus on my voice," someone snarls.

Oh no. There's vomit on my tongue. On the bed. I feel it running down my chin, hot like blood. Someone tries their best to wipe it away, utilizing a handkerchief.

"L-let me go!" I swat at his arm, but this time, he backs away.

It's unfair how easily he maneuvers, even in the dark. My eyes blink rapidly as I adjust to the loss of his heat. Too cold. Shivering. My fingers fan out, searching until they brush silk and curl around a fistful without permission.

"I'm here."

God, he's the last person in the world I should hear uttering those words. The last man on Earth whose reassurance should ease my heartbeat.

The last man in the world to drag me from a nightmare.

"Get out," I croak.

He doesn't move and the minutes of the outage tick by, longer than the first. Too long.

"Let's play a game," he said. "Eeny, Meeny, Miny, Moe or rock-paper-scissors? What about you, little girl in the purple... Tell us what to play."

"Are you listening to me? I think I just insulted you, Ms. Thorne."

Huh? I blink. Still here, in my room. With Damien...

"I said," he says, infuriatingly calm, "that your bed is a travesty. *Sí*, no wonder you've been moaning every night."

Heat creeps into my cheeks. "B-bastard."

"I thought women like you lounged on silk?"

"Fuck you." The retort trickles out of me, more as a whisper than anything else. "Go away."

"I would," he says thickly. "If you let me go."

I stiffen, aware of my grip on him, but I can't seem to loosen it. Out of self-preservation, of course. If this is a stunt, I'll make sure his DNA is beneath my fingernails. I'll make sure the world knows that Damien entered my apartment and...

"Your heart is racing," he declares, sounding more concerned than taunting. "You're afraid—"

"Get out!" This time, I manage to shove him off just as a ripple of thunder reverberates through the walls.

"Pick," a cruel voice demanded. "Who will live and who will die?"

"Damn." The harsher, deeper baritone doesn't belong in my memory.

Blinking, I return to the present. I'm in my room. On my bed...

Someone's fingers are in my hair as more warm liquid drips from my mouth and down my chin.

"Get off," I croak, swiping at my lips. Panic melds in my blood, making everything too loud. Too sharp. Too hot.

"Breathe," someone urges against my ear. Their hands slip from my hair, following the curve of my spine. "Breathe."

My lungs obey him, sucking in air as the chilling reality sinks in. There's vomit on my shirt. I'm shaking and the past looms, waiting for another roll of thunder to overwhelm me again.

And Damien is here to witness every terrible second.

"Get out." I shift away from him and brace my feet on the floor, but he follows, his heat like a wall, keeping me upright.

"Close your eyes," he commands against the nape of my neck. "Now."

I do, and the darkness doesn't help ease the shame setting my cheeks on fire. "Lucky you," I rasp. "You have a wonderful story to sell to the tabloids—"

"Take off the shirt."

My blood goes cold and the reality of the situation descends at full force: I'm alone in my room with a stranger.

"W-what?"

"It's filthy." He sounds so calm. So logical. "You need to change."

But my closet is too terrifying a territory to venture into now.

"You're disgusting," I spit, even as I shrug the shirt over my head and toss it aside. "Only a pervert would get a woman naked at a moment like—"

"You can insult me," he counters, still so damn unshakeable, "if it helps distract you. I can make an exception this once."

An exception?

"Get out—"

"I can think of a better distraction than anger, however." The shift in his tone sends my pulse racing. Another roar of thunder echoes, but it sounds too distant now, no match for his low, dangerous rasp. "When you performed your little exhibition, where exactly did you touch yourself?"

I can't breathe, but this time, it's not because of terror.

"You disgust me," I hiss.

"Show me," he counters. "Or was it all an act?"

A shiver runs down my spine as he adjusts himself behind me. On either side of my hips, his hands appear outstretched, painted silver as lightning flashes.

"You want me to paint you," he reminds me, his breath hot on my skin. "You think you can bare every inch of yourself to me? You truly believe you're brave enough to face that woman? I think you're lying to yourself, Juliana." Thunder mingles with his words, sending a thrill through me. "I think you're damn good at lying—"

I grab his hand and place it against my thigh.

We both go rigid.

His fingers are too damn soft. Mine shake as awareness of the storm threatens to shatter even his twisted "distraction." I can taste the forest again. See it…

Just as the memory unfolds, Damien asks, "Was it here?"

I gasp.

His fingers travel without permission. I'm back firmly in the here and now, suffocating as the tip of a thumb nudges tender flesh.

"Or here?" He drifts higher, sweeping his touch up the ridge of my belly. "I doubt you're bold enough to go lower."

"I-I told you," I manage to reply in a rush. "You'll never have—"

"Or maybe here?" His other hand cups the opposite hip, applying just enough pressure to tease an ounce of fear from my frayed nerves.

For a second, I toy with the potential danger. He could rape me.

But he won't. A man like him wouldn't see the fun in that.

"You wouldn't dare," I tell him, confident of that fact. My eyes are closed again and reading him now is easier than ever. He's brutal, Damien. Never reckless. He wouldn't give me the satisfaction of ever claiming assault. "Men like you don't get their hands dirty."

"No?" he retorts in a low murmur. "If not to hurt you, then what might my motives be?"

He's distracting me, as much as it stings to admit that. His fingers are my only anchor against the past and Simon. Two monsters go to war on my psyche, but one wins out.

"It was lower," I admit, breathless. His fingers twitch, hesitant to move. "A place you will never, ever touch—"

"But I have touched you there," he points out, chuckling in a grated, tortured way. "In fact, I doubt many men have. So tight. Barely accepting of one finger."

There's awe in his tone. Smugness too.

"I can accept my fingers just fine," I snap.

"I can imagine."

I jump at the barely concealed dare. *So do it, then.*

My fingers tremble as they brush over the fabric of my pants. Every cell in my body warns me to run. But I don't. I find the drawstring instead, arching my hips to undo it.

And the atmosphere changes. His grip tightens, biting in deeper.

"It was here," I tell him, sliding a hand between my legs. He shouldn't be able to tell. I could be lying.

But he knows the second I make contact. His breathing changes. His posture tenses.

I've won the game.

But the rules have changed from here on out. It's not enough to accept his dare. The second I attempt to pull my hand back, his falls over my wrist, conveying a silent command through only a subtle bit of pressure.

Show me.

I squeeze my eyes shut as traitorous heat builds and spreads. My legs drift apart before I can help it. My hand slips lower. His becomes a vise.

And nothing else matters. Not the thunder biting through the silence. Not lightning. Not Simon.

I touch myself.

He listens, inhaling harshly against my earlobe, his touch tracking every shameful motion.

It's my previous show in HD surround sound.

And I don't care if he records this moment and sends the tape to the news.

He makes for a chilling barrier against the darkness as heat builds inside me. For a dangerous second, I imagine his hand drifting lower and pushing mine out of the way...

A gasp slips from my throat and wetness coats my fingers. Too much. Too real.

"You're close, aren't you?" His lips part near my jaw and my nerves rattle. With one quip, he could devastate me. Humiliate. "Let go," he demands instead, his voice like a spark over tinder.

I catch fire.

My eyes flutter shut as my back arches. I'm leaning against him. Into him, letting the heat drown out shame until all I can feel is an agonizing inferno.

"Should I paint you like this?" He sounds on the edge of a groan as I spasm against his chest.

At the back of my mind, I know I should be embarrassed. Horrified, even. Not writhing through every tortured second he extends his nearness.

"Coiled muscle, sweat-slick skin, panting," he murmurs into my ear, painting a picture with his fucking voice alone. "Hang it where your father might see? His beautiful girl… So broken. So shameless."

My face inflames at the thought and enough shame leeches into my dazed brain that I withdraw my hand. "Would you?"

A brush of his knuckles over my wrist doesn't give me a solid answer. "How many fingers was it?" he wonders, half taunting, half serious. "That you used that night—"

I force out a laugh. "Wouldn't you like to know?"

His own fingers flick my skin in tandem as if to convey silent guesses. One? Two? Five?

But he doesn't force me any further, dragging me right to the edge of some invisible boundary that I didn't even know was there.

He waits, letting me keep the fragile reins of control.

And only now do I realize that the rain has stopped.

The storm has passed.

SIXTEEN

*U*h-oh. The ominous thought tugs me awake and my brain sluggishly tries to decipher why. There are the usual suspects. Uh-oh, I'm late for work. Uh-oh, I'm having a horrendous flashback. Uh-oh, Daddy's pounding on my door, demanding I reassure him of how happy and healthy I am.

All of those would be preferable to the slow realization that someone else is in my bed. Someone large, their limbs skewing the surface of my mattress to one side. Someone who smells of sin and cognac, and inexplicably of roses.

Uh-oh.

I peel my eyes open to a view of my ceiling. Gray daylight streams across it, alluding to a final break in the storms. If only that peace could translate into my current reality.

Even his breathing resembles thunder. Low and unassuming until I finally notice it. With every additional note, I find myself tensing with the next unnerving rumble.

I turn in his likely direction, all the while desperately gathering up the nerve to do what must be done. Scream. Fight. Kick him the hell out.

Or stare.

He's a creature made of shadow who has an unholy affair with sunlight. No matter how faint, it paints detail into his skin, fleshing out what dimmer surroundings disguise. Like the subtle lines around his mouth that hint at his age. The faint gold in his skin. The blue-black tint to his hair, and the slight quirk in his jaw that betrays when he's awake.

"Good morning, Ms. Thorne."

"I could have you arrested for trespassing," I tell him, hoping I sound intimidating enough. Not exhausted. Uh-oh, uh-oh. There's a bitter taste on my tongue. Residue from a horrific flashback. I can only recall snippets. Good. I don't remember the gist. Just that…

I clung to someone. Someone who coached me through the nightmare, their voice a rugged anchor. Someone who held me through gasping sobs. Someone with an accent like hellfire.

"You vomited," he says. "Afterward, you removed the shirt."

The blunt warning precedes the moment I finally look down and realize the horrifying truth. It comes in the pair of gray panties I'm wearing—nothing else.

"Y-you stripped me." I instinctively cover my breasts with my hands.

"I'll avert my gaze if you'd like," Damien says dryly.

So the man has jokes. Apparently, my realizing that I slept mostly naked next to a psychopath amuses him.

Or not. His expression is tense. I can decipher the emotion conveyed on his face clearly, even with the blindfold obscuring most of it. Annoyance.

"Why…why did you stay?" My confusion confounds me almost as much as my lack of real anger does.

He's right. A foul stench taints the air, and my vomit-soaked shirt is on the floor, neatly folded. I have a vague image in my head ripping the soiled clothing off by myself.

And I huddled against him rather than move. Something I rectify now by lurching from the mattress and into my closet. I snatch the first garment I see from its hanger and pull it on: a black cocktail dress worth more than Sharla from accounting's weekly wages. And I just ruined it with vomit and tears.

To save face, I enter my room with my head held high as though I'm totally unaffected by the sight of Damien standing near my bed.

"I assume your father had good intentions when he hired your current security detail," he says, sounding oddly neutral. "However, I shall take the liberty of installing my own men from now on. I can assure you that you won't have a repeat of last night."

Did he mean the near break-in, his impromptu visit, or both? I shake my head to clear it. Neither matters.

"I suppose I should feel flattered," I admit. "Bodyguards installed by a criminal. I'm sure they excel at murder, and extortion, and whatever sordid talents men like you value."

He doesn't even wince. "When necessary."

God, he actually sounds serious. A concerned Damien is the last thing I need.

"Why should you care?" I demand, placing my hands on my hips. "You hate my father. I bet you loved seeing me terrified—"

"You're right. I despise your father, and you are the single most devastating weapon I can use against him. But I prefer to utilize you on my terms, as I see fit."

Can't blame the man for honesty. "Well, you certainly don't mince words," I quip.

"And you aren't foolish," he counters. "Accept my offer."

I should refuse. That would be the smart, logical thing to do. But smart and logical don't apply to seeking safety in the arms of a psychopath.

As if reading my mind, he adds, "I won't always be there to listen for your nightly performances, Ms. Thorne."

I puff up indignantly and bite back a sigh of relief. Anger is a weapon I need now more than ever—I won't acknowledge the fact he gave it to me.

"Do what you want, Mr. Villa." I make a show of marching into the living room. Loudly. My heavy footsteps barely drown out the slower, heavier ones in my wake. "Just so long as your offer doesn't include *you*."

"This one doesn't."

I look back and find him advancing from the hall.

"My next proposal, well… That will require some negotiation."

I don't take the bait right away. I nearly run to my coffee maker and fumble with the settings until something dark and steaming pours into a mug. Only after I've drained every last drop of liquid do I bite. "And what proposal would that be?"

"Dinner. With me. Tonight."

"Dinner." I hum thoughtfully and tap my chin. "Let me guess. You'll take me to an orgy this time—"

"Dinner," he insists. "A meal. You and I. Entirely business in nature. We would both be allowed to question each other, and both be required to answer. Honestly."

I frown and search through my cupboards for another pack of instant coffee. "Frankly, Mr. Villa, I have to wonder why you'd want to question me. I'm Juliana Thorne, and as you've said more than once, there isn't anything interesting about me."

"I'm sure there is plenty you would like to know about me," he counters as he starts for the door and opens it. "The next time you search for me online, remember that there are two Ls in my name. Enjoy the rest of your day, Ms. Thorne. Oh, and Julio will be your guard for this evening. He'll stay out of sight."

"Dinner…" I draw the word out, only mildly entertained by watching him linger. Oh, he doesn't want to. I could bounce pennies off the tension coiled in his shoulders. "I'm terribly busy, Mr. Villa."

He takes a step.

I raise my voice. "But…"

Again, he pauses. For a second. Two. The fact blows my mind. He's a man with a criminal empire to run, frozen at my doorstep in anticipation of whether or not I'll accept a dinner invitation. "If I can find the time, how should I reach you? Scream into my wallpaper?"

"Ah…" He chuckles darkly. "But as you yourself have said, I have more important matters to amuse myself with than the life of Juliana Thorne. Have a good day. *Adiós*."

He leaves, for real this time. I don't bother taunting him back.

I sip fresh coffee like the antidote to his poison only to find myself eyeing the very real toxic gift he left for me. I don't normally keep plants on principle. They require even the bare minimum attempts at nurturing—something that was never my forte. Still, I take a stab in the dark and assume this one needs water. Surprisingly, its delicate petals haven't started to wither.

They cast the faintest aroma that itches my nostrils. It's deceptively sweet. Like roses, laced with sugary candy. You'd never know that one nibble could be deadly.

If there were a person as sweet and as innocent as oleander, Daddy wouldn't think twice before letting them off, despite what the evidence may say. They weren't menacing. Not like Damien or his brothers who alarmed and inspired unease on sight.

Therefore... I drag my finger across my neck and mouth another one of Daddy's chosen phrases, "Guilty as sin."

But what does that make me? Oleander, or snarling imposter weeds?

The question haunts me as my cell phone rings.

"Juliana," my father says from the other end. "I've made all of the arrangements for tomorrow. All you have to do is attend."

"T-tomorrow?"

"The press conference," he says, exasperated. "I'm having a dress sent over. It will be at ten sharp, and I'll have a car sent for you an hour before."

"Of course... See you then."

The looming prospect of media attention makes for the perfect foil to Damien's visit last night. I'm haunted by both as I strip my dress and shower, scrubbing vigorously to erase every trace of the blind psychopath. When I return to my room to tidy it, I groan and wring my hands in exasperation. Someone already has—attempted to, anyway. They straightened my sheets. Removed the soiled clothing from my floor and placed it in the hamper near my closet. They also presumably tripped over the heels I left scattered near the door.

I don't clean for him. Neither is he the reason why I strip my sheets and replace them with fresh ones. So maybe I rustle the sheets loudly enough for a speaker to pick up from some hidden location. According to his smug insinuation, he won't be listening. So he certainly won't hear the reluctant sigh that tears from my chest.

"Dinner," I blurt, hating how my voice echoes in the silence. "We do this on *my* terms. Nowhere public, but somewhere with plenty of exits in sight. If I feel cornered, I'm leaving. If I feel threatened, I'm leaving. I decide what we eat, and most importantly—I ask the first questions." I pause, belatedly realizing that he won't answer back. Feeling my cheeks flame, I soldier on. "Have a car waiting for me at seven. A minute later and I'm not going. Though I suppose I might as well not bother at all. You're far too busy to be listening."

There. Empowered, I shrug nonchalantly as if performing for a camera—though, who knows, maybe I am. Good. I hope the bastard has someone there to give him a very vivid description of my ass as I stoop for a pair of heels, grab my coat, and promptly escape my apartment.

I enter a hall and jump at the sight of a large man leaning against the wall at the other end. Only his vaguely familiar features keep my heart from pounding its way from my chest. He nods to me slowly in greeting. When I head to the elevator, he doesn't follow. Yet I can't shake this lingering suspicion that I'm never alone. Someone is watching me—and not quite as predatorily as Simon.

Speaking of which…

My old friend hasn't asserted his existence yet. I should feel relieved, but I don't. Just tense. It's not a matter of if he'll resurface.

It's when.

SEVENTEEN

*S*even rolls around and I'm still in my apartment, blissfully unhurried. After all, there's no point in waiting for a ride that will never show—or so I tell myself.

Following that logic, there was no reason to get dressed, either. No reason to wash and blow out my hair or paint my lips in the one shade I have other than red: a slightly lighter pink. There's certainly no reason to glare at my reflection and wrestle with the idea of changing for the umpteenth time.

In the end, I'm still scowling when I finally leave the bathroom and don my coat. I'll head down out of pure curiosity. Being stood up—in theory—will just give me more ammunition to use against Damien. At least I'll prove he was lying about the bugs.

Just for fun, I pause near the foyer and tilt my head toward the ceiling, scanning for little black devices. "I want pizza," I say. "The extra-cheese special from Georgianos. They know me there, and I'm the only one in the world who orders that special, so there will be a record of your address that my father can trace if I go missing."

It's a bald-faced lie. I haven't ordered from Georgianos in months —though he doesn't know that. Then again, the bastard did bug both my home and my office for an undetermined amount of time. In any case, I can take comfort in the fact Mr. Damien Villa has already expressed boredom from spying on me.

Though I still find one of his men in the hallway when I step out of my suite. Dressed in black, he greets me with a nod. Downstairs, I spot two similarly dressed men lurking amongst the crowd. They don't acknowledge me directly, but I sense them watching as I head for the main doors. Outside, a sleek vehicle is waiting for me. The driver stands beside the passenger's door and opens it as if on cue.

"Good evening, Ms. Thorne."

Damn Damien. So the bastard called my bluff after all. In the process, he gave himself away; he's been listening to my boring life in real time.

Gritting my teeth, I enter the car and try to ignore the alarm bells going off in my mind. This could be a trick. A rather elaborate one, admittedly. Any time during the day, Julio could have barged into my apartment and done whatever he wanted.

Perhaps Mr. Villa preferred to do the deed himself? Luckily for him, I'm being hand-delivered.

He isn't far. My destination turns out to be only blocks from my building, in the same upscale part of town: an even taller skyscraper formed of black glass and gold accents. It's a breathtaking bastion of wealth, but there's no clear indicator as to its purpose. Evil lair? Reclusive penthouse dwelling?

Inside, a plain lobby with granite floors and dark walls funnels any visitor to a gilded elevator.

"Take it to the roof," the driver instructs, having come inside with me.

He leaves, and I ride the elevator up alone, desperate to quell my staggered heartbeat. When the elevator doors finally part, I'm forced to acknowledge my first concession of the night: Damien followed my instructions perfectly.

The private roof, several stories above most surrounding buildings, certainly isn't within obvious public view. Score one. The low barrier keeping an occupant from plunging to their death could technically be viewed as an abundance of "exits." But only a sadist would interpret "I don't want to feel cornered" as a license to host their morbid soiree inside of a structure composed almost entirely of glass.

It dominates the center of the rooftop, illuminated with golden light. I blink several times before I dare put a name to it: a greenhouse.

A real one.

I can smell the flowers from here. Sweet. Fresh. An amalgam of color bolsters the different scents: spicy, delicate, aromatic. Too many to name. I'd stake my life on the assumption that roses are among them.

When I don't spot Damien lurking within the shadows, I warily approach the pair of glass doors serving as the greenhouse's entrance. They open easily, and I smother a sigh as a comfortable warmth replaces the frigid night air. My eyes blink to adjust, and for good reason.

It's like I left winter and entered spring—if mother nature happened to be a passive-aggressive perfectionist.

Countless plants are arranged neatly in black planters, spread out at meticulous intervals. There isn't so much as a wayward petal on the stone flooring, and I could walk the orderly paths…well, blindfolded. A vital feature, I'm willing to admit, given the limitations of the man sensing my approach from beside a selection of his signature flowers.

Red. White. Yellow. Pink. Roses in every hue imaginable sprout around him, a morbid rainbow, clashing with the black of his suit and matching blindfold. Here, Damien sticks out more than ever: a glaring stain on this otherwise paradise.

"I hope this is suitable to your terms," he says dryly.

"It's not a sex club, at least." I fight to keep awe from my tone. "I hope you don't think that bringing me here will make me let my guard down. I've never been that sort of woman."

The kind to fall for extravagant gestures such as a private dinner among a makeshift field of flowers. Then again, I've never been the sort of woman whom men made such gestures for on a regular basis.

"I'm not sure what you mean."

He has his head cocked, confused as he processes my words. Oh. I could kick myself. Obviously, he isn't aware of how this venue might appear to someone. Which makes it doubly infuriating that he brought me here. Why?

Could the choice be entirely personal rather than meant to intimidate? Maybe. He wants to confront me on familiar ground.

"Did you plant all these yourself?" A tendril of appreciation makes it harder to seethe. I'm wandering the nearest row before I can stop myself, reaching out a finger to brush a soft bloom—a dangerous act in the world of Damien. "I hope this isn't oleander?" I ask belatedly.

"Toxic shrubs are in the righthand alcove," he replies. "And I require assistance, but I care for what I can."

He sounds…hesitant. Each word is clipped. Defensive. The same way he sounds whenever I mention one of his paintings. He thinks I'm mocking him.

"It…it's beautiful." My body deflates with the admission and I keep wandering, brushing flowers as gently as I can. Just to make sure they're real and not plastic.

He follows me, keeping a cautious distance.

"I'm assuming this is where my 'toxic shrub' came from?" The righthand alcove. I find an area slightly set apart from the main display. Those boxes are silver, which gives the plants they hold a mysterious air.

"No. I know a supplier whom I trust, but I would never discard one of my plants." Judging from his tone, he could have substituted another word: *I would never murder one of my plants.*

Not for the first time, he displays obsessive protectiveness of his work. Even sending a thinly veiled threat to a target is seen by him as wasteful.

"And the roses?" I wonder. Unsurprisingly, his appear unmolested. I doubt my floor is good enough to be graced with Damien's hand-grown creations.

"Also purchased." He sounds closer.

Perhaps because I've stopped walking, riveted by a blossom unlike any I've ever seen. Ebony petals form a cup with a wash of light pink inside. I tentatively finger a petal; it's so soft, one touch feels liable to tear it.

"A black orchid," Damien explains. He must have the layout memorized, down to the location of each blossom. "Ironic, considering you don't seem to be wearing that color tonight…"

His nostrils flare. Maybe the bastard really can sense color by smell.

For the first time since leaving my suite, I look down at my dress and lament forsaking my chosen color. I went to the boutique earlier today—one I've frequented for years. When I requested something in "a more colorful shade," the saleswoman looked as though I'd proposed ending world peace with a wave of my manicured hand. In a daze, she wandered into the back room and returned with this.

A blood-red number in the same shade as his massacred roses. The fabric feels too thin, a mixture of satin and lace. The neckline plunges a hairsbreadth too low, displaying nonexistent cleavage. All in all, it's a garment so unlike my usual style that I wouldn't recognize myself.

"Well?" I confidently appraise my opponent. No earpiece tonight —unless he hid it. No lackeys nearby to feed him all the right answers either.

Just me and him. A level playing field for once?

"What color am I now?" I extend my arms, offering myself up for his scrutiny. "Oh, Damien, all-knowing stalker of Juliana Thorne. Tell me how I look. Bonus points if you can describe it based on *smell*."

Mocking a blind person may be wrong in a different context, but I'm prepared to make an exception. Until he steps forward and inhales me deeply, without warning or permission.

"Oh, I can't be sure, Ms. Thorne, what with my *disability*..." He reaches for me, finding my shoulder. Two of his fingers tease the spaghetti strap of my dress and follow it down to the lacy neckline, heedless of the exposed flesh beneath.

He knows just how to unnerve me. Where to touch so I can't claim indecency. As well as the exact moment to pull his hand away and bring it to his mouth.

I expect him to rub his chin thoughtfully. Not run his thumb directly over his lower lip as if tasting scarlet on my skin.

"Why, Juliana, I have to say, you smell divine in *red*."

Bastard. "You cheated," I snarl, turning away from him. "What, did you have me followed to the boutique?"

"Come here." The command lacing his voice alone should give me the cue I need to leave.

He doesn't own me. He certainly can't order me to do his bidding. But perhaps that's the infuriating part? He isn't. No matter how many seconds tick past, he doesn't come after me. Doesn't reach for me. I don't even hear him breathing heavily to indicate anger. No, he merely proposed a dare. *Come here and learn the answer for yourself.*

I don't give him the satisfaction of responding. Instead, I turn on my heel and cross to him.

He captures my forearms from either side. A gasp escapes my throat, but before I can even think to fight, he loosens his grip and one of his hands drifts up to my chest.

"Your heart is racing," he explains, grazing a nail over the muscle in question. I feel it lurch, assaulted by his touch even through layers of skin and bone. "You're uncomfortable. Red is a bold color. You feel unsure wearing it. Though I did accuse you of being dull. It's only fitting that you would select the boldest hue in response."

He sounds so damn smug, as if he has me pegged down to the last cell and strand of hair. When I raise my hand, he predictably seizes my wrist.

"I wasn't going to slap you," I admit.

After a deliberate second, he lets me go and I bring my hand inches from his face, hating how my fingers shake. With effort, I calm them enough to trace the line of his jaw, shivering at how he clenches it against me. So damn suspicious.

"You think you know me, but I've already got you sussed," I tell him, fighting to keep my voice steady.

Touching him at all was a mistake. His heat isn't repulsive even in the humid greenhouse. His skin feels as soft as his hands, and the closer my fingers drift toward his mouth, the more I'm reminded of how his lips felt against mine. Swallowing hard, I step back and flatten both of my hands against my hips.

"You think I'm so predictable," I say, "but you're worse. You're infallible. So desperate for control you can't have one little thing go wrong. Can you?"

Alarm drips down my spine even before I follow through on my foolish impulse. I reach for an orchid and use both hands to snap a bud free. The violent crunch echoes like a gunshot and Damien looks...

Consuming.

He advances on me swiftly, capturing my chin in his grip. His nostrils flare with the aroma of his ruined flower. His shoulder tenses. I know he'll hit me. I'm ready for it. Maybe I want him to.

Violence would give me a reason to hate him more. Something to counter the image of the man who held me while I broke. The same man shamelessly haunting me, claiming to know me better than I do. I'd take any reason.

All he does is cruelly drag his thumb up to my mouth and apply enough pressure to force my lips apart. He steps in closer at the same time, allowing his breath to fan my throat in a teasing swipe.

Anger has a smell on him too, but I wouldn't dare attach it to a color. Maybe a phenomenon: *lightning*. Striking without warning and inflicting untold damage. Breathing is an ordeal. Sweat slicks my skin, affecting his grip. It tightens, tilting my head back farther, in the prime position for his mouth to claim mine if he wanted. Bite. Consume.

Suddenly, he lets me go and I cling to a nearby planter for balance, still holding my severed orchid.

"Put it on the table, *por favor*," he snaps to a man who I didn't even notice has entered the structure.

Wearing a suit and tie, he blends in with the other nameless men who I assumed work for Damien—minus the object he's carrying. I do a double take and wind up tightening my grip on the planter. The rich smell flooding my nostrils proves that the sight isn't a figment of my imagination: a large box of pizza fresh from Georgianos.

"Shall we?" Damien inclines his head. "I believe we've wasted enough time."

We have. Back to the task at hand, the only reason why I came here in the first place: for answers.

"Fine." I follow him down the aisle and into a small section cordoned off from the main greenhouse by a wall of glass.

The man with the pizza sets it onto a small table flanked by two strategically placed chairs.

"Dismissed," Damien says to him, and the man leaves without a word. Then my host tilts his head toward me. "Sit."

I eye the table warily. Pizza with a madman. Oddly enough, I've had worse dining companions. The governor's disgusting son who spit food while he ate. The lecherous old senator Daddy tried to woo for support.

Damien Villa isn't the least appealing, admittedly. So, I take the chair nearest to me while he claims the opposite one. Once seated, he gestures toward the box of pizza.

"As you requested."

He's not gloating for once. Something tells me that pizza wouldn't be on the menu if he had his way. Good. I drag the box toward me and flip the lid open. It smells even better than I remember, cooked exactly to my preference.

"How do I know it's not poisoned?" If so, it's too late; my fingers have already staked claim over a slice.

"It isn't," he says. "Though I'll admit that I've considered it."

I wrench my fingers from a strip of crust. "What? Why? Have I bored you to the point of murder?"

"Who said anything about killing you?" The grudging honesty in his tone is enough to help air trickle back into my lungs. For now. "No. I'm nowhere near finished with you yet. So eat."

"So…" I toy with a different slice. "Was your aim to paralyze me, then?"

His glowering posture makes me aware of how I'm sitting: legs crossed, my free hand knotted in a fist to hide how it trembles.

"That is a matter we will discuss at another time. For now, I've humored your requests, so get the remaining one out of the way and ask your questions." His tone reveals the threat he's holding back. *Then I'll ask mine.*

I find myself eyeing the corners of the room, desperate to stall this moment. There are so many damn things to ask. Looking at him, I settle on the most obvious. "Were you born blind?"

I already suspect the answer before he shakes his head. His drawings are far too detailed. Too raw. He must have some prior knowledge of the human body. Of women, and flowers, and lust-filled glances.

When he doesn't speak, I'm prepared to accuse him of breaking our agreement. Before my lips can even part, he reaches behind his head. One tug of his fingers and the blindfold falls away.

"I apologize in advance for your appetite."

Food quickly becomes the last thing on my mind. Faced with all of Damien, I can't breathe.

I knew he was handsome, even with so much of his face obscured. Taking him in fully, I'm forced to admit that the man is nothing short of beautiful. Strong nose. Elegantly arched eyebrows. Chiseled cheekbones. He's striking, despite the two vertical scars sealing his eyes shut. They're silvered. Old. At least one of my theories is thoroughly debunked: He can't see at all.

Horror robs me of any snarky response. I move my lips several times before I can croak out an actual word. "H-how?"

He bears the scrutiny for a few seconds longer before retying his blindfold with an ease that betrays years of practice. "I'll spare you the dramatics," he says simply. "One might say that I blinded myself."

217

I'm not sure if I gasp or say something intelligible. Whatever I do makes his jaw clench, and he's suddenly stone.

"I'll preemptively answer your next question. Why? I can assure you that you wouldn't understand the reason."

He's lying. No one could inflict wounds like that on their enemies, let alone themselves. I wouldn't wish that agony on anyone. Even Simon.

"H-how long?"

He frowns as if he's never stopped to tally up the years before. "Fifteen years," he says finally. "I... It happened when I was nineteen."

Which makes him only a few years older than I am. Odd. He seems so much older. A wizened man trapped inside the body of an exotically colored Adonis.

Curiosity keeps me questioning, even as the image of his scars lingers in my mind. "Where are you from?"

"A village in South America," he says, "in a region you've most likely never heard of, with a name you'll never be able to pronounce."

Fair enough. "What made you come here?"

"My father was...let's call him a judge, though not in the general sense. He was never elected, nor appointed to his position. He merely woke up one day and claimed it for himself."

"Oh?" I'm simultaneously riveted and repulsed by his tone. He doesn't speak of his father the way I speak of mine—Heyworth Thorne, anyway. There's no love lost or hostility spared. No hero worship.

"Some might consider my old home less than conventional," he adds, leaving it at that.

Which is an understatement if whatever he experienced forced him to blind himself at the age of nineteen. I'm tempted to ask, but I can take a hint. He won't hold back, and what he might say could disturb more than my appetite.

Changing gears, I decide to ask a far more pertinent question. "How long have you been watching me?"

"Now be specific, Ms. Thorne. Do you want to know how long I've been aware of your existence or just how long I've taken a *personal* interest in your welfare?"

I suck in a breath. His tone dipped just one octave above the danger zone. "B-both."

"A little over four years."

"After your brother's first appeal."

If he's surprised that I choose to divulge that bit of information now, he doesn't show it. He's stone again, completely unreadable. Though not quite…

I close my eyes and brace my palms flat against the table. Strange. He reveals more to me in darkness than I'm comfortable deciphering. Tension resonates from his end. His hand is braced against the wooden surface and vibrates ever so slightly, indiscernible to the naked eye.

"So you remember now," he says.

"That's why you hate my father," I admit, opening my eyes. "Because of Mathias. Isn't it?"

He inhales deeply as if just hearing the name stings. "A better man than Heyworth Thorne would have handled things differently. With Mathias. And with you."

But how? I'm not brave enough to ask out loud. Instead, I pose a different question. "What was he like, your brother?"

"Human," Damien replies. "A particularly decent one, but human nonetheless."

"And…" I swallow hard to gather up the nerve to broach this topic. "You think he's innocent?"

"I know he was." The grit in his tone warns me to back off. Discuss something else.

So I pick the obvious route of questioning. "So how did…*do* you plan to use me against my father? I'm sure you know all about the press conference tomorrow. I bet you have some brilliant masterplan to derail it."

I expect dramatics. Laughter. Or for him to throw his head back and announce some villainous plan so evil that I'll quake in my heels.

"How to use you? I don't know," he admits, each word sounding as though he had to rip it from his throat. "Expose you? Corrupt you? Your fate presents an interesting conundrum."

"How so?"

"Well…" He tilts his head thoughtfully and shrugs. "I can't decide whether or not your disgrace or your death would matter in the end."

Honesty. That's what he promised. I tell myself that as horror descends like a punch to the stomach. He promised me cruel, bone-chilling honesty.

"Y-you've thought about killing me?"

"I have once," he replies, his tone level. "The way I'm sure you've fantasized about destroying all of those who have wronged you."

"Punching, maybe," I rasp. "Not murder."

His cold laugh undercuts the intensity in his tone. "You may lie, but we both know the truth."

"So why haven't you killed me, then?"

"Therein lies the dilemma, Ms. Thorne."

Coming from a normal man, those words would be the punchline to a terrible joke. I could choke out a *haha,* throw my drink in his face, and storm away. I wouldn't be driven to dissect his answer into a million tiny pieces. One of them being: Did his supposed change of heart come before or after he met me in person?

"This has been very...illuminating, Mr. Villa." I flex my fingers against the table, though I'm not sure if I intend to stand.

His hand captures mine before I can decide, pinning it flat with the barest amount of pressure. "*Sí.* I'm glad, Ms. Thorne. Now, I would like you to extend the same favor, *por favor.*"

The amount of patience he's shown tonight has me worried. What could he possibly want to know that four years of spying— a timeframe I'll stress over later—couldn't garner him? Nothing good.

"Fine. Ask away, Mr. Villa." I reach for a slice of pizza to disguise how my teeth are chattering with nerves. One impulsive bite later, I remember his murderous intentions. "Wait. You can ask me whatever you want *after* you prove this pizza isn't poisoned. Take a bite."

He doesn't move. A refusal? Not quite. He reaches into his pocket instead and withdraws a device too small to be a cell phone: his earpiece. "Bring a plate and silverware to my location, *gracias*," he snaps into it.

Damn. I'm suddenly aware of the grease on my fingers. What kind of man, no matter how polished, uses protocol for a slice of pizza? Then something clicks. No one even remotely familiar with Georgianos would ever show such disdain for it.

"You don't like pizza."

A muscle in his jaw jumps, a rare display of displeasure. "I've never tried it."

I wait for another punchline that never comes. In fact, he looks far too uncomfortable to be lying. He's tense: a mountain of man perched on a delicate wooden chair.

"Tell your slave to forget the silverware—"

"My men are family, not slaves," he insists. Quietly. Calmly. Even so, the tone conveys an unmistakable warning to never utter that word again.

"Your man, then. Tell your *man* to forget the silverware. Then give me your hands."

Now, it's his turn to look wary.

"We could sit here all night," I tell him, "or you can ask your questions before I get tired and go home. Now, I'm starving. Hands."

He raises the object to his mouth and mutters something in Spanish. Then he stows it and slams his hands onto the table. Pushing the box of pizza aside, I reach for one and bite back a swallow. I'll never get over how soft he feels. Perhaps our surroundings have something to do with it. His fingers are petal-soft.

With my free hand, I heft a slice of pizza onto his palm. "Now, bring it to your mouth," I instruct, "and take a bite."

His lips move, murmuring something I can't understand. Spanish? One word stands out. *Amen.* A prayer?

I don't have the chance to reconcile the pious nature to his criminal one. He grimaces. His fingers flex against the crust as though he's unused to the texture and slow ooze of melted cheese. Unlike how he handles flowers, or maneuvering, or—admittedly —women's bodies, I suspect pizza is something he's never been subjected to before. He's never seen it.

"It's shaped like a triangle," I explain. My fingers curl around his, helping him guide the slice to his mouth.

His brow furrows at the teasing swipe of sauce and dough against his lip.

"Take a bite," I instruct.

He does, only to promptly set the slice onto the bare table while he chews. I sense that pizza will not be a returning item on the Villa menu. As he swallows, he fishes through his pocket for a handkerchief and dabs at his mouth.

"Heyworth Thorne used to have lunch from an expensive French café hand-delivered to him when he sat on the bench. I assume that *this*"—he nods toward the barely touched pizza—"was not a regular entree on your dining table growing up."

I start to correct him only to realize that he's right in a sense. Daddy had our cooks prepare family-style meals every night and a healthy breakfast in the morning. Pizza or cheap snacks were treats I typically sampled only at school occasions or birthday parties. Before I became a Thorne, however, stale crust eaten out of the box while surrounded by the smell of booze had been a daily occurrence.

"I ate it more often before I was adopted," I admit.

He nods. "When you were eight."

If he expects me to react to his knowledge of yet another intimate detail of my life, well... I don't.

"Ask your questions, Mr. Villa," I quip. "I'm getting tired." I yawn loudly for dramatic effect, but he hunches forward, like a wolf readying to go in for the kill.

"Are you a virgin, Ms. Thorne?"

I nearly choke on my next bite and wind up coughing. Calmly, Damien offers me his handkerchief as I sputter, my eyes streaming.

"What does that have to do with anything?"

"Answer the question."

"And if I am?"

A muscle in his jaw twitches, betraying his impatience. "I would prefer a yes or no answer."

"What made you ask that question anyway?"

His teeth audibly grind together. "You didn't...feel like other women I've been with. I'd also like to give you the benefit of the doubt by assuming that you aren't skilled enough in acting to have put on the performance that you did."

Performance? I'm not sure just which show he's referring to. When he drugged me? Or all those nights of taunting him through his bugs?

"Again, what if I am?"

"So that's a yes, then." He sits back in his chair and folds his hands before him. If anything, he doesn't look satisfied with the answer he stole. His chest rises and falls, betraying harsh, slowed breathing. I do believe I may have upset the stone-cold Mr. Villa. I just wish I knew how.

"I'm invoking my rule," I say, hating how my voice shakes. Damn him for making me feel even a shadow of self-consciousness. "Why the hell does it matter to you?"

He breathes in sharply. Exhales even more harshly. "Because I want to proposition...*propose* an exchange."

"An exchange for what?" I ask stupidly.

He frowns, and then it clicks. *Oh.*

He wants to take my virginity. I let my eyes close again, for longer this time. My head spins. A part of me assumes I misheard him, but no. He throws off anger like heat from a furnace, infuriated. Annoyed. At himself? As strange as it feels to consider, I don't sense that his rage is directed at me.

No bother, because I feel more than enough fury for both of us.

"So no wonder you 'apologized.' Have you decided to replace murder with rape?"

He's a more equally matched opponent when I can't see him. I'm forced to feel what my eyes overlook. The tension lacing his posture. The unease emanating from his end. Every forced breath he takes in his desperate quest to maintain control.

"I don't want to rape you," he snarls, sounding disgusted by the prospect. I open my eyes and find him scowling. "How should I put it in a way you might understand? I want to fuck you,

Juliana. More specifically, I want use of your body, at my discretion."

He could have said, *"I want to shake your hand and be done with it,"* and I doubt his inflection would have changed any.

"Let me guess. You want to deflower me in some sick way of getting back at my father?" I push back from the table so violently that his pizza slice falls to the floor. "Have a good fucking night in the literal sense. I'm sure your right hand will make a nice substitute for me—"

"Sit down."

I don't. But I don't storm from the room, either. I wait, breath bated, shoulders squared, my body thrumming with more indignation, hate, rage, and shame than I have ever felt at one time.

"I don't want you because of your father," he snaps. "I could think of several much less taxing ways on my part to humiliate him."

He sounds far too stern for jokes. It's the truth. And I now feel a sudden urge to warn my father of the danger he's really in. First things first. "So then why?"

"The experience," he says, as if he's used to picking and choosing which life milestones to conquer on a whim. "I've never had a virgin."

I scoff at the word use. Had. "So, I'd be just another trophy in your collection?"

"I'm willing to abide by your terms." He doesn't bother denying it.

Ah. No wonder he's been so accommodating with dinner.

"Take your offer and shove it up your ass, Mr. Villa," I say sweetly. "My body isn't for sale. Though I have to commend you for being the first man I've ever met who was so disgustingly honest about only wanting to get into my pants."

"Don't play coy with me." He pushes back from the table as well but remains seated. "I was there, Ms. Thorne, when you kissed me—"

"You kissed *me*!"

"I felt you. I heard you, if you haven't forgotten your little display. And…"

I don't see him reach out until it's too late. He snatches my wrist, tugging me against him. My hands scramble for purchase over his shoulders, but he tugs harder, nearly forcing me onto his lap. His free hand cinches my waist with breathtaking familiarity. I'm trapped.

"I must remind you that I have a remarkable sense of smell."

I bite my lip, torn between slapping him again and running. Or both. I attempt to wrench my wrist free, but he doesn't let go. He doesn't tighten his grip, either, teasing me with a glimpse of freedom.

"What is that supposed to mean?"

Suddenly, his face is parallel to mine, which allows him to speak directly into my ear. "It means that I know when you're lying." He lets me go and I scramble away from him, smoothing the front of my gown with trembling fingers.

"Well, try this one on for size: Goodnight." I storm toward the main room of the greenhouse only to falter over the threshold. He hasn't moved from his chair. Maybe that little fact makes me brave enough to utter one last taunt. "Let's say I was interested in 'negotiating.' What would you offer in exchange?"

I'm ready for something truly wicked. An insult that will justify more than a slap. A kick between his legs. A punch. Something vile enough to warrant assaulting a blind man and ruining what little shred of gratitude I may feel toward him once and for all.

"It's simple," he says, sounding more than willing to take the bait. "I'd give you whatever you wanted."

"W-what?" I shake my head. No way I heard that right.

"I said, you could have whatever you wanted. Within my means, of course."

I force out a haughty laugh the likes of which would make Sharla from accounting proud. "So if I asked you to get on your knees and kiss Heyworth Thorne's feet, you would?"

"I'd consider it." He doesn't even cringe at the prospect. "Though there is no telling what I might do to him after fulfilling your request."

Fair enough. "What if I asked you to give me your fortune?"

He shrugs. "I've had nothing before."

I blink. "Your studio?"

"Property," he tells me the same way another man would say *plastic fork*. Referring to something easily disposed of and replaced.

"What if I asked you to paint me every night for the rest of my life?" I ask. Though he had already expressed a fleeting interest in shortening it.

"Really, Ms. Thorne, I would have thought you'd have some imagination."

"Oh, Mr. Villa, I'm afraid my imagination couldn't come close to a man so desperate to get laid that he'd…"

Do anything.

"Understand one thing about me, Ms. Thorne," he says, flattening his hands on each corresponding knee. "I know at least ten women within a block radius alone who I could call to, as you put it, 'get laid.' Sex isn't what I want from you."

I'm frowning. "Then what?"

"The same thing I was after when I met Daphne from Moscow. I was curious how her accent might sound when she orgasmed. In exchange, I paid to have her family relocated and supplied with the adequate documents. I wanted to experience a woman with age, hence I gave Catarina from Madrid a quarter of a million dollars. Marnie from Kentucky had never experienced, as she put it, 'kink.' In exchange, I jumpstarted her career as a successful model in Italian vogue." He ticks them all off like accomplished chores. *Daphne. Catarina. Marnie.*

I know without having to ask that each starred in a painting of his. One of them could be the figure hanging on my wall.

"Everything I do, I do for my art. Human nature cannot be copied. It must be experienced."

And, for some reason, he wants to "experience" me.

"I'm sure your previous ladies had a wonderful time, but I'm not for sale." My voice shakes, but damn it, I don't care.

"I do not purchase women." He sounds genuinely insulted by the idea. "Every encounter is a mutual one. And I can assure you that the curiosity went both ways. I'm sure you've thought the same thing, even in that sheltered head of yours. Can the blind man fuck?"

"Don't mock me," I hiss.

With equal vitriol, he says, "Don't underestimate me."

"You should take your own advice. Maybe I want my first time to be with a man who gives a damn about me, hmm? Have you considered that?"

A man who could understand my night terrors. Who could hold my hair when storms have made me vomit. Who wouldn't run at the mere mention of Simon.

It's a laundry list I stopped wishing for years ago. And I won't even consider how many boxes Damien has already check marked.

"A man who gives a damn," he repeats. "What about a man who gives a *dime*? My men earn a salary of no less than a grand per day."

And I spotted at least three watching over me. "Oh, congratulations!" I clap my hands. Thwack. Thwack. Thwack. "Give the man a medal! If you want to throw your money in my face, then fine. I'll send you a check to cover the expenses—"

"I don't expend my resources or time on people or things that hold no value to me." His tone resonates unlike any I've heard from him before now. Cold. Ice. Soulless. "You'd do best to remember that. I've taken an interest in your welfare, whether you like it or not."

"And *I* always honor my debts." Though I pray to any deity who will listen for the strength to forsake my pride now. "So ask your final question, Mr. Villa. I'm waiting."

From the set of his jaw, I know it will be devastating. Simon? Or something far more taboo, like the meaning behind that yearly bottle of wine? I feel every muscle in my body tense in anticipation.

I'm ready.

"I…" He sits forward, his head cocked. Then he stiffens. "Get out."

"W-what?"

He rises to his feet and advances toward me without warning. "Go."

"What are you—"

"Now!"

"*Con permiso*, brother." The voice of another man drifts through the glass walls of the greenhouse.

I turn and find a figure strolling down the main aisle, tall like Damien, with the same incredible bone structure. Only this man's eyes are fully intact, a haunting shade of amber, and his hair is closely cropped to his scalp. He's leaner as well, wearing a black shirt and jeans. Despite the casual attire, he holds himself with an air that rivals even Damien's swagger.

"I thought I should join you tonight and introduce myself." He turns that chilling gaze on me and smiles in a wicked display of white teeth. "*Buenas noches,* Juliana Thorne. I wondered when you would pay your respects."

EIGHTEEN

"*M*ateo." Damien pushes past me and nearly trips over the discarded pizza slice in his haste.

I've seen him angry, but never like this. His mouth flattens into a harsh line, stripped of emotion. It's how Daddy used to look whenever Danger, his prized mutt, ran out of the house off his leash.

"Whatever you want, we can discuss it later."

"There's nothing to discuss." Mateo shares the same light accent as his brother, but where Damien's words fall like haunting music, Mateo's are all sharp, thundering notes. He smiles and lowers his hand over his brother's shoulder, hard enough to jar his balance. "I merely wished to join you. I'm so lucky to have made it to dinner in time." His tone conceals a hard note that I sense is solely directed at Damien.

A warning.

"Pizza tonight?" He eyes the offering on the table and shrugs. "*Lo siento.* I'm being rude." He cuts his gaze to me: dark, cold eyes. "Ladies first."

"She's leaving," Damien warns. "Goodnight, Ms. Thorne—"

"Ah, but we have so much to discuss, Juliana and I." Mateo grabs my vacated chair by the back and deliberately angles it toward me. "Have a seat."

"Mateo," Damien warns through gritted teeth. Blind or not, his voice rings with an authority few men would ignore.

His brother laughs. "Oh, but I was so looking forward to our conversation," he says softly. "*Sí*. Who better to understand our recent troubles than another so-called murderer?"

Silence. It falls so thick that I can hear my heartbeat surging wildly beneath my skin. Like a tune composed of one haunting lyric: Murderer. Murderer. Murderer.

"Let's play a game. The life game." Smiling wide, Simon glanced from me to Leslie and back. "Who matters more?"

"*Sí*," Mateo says, sounding miles away. "If anyone could understand my predicament, it's this woman. A killer at the age of eight, self-professed, even—"

"Mateo!" Damien slams his hand against the table so hard that he knocks it off its axis.

I'm in the present again, stunned as what's left of the pizza lands on the floor.

Grinning, Mateo stoops for a piece and takes a bite. "It's no wonder she came calling," he adds after swallowing, "Did you want to know what it's like, hmm? To actually be punished for a crime?" He laughs and nods toward the half-eaten slice in his hand. "It's good. Much better than what they serve in prison. Plus, I don't have to stab a *pendejo* in the back for it—"

"Enough."

"I just want to know what it felt like," Mateo insists, his voice dripping with derision and charm. "To take away someone who mattered from a family who loved them. When you had nothing. No one. Though you did score yourself a rich daddy, eh?"

"I said *enough*."

"Oh, but we're having such a thrilling conversation. Aren't we, Juliana?"

"You." He pointed to me, grinning wide. "You pick. Remember the rules—"

"Juliana." Damien's voice has never sounded so cutting. It sinks into my skin, demanding my obedience. "Look at me."

I do. He's a blur, fading in and out of focus.

"This one matters, doesn't she? She's important, isn't she? She'll be missed, won't she?

"Watch." I had no choice.

He put the knife to Leslie's throat. Dug in hard enough to make her whimper. Then scream. And scream…

"Look at me!"

I blink and the flashback melds into Damien. Then the forest. Damien. The forest. Simon. Leslie.

A sound I vaguely recognize as coming from me fills the air. A wheezing gasp. Can't breathe. My fingers claw at my chest, but air won't go in.

Can't breathe!

"Enough!"

Warmth brushes my shoulder and I'm shoved toward the door.

"Go," someone commands.

"No." The second voice is harsher. "Let her stay."

I'm dragged another step forward. Another. Suddenly, the world sways and I'm pushed aside. I stumble against the wall, fixated on the scene unfolding before me.

Mateo grabs his brother's arm, his knuckles whitening over coiled muscle. "I said let the *puta* stay—"

Boom! In a flurry of motion, someone careens into a nearby planter, sending soil and crushed flowers sailing through the air. They groan, lying dazed in the aftermath. Thin. Mateo. His brother stands over him, his hands clenched into fists, his body radiating fury. *Madman*, Daddy called him. Now, I know why as his head swivels in my direction, his voice a slap.

"Go!"

My limbs jolt into motion. I run for the exit and across the roof without looking back. Panting, I reach the elevator and take it to the first floor. A man barges into the lobby at the exact moment the elevator doors open. I ready my hands to fight, my throat already clenching around a scream.

"It's all right," he says, crossing to me. His face looks familiar. Faint sound crackles from an earpiece he's wearing. "Mr. Villa sent me. I'm to take you home."

Home.

Where Simon's probably waiting for me. Where memories definitely are.

The home I don't deserve.

The life I stole by killing Leslie.

Damien's man hustles me onto the street, muttering something about a car being sent around. While he speaks, my eyes latch onto a yellow cab and I break away from him to flag it down.

"Wait!"

The guard can't catch up before I fling myself into the back seat and slam the door behind me. The bewildered driver watches me from the rearview mirror as I slap my hand against the back of his seat.

"Drive!"

Damien's man is already pawing at the door, but the cabbie doesn't need to be told twice. He plunges into the thick of traffic without waiting for a destination.

Not that I have one to give.

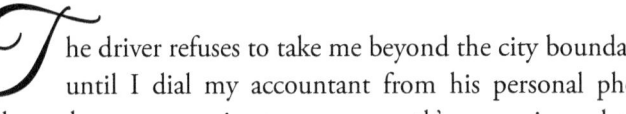

The driver refuses to take me beyond the city boundaries until I dial my accountant from his personal phone and have the man promise to pay a month's wages in exchange for taking me where I want to go.

A lonely stretch of road four hours away.

I make him drop me at a rest stop, where I attempt to buy a cheap bouquet of carnations before remembering I don't have a dime on me. Still, the cashier lets me have them out of pity, and I continue my pilgrimage on foot as the wind howls and nips at my hair and bared skin.

My flowers are frost-bitten when I finally reach a foreboding bend in a winding road. *Sorry, Leslie*, I mouth. They're not even her favorites, lilies. Just dying, pink petals and crumbling leaves.

It's so damn silent here, even now. Houses have sprung up close to this spot. There's a newer development in this part of town, a hint of civilization where there used to be nothing.

I don't have any trouble finding that small, dank crevice only a child could fit into. A matted layer of weeds has grown over the opening, remaining even as winter approaches. I perch my meager offering against a tree and then use both hands to tear the underbrush apart.

Twenty years later and it's never felt realer. Leslie's screams have never been louder. Simon has never felt closer.

I can hear him picking his way through the forest to find me and finish off the deed he taunted me with all those years ago. I hid here, holding my breath, shielded beneath a surging storm.

"You made the right choice," he told me then. "You won't be missed like this one will be—"

"Juliana!"

I jolt into awareness as reality makes itself known in varying degrees of pain. My burning, frostbitten skin. My cramping knees and my aching back. I'm hunched against the hillside, partially huddled within the crevice. Daylight stings my eyes as my ears catch footsteps prowling the woods nearby.

Fear grips my heart. Simon?

Whoever the figure is, he's persistent. "Juliana!"

Wait. I flinch. That voice doesn't belong here. Even the wind seems confused by his presence. It plays with the lilting notes of his accent, distorting them.

"Juliana! Answer me—"

"I'm here." My voice is a whisper promptly swallowed by the wind as I fixate on the imposing man wandering the woods just a few feet away.

He stops, his head cocked, sensing me regardless. "Where are you?"

I can't bring myself to move, even as he staggers within my reach, each step hesitant over uneven terrain. Somehow, he appears regal while tentatively feeling the space in front of him. He's still wearing his suit from dinner, a sauce stain along the lapel.

"Where?"

I stand slowly, biting a groan back. Is he here to finish the game his brother started? Or because of his stupid wager? Or because…

"Juliana, *por favor*. Where are you?"

"Here." I stagger toward him and grasp his outstretched hand in my own.

He's an inferno, clamping down like a vise. "You're freezing." The next instant, his coat is around my shoulders and he's shouting something into his headset.

"You…you found me?" I sound dazed. I *am* freezing. I don't have my coat, and frost glitters on my dress.

Damien says something else into his headset. Moments later, a man I recognize as Julio appears, panting by his employer's side.

"This way, sir."

For the first time, I realize that Damien literally went searching for me blind. He's unfamiliar with the landscape, using Julio's guidance to steer me forward. But his grip is sure and I'm so damn tired. When I lean against him, he doesn't even flinch. His arm slides around my shoulders instead, offering more support.

So strange. So surreal. Too fragile to question.

So I merely observe.

He and his guard came by car. It's parked along the road, and I'm guided into the back seat while the guard circles around to the driver's seat. Damien, on the other hand, takes the seat beside me. He says something to the driver in Spanish and the car begins to move.

I'm too busy shivering to pay attention to our surroundings. He could be taking me anywhere, for any purpose, yet I can't muster up the energy to care.

Though my silence, ironically, must worry him. "Don't sleep," he warns as if sensing my slowed, heavy breathing and how my eyelids drift lower by the second. "What the hell were you thinking?"

His anger sears my skin, hotter than the heat he orders the driver to turn up.

"Sorry," I murmur, unwilling to lift my head from his shoulder, even as I direct what little anger I feel his way. "It's not every day that I'm called a murderer to my face."

Recently, anyway.

I sense him stiffen.

"I…apologize."

And I *must* be delirious. My body reacts violently to the sudden warmth. My teeth chatter. I can't stop shaking, and the worse my tremors become, the more words in Spanish Damien snaps at his driver.

"*Vámonos!*"

The man must be used to the pressure, because he doesn't so much as flinch while maneuvering seamlessly through traffic. My old town flies by in a muted blur. The school where Leslie and I spent our last few hours of innocence. The old park. The library.

Nostalgia hits like a punch in the stomach. I squeeze my eyes shut against it and find myself sinking even further against the firm body serving as my sole support.

"No." His finger grazes my chin disapprovingly. "Stay awake."

"I'm fine." I grimace, but with a sigh, I peel my eyes open. His concern shouldn't affect me so much.

"Say something," he growls.

"My father's going to kill me."

The press conference is today. His big announcement. His triumphant return to the political sphere. All of it tarnished slightly by me.

"He delayed the press briefing," Damien says dryly. "It's later this evening."

"Good." A funny thought occurs to me. "How did you find me? Do you have me LoJacked?" Then again, the prospect isn't so funny.

"Julio followed you long enough to get the license plate of the cab," he explains. Not because he wants to, I suspect. He's stiff, resembling stone again.

I have a sudden urge to run my fingers along his jaw, testing the give of his flesh for myself. I do and frown. Soft like always, though he flinches at the contact. My fingers look like a stranger's. I've never been so pale.

"Why?" I croak.

"I have contacts who tracked your position out of the state," he adds without answering my last question. "Once I realized where you were headed, I knew where to find you."

"You were very thorough in your research, it seems." My fingers are still on his jaw. "Did you break into my old file?" I've been told the case has been declared indefinitely cold. "I guess you really do know everything."

"Not everything." Glowering, he removes his arm from around my shoulders and takes my hand, lowering it to my lap. But he doesn't let go. If anything, his fingers tighten as if he can force out the numbing chill through brute strength alone. "For example, I don't know what lasting damage you might experience from being in freezing temperatures for several hours wearing only a dress."

"You don't have to do this." But even as I watch his fingers intertwined with mine, I can't bring myself to pull away.

"New wager." His tone warns that, this time, there will be no negotiation. "Give me this one moment to give a damn about your welfare and tomorrow you can berate me all you'd like. *Por favor.*"

Apparently, he's not interested in receiving permission, because the car comes to a stop a heartbeat later. While the driver circles around to his side, Damien tightens his grip as if he's expecting me to resist.

But I don't. I allow him to steer me from the car and then through the halls of what I assume is a modest hotel, so unlike the posh, luxury high-rises we both frequent.

Julio enters our room first. He prowls the area, spitting out simple phrases all the while. "Bed at twelve o'clock, sir. Bathroom at three o'clock. Ten paces each way."

"Thank you," Damien says. Only now does he guide me inside, and I realize that this must be one of the many ways he navigates without his cane. "You can leave for the moment, Julio. See if you can have clothing brought for Ms. Thorne."

"Right away." Julio embarks on his mission while I'm marched into a modest bathroom.

Damien feels along the wall until he finds the light switch—for my benefit. Then he keeps going until his fingers brush the cool tile above the tub and then continue to the water fixture. "Remove your clothing," he commands as he switches the faucet on.

"I'm late," I realize as—of all things—my commitment to Daddy enters my mind. "My father's press conference. I've missed it—"

"It's been rescheduled," Damien says calmly. "Arrangements have been made. You don't need to worry about that now. What you do need to worry about is your internal body temperature." He gestures toward the tub. "Now, take off your clothing."

Memories of Simon must have stripped me of my free will. I'm an obedient little girl again, jumping to the rasp of a monster's growl. This one doesn't rest until I'm standing naked before him as he fills the tub to his preference.

Taking a step back, he nods to the water. "In."

My body rebels once I'm submerged in the deliciously warm bath. I can't move. I'm so damn tired—to the point where someone has to assist me when seconds pass without my cleaning myself. They hand me a washcloth, and then they wet it for me and drag it along my back and my shoulders. They work their fingers into my hair and lather it with shampoo. Finally, they dry me off into a towel and perch me on the ledge of the tub, apparently while waiting for Julio to bring me fresh clothing.

They stay. All without reminding me to smile, or hush, or be brave, charming Juliana.

I know they hear me crying, and they say nothing.

NINETEEN

I thought Daddy overreacted to the smallest crisis. Damien puts him to shame.

Heyworth Thorne could have found me neck-deep in a snowdrift, but I doubt he'd have his driver speed across state lines and all but drag me into my suite, where I find a private doctor waiting to examine me. It's a concern that borders upon... obsessive: a collector ensuring the objects in his possession remain unharmed—by anything *but* him.

I should resist.

Fight him off.

I shouldn't let him stay.

Damn Damien.

He waits in silence as the doctor pokes and prods me before declaring me healthy, though sleep-deprived and dehydrated.

"Primarily, you should get some rest," the man suggests, gathering up his supplies.

He's barely out the door before I find myself being manually steered into my room by a more formidable opponent.

"Wait…" I sway on my feet as Damien drags his fingers over my duvet and folds it back. "You don't have to stay—"

"You need to rest. At least for an hour. Especially if you are attending the briefing tonight. It will be starting soon."

"My father…" I groan, bracing my hand against my forehead. "He's probably called the FBI by now."

"Not quite." With a knowing tilt of his head, Damien proves he's outsmarted me yet again. "I had your building manager distract him with some lie about you losing your phone to explain why you're running late. You can arrive at his media blitz on time and he'll be none the wiser. Now, rest." He sounds so damn stern.

Not that I'm helping my case any; I can barely stay upright. I've never felt so drained. So exhausted. So vulnerable.

I can't ignore the subtle disgust tainting his tone—or the fact that he's trying his best to disguise it. For me.

"You want to tell me something," I blurt, sensing the truth in his tense posture. "About my father? Just say it. Please…"

"You need to rest."

"Just tell me." The desperation in my voice startles me. "That's why you've been so patient, right? To deliver the blow when I least expect it? I'm at rock bottom now, so just tell me now."

Of all reactions, he…flinches. "Juliana—"

"Are you going to have nudes of me plastered around city hall during the press conference?" The thought makes me shudder—but it's surprisingly low on the list of potential revenge plots. There are so many much worse. It's a dangerous game to play, jumping into the brain of a criminal mastermind. He already knows more than enough to decimate me. "Will you have my little recording play on the speakers? Tell me. I know you have something planned."

"And if I don't?" His tone cuts into me, sharp and demanding. *You think you know me, Ms. Thorne? Think again.* "What if my plan was far simpler?"

"What?" I ask. "If you truly give a damn about my 'welfare,' like you said, you'd just tell me—"

"What if I only had to tell you the truth? That your nightmares and your pain and the terror you feel at night could have been resolved years ago? That the man you worship hasn't done a damn thing to protect you. If anything, he's used you as a pawn in his own sick, twisted scheme meant to cover his tracks."

I swallow hard, hating the gruff earnest in his voice. It's harder to ignore than his usual smug mocking. "Like how?"

"All this time… You have no clue, do you? Think back to when he first adopted you, Juliana. Did you ever ask yourself why a man like him would take in a child like you? Why *your* case in particular drew the notice of such a cavalier defense attorney who rarely participated in even charity events?"

"Are you blaming my father for Leslie's death too?" I scoff. "Very funny."

But he isn't laughing. "Nothing could prevent what happened to you, except justice. Justice served to the man who hurt you before you could ever cross his path."

"The police never found him," I croak. "Does the all-knowing Damien claim to know his identity too?"

"What if I told you that you weren't the first or the second victim of this man. This killer? That several girls your age had suffered through a similar hell. Died. Mere shreds of evidence tied them to one suspect who escaped prosecution—not through fate, but intention?"

"What are you saying?"

"I'm saying, what if that monster had a damn good lawyer? A lawyer who got him off scot-free and had the records expunged so that the world would never even learn his name? A powerful man, with a powerful lawyer who allowed him to terrorize two little girls, killing one and leaving the other traumatized for life? Only after his mistake did that same lawyer adopt a victim of a crime he himself enabled and yet pretended to have suddenly grown a heart? A lawyer who likes to think himself a beacon of all things just."

His words create an invisible noose that wraps around my throat, tightening by the second. "No…"

"Should I be blunter?" Damien wonders, cocking his head. "What if that lawyer's name was Heyworth Thorne, and that everything he claimed to believe in was a lie?"

"You're lying."

"No. He has been lying. To you, most likely since the day he came into your life. It wasn't an act of goodwill that led him to you, Juliana. It was guilt. But guilt that hasn't led him to do the right thing and name your tormentor, even after all these years. He knows his name. He's known all along—"

"Stop."

"Why else erase the records?" He sounds so calm, though it feels like he's shouting. "Why else suddenly take an interest in supposed 'justice'? Heyworth Thorne never loved you. He merely used you like a trophy to assuage his own fucking conscience—"

"Stop!" Tears spray down my cheeks like bullets as I scramble to my feet and stagger toward the door. "You're lying!"

"Juliana, wait—"

"Leave me alone!" I'm running, escaping into the hall without bothering with a coat or shoes. Downstairs a car is waiting as promised, but when I enter it, I break.

Because I know that Damien wasn't lying.

If he could turn me against my father, he'd have everything to gain.

But Heyworth Thorne has a lot more to lose.

Enough that he'd use me as a pawn to keep it all.

own Hall sits within a maze of reporters jostling for the right vantage point to cover my father's moment of triumph. It's a buzz of activity I quickly adjusted to while growing up in the Thorne family. From the age of eight, I learned how to smile on cue and nod solemnly when asked to explain how grateful I was to my father for adopting me.

When all along…

He might have known the identity of the specter haunting my nightmares. And all this time, he's said nothing.

Could such a man really be deserving of all the hate Damien feels toward him? Could he have allowed prejudice to cloud his judgment in the case of Mathias Villa?

The answer makes my stomach churn. Deep down, maybe I've known it all along: yes.

Heyworth Thorne is human—and I've learned the hard way that every human, at their core, has the potential to become a monster.

"Where to, miss?" the driver inquires, which makes me jump.

"H-here." I exit the car a block away from the press queue and spot my father amid a crowd of assistants near the entrance to the sprawling, Romanesque town hall building. It's a ritual of his: show up early, prep his speech, and ensure that all optics are picture-perfect.

My heart throbs as I observe him and try to see the man most of the world has turned against. His gray, balding head. His warm, gentle smile that eased my fear when I needed comfort the most. I try my best to strip away twenty years of loving Heyworth Thorne.

But all I see is an old man preening for the cameras, desperate to salvage the one thing he's cherished above all: his career.

I don't even realize I've slipped through the throng of onlookers until he spots me from the top of the steps, still smiling in his charming way.

"Sweet pea..." He frowns, looking me over. I'm in pajamas, my hair a mess, my eyes bloodshot. This isn't the perfect daughter he envisioned parading around today. "Didn't you receive the dress?"

"Why?" It's the only word I can get out as cameras flash and reporters shout questions. "Why did you lie to me? Why?"

"Juliana—"

"They said I was a liar. All the papers. The people. My own parents didn't want me because they thought I was..." I can't even say it. *A murderer.* "And you lied to me. Tell me he wasn't one of your cases. Tell me that you didn't know—"

"What on Earth are you talking about?" Diane asks, placing her hand on my arm. Beside her, Heyworth Thorne just stares at me, his eyes wide. "Darling?"

"Was taking me in some kind of pity party? A way to assuage your guilt? Or was it pride? Was that all I was to you?" I demand of them both. "All I am to you? A trophy?"

"Juliana." Daddy blinks, reassembling his mask. How ironic. He used to punish those who hide behind lies, but that's all he's ever done around me. "We need to discuss this in private—"

"No!" I turn, my eyes streaming as I scan the crowd for an out, any outlet. I find one in darkness: a sleek black vehicle with a hand beckoning from the back seat. Of all the things to fear, relief shatters the pain ripping through me—and I cling to it like hell.

"Juliana!"

I push through the throng of spectators and climb into the car. Black leather upholstery makes for a chilling escape. So does the man seated beside me.

"Drive," Damien commands, and I don't give a damn where he takes me.

Just somewhere far from here.

TWENTY

"Have you known all along?" I demand as the car melds into the thick of traffic. "That my father defended him? Leslie's killer? Do you know his name? Who was he?"

Damien says nothing. Too busy savoring the moment? Fine. I'll give him plenty to gloat over. My tears continue to fall unabated. I don't even try disguising the sobs ripping from me one after the other. "Who was he? I... I could press charges. Testify against him. Do something."

I try to picture him. Simon. My father and Simon. Could Heyworth Thorne have known more about the attack on me than he let on? No. Even thinking as much triggers a wave of bile up my throat that I have to choke down.

But the sinking thoughts nibble away at what little sanity I have left.

All those years of Simon's presents. Perhaps the man wasn't as omniscient as he appeared—maybe my father let him in. Let him taunt me with those memories. Could the home I'd thought was a haven have been little more than a kennel, with me as the pet, locked inside for others' amusement?

"I don't know his identity," Damien says, sounding eerily calm, no glee to be found. "I merely discovered the inconsistencies in Thorne's prior cases. But the records were expertly expunged and I never learned a name. I will say that only a powerful man could ensure that. Someone in politics most likely—"

"He never stopped after that night," I admit, my voice breaking. "S-Simon—that's what I call him. Simon. Every fucking year, on my birthday, he taunts me with the same fucking 'presents.' Like the doll, and the rose, and the ribbon. It's so I won't forget. He's still out there."

The silence greeting my confession is too much, too thick. Desperate to shatter it, I keep talking. "He made us play a game, you see. I had to pick. Who he was going to kill. We were near the woods. Leslie and I were walking home after I got jealous of her stupid doll and…"

We fell into a madman's trap.

I close my eyes as the memory threatens to unfold. For the first time in so damn long, I don't resist it. I *let* myself see the forest. Smell the blood. I can taste the fear, so thick and real…

"He made me pick which one of us would live or die. My rich, pretty, popular friend or me, the poor, pathetic pauper? And I…"

"You don't need to tell me this," he says. His accent dips in an unfamiliar way. Horror? Disgust?

Confused, I look up and find his jaw clenched, his posture tense. Men like him don't like to get their hands dirty after all. Not even figuratively.

But I can't stop.

"I-I picked *me*. I picked me," I repeat, choking out the secret I've suffocated on all this time. "I wasn't important. I wouldn't be missed. He *told* me. And he stabbed Leslie anyway! He…he stabbed—"

"Enough."

"He killed her," I whisper in defiance. "And he's hunted me everywhere I've gone ever since. So that I will never forget. My life is worthless.…"

And all along, Heyworth Thorne might have known his identity. Yet I wasn't worth bringing that monster to justice. I wasn't worth justice.

"You win, I guess," I quip, laughing at the irony. "I never want to see Heyworth Thorne again. Does that make you happy?"

"You still sound weak," Damien says, ignoring my question entirely.

I look beyond the windows and realize his driver has pulled up before the private entrance of the Lariat. There are no reporters lying in wait, surprisingly. Through his doing, I suspect.

"You need sleep—"

"Don't pretend like you care." My hand shakes as I wrestle for the door handle. "After all, this is what you wanted. To see the look on my father's face as my world fell apart—"

"You shouldn't be alone."

Damn him. He should be gloating. Smirking. Smug. But the stern tone of his voice robs me of my anger and all I can do is follow meekly as he takes the lead and escorts me inside.

His face reveals nothing once he's herded me into the elevator and we ascend to my suite. As we cross the threshold, guilt and gratitude feed off the potency of my fatigue. Only one thing can combat both: control.

"Fine," I hiss as he steers me into my bedroom. "We can play this game so that you can end this charade that you give a damn." In all honesty, the bastard's left me no choice after today. I have just one thing to leverage against him. "I'll agree. I'll do it."

He grabs my arm and pushes me firmly toward the mattress. "Do what?"

I climb beneath the sheets while he lurks there in utter silence. He's right: I'm exhausted. All at once, the gravity of everything slams down like a hammer. Delirium sets in, skewing my priorities. Heyworth Thorne and Simon are a million miles away. As my head sinks against my pillow, I watch him. His jaw has never looked so comparable to steel before. I bet he could crush diamonds with the weight of his scowl alone.

"Sleep with you," I say. "Now you can hold something over my father's head, like you've dreamed—"

"You're delirious," he says with obvious restraint. *Therefore, I'll ignore the fact that you're mocking me.*

"I'm serious." Am I? Maybe. The thoughts in my head all feel slurred and run together, but oddly enough, one seems startlingly clear. "I'll let you have my virginity."

He frowns and starts for the door. "Get some rest, Ms. Thorne."

"In exchange—"

His footsteps falter.

"I want you to…"

"Yes?"

The grated word makes me realize that I've trailed off, lost in my thoughts. I want more from Damien than a smart woman should. Small things. Stupid things. Tiny, inconsequential things that suddenly appeal to me more than any couture gown or high-rise apartment would. Maybe because I know deep down he'll never let me have them.

"I want you to find out who Simon is. I…I want justice." That elusive thing Heyworth Thorne spent his entire life promising to deliver. "Is that a fair enough trade?"

"I can give you that," he says quietly, as if it really is that simple. The powerful Damien Villa can do anything. So why stop there?

"And," I add, "I want you to stay with me. Until my birthday, anyway."

"Stay with you."

"In theory," I reply, murmuring.

"For a year?"

I can't tell if he believes me or not. To him a year must be a lifetime. For me, it's merely a brief lull before a recurring nightmare. "Yes."

"And I would stay with you?"

Suddenly, my eyelids weigh an unbearable amount and I let them drift shut. "It shouldn't be hard." Ironically, considering this is the price I'm naming for my body. "Send me fresh flowers every day. Stay with me when it storms. I'll even let you stalk me if you have to. Keep me away from my father if that's what you want. Just…"

"What?"

I almost forgot he was there, listening avidly to my slurred, disjointed wish list. "Just pretend that you actually give a damn… Pretend you want to keep me."

Maybe then I'll stop hearing Simon's voice slithering inside my skull: *This one will be missed. This one matters.*

You made the right choice…

And I'll never let you forget it.

For the second day in a row, I wake up only to be bombarded by a million chilling realizations. One, I'm not wearing my own clothing. Soft cotton has taken the place of tailored silk.

Two, someone tucked me into bed, drawing the blankets over me with unnerving care.

Thirdly, and most confusing of all, I'm alone.

My breathing echoes loudly in the silence as I peel my eyes open to yet another overcast, stormy-gray sky. I'm not worried. Gritting my teeth, I climb out of bed and strip the gray pajama set someone dressed me in. I'm partially within a trademark black-pantsuit ensemble when I hear it.

A man's voice.

The sound comes from my living room: a speaker rapidly communicating in a mixture of English and what I suspect to be Spanish. From his tone alone, I can tell he's in the middle of what he seems to do best: dishing out orders.

Partly convinced it's all a figment of my imagination, I leave my room half-dressed, only to be faced with a furious Damien pacing before my coveted view.

He must carry around impeccable suits wherever he goes. Today, his outfit of choice is gray with a muted tie in a similar hue. The moment I step closer, his head swivels in my direction. "Find him," he snarls into a cell phone before shoving it into his pocket. "You're awake," he says gruffly.

I swallow hard, surprised to find my throat dry and my lips cracked. "You're still here." My tone inflects at the last second, turning the statement into a whispered question. *Why?*

"How do you feel?"

Exhaustion robs me of my usual filter. "Tired," I admit. "I'm thirsty. Starving—"

"Side effects of hypothermia," he interjects in a fittingly icy tone. "I'll have something brought up."

Before I can blink, the phone is at his ear and he's snarling even more phrases in Spanish.

A glance beyond him reveals that he's been busy. My couch looks as though a man roughly the size of Damien has occupied it for quite some time—God forbid slept on it. A nondescript stainless-steel mug rests on my coffee table. One sniff and I can tell the blend isn't mine but the concoction of someone who prefers their caffeine black.

Do I dare believe he slept here overnight? Of course not. That would mean assuming he considered taking me up on my offer— and I already have an *I was just delirious and joking, obviously,* quip poised on the tip of my tongue. Seconds pass, but it never leaves my throat.

"You didn't have to stay."

He pauses in his solitary march, facing the view from the windows. Even though I know he can't see the dreary clouds through a jungle of concrete, his posture stiffens.

"I apologize again for the other day," he says, leaving me scrambling to wonder which night he referred to. "That was not my intention. For you to learn the truth in that way."

"I can believe that," I say. A man like him would have envisioned something far more devastating than a woman's minor mental breakdown in front of a throng of reporters.

In fact…

I know deep down it could have been so much worse. "I'm surprised my father hasn't come by or called…"

The subtle tensing of his jaw makes me suspect that he may have something to do with that fact.

"I don't want to see him," I admit before he can voice an excuse. "Not now. I-I can't…"

His lips part, but the door opens at the same time and Julio strolls in as boldly as if he lives here. He places a steaming cup of commercial coffee and a white takeout box on my counter. He nods to me and greets Damien out loud. "Sir."

Then he leaves, and Damien decides that taking charge of my welfare would punish me more than any comeback could.

"Eat," he commands, stressing the word.

I'd refuse if I weren't so hungry. My stomach growls as I cross over to the food and lift the lid of the container. The meal certainly isn't fare comparable to pizza. The buttered croissant and blueberry jam taste both heavenly and suspicious. Could they be a peace offering?

Looking at the man, I can't tell. He almost seamlessly blends into the background of the stormy city landscape. Sharp, harsh edges and sleek lines with streaks of odd light where there shouldn't be any. Like the fact that I can tell—whether on my couch or not—he hasn't slept much. The lines around his mouth are more pronounced than usual. He looks weathered and weary.

Because of me?

"I can pay you for the doctor's visit," I suggest. "And the gas you spent to—"

"I don't want money from you."

"Oh, that's right," I say softly. "You want my virginity."

I was wrong before in thinking that mentioning Mateo had triggered the worst of his anger. Sorely mistaken. This cold, silent creature, with his head dangerously cocked to the side, is Damien at his most volatile. My, how the man hates being mocked.

And in this moment, I'm poised to deliver the most crushing comeback I can and save face once and for all. Because I remember in cruel, crystal-clear detail everything I said to him. The price I deliriously dreamt up for myself. *Stay with me. Be with me. Pretend for me.*

Most pathetic of all: *Keep me.*

"Well?" I croak after choking down the last bite of my breakfast. "Have you considered my terms?"

I don't know which one of us is more shocked. My knees knock together. I feel liable to melt into a puddle on the floor.

And Damien looks like the definition of a man caught stepping on a landmine. "You remember?" His tone betrays more than mere caution. It's deadly.

"I require a yes or no answer, Mr. Villa." My God, how do I sound so calm? So in control when I feel anything but? "Did you find my terms agreeable?"

Of course he didn't. And his silence proves it. Without warning, he heads for the door.

"I have business to attend to," he tells me while straightening the sleeves of his perfectly crisp jacket. "It may take the rest of the day."

I still expect a direct refusal. Or for him to laugh and utter some parting cheap shot. Not to leave, shutting the door behind him. I can hear his footsteps retreat down the hall as my words hang on the air, sounding less calm the more I think on it and more...desperate.

Have you considered my terms?

No wonder he sounded so surprised that I'd mention them. He hoped I'd forgotten. Apparently, he wasn't willing to pay any price after all.

Bastard. My fingers tighten around the cup of coffee and I wind up throwing it across the room. It strikes my wall with a thud, splattering brown liquid over the industrial gray surface. Who needs Damien when I can create my own fucking art?

"Miss?"

I flinch as the accented voice accompanies a knock on my door. "Y-yes? Um...come in."

The door opens to reveal Julio, his expression stern—which makes the fact that he's holding a delicate vase of flowers in his hands even more comical and chilling. "Where would you like these, miss?"

Son of a bitch. I blink and find myself staring at the vase in a daze. The container itself is silver. From it sprouts a single black orchid with a telltale dash of pink across its center.

It's one of *his*, ripped right from the oh-so-private collection. I recognize the shape. The smell. The jagged stalk missing a single bloom.

By some miracle, I manage to point to the counter, and Julio obeys my silent command before leaving again, presumably to take up his post in the hallway.

Swallowing hard, I observe the petals of the bloom up close. It could be some sick version of a goodbye message or a threat. I'm almost content with that scenario.

But then I remember my own slurred, incoherent words.

Send me flowers every day.

Only a man like Damien Villa could make such a gesture feel like a warning.

<h2 style="text-align:center">~ END OF PART 1 ~</h2>

A TASTE LIKE SIN

A Taste like Sin

A Taste like Sin By Lana Sky

Cover Design by Charity Chimni
Editing by Mickey Reed Editing
Formatting by Charity Chimni
Proofreading by Charity Chimni

ONE

*R*eal monsters hide their true identities behind their polished masks. But broken little girls? We disguise our pain with rebellion.

For instance, when faced with her father's betrayal, in what ways might a sheltered socialite lash out? Why, by selling her virginity to none other than said father's sworn enemy.

And where might such a man take her in order to culminate her pain and humiliation?

To view an orgy, of course. In all fairness, I all but dared him to.

Distract me was the challenge I proposed to Damien Villa after spending forty-eight hours locked inside my apartment. It's only fitting that he picked his favorite arena to amuse me within—as well as to reinforce the bargain we've struck: I've sold my virginity to him for a dangerous price. *His* company.

"You're shaking, Ms. Thorne," Damien acknowledges, his coarse tone like velvet against my eardrum. He's seated on a leather chair beside the identical one I'm perched on the edge of. Only a sliver of space separates us and, this close, his heat is a cruel, mocking taste of what I can't seem to feel: anything.

The aftermath of Heyworth's deception has rendered me hollow.

Empty.

Numb.

Though my nails dig into my palms—I'm clenching them that tightly—nothing cuts through the fog in my brain. Nothing except *his* voice.

"I can smell the sweat on your skin," he says, utilizing his skills of perception the way an assassin would a knife. To reinforce that comparison, the blindfold obscuring his vision is the same ebony shade as his suit, helping him cut a chilling figure against the blood-colored backdrop. "If you are nervous, we can leave. I'm sure I can devise another form of entertainment."

"N-No." The appearance of an easy out makes me shudder—this man, despite how short a time I've known him, doesn't strike me as the merciful type. More devilish if anything.

Because we've made a deal, he and I. It's only fitting that he brought me to Hell in order to honor that pact.

To be fair, his version of Hell is a stylish affair. Scarlet walls enclose a private booth resembling one that might be found in an opera house. Admittedly, an opera house that stars naked performers writhing upon black silken sheets rather than a stage.

In a sick way, there's beauty in it all.

Down below, two men and a woman lie entwined, their pale limbs entangled. Hoarse groans allude to their activity, but as far as I can tell, there's been no penetration. Yet. A strange detail to notice with a madman seated beside me.

Fully aware of him, I sense my inner thighs tense in a way that makes me stiffen and cross them tighter.

"I'm fine," I lie. "And I laid out my terms. It's only fair that you get to specify yours."

Like "dinner" here, again.

The first time he brought me to this taboo venue, the layout was admittedly different: a single couple viewed through a sheet of glass. Tonight, shadowed balconies reveal the vague hints of other people watching from across this wide atrium. At a glance, I count six booths in total, all with a bird's-eye view of the trio, their occupants rapt at attention.

"I will admit," I whisper, "that when you mentioned sex, I wasn't aware that you meant in the context of...an orgy." God, I can barely spit that word out. I breathe it instead, a gasp tinged by so many connotations. Dirty. Disgusting. Debasing.

Least of all: My father wouldn't approve.

The man who, as of two days ago, I considered to be my father, at least. Maybe that stubborn fact is why I haven't left yet? Why I can't seem to take my eyes off the naked woman being pawed like a toy doll between two different men, either.

Spite.

At least she's enjoying her stint as a pawn.

"I won't insist on anything you are not comfortable with," Damien warns, a rather polite non-denial. "You will have the final say in that matter when it comes to it. This is merely a diversion."

"From the saga of Heyworth Thorne," I snipe. "I know he's been trying to contact me." And I've avoided every message, call, and text. Something tells me that Damien hasn't strived to be as ignorant as I have, however. "How many times has he called today? Let me guess, he apologized? Promised to buy me a pony if I forgive him for protecting the identity of the man who made my life a living hell for twenty years? Or perhaps a new dress?" The vitriol undercuts the sensual murmurs drifting from below, and I have enough sense to feel some semblance of guilt. I'm ruining the show. "I'm sorry—"

"Don't be ashamed of your anger, " Damien growls, displaying his uncanny knack for sensing my emotions, even as I try to ignore them. "You have every right to express it."

"Do I?" I tilt my head thoughtfully, blinking back a burning sting from my eyes.

The loss of a loved one is an awful, ripping kind of pain. I've suffered it before—and I should be able to survive anything after that.

But I was wrong. So *wrong.*

My birth parents were absentee, barely imprinted in my memory —but Heyworth Thorne is my *father*. My mentor. My protector. My hero.

And beneath his well-crafted mask, he is little more than a fraud.

And a liar.

"Several," Damien says, shrugging the question off. Before I can command him to elaborate, he inclines his head toward the balcony. A not-so-subtle reference to the high-pitched moan emanating from below. "I must admit I'm curious as to the act encouraging our current soundtrack. Would you kindly narrate?"

I lean forward just enough to view the trio again. "They're fingering the woman," I dryly convey. "It looks rather uncomfortable, if I do say so myself—"

"Oh?" He laughs while copying my movements, his breath on my throat. "Do add some more theatrics to your descriptions, Ms. Thorne. I would like to visualize the scene, if you will. Is it one finger or two?"

I stiffen. Only he could pleasantly request something so obscene yet make it seem tempting to comply.

"They're…positioning her," I say. "On her hands and knees. The taller one is looming over her from behind and—"

"Ah, but what is she feeling?" As if such a thing could be discerned just at a glance.

Surprisingly, I think it can be as the woman in question arches her back into the taller man while brushing her fingers along the chest of the other.

"She's not ashamed," I hear myself croak. "I think…she's enjoying it."

"Is that so?" He's even closer, his scent flooding my nostrils with every breath I take. Wine. Cologne. Sin. My eyelids flutter as my gaze darts from the show to him and back again. "How could someone *enjoy* something so vulgar?"

"Her eyes are wide," I admit. "She's trembling. Moaning. I suppose you can hear the rest."

"That I can."

I turn in time to catch a flash of teeth as he grins. But just as quickly, a frown replaces the expression.

"I'm afraid our entertainment may be cut short."

"Huh?" I look behind us and find a hostess entering the booth, her teeth clenched.

She crosses to Damien and leans down to murmur something into his ear.

"I see," he replies, reaching for his cane. Extending his hand toward me, he nods to the door. "I was correct. After you."

"What's going on?" I warily place my hand on his and allow him to pull me along after the hostess, but he doesn't offer up an explanation. Near the mouth of the lobby, I deduce the reason for this unceremonious interruption all on my own.

Two police officers are guarding the door, glaringly out of place. Their twin stern expressions fixate on me simultaneously and one of them advances, his hand extended. "Miss Thorne?"

"Yes," I croak. "Can I help you?"

The two share a look. "Have you heard from your father recently?" the first one asks.

My heart falls into my stomach. "Is something wrong? Did something happen—"

"No," the man says quickly. "But he seems to be…concerned for your welfare."

"My welfare?" My brows furrow. "He didn't—"

"As you can see, she is safe and sound," Damien smoothly says before I can complete my suspicion out loud. "We apologize for the confusion, officers. Goodnight."

His careful tone implies the worst-case scenario. Like the fact that these officers didn't randomly show up to a sex club for the hell of it. They had been sent here.

For me.

"He called you, didn't he?" I demand of the nearer officer, who looks back at his partner. "My father?"

"We're just doing our duty, ma'am." A confirmation if there ever was one.

"Well, you can tell my *father*..." I grit my teeth over that word and choke it down. "*Heyworth Thorne*. You can tell him to stop contacting me. I'm fine."

"And you feel safe?" the other officer inquires, his eyes darting in Damien's direction. "Your father would like you to give him a call if you can. Just to reassure him that you're okay."

"Why?" I demand. But then another, more pointed question escapes. "Or what?"

Isn't the answer obvious?

"He wants you to arrest me, doesn't he?" I suspect, my voice breaking. "Or commit me, or whatever you can do to lock me away—"

"Juliana." Damien's hand lands over my shoulder. Even I know how insane I sound out loud. Paranoid. Irrational.

Days of obsessing over Heyworth's next move might do that to a person.

"You can tell him to go fuck himself," I hiss. "Tell him to—"

"I believe you have witnessed more than enough to be assured that Ms. Thorne is perfectly safe, as well as in her right mind," Damien says over me. "If you please."

When he touches my arm again, I have enough sense to follow, allowing him to guide me into another section of the shadowy lobby. Then through a door and into a small sitting room.

"That will be all," Damien says to the attendant, who scurries off. "Breathe," he commands me. "Getting upset now would only play into Thorne's hands."

I hate that he's right. That he can read me—and my father—so damn well. Like pawns on a well-studied chessboard. That's all we are to him really. Mere pieces in a giant game.

"You think like him," I croak, tearing my hands through my hair, desperate to keep them from shaking—it doesn't help. Helpless, I tug at the sleeves of my coat instead, straightening it over my black cocktail dress. He suggested formal attire for tonight's engagement—a bit of irony all things considered. My life is in shambles, but at least I'm well dressed for the occasion. "Always about appearances and propriety, and—"

"My reputation doesn't depend on you," Damien argues. "Frankly, we haven't been publicly linked, so I have no stake in ensuring the paparazzi doesn't capture a front-page story of you having a meltdown in a private club. So scream if you so choose. Rant. I will not judge you."

God, it's the wrong thing for him to say. Patient. Understanding.

Disarming.

"I would rather you be an ass right now," I admit. "It would be easier to be furious."

And I need to stay angry. Bitter. Callous.

Because if I can't...

"Forget the rest of the world." Like a wall of muscle, every contour of Damien hardens against me from behind. "If you don't mind, I'd rather we return to the show. Your sanitized narration has grown on me—"

"Is that what you want from me?" I ask.

His silence intrigues me, overriding the ache in my chest—for now. Like a drowning victim presented with a life rope, I latch onto it.

"Want to *do* to me, I mean. F-Fuck me in front of a room of people like some kind of pathetic porn—"

"I believe you weren't paying close enough attention, Ms. Thorne," he scolds, his lips grazing my jaw, a whisper of lethally soft flesh. "There is nothing pathetic about that woman. She holds all of the power in that instance. I would ask you not deride her method to express her empowerment. However, these excursions are diversions meant to occupy your attention. Nothing more."

"Diversions." It's as if tasting the word out loud unlocks the hidden meaning. Perhaps I ignored it until now. Here, in his private fantasy club, Heyworth Thorne would never dare follow. In fact, there is only one way anyone knew where to find us at all, I suspect. "Did Julio direct the police here?" I ask, referring to his lead bodyguard.

An uncharacteristic grunt escapes him. Then he sighs. "I have *friends* in law enforcement, shall we say. Your father has been persistent—belligerent, even. To placate him, they threatened to mount a more…public search. This way, they can be satisfied with seeing you safe and whole. For now. And the police chief can't use your association with me as fodder for his son's political machinations."

I raise an eyebrow. "And you didn't warn me?"

"Would you have come?" he inquires. "Would you have stayed?"

"I… Damn him." Ignoring his question, I refocus my irritation on the one person who deserves it. "Damn him—"

"But can you blame him? You have been avoiding him for two days."

"Don't pretend you care." Only as the words leave my mouth do I realize how ungrateful they sound. "I'm sorry. I just mean… After everything he put me through, the silent treatment isn't the worst method of revenge I could resort to."

What are a few days of shunning in comparison to over twenty years of lies? Deception designed to make me believe my best friend's killer was an unknown assailant. A specter. A shadow. When all along...he defended the man in court. He knows his identity. And even now, he has yet to tell me.

All to protect his pride.

"Have you learned anything?" I ask Damien, turning to face him. "About Simon?"

"I'm afraid not." He shakes his head. "The records are proving harder to track down than expected. But when I do discover anything at all, I'll alert you immediately."

"Thank you." I squeeze my eyes shut, even though it's futile around him. He may not be able to see my tears, but he can sense them. Smell them. I tremble as what feels like his thumb swipes at a fresh bead of liquid, wicking it away.

"I *will* keep looking," he promises. "In the meantime... Let me take you home—"

"No." Opening my eyes, I turn away from him and find myself nearing the threshold of the hallway. This place is so strange when given more scrutiny. Private. Discreet. Yet within these walls, anything but takes place. How strange that, of all potential hiding places, he would let the police find us here—because I have no doubt in my mind that they wouldn't be here otherwise. "Don't you value your privacy? I mean, if one of those officers decides to leak to the press that you were found in this place..."

"They could," he says. "Or perhaps, they *would* if I hadn't had Julio educate them on the strict privacy guidelines of this establishment before bringing them here. I've also ensured that their chief is aware to remind them. Though it was only a matter of time before they came here looking regardless."

Such a harmless statement reminds me eerily of the tensing of a trap readying to spring. Like a good lamb to the slaughter, I blindly step within its snare. "Why?"

"Because I own it," he explains. "And while its true purpose is private and its clientele strictly guarded, public documents are alas public. Though I did have the officers come in through a private entrance, preventing any unnecessary dramatics."

Which sounds like a lot of trouble to go through for a welfare check.

"Why not just take me home? Unless... You wanted them to find me here specifically. Or, to be blunter, you wanted *Heyworth Thorne* to know I was here. With you."

At a sex club.

His smile should unsettle me more than it does. "If I admitted as much, would that bother you?"

The bastard. He makes it sound so casual, as if he's truly offering me a legitimate choice.

But I've never had a choice, have I?

"You and my father can play your mind games," I tell him tiredly. "But..."

"But?"

"Don't ever do this again. Manipulate me like a pawn. I'm tired of power plays. I'm tired of being controlled. I would like to be in charge of my own damn life for once, if that's not too much to ask."

He nods. "*Sí.* I apologize if I have offended you."

"No…" I'm partly alarmed to find that he hasn't. Not entirely. Overall, my ex-father will learn tonight that I am at a sex club with Damien Villa of all people. How unfortunate that, all appearances aside, our visit has been rather platonic thus far.

Merely a three-way orgy starring a woman being fingered.

"What you said, about the woman being in control," I start, licking my lips. "What did you mean? How could someone possibly be in control in that situation?"

Such a scenario is the pure antithesis to everything I grew up believing about power. Like that it should be carefully controlled and kept on a leash. Never relished or flaunted.

"Do you feel in control now?" he counters. "You are constantly ogled by hundreds, if not thousands of people, hounding your every waking moment, waiting for a single flaw to pounce upon. I can only imagine how exhausting that could feel."

"I do feel powerless," I admit. "I am never in control—"

"And yet *that* woman is in an environment where she can feel safe. Where all who enter come for her. She sets the tone, the pace. Without her enjoyment, there is no…entertainment, shall we say. Her partners, the audience are at her mercy. She wields her power over the entire damn room, whether the occupants admit as much or not."

"And do you want to do that to me?" I wonder for the second time. "Put me on display?"

"No." His hesitation is even more apparent in the careful clearing of his throat. "I am not sure it is the type of control you would enjoy having."

"Why not?" I cross my arms over my chest, envisioning his potential replies. "I'm too much of a prude? I'm too weak? Too sheltered—"

"You are too *haunted*," he clarifies. "Laying yourself bare in front of strangers may be an experience you are not ready for. I will, however, take you up on your first suggestion." He steps forward, coming to my side. "Allow me to take you home."

"No." I shake my head even as I take the hand he's extended toward me and fall into step with his pace. "Not there."

Because police or not, I know Heyworth. He will have the SWAT team waiting to ambush my suite at the Lariat hotel the second I step inside it.

"Take me… Oh, I don't know." My temples ache, making it hard to settle on one of the many hotels within the city. Which one would my father—or the paparazzi—most likely overlook? "The Harrison?" I guess, thinking out loud. "Or maybe the Madison?"

"If I may make a suggestion," Damien murmurs. "I know someplace neither your father nor anyone else could enter. Not even the police."

"Oh?" It sounds too tempting. Another trap? "Where?" I ask, taking the bait regardless. Then, from the corner of my eye, I catch his teeth flash in a sinful, savoring smile.

"I believe it would perhaps be more impressive if I just showed you."

TWO

*B*utterflies unfurl within my stomach as his driver pulls up in front of a building I vaguely recognize in the darkness. Multicolored streetlights illuminate an impressive skyscraper—one sporting an incredible glass greenhouse on the roof and owned by the man sitting stoically beside me.

"You can stay with me," he says, dropping all pretense. "My suite is large enough for you to have a section of rooms to yourself. If it makes you feel more comfortable, I will agree to stay within mine—"

"Considering you bought my virginity for all intents and purposes, you sure are"—I mull over the right phrase—"beating around the bush."

He laughs. "How crudely apt, Ms. Thorne. Though I *do* fully intend to collect on my half of our wager," he says with a fitting hint of malice. "But I believe my future plans may have a better reception if I tread carefully."

"Fine." I unbuckle my seat belt and reach for the door. Before I even touch the handle, Julio opens it from the outside.

Given the lack of a doorman and keycard entry, I assume this is yet another private entrance. Inside, a narrow black hallway leads to an elevator, but rather than the one for the roof, Damien strikes the button for the floor below it.

My heart pounds as the doors finally part and I follow him out. Unsurprisingly, the décor is black, but the floor plan is more open than I expected, given his penchant for shadowy, decadent places. A modest living room consists of black leather chairs and chaises positioned in front of a massive window displaying a view of the city. Beyond that is an open kitchen with bar seating, a dining room, and then two hallways that branch off in different directions.

Damien heads right. "This is the way to your suite," he explains, throwing the term out as easily as some people might discuss a spare pair of shoes. "You should have everything you need. If not, Julio or I will see to it."

I hold my breath as I glance over his shoulder into the first of the rooms: a beige décor sets it apart from his typical color scheme.

"Let me guess: You told your designer to have free rein in this section of the penthouse?" I snipe.

"Oh, no." He laughs and shakes his head. "Far from it. I told her to design a room that Juliana Thorne would be mildly comfortable dwelling within."

I can't tell if he's joking or not. Neither can I muster up the energy to ask. Instead, I step into the room, spotting all the little details that would prove his remarks twistedly true. The décor, disregarding the beige, mimics that of my suite at the Lariat: simple though luxurious furniture and an open floor plan. On its face, it's the style someone would assume the heiress daughter of a powerful judge might be used to.

"Impressive," I admit, aware of him advancing on me with slow, precise steps. "Though the color scheme is a bit more muted than

I would expect."

"Oh?" His chuckle tickles the back of my neck, lingering even as his steps retreat toward the hall. "I hope you find the bedroom equally as…comforting. I'm afraid you may describe it as far too conservative for a woman of your talents. Alas, it should suffice. Goodnight, Ms. Thorne."

Wary, I continue through the suite as his steps fade, inching toward the room I assume the bedroom in question to be.

For a second, I forget that Damien isn't in earshot as I mutter, "Very funny. You think you know me so well."

Maybe he does considering he supposedly designed a room damn near tailored to make me feel entirely out of my element. Conservative my ass. The walls are red, the floors a plush, sensual black. A luxurious bed draped in red satin sheets serves as the most intimidating focal point.

And on the ceiling is an enormous gilded mirror. Because of course there is.

So the blind man has jokes. Very funny. I laugh to prove I'm unaffected as I shed my jacket and brace myself over the edge of the mattress. But without him here…

I don't have a barrier from the guilt. Not the pain or the crushing realization that the past twenty years of my life have been one monstrous lie. Only one person holds the answers.

Why, why, why?

As I fish my cell phone from my purse, I'm determined to discover that very fact once and for all.

"Thorne residence," a gruff voice demands from the other end of the line. "How can I assist—"

"It's Juliana," I say over who must be a bodyguard. "Put me through."

"Of course, Ms. Thorne."

Not even a second later, a familiar voice drips into my ear. "Juliana? Sweet pea, please tell me what is going on—"

"Why don't you tell me?" I counter. "Starting with who exactly he is: Simon. You've known all this time, haven't you? Who he really is?"

"Darling…" The background noise shifts and mutes behind him. He must have secluded himself into another room. "We need to discuss this in person. Please. I've been worried sick about you. Come home and we can—"

"If we talk, it will be somewhere public," I blurt. "The Lariat. This time, maybe you can leave out the police?"

An audible grunt escapes him. "Darling, can you really blame me?"

"Tomorrow morning at nine," I snap. "Be there and…and tell me everything. I mean it. Or…"

I can't even say it. *Or consider me your daughter no longer.*

"I will," he insists. "Just tell me where you are. That you're safe. The police are—"

I hang up and crawl beneath the sheets before I can regret contacting him in the first place. It's pathetic how your entire identity can be wrapped up within one person. Their aura. Their persona.

If that's stripped away, they become a stranger, and you…

You become a shadow.

THREE

J creep from Damien Villa's lair to the first floor of the building with him none the wiser—or so I think.

A man's lurking near the mouth of the building's lobby. As the elevator doors part, he steps forward, and my knees buckle. Tall. Golden skin. Cropped raven hair. He could be Damien…if it weren't for his whole, dark-brown eyes.

"Mateo Villa," I croak, inching back as the elevator doors close behind me.

"Juliana Thorne," he coldly replies. "How strange to find you here, of all places…" In lieu of his brother's trademark suit, he's wearing a pair of jeans and a leather jacket. A mocking half-smile sets him further apart from Damien, but a steely nature reinforces his gaze, leaving me uneasy. "Though I shouldn't be surprised," he adds. "My brother did pay for the privilege to play with you in private."

"Privilege?" I fight to keep my chin in the air.

"*Sí.*" He scoffs, his mouth quirked. "He didn't tell you? Maybe I should have pressed him for more in our bargain?"

"What do you want?" I consider running. Calling for help. Before I can make the decision, he turns and strolls toward a hallway.

"Don't bother calling my brother to heel," he calls back. "And as for what I want? Why to warn you, of course." He pauses and cocks his head.

"Of what?" I croak when he doesn't elaborate. "Trust and believe I'll report every threat to the police."

"My brother is a dangerous man, Ms. Thorne. You should do your best to remember that. He may put on his charming act around you"—he flicks his gaze up to my face and chuckles—"but don't be fooled by his blindness. You must have given him quite the roll in the hay. I've never seen him so fucking whipped."

Heat floods my cheeks though I fight to keep my chin in the air. "E-Excuse me?"

"I'm surprised he got much use out of you, all things considered." He nods pointedly toward my body in general. "You aren't his type. Not a trophy, I think. Just a toy for his amusement. One he isn't inclined to share though. Not yet. He damn near threatened to kill me if I touched you. But still." He shrugs and heads farther down the hall, briefly turning to toss his parting words my way. "I pity you. Even I can find it in my heart to warn an easy mark. Your father is a selfish, moral-less cunt, but Damien thrives on vengeance. Don't trust him. Considering that just by touching you he's spitting on Mathias' memory, the *hijueputa* has no loyalty."

He retreats, and my blood runs cold, my heart solidifying into a painful lump in my chest. With difficulty, I ignore him and focus on the task at hand: escaping.

One fearful peek beyond the lobby reveals a familiar black car waiting for me along the curb. *Damn.* The moment I exit the building, Julio climbs from the vehicle and the jig is up.

"Good morning, Ms. Thorne," he declares, opening the door to the back seat. "Mr. Villa thought you might appreciate having him supply your transportation this morning." His stoic expression reveals nothing. I can't tell if he knows about my brush with Mateo—but I suspect that this "offer" isn't by coincidence, either.

"Does Mr. Villa have the room I stayed in bugged?" I ask without expecting an answer—because it's obvious. Given his track record, I wouldn't put another instance of espionage past him.

Luckily for Damien, I'm not in the mood to resist him this time. Mateo's little warning made it clear that navigating this uncertain landscape alone may not be in my best interest—especially where my father is concerned.

So I climb into the car without complaint, and minutes later, Julio deposits me in front of the private residential entrance of the Lariat, safe from any prying paparazzi. It's a short, unnerving trip up to my apartment.

But Heyworth is nowhere to be found.

Julio stands guard in the hallway while I wait, passing the time by alternating staring out the window and checking my phone. A quick scan of the top news stories doesn't reveal any unusual traffic jams—but a flashing headline chills me to the core.

The Borgetta Murder Case: five people connected dead within a month of overturned conviction.

Perhaps my father's security detail took extra precautions this morning, thus delaying him over thirty minutes?

After nearly an hour, I finally breakdown and call.

"Thorne residence," the same man from last night announces.

"Where is he?" I demand.

"Mr. Thorne is…indisposed at the moment. I'm afraid he'll have to reschedule."

"Reschedule?"

The line goes dead without further explanation and my heart twists inside my chest. Could something be wrong?

Or perhaps something more important has come up. More important than mending fences with me. A coveted interview? A donor meeting? The possibilities mount and each one feels increasingly plausible.

Heyworth pushed me aside for yet another political calculation.

It's nothing new, but this time…

Tears spill down my cheeks like liquid fire as I tear into the hallway, heedless of who may be spying from the shadows.

"Ms. Thorne?" Julio calls after me as I surge into an opening elevator. "I suggest we take the private exit—"

The elevator doors close behind him and part seconds later to reveal the lobby, where a sea of flashing cameras stops me dead in my tracks. Reporters—too damn many of them to be here by accident. Panic renders me frozen as a million shouted questions descend in a barrage of clashing voices.

"Miss Thorne! Is it true that you are in a relationship with Damien Villa, the brother of the man your father sentenced to death?"

"Miss Thorne, care to comment?"

"Juliana! Do you have any comment on the fact that people related to your father's case have died recently—"

"Juliana!" A balding man with a beer gut comes from nowhere to shove a microphone in my face. "Your father has been accused of racial bias. Given your birth mother's heritage, did you witness anything of the sort growing up?"

I don't know what happens. One second, I'm staring down at my trembling fingers. The next, my knuckles are connecting with something alarmingly flesh-like and blood is flying through the air. Alarmed cries go up as the reporter crouches, clutching his nose.

"You crazy bitch!" he shrieks as he, and the rest of the world, come back into focus.

Crazy bitch. Those two words are all I hear as I push through the mass of people and somehow make it out of the building. Blindly, I run, crossing traffic and intersections until I reach some semblance of quiet what seems like an eternity later. A park, I assume, judging from close-set trees and scattered benches.

Here, I can hear myself think. About how much of an idiot I am. Gullible. Desperate. Pathetic.

And worthless, apparently. I sure hope Daddy's meeting or television appearance was worth it.

At least I keep it together until I find a bench tucked within a copse of trees. Only now do I finally break, burying my face in my hands.

I don't hear him until it's too late. By the time I stiffen at the sound of approaching footsteps, he's already close enough to swipe his finger along my cheek.

"You know how to make quite the scandal," he murmurs, his accent especially pronounced.

Despite the overall polished elegance conveyed by his black coat and scarlet scarf, he's breathing more quickly than usual. A bead of sweat glints on his jaw. Like he rushed here?

"The reporter is pressing charges, or at least he *was*," Damien adds. "May I?" With what I presume is a practiced motion, he finds the back of the bench with one hand and uses it as a guide to lower himself onto it.

I doubt he's omniscient enough to find me without help—and sure enough, I spot Julio in the distance, muttering into a headset, feeding his boss my location, I suspect.

"A rather dull man from a paper few read anyway," Damien continues as if uninterrupted. "A bit of money to pad his next check and an inside scoop on some tawdry celebrity scandal and the man changed his mind."

"Why?" I demand, swiping at my face with my sleeve.

"Hmm." He tilts his head. "I assume because he enjoys money and notoriety—"

"No, I mean…why help me?" Is what Mateo claimed true? He bargained to keep even his brother from me?

"Why?" A frown distorts that stern, beautiful mouth, confusing me further. "Unless you've forgotten, you yourself laid out the terms of our agreement."

That I did.

Stay with me.

Protect me.

"Then you should have no trouble humoring me," I say. "Or with telling me the truth."

"Of course," he says without a hint of hesitation. "You only need to ask."

"You spied on me last night. You knew I was meeting with my father."

"*Sí.*" He cocks his head without an ounce of shame. "Seeing as I appointed myself head of your security, I feel no need to deny that."

Touché. Once more, I'm forced to admit that he has a point.

"Did you know that he didn't show?" I demand. "If so, then tell me. Did someone powerful come along and make him an offer he couldn't refuse?" I force a smile while telling myself I can handle any explanation. But my stomach churns more the longer Damien's silence extends. It's not out of ignorance, I suspect. He's hiding something. "Just tell me."

"I'm not sure," he concedes. "Just that he canceled all appointments for the day."

"You don't think something's wrong, do you?" The concern in my voice isn't fake. Heyworth Thorne may be many things. But for twenty years, he was my father. Go figure, those emotions can't be shaken overnight. "Maybe I should go to the house?" I start to stand.

"I can have Julio take you there now," Damien suggests without moving. "Merely say the word."

"Or it could be a trick," I find myself blurting, lowering beside him again. "Lure me to the house. Ambush me with the police present. Declare me mentally unfit. Have me committed—"

"Well, you did physically assault an innocent, prying journalist," Damien dryly interjects. "In the midst of cursing you to hell and back, the man did admit that you have a decent right hook."

I laugh, alarmed by how real it sounds. A real laugh in this shit-storm of a morning.

"Can I ask you for something else?"

He doesn't even bother to answer me this time. A stern grunt is all the encouragement I need to confess.

"I…I want to forget everything about today." My father. Mateo. The press. "You can pick the distraction." Even as the words leave my mouth, I know how dangerous they sound. "Just take me somewhere far away where I don't have to think. Please."

"A brave request." He stands and murmurs into his headset, "Julio, bring the car around *por favor*." To me, he offers his hand and helps me to my feet. "That I can do."

Of all places he could take me, he fittingly picks one of the last I'd assume.

His waterfront studio. The place where he sketched me for the first time on his wooden table. Naked. Today, a blank canvas dominates an easel placed strategically in the center of that same room. Beside it is a flat marble slab with a mattress covered in a black sheet balanced on top.

A brave request, he said. Now, I'm starting to realize why.

"Strip," Damien commands, shedding his own coat, which he tosses onto a leather chair near the entrance. "You can leave the dress on the floor. I assure you it's clean. Then, we can begin."

"You plan to paint me?" My gaze settles on the marble slab and then the easel set up beside it.

"You sound skeptical," Damien points out, pouncing on my unease. "Not quite what you had in mind?"

He doesn't seem disappointed. If anything… amused, like a master puppeteer waiting for his pretty little doll to notice her strings.

"Lying still for a long period of time utterly motionless isn't exactly conducive to helping me forget." Even still, my hands graze the front of my coat. Slowly, I undo the first button.

"Motionless?" Damien echoes, tapping his chin with an extended finger. "Who said I would use the drug this time? In fact, I will offer you a choice."

"A choice?" Intrigued, I track his trek across the room.

When he reaches the marble slab, his cane in hand, he bends in an elegant motion, lifting something from a shelf built into the side of the structure. A tray, I see as I come closer. On it are a few assorted objects. A mirror, a small box, a swath of black silk…

"A blindfold?" I question.

"*Sí*," Damien says, his mouth quirked. "You may pick between it and the drug—"

"The blindfold," I blurt while snatching up the strip of silk. I'm relieved for reasons I can't explain as the fabric settles into the palm of my hand. "Now what?"

"Now…" He turns his attention to the small box and lifts the lid, revealing the round objects lying on a bed of red velvet. "Pearls," he explains. "Harvested by hand and chosen for quality. They are damn near priceless; I can assure you of that. Each one is exquisitely unique."

"Oh?" It's hard to keep the awe from my tone. Only a man like him would have priceless items lying around out in the open, their purpose unknown. I tentatively finger one bead, impressed by the quality. "Are you planning on bribing me with a necklace, Mr. Villa?"

"Something like that." His deep, rumbling laugh sends tendrils of unease lancing through my blood. "You will lie back while I paint you," he explains, his tone professionally level. "I will place these pearls on your body and you must not allow them to move. Does that make for a fitting diversion?"

I swallow hard, intrigued despite myself. "And if they *do* fall off?"

He smiles, and I have never witnessed something so devastatingly beautiful. Rather than answer me right away, he extends his palm, and without being prompted further, I surrender the blindfold. As easily as if he's memorized every inch of my body, he reaches out and finds my cheek.

"Turn around, sweet girl." His use of the endearing term sets my nerves on the edge of a cliff.

When I comply, he draws the silk over my eyes, using my ears as a guide. After tying the knot, he steers me back until what I assume to be the ledge of the platform brushes my hip.

"Every pearl that falls is one I will be allowed to use," he says, casually picking up the thread of our previous conversation. "As I see fit."

"In what way?" I question.

Subtle sounds are all I have to discern his next movements. A soft click, as if he propped his cane against an edge of the platform, followed by the creak of the leather-topped stool placed halfway between the platform and the easel. It makes sense. From that position, both are within his reach—as will I be.

"In a way that will allow me to explore your body in a manner entirely separate from my art."

Heat sears my cheeks. A nun could hear the innuendo in his tone —and he's done so well to disguise it until now: the restrained lust oozing from him, as tantalizing as his cologne. A part of me shivers in response. Flinches. I'm painfully aware of the thin fabric of my dress whispering over my skin.

"Have I startled you, Ms. Thorne?" he wonders innocently. A soft hiss makes me imagine him picking up the brush, dipping it into paint before testing a streak over the canvas. "Perhaps you find this proposed diversion too stimulating? We can skip the blindfold, if that appeases you."

"No. In fact, I think you have a deal, Mr. Villa." I wrench my coat open, fiddling with the buttons as I go. Once it's off, I toss it aside and shed my dress, feeling the chill in the room. My nipples tighten as I wad my panties up and discard that as well. "Now what?"

"Lie down." His voice has deepened. Gone is the mocking, playful edge, and I can't stop my arms from flinching toward my breasts, despite his lack of sight. An artist has replaced the powerful, reclusive billionaire—but he's a more dangerous animal. One who communicates with grit in his tone and an authoritative aura. "On your back," he prompts as I feel for the platform and perch myself on the edge of it. "Don't worry about positioning your limbs. I will arrange them for you."

An ominous sentence if there ever was one.

"Arrange?" I can't resist parroting as I run my fingers along the silken sheets, testing their quality: luxurious. "You make it sound more in-depth than painting."

"*Sí.*" A wistful sigh rips from his throat. "It always is…"

"Ah, how could I forget? You've done this before."

Painting naked women is a pastime that's garnered him acclaim. Though it's the first time in a while that he's referred to his other subjects—a deliberate tactic, I suspect. Deciphering his reasons why is like playing an elaborate game of chess with a master far out of my league.

So I forge a change in subject.

"I'm lying down." Twisting, I lift my legs and lower myself onto the platform. "So when do the pearls come into play?" I ask, sounding bolder than I feel.

"Now."

I sense him stand again and my ears strain to catch his every movement. There is a practiced grace to how he moves, supposedly pivoting on his feet to navigate the slender path between his stool and the platform. From this angle, I have no idea where he's positioned. My only clues are the nuanced shifts in the air. His breathing. His scent.

"Are you ready?" Gone is the smug mocking from his voice. I picture his nostrils flaring, his tongue flicking along his lower lip.

With what I suspect is another practiced motion, he finds the tray near my hip and noisily drags it closer to him, allowing the edge to brush my skin so I can feel every single inch.

Tiny pings make me assume that the pearls are colliding with the sides of the tray. Each delicate click sends my heart surging just a bit faster. There are too many possibilities for him to implement the words he said. Use the pearls to explore me. But how?

I'm so lost in thought that I almost miss the moment he seizes one of the ivory balls between his thumb and his forefinger: the only solution I can envision when the tiny noises suddenly go silent. I can almost see him rolling his chosen pearl between his fingers as if memorizing every slight flaw in its surface. Satisfied, he'd cock his head, a dangerous grin shaping his mouth.

"Do you want to place them initially, or should I?"

"Is that a trick question?" I counter, resorting to the only weakness of his I can use to my advantage: his blindness. "Just tell me where you want them and I'll—"

He laughs. "Oh, I'm sure I could manage. Your hip," he announces before the silk pad of a finger brushes along my side, persistent even as I jump. "Your stomach. Your navel. Should I utilize this spot in particular?"

I shiver as he flicks the dip in my belly. Rather than move on, he lingers, imparting his heat into my skin merely to prove a point.

"Yes, here," he declares before replacing his touch with the unmistakable round shape of a pearl.

Panic spreads down my spine like wildfire as the slight weight settles there precariously. One wrong move and it's gone.

"And if it falls?" I struggle to ask while keeping my stomach flat.

He laughs again, but the sound is an octave deeper. "I'll let you imagine what the consequence may be."

"B-But—"

"Next one," he declares, cutting me off. The hiss of silk and flesh teases my ears as he presumably rummages through the contents of the tray to retrieve yet another pearl.

"Open your mouth," he commands as the noise ceases.

"W-What?" Heat brushes my cheek, easily finding my mouth—his thumb, I think. He teases my lower lip with the hardened tip of a nail. "Why?"

"Just open."

My lips part on command and I'm rewarded with the hint of salt. From his *thumb*. The rigid shape is recognizable as my tongue skims the ridges and whirls on the pad of it. With every tentative lick, my stomach twists into knots, registering his unique taste. Sweat. Sin. His finger withdraws before I can decipher more, and something new replaces it. Smooth with a slightly gritty surface, not completely round. And...

It's wet, tainted with flavor. The sinful taste triggers my memory as heat ignites near my belly: expensive wine like the kind he owns. A dangerous thought worms its way into my skull, robbing the air from my lungs. Did he taste this before giving it to me?

The pearl withdraws before I muster up the strength to decide. For a painful few seconds, he remains silent.

"Perhaps here, next?" he murmurs as a soft touch teases the space between my breasts.

I gasp, remembering the first pearl before it's too late. Moisture paints my skin in the wake of the second pearl, leaving a path that cools instantly in the air. I shiver as he guides it up...over...

There's no disguising my body's instinctive reaction. A low hum taints the air as the pearl meets the stiffened peak of my nipple.

"Here?" he wonders thickly before rolling the pearl down my breast. There he leaves it, balanced on my breastbone.

He's quiet again, only his breathing gives me any clue where he is —more distant as if he's moved near my feet. The next moment, his touch is back, at my ankle this time. I can feel the heat of his hand, but only a newer pearl contacts my skin, gliding up my leg. I feel all its imperfections, its dents as it grazes my calf. It's surprisingly gritty like sand, teasing the flesh on my knee.

"Here?" he murmurs, lingering again.

My lower half trembles, muscles tense to ensure the other pearls don't move.

"Or here?"

Coldness swipes along my inner thigh, inching higher…

I barely register the unnerving sensation of the small bead between my legs before a firmer touch continues its original path. I have no trouble naming the culprit: his hand. The individual shape of every finger sends my senses spiraling. My spine stiffens, aching to arch—into him? Away from him? The thinnest shred of pride keeps me still, a slave to his touch. One by one, he spreads his fingers over my hip. Slowly…so damn slowly, they dance across my pelvis, stopping just short of the thatch of curls at the base of my abdomen.

And another pearl settles, jarring my dazed thoughts.

"Last one." Alarm sets in as his finger caresses a path up my throat and finds my lips. "Open," he commands again.

This time, I definitely taste salt as his finger glides across my tongue. "Close."

Once my lips meet, a gentle pressure seals them shut—the final pearl.

"There." He turns back to his canvas and the stool creaks beneath his weight. "Now we can begin. I hope you are comfortable, Juliana?"

He chuckles in that slow, callous way when I don't answer.

"Good. Now that I have your full attention, we can discuss in detail what I plan to do to you. When I finally decide to take what I am owed."

My lips twitch and the pearl slips—thank God it doesn't fall. It's certain now; the man is evil. Pure, unadulterated evil.

"I'm sure you've wondered about it," he taunts. "Obsessed over every little detail—you may let your gilded world control every aspect of your life, but you still can't stand it. And yet you haven't asked me."

So he has noticed my silence on that topic. Has he been waiting for me to broach it first?

The pearl feels like a lead weight, keeping me silent. And like a true torturer, he knows exactly how to twist the knife.

"Shall I tell you?" That dangerous chuckle rumbles from him again. "Though I'm tempted to let you stew on it. There are so many ways to rob you of that one shred of innocence you cling to —because you *have* clung to it. I know you've dated before." He throws it off like a casual observation, but it conveys so much more. Like the fact that he's delved into more than just my past. Perhaps he's spied on more than my intimate moments as well. "All powerful, pretty men, none of whom last the month with you. And not because *they* leave *you*," he adds, proving my suspicions correct. "You never let them in. Not to your apartment. Not even the damn building. You've built a wall between the world and your private life and I doubt you even know how to break it. Because of him."

He doesn't say the name. I flinch regardless—and the round bead on my breastbone shifts, threatening to roll off. Holding my breath is the only way to keep it still.

"He hurt you, didn't he?" There's an uncharacteristic softness to his baritone. "In more ways than killing your friend."

No. I squeeze my eyes shut and inhale, heedless of the way the pearls on my body lurch in response. A frantic sound builds up in my throat but doesn't escape my mouth. Yet. A plea. *Please don't.*

"I'm not mocking you," he clarifies like it matters—but the gruff, bitter note in his voice makes me bite back a scoff. "Your limits. Your fears. *Those* are the things I must know before I can fully take what you wagered. I refuse to traumatize you, for lack of a better word. Despite what happens between us, I have no intention of harming you."

And perhaps that's why he claimed to be willing to offer up anything in advance. The price of my deepest, darkest secrets is one worth paying to a man like him.

So that he can use my past against me?

"I believe the best course of action would be to have you demonstrate for me," he muses amid the scrape of the brush on the canvas. "Where to touch you. How. Exhibition seems to be one of your defining traits. I'm sure you'd enjoy the experience more than I—"

"You're insane." *Ping!* The musical sound chimes a faint warning as my lips part again. "You wouldn't!"

"Wouldn't what?" he murmurs.

With my mouth free, I don't hold back. "Take me to your creepy little club," I spit hoarsely. "Make me…in front of—"

"You think I meant publicly? Oh, no. Some experiences should remain private between two individuals. Like how you sound in the throes of an orgasm. *Sí…*" A grated sound resonates in his throat. "The members of my club don't pay nearly enough to partake in that kind of entertainment."

"Why even own a club like that?" I spit without parsing the possession evident in that statement. A nefarious reason worms into my brain. "Do you participate in the 'entertainment' yourself perhaps? At an owner's discount?"

"*¿Qué?*" Another heartless laugh conveys he's anything but insulted. "No. I am afraid the true reason is rather boring, Ms. Thorne: leverage."

"How enterprising of you," I counter. "Naked, undisguised blackmail. There is a poetic irony to it."

"*Gracias,* though I'm not sure you fully appreciate what I mean. Humans are such strange creatures, you see. They'd give one man the absolute power to destroy their lives in a heartbeat, all for the promise of freedom to indulge in the most wicked of pastimes. It is quite the Faustian bargain."

"Leverage?" I echo. "That sounds more like blackmail. I thought you valued discretion and ensured privacy?"

"And I do," he insists, but I sense another half to that statement that he doesn't voice. *And I do…for now.* "But if you're wondering if I fuck the performers in my spare time, I'm afraid the answer is no."

"Why not?"

"You still don't understand me at all, do you?" He sounds so amused by the prospect. But maybe he's wrong in this case.

"Because you expect to gain something from every encounter," I answer before he can say anything else. "To learn something. For your art—"

"And I wonder how much I'll learn about you via this delicate, single pearl. Do drop another *por favor.*"

The air in my lungs escapes in a gasp. Damn it. That's right. I've given him a victory already: one pearl lost. I'm suddenly aware of the remaining three balanced precariously on their respective positions.

"Hmmm." The floorboards protest as he stands.

I imagine him swiping his fingers along his chin. Specks of dark liquid most likely coat the tips. Paint. I can even smell it, sharp and chemical, melding with the amalgam of scents that enhance his persona.

Circling to my direction, he grasps where I suspect the tray of pearls to be. An array of soft clinking noises conjures an image of him fondling every round bead, looking for the perfect one. Despite the blindfold, I can almost see him as he finally raises his selection trapped between two fingers.

"Shall I make a confession?" he muses. "It's not every woman that I would allow to make demands of me. Flowers every day…"

He's referring to one of my delirious requests made in the aftermath of a world-altering betrayal.

"Those were *your* terms," I point out, fighting to keep every muscle still. "You said anything—"

"And I meant that. But I am sure you love a good bargain as much as I do, and I believe it would only be fair if I were to make a request in return."

My body twitches in response to his deepening baritone.

"So what do you say? I continue to send you your flowers. You perform a daily task of my request, and in return, you get to bargain something else from me."

"Like what?"

"By now, I'm sure you know the answer." He pauses for drama's sake and then rasps, "*Anything.*"

"Fine. Then whatever you're planning for when you take my… I-I have to agree to it," I propose in a rush. "You can't force me to—"

"I'll do you one better; I'll make you beg for it. Fair enough?" He waits for a reply that never escapes my throat. "As for now... I believe I am required to do something with my pearl."

Heat runs through me like a lance. *His* pearl. God, such a tiny object has never seemed so menacing.

"Do I have your permission, Ms. Thorne?"

He's serious. If I say no, I have no doubt he'll drop the pearl and leave—yet lord my fear over me in some way down the road. A man like him demands his payment. An eye for an eye.

Always.

"Y-Yes."

"Good."

I track a sudden series of movements coming from near the end of the pedestal.

"Do you want me to tell you what I plan to do?"

I nearly jump as his touch teases my lower lip yet again, urging me to open. "Y-Yes," I murmur against his fingertips.

"I feel a demonstration may be more...telling." He sounds closer, his scent strong enough to taste. All of him. "So do I have your permission to utilize a pearl as I see fit?"

"W-Wait." I jolt upright, braced on my elbows. Distant pings allude to the fact that the other pearls have fallen, but I can't even spare enough concern to truly despair. Damn, I almost wish he'd used the drug instead.

There's something about the idea of him hunched between my spread legs. I can hear every cadence in his breathing, slow and deliberate. Labored. He's disguising just how much he wants to touch me, but his finger twitching against my tongue betrays him. I doubt he's even aware of it. Wanting. This man can display the deepest emotions of others so easily.

He has no clue how much he himself can give away.

"And if I refuse?" I manage to whisper as my inner thighs twitch, aching to clamp together. "What if I say no?"

"You won't." His accent thickens with confidence. "You're too curious. Too daring for your own good. You want to know even more than I want to continue. So shall we both drop the pretense? *This* is what I plan to do with the goddamn pearl—"

His fingers slip between my legs, pressing against sensitive flesh. I jump, clawing at his forearms, as the unmistakable shape of the pearl toys near my entrance, guided by his swiping thumb. One flick of his wrist nudges it farther. Another pushes it *deeper*.

Explore, he said. The word he meant was *invade*.

And there is no escape. The broadness of his callused palm captures me, but the pearl is a terrifying bit of leverage, probing with the right amount of pressure. Too small. I feel him more than it, easing inside me.

And it is sin. Hell. He has me on a string, arching with every touch.

"Let the world see you like this?" he growls, his voice dripping into my ear, easily overpowering the pathetic gasps escaping my throat.

There's a method to his madness. His finger caresses me first. Then the pearl strikes a tense ball of nerves, making every thought in my brain go haywire. Explode. Unravel.

"Let them see you in the only way I cannot? Like hell. This is *mine*." He quirks his thumb, making my spine contract, manipulated like a marionette. "Your heavy pants, mine to taste.

Your wails of ecstasy, mine to hear." He teases me with a second finger, spreading me open. "The tightening of every muscle just before you lose control, mine to feel. The scent of your arousal that lingers long after, mine to smell."

I can't stop what he unleashes within my body. A torrent of fire robs me of everything but sight. Feel. Sensation.

His taste is on my tongue, his mouth at my throat, his fingers inside me, thrusting so deep that it toes the edge of pain. Lust has a razor's edge with him. Too sharp.

He'll cut me with it.

Or kill me.

But the prospect of death by his hand is alarmingly tempting. There's no noise in this shadowy realm of pleasure. No secrets or lies to combat. The world fades as all the darkness gives way to blinding white. My brain separates from my body—all I know is that an unyielding strength supports me as I writhe through the tumult of ecstasy.

Until it's over.

Reality inevitably descends and I find myself panting against a stranger. A stranger who's murmuring into my ear, grated sinful things. "Wet for me... *Dios mío.*"

He's still touching me through the praises. Stroking. The pearl plays tag with the thickness of his finger. I'm full of him. Teased with his substitute. Full again.

Over, and over, and over...

"D-Damien." Rippling muscle serves as my only anchor as I curl my fingers, nails drawn. Anything to retaliate. But my attempts just make his touch all the bolder.

"You hold your breath when you're on the verge of coming," he grates against my throat. "So desperate for control. You don't want to scream—it feels that damn good."

Heat fans my lower lip. Both of mine part. His come down to devour them whole. The thickness of his tongue is a disturbing contrast to his thumb. He times his strokes so both thrust into me at the same time. I'm overwhelmed. Empty. Bursting.

"You don't want to moan," he grunts, drawing his mouth back. "So you bite your tongue. But I can't stand your silence. I won't coddle you. Shelter you. I can *give* to you, sweet girl. You only need to ask nicely."

Another kiss consumes any sound I might make. My hands leave his arms and move into his hair, grasping at the thick strands. He copies me, cupping my scalp, using it to deepen the contact between us. His teeth nip at my lip and the pain makes me reckless.

Reckless enough to bite him back. Grip him back. Push back, urging him inside me. Harder. Deeper.

Consequences no longer matter, neither do his calculated little plans.

In this moment, I need him like I've needed nothing else.

"Mr. Villa?"

A heavy knock on the door feels too surreal, like a random moment from a nightmare. I ignore it first, swatting it away like a buzzing fly—but Damien goes rigid, his lips still on mine.

Fury is palpable in the way he harshly exhales as he withdraws. "*Meirda.*"

Just like that, I'm back in my body. Back in the real world. Arched on a pedestal with Damien Villa's hand between my legs.

He's already sliding his fingers away, taking the pearl with them.

It isn't until another knock echoes off the walls that I realize I'm not hallucinating. We've been interrupted. Within seconds, the world is a serious, shadowy place again. And the man in front of me is someone to never underestimate.

"You are to never disturb me," he bellows in a thunderous tone that radiates throughout the room. "In fact, I don't know whether or not to fire you—"

"It's urgent, sir," Julio replies, sounding muffled, as if he's speaking from behind the door, as calm as ever. "I apologize for the breach in protocol, but…I assumed you would want to hear it before Ms. Thorne had the chance to catch the news coverage."

News coverage? I undo the blindfold one-handed and blink, finding Damien scowling near the edge of the platform.

"Get dressed," he says before moving to the door.

I slip from the mattress and stoop for my dress and panties. Hunched away from Damien, I slip it on over my head, but he's already marching across the room, radiating rage with every thundering step.

"Are you dressed?" he barks at me.

I pull my coat on and fumble with the buttons. "Y-Yes."

He wrenches the door open, revealing Julio on the other end. The man leans toward him and murmurs into his ear.

"I see," Damien says, his tone degrees cooler. "Yes, I understand. You made the right call, as always."

Julio nods and presses something into Damien's hand. "Sir," he says before stepping back into the hall. He doesn't go far, I suspect.

"Juliana…" Damien extends his hand in my direction, revealing just what he's holding: my cell phone. "Call your stepmother."

"Diane?" Nerves unfurl in my stomach as I approach him, feeling too uneasy to voice my suspicions out loud.

Has my father made a more public plea this time? Accused me of being insane on national television? No, his reputation matters too much for such a stunt.

Right?

"What's wrong?" I take the phone and glance at the screen. There are four missed calls from my father's office and four more from Diane's direct cell—all within the span of an hour.

"Hello?" Diane picks up on the first ring. "Juliana?"

"What's going on?"

"Oh, thank God! I told him to tell you sooner, but he didn't want to worry you. And now I don't know what we're going to do. The doctors don't—"

"Slow down," I urge. "I don't understand. What's wrong?"

"Your father is in the hospital," she says. "He had a stroke. Juliana… It's not good. Please come…"

The phone falls from my grasp, sliding across the floor as the world dips in and out of focus. One minute, I'm standing; the next, I'm on my knees, supported only by a strong hand on my shoulder. Like an anchor, a gruff voice sinks through the chaos of my thoughts, tethering me to reality.

"I'll take you there," Damien says, though I don't even remember asking him to out loud, let alone saying anything. "I've got you."

FOUR

*E*ven now, whenever I picture Heyworth Thorne, it's always as he was the day we met: a knight in shining armor, rescuing me from a nightmare. I'd been sedated that morning, three days after Simon's attack. Lying tucked beneath the stale, stiff blankets of a hospital bed, draped in tubes and wires meant to monitor my vital signs, I never felt more alone. My mother and father hadn't been to see me. Besides the police, doctors, and the average nurse, no one had.

I think my case manager back then explained the fact away with some spiel about reducing stimulus to help me adjust.

But I knew the truth they had been too polite to say: Leslie was dead. I wasn't. And while the townspeople may have crowed their relief to the local papers, few of them could look me in the eye.

Until he came, Heyworth Thorne. A pudgy, stout man with thinning brown hair, wearing a green suit that stretched at the middle. He stood tall despite the diminutive size, carrying himself like someone who mattered. Someone important.

Asked to consult on my case by the local police chief himself, he entered my hospital room with little more than a teddy bear and a strained smile. There was something rare tucked into the corners of his mouth though: genuine concern.

"Hello, Juliana," he said, dropping the crisp, polite tone everyone else used around me. His was blunter. Honest. "I know that nothing I could say would ever be good enough, or empathetic enough..." He cleared his throat and nodded to my empty bedside table. "So would you prefer we skip the introductions and I smuggle you some ice cream from the parlor down the street?"

The memory stings as I enter a different hospital room in the present day. God, I've always hated the crisp, antiseptic smell of the sterile environment. A chill seems to permeate the whole building—no different, no matter the state or year it's in, apparently.

The hushed, startled faces of everyone you pass are all the same: wide eyes, mouths contorted in pity. A hellscape of sympathy. Or perhaps an alternate reality serving as a gruesome juxtaposition to my memories.

My father is lying in my old place, tubes snaking from his body to feed various beeping machines. He looks so old. A frail stranger buried beneath white blankets.

"What happened?" I ask the room's only other occupant.

"Juliana." Diane, my stepmother, rises from a chair near the bed and swipes at her eyes with the sleeve of her cream sweater. "It started the other day. He didn't feel himself, enough that the doctor kept him overnight. Then this morning..." She shakes her head and buries her face in her hands. "Oh God, I don't know what we'll do if he doesn't..."

"I'll be in the hallway," Damien announces, releasing me as I step forward and throw my arms around Diane.

It's almost funny in a sense. I thought Simon and the horrors he put me through were the worst possible things I could face. I was wrong.

Seeing Heyworth, a man I spent more than half of my life admiring, lifeless cuts me to the core. I despise all the lies, the deception, and the pain he put me through.

But at the end of it all, he is still my father.

And I don't know if I can lose him for good.

"*J*uliana?" Someone taps my shoulder, their voice a whisper. "Go home, dear."

"H-Huh?" I startle upright and blink to bring my surroundings into focus: a plain white room with linoleum floors and a sterile view of the city beyond a wide window. Heyworth's hospital room. One glance at him, his eyes resolutely closed, and my body deflates. "I'm fine," I murmur, returning to the position I was sleeping in, with my face resting on my forearm. "I'm just resting for a second."

As my eyes drift shut, the person beside me sighs. Diane. "Sweetie, it's been two days."

I reopen my eyes and observe my body, contorted within an uncomfortable armchair. I'm still wearing my dress from Damien's studio. Two days. It's almost surreal, considering that in all that time—punctuated by a stream of doctors and nurses flooding in and out—my father's condition hasn't changed.

His prognosis is grim. They were able to destroy the worst of the clots in his brain, but each professional consulted on his case seems unsure of the long-term damage. If he wakes up at all, he might not be the same man.

It's so selfish to feel the way I do. Annoyed. As though he got the last laugh. I'll never learn the truth about him—or about Simon. But even as the thought unfurls, I cringe from it and reach for his hand, gripping it tight.

"I'm fine," I say, shrugging Diane off. "He could wake up any minute. I need to be here—"

"Juliana." She doesn't move. "You need to shower at least. And eat. And sleep. Think of what he would want? It certainly wouldn't be for you to jeopardize your own health, worrying about him. Besides"—she clears her throat and darts her gaze toward the door—"your friend may want some rest as well."

My friend?

Damien.

A familiar shadow is hovering near the doorway—the same spot I suspect he's periodically occupied during the past forty-eight hours. Not constantly, of course—but long enough.

I can't tell if Diane knows his identity or just doesn't care. Her pained expression is fixated solely on me.

"Please, darling." She cups my cheek against her palm, her blue eyes watering, her blond hair damp. She must have left and showered while I was sleeping, only to return wearing a fresh sweater and slacks. "I'll take over from here."

"Okay…" I've barely voiced the surrender when she takes my hand and helps me stand. Then she all but drags me to the door.

"I'll call you with any updates. I think you should take the day for yourself. Rest."

Rest. But how?

"No." I start to turn back. "I need to be here. I need to—"

"I believe you have been exiled." A firm hand captures mine before I can take another step, and its owner tugs me farther into the hall.

"But—"

"*Dulce niña.*" Lips tinged with the hint of cologne brush my earlobe. "I'll bring you back later. But I encourage you to take her advice."

God, I can only imagine how I look to have warranted the raw concern in his voice. How I must smell.

Surprisingly, Damien himself may give me an idea. Haggard. Even his blindfold can't disguise the full extent of his exhaustion. Shadows paint the hollows and contours of his jawline, making his age more apparent than ever. Stray strands have escaped from his usually slick ponytail. Unfairly, the lack of polish only adds to his intrigue. A passing nurse can't seem to take her eyes off him. At least until she glances at me and then shakes her head in pity.

"Come." His arm slips around my shoulders—a surprisingly intimate gesture. I stiffen until I realize why he's chosen this method: He can guide me without his cane. "Julio, if you please."

"*Sí.*" His guard appears as if conjured from the shadows. "This way, sir."

Damien herds me along after him, presumably tracking the sound of his footsteps. Far too soon, he's easing me into the back of his car, claiming the seat beside me.

"I need to make sure the nurses have my direct number," I say, toying with the idea of returning to the building. "What if—"

"You need to care for yourself," he insists. As if to demonstrate, he leans over me, finds my seat belt through feel, and fastens it over me. "You can return later. I will see to it. Julio, *vamanos*, if you please."

Given the sparse amount of vehicles surrounding us, we must be in a private section of the hospital's parking garage. As the car exits the structure, reality makes its presence painfully known. Hordes of reporters from various news outlets are camped on the outskirts of the property. Like vultures, they stand at the ready, waiting for a carcass to pounce on.

"They're here for me, aren't they?" I blurt.

"I've increased your security measures," Damien says without answering the question. "What happened the other day will not happen again."

"I...I need to go home." The hitch in my voice must betray exactly what I mean—*home*—because he nods and utters something in Spanish to Julio.

Minutes later, the car pulls up not in front of the Lariat, but my father's beautiful mansion in the hills. The reporters have made their way out here as well, clamoring near the front gate. Julio fearlessly navigates the spectators to the security checkpoint. One look at me and we're allowed through.

"I just need a minute," I tell Damien before slipping free of my seat belt and escaping the car altogether.

The front door opens when I turn the handle, but I'm not ready for the scent that hits me like a punch: Daddy's cologne.

His aftershave.

His old, comforting identity before lies revealed him as a stranger.

Tears flood my eyes and escape down my cheeks. I can't stop them, so I move instead, navigating the front hall until I reach his office.

Someone's been in here recently—or perhaps no one's touched it since my father last entered. God, his scent floods every ounce of space. I imagine him sitting at the desk, rummaging through his documents, plotting his triumphant return to politics. So concerned with appearances.

He couldn't even tell me that he'd blown off our meeting due to his health. Why? Did he think I'd accuse him of lying?

Maybe I would have.

Or maybe I'm the reason he's in the hospital in the first damn place. Did guilt exacerbate the blood clot? Guilt for lying to me...

Or fear? His perfect little doll might run away from his dollhouse forever. He's been keeping tabs on me, or so I infer from the newspaper clippings strewn all over his desk. Every single headline features my name, dating back weeks ago.

Juliana Thorne Takes Leave of Absence Amid Father's Scandal.

Juliana Thorne Linked Publicly with Family in Father's Botch Judgment.

Juliana Thorne, Rescued by a Hero: An Adoption Story.

Blinking frantically, I approach his coveted trophy case, displaying all of his awards. Heyworth Thorne, the golden citizen. Heyworth Thorne, a man who knew the identity of a monster and shielded him for over twenty years.

Heyworth Thorne, the very worst monster of them all.

My hands shake as I wrench the cabinet open and grab the first award I can reach: one for exemplar contributions to the city, shaped like a shooting star. Whirling on my heel, I throw it as hard as I can, narrowly missing a framed diploma hanging on the wall. As my vision blurs, I grab another. Another. They crash like missiles into various objects, knocking books from his shelves or careening into prized knickknacks. Was every bit of metal and glass worth more to him than I was?

They don't seem to matter so damn much now.

Panting, I yank the drawers out of his desk. The one near the bottom is already open and the edge of a folder is sticking out of it, as if shoved there, the last thing he may have read. His precious, coveted donor list? I grab it and callously scan the familiar, small handwriting scribbled on the front: *For Juliana.*

My body goes cold. As if from miles away, I hear a thud, and when I regain focus, I'm on my knees, hunched over the slim stack of documents. They're faded and dog-eared, delicate with age. Oh God... I recognize the crisp, cold layout of the topmost one as that of a police case file. Across the header reads *Juliana Mirangas, age 8.*

Numb, I scan each line, discovering nothing new. It's merely a summary of my statement and the events described. But the last page...

I've never seen it before: a different briefing referring to another case. Yet, in some ways, the events described are chillingly similar. The girl's name may be different, but the scattered bits of her statement resonate within me down to the bone.

"Wanted to play a game." "Didn't see a face." "Simon says..."

The date is a full year before my case, but unlike mine, a single suspect was questioned in this horrific crime. His name, however?

It's been blacked out entirely. Even when I flip the page over and hold it up to the light, I can't read the letters marked over with black ink.

"Damn it!" I throw the file and watch the pages slowly drift down.

Even now, Heyworth refuses to divulge the answers I need. Answers only he can give.

Though no. He's not the only one. I flick through the pages for the older case file. The name of the girl... I read it over and over until it's cemented into my brain.

Lynn McKelvy.

Scrambling upright, I snatch up the remaining pages and carefully return them to their file, but when I reach an unfamiliar series of paragraphs, I freeze. *Psychiatric evaluation* screams across the top of the document, and the person described within the lines of text I know all too well.

__Juliana Mirangas__, age 8, female. School records convey poor attendance, average grades. Described as withdrawn and isolative by teachers. A fellow student referred to JM as "weird. Leslie was her only friend I think." No outward signs of prior trauma or psychiatric history. Family psych history of depression in mother. Father alcoholic with repeated parole violations stemming from an assault charge. Upon assessment with this writer, JM presented with a flat affect and mood and was evasive when asked about 10/28. Reports poor sleep, night terrors, anxiety. Current guardian reports that JM is fearful, guarded, and prone to emotional outbursts. Final impression: post-traumatic stress disorder, rule-out psychotic features.

Fearful, guarded, and prone to emotional outbursts. No wonder Heyworth watched over me so closely, tightening the leash whenever he felt I could threaten his precious political chances.

To him, I was always the same stray mutt: a damaged little girl with undiagnosed psychological issues. A threat to his reputation if left unchecked. A trophy to display for his benefit.

A toy to manipulate.

He never loved me.

He merely possessed me.

FIVE

*D*amien is standing outside the car when I finally escape the house, battered file in tow. His clenched jaw betrays an unusual amount of concern. I wonder if he heard the chaos from here. Breaking glass. Broken trophies. A broken soul.

"You need rest," he rasps as I come closer. The authority in his tone warns that I won't be able to dissuade him this time. "I'm taking you to my—"

"Do you want to know what I really want?" I laugh. It's a trick question, no one ever does.

But he...

Damien goes silent, his head cocked. When he extends one of his hands toward me, I take it, surprised by how damn warm he feels. How much I crave that warmth. I'm freezing.

"Tell me," he demands.

"I want..." The sob I can't swallow has him pulling me closer. Too close. More tears spill into his jacket. Within seconds, I'm howling and nothing can keep the gasping cries from coming.

What do I want?

"Control," I wail brokenly. "I want... I just want answers! I'm so sick of being coddled, and watched, and whispered about. Did you know he put more effort into stalking my tabloid mentions than actually talking to me? I want to give them something to stare at! I'm so—"

"I know." His words undercut my high-pitched whine, low and steady. So damn assured. He knows. All of me. More than I care to admit to myself or name out loud. "I know, sweet girl. *Dulce niña.*" His fingers sink into my hair, finding my scalp. "And I'll give it to you. But first..." He pivots, guiding me toward the open door to the back seat. "You need rest. I won't take no for an answer, so don't resist just this once. *¿Sí?*"

Despite my pathetic little pleas, I nod. "Okay."

I let him control me.

Just this once.

Contrary to Damien's wishes, I can't sleep in spite of the exquisite quality of the bed and its luxurious sheets. I toss and turn for hours before eventually crawling off the mattress in defeat. I manage to shower at least, and I call Diane shortly before midnight.

"No change," she tiredly conveys. "And if you went by the house..."

"I'm sorry." I clench the fingers of my free hand, wincing as the nails dig into my palm. "I just—"

"It's okay," she says over me. "Don't worry about the damage. I've taken care of it. Just get some sleep, darling."

But I'm not tired.

I'm too damn hollow.

I hear him first, rounding the hallway beyond my room. His assured, slow steps betray just how well he has the layout memorized, though I doubt he's the type to intrude upon a sleeping woman without an invitation. No, I bet he heard me first, aware of me as much as I am of him.

When I turn to watch him appear in the doorway, the mug of steaming liquid in his hand confirms it.

Wordlessly, I approach him and accept the beverage offering: coffee, made to my preference. It's a gesture that conveys more than kindness: it's an acknowledgment of the obvious. I need to be awake.

"You brought these with you," he says, revealing something slender clutched in his other hand: the file from Heyworth's office.

"I'm sure you had Julio read them to you," I blurt—but I didn't intend to sound so hostile. "Thank you," I add, trying again. "But it's just trash. In fact, I should throw it away."

I reach for the file.

He doesn't extend it. "Trash," he murmurs, deceptively soft. With barely concealed interest, his fingers stroke the worn pages poking beyond the edges of the folder. "Your past. The truth you seek. The answers he hid from you. You call that trash? No, I don't think so."

Suddenly drained, I sip from the coffee and wander to the mattress, slumping onto the very edge. "That's not what I mean. I…" A watery giggle serves as the herald for the torrent of words I can no longer hold back. "Is it funny that I'd forgotten most of it? The details, I mean." Never Simon himself. "In some ways, I think I repressed it. Can you believe I forgot what my old name was? My real name: Juliana *Mirangas*." Another hollow laugh helps keep the tears at bay—for now. "At least that blows the whole 'Heyworth Thorne is racist' question out of the water. My mother had Spanish ancestry. Though, hell, maybe he is a fucking bigot and that made it easier for him to use me at all."

"Did you learn anything about your case?" Damien wonders. "Anything you might have forgotten?"

"No..." I shake my head. "But there is something I never questioned before. The local police chief back then asked my father—Heyworth Thorne—to consult on my case personally. But he was a defense attorney." I frown. It sounds even more unusual out loud. "Why would he ask a defense attorney to consult on a murder case?"

"Let alone one who practiced in a different state and jurisdiction?" Damien adds, stroking his chin. "Interesting. I intend to find out. I may have a contact at the city police department who may be able to help—though their chief is a man I don't particularly enjoy interacting with."

I raise an eyebrow. "Don't tell me. He's not a friend of yours? Not even after you insinuated blackmail to keep his men quiet about your sex club?"

"I would suggest you not extend your pity to Chief Harrison," he warns. "Trust me on that. Some men aren't nearly as righteous as they appear to the public."

"It takes one to know one, I suppose," I say.

"Perhaps," he admits. "But I will extend any resources I can to assist your search for information, whether or not they involve Harrison."

"There was something else," I murmur, running my hand through my hair as if to help shake the thoughts free. "In the file, there was information about another girl. Lynn McKelvy.

Her case was similar to mine. She was attacked by a stranger, a man who had a knife and wanted to play a game of Simon Says…" I shudder, closing my eyes against the memories that threaten to descend. When I open them again, Damien is still here. "Can you help me find her? Maybe she knows something."

"Done," he says without hesitation either way. "But now we focus on you. You're upset—and I'm not just referring to what happened today. What can I do?"

I blink, overwhelmed by the genuine concern in his voice. The only way to smother the confusion is to drink more coffee, inhaling every drop until I've drained it all. Sighing, I shrug. "Make my father wake up and force him to tell me the truth?"

"If only I could." He laughs, but it's muted compared to his usual rich chuckle.

And I hate the fact that he's on edge around me. Wariness doesn't suit a man like him the way it does my father. Heyworth merely pretended to care; I see that now. But Damien?

He's too damn calculating to put on such an act. So what is his aim?

Watching him, I can't tell—and I do so for so long that my mug feels cool to the touch when I startle back to awareness.

"What can you do?" I whisper, recalling his question. "You taunted me once for being sheltered," I remind him. "Pathetic. Weak. A prude."

Not his exact words but close enough. The point was all the same.

"My father kept tabs on me," I admit. "Every fucking mention of my name, he collected from the tabloids, obsessing over them.

My every move is cemented in ink, but that woman? She feels like a stranger. I…"

I stand and take a tentative step in his direction. My tongue flits along my lower lip as I process just how twisted my reality has become in only a few short days.

My father is lying in a hospital bed. He may be dying.

Yet I'm in the lair of Damien Villa, and for some reason, he seems to be the one damn person unwilling to treat me like a goddamn idiot. So what does a sheltered heiress do with her dangerous, masculine lifeline?

Test the hell out of him.

"Do you remember what you told me about the women at your club?" I ask. "That they have all the power?"

"*Sí*, I remember." He frowns and I can almost see him wrestling with the idea of humoring me or not. Indulgence must win, the cause of the slow smile that shapes his mouth. "Those women… In their hands, the obsessive attention of others is a weapon. They hone it sharp to their advantage. But few are brave enough to wield the same amount of control." His heated tone sends my blood racing. It's like he's invaded my mind again, goading me to voice my naughty desire out loud and in the open. "If you are curious, Ms. Thorne, I will ask you to admit as much *por favor*."

Holding my head high, I try. "So tell me, Mr. Villa. How…how does one feel in control like that?" My cheeks catch fire. I'm cringing at the raw vulnerability exposed by such a question.

Until his mouth quirks, a lethal smile. "I will tell you, sweet girl," he swears. "*But* I am not sure if I should. Sharing experiences is not one of my strong suits. From an entirely selfish standpoint…I should dissuade you."

God, the way he said that word. *Selfish*. It contained way more than possession—a grit making every syllable harder than it should be. I should be terrified. In fact, I am, according to the pitching sensation jolting my stomach. Terrified. Intrigued. Curious.

And in this moment, I can no longer beat around the bush.

"Make me forget, Damien," I say. I beg. "I need to forget. I need to…" My fingers tear through my hair, ripping at stray strands. "The reporters are everywhere I look. I can't even hate my father despite all he's done to me. I feel like I'm going insane—"

"*Sí.*" He's close before I realize it. Like liquid fire, his fingers find my chin, tilting it so our mouths are within dangerous reach. To heighten the nearness, his breath fans mine, searing and potent. "I will give you a taste of control. But I need you to promise me one thing."

I suck in a breath. "What?"

"That you will trust me."

Trust. That word takes on an entirely new connotation coming from him. It's more than a mere surrender of doubt—it's a surrender of sanity.

Of instinct.

Of safety.

To trust him will mean forsaking the one thing I've just begged him for.

I'll lose any shred of control.

I'll lose my goddamn mind.

"Can you do that for me?" His thumb traces the line of my jaw in a distracting, teasing swipe. "Give me your trust?"

"It's not like I have much of a choice," I admit in a whisper.

It's either him…

Or the horrors in my head.

With only a second to decide, I nod. "Yes."

"Good." His resigned frown takes my breath away. Like he said, he's breaking his own rules. For me. "Then get dressed. I will make the arrangements."

I watch him go, my nerves in knots. When I finally remember how to move, I start in the direction I assume the closet to be, trying to decide what one wears to regain control. Halfway across the room, I remember I'm not home.

"If you need something to wear, feel free to check the wardrobe. There is some clothing," Damien calls from down the hall as if realizing my dilemma. "You are welcome to wear whatever you like. I made sure to cater to your specific tastes."

Only he can make generosity seem like the most unsettling of threats.

Wary, I creep to a set of closed double doors and open them to reveal a luxurious walk-in closet. *Some clothing,* he said. More like a complete wardrobe, stocked with everything from shoes to items of jewelry displayed in a glass case. How thoughtful. How…prepared.

Flattery feeds a swarm of butterflies in my stomach until I recall his past muses.

Oh. No wonder he has a full boutique in house, given his proclivities.

Eyes narrowed, I flick through the items dangling from hangers and realize that they are all in my size. Every last item. Some are dresses in varying shades of crimson and navy. Some are simple blouses and slacks.

None are my customary bulletproof black.

I imagine him chuckling over that fact. Gloating. Any other day, I'd march toward him and deliver some haughty, scathing remark to prove how unaffected I am. Tonight, I bite back my pride and settle on a rich blue dress with a modest neckline and a knee-length hem. While outside of my usual wheelhouse of couture black, it's beautiful. The A-line shape hugs the contours of my body without feeling too restricting or revealing.

A fitting suit of armor to face an opponent like Damien Villa in. *Touché.*

He's in the foyer when I finally leave my room wearing my own pair of heels, clutching my purse to my chest. "So where are we going?" I muster up the courage to ask. "To your club?"

"I'm afraid not." He cocks his head in that predatory, hawklike way, and I swallow whatever else I meant to say. "Learning to take control is a methodical process, sweet girl. The first step is to cede it."

"I think I've been doing that my whole life. Ceding control," I add. God, I sound so petulant. "Letting everyone else manipulate me at every turn. I doubt you follow that step yourself."

"I do." He grabs my arm, pulling me closer before I can react. Soft and gentle, his fingers slide down my wrist and capture mine with a knowledge I will never get over. "When it matters," he insists, tightening his grip. "When a brief moment of control can tip the scales in favor of someone who needs that security. I can cede it, even despite my…preferences."

"Oh." My heart races, throat thickens. He's too close. His voice is too damn deep. Too earnest.

"However," he warns. "This will not work if you do not trust me."

"I-I can. I mean…I do."

"Good." He turns, guiding me to the door. "Then let us begin *por favor.*"

Unsurprisingly, Julio is waiting in the hall to lead the way to the lower level. Given his appearance, I assume our destination is outside to a waiting car. Instead, we turn down a different hallway that leads deeper into the building. Eventually, we enter an elegant dining room, so out of place that it could have been conjured from thin air. Dark walls and wooden floors create an ebony backdrop for the round table draped in a pure white tablecloth, adorned with golden utensils.

In a way, it's a more terrifying battlefield than lying naked in front of a horde of strangers.

"Dinner?" I say thickly. "An interesting lesson, Mr. Villa."

"Patience," he replies, his upper lip quirked. With his free hand, he finds the back of one of the two chairs at the table and angles it toward me. "Yet another step that must be taken."

"And then?" I ask as I sit and watch him navigate his way to the chair opposite me. "Tell me: Is food the gateway drug to control?"

"No," he admits once seated. "But *knowledge* is. And to ensure your safety and comfort during our…arrangement, I need to know as much about you as you are willing to share."

"Oh?" I jut my chin haughtily into the air. "I thought there wasn't anything about me worth learning?"

His stern frown stubbornly remains. He wasn't joking. "I can admit when I have miscalculated. In your case, perhaps I have—

enough to realize that, with you, I may have to adjust my own boundaries. So allow me to rectify that. I need to know your limits. What you are comfortable with. What you will not allow. And…" He pauses and an uneasy realization worms into my mind. He's hesitating.

"And what?"

"I need to know if you have any lingering trauma that may make our arrangement…unpleasant for you."

Ah, as polite a way of beating around the bush as I've heard.

"If you're asking if I was sexually assaulted, I wasn't," I say softly. "As far as monsters go, Simon was a different breed. He wasn't interested in my body, I don't think. Just my psyche. My sanity. My soul. But as far as the psychological trauma scale goes, we can check off daddy issues, trust issues, and post-traumatic stress disorder."

Is he relieved by that information? I can't tell. He sits like stone, his head tilted toward me, conveying that I have his full attention.

And yet…

I can't shake the sense that he's hiding something. Or perhaps avoiding.

"You're uncomfortable with the notion of sex," he points out. "Though not sexuality. You seem to have no problem relishing in your mastery on that front."

My cheeks burn as I remember all of the many ways he's gotten to experience me relishing in said sexuality.

"In fact, if I may be so bold…"

I swallow hard and scan the table in search of wine. There is none. I have to fight this battle of wits with no armor to hide behind.

"Yes?" I croak when the passing seconds make it clear that he needs an answer. "You can be bold."

"I'm curious if you are partial to exhibition."

I nearly choke. By the grace of God, I spit out a reply instead. "Like what takes place at your little club?"

"Yes." He nods. "Like what takes place at my little club. Women, comfortable in their sex, empowered enough to bare it all for the rich, closeted clients willing to pay through the teeth to watch. It's the clients who pretend as though they have the upper hand —the dignity in the situation, you see—but no." He scoffs, shaking his head. "The woman they sneer down at. Scorn. Ogle. She knows who has the real power. They all wish they could be so free."

"Free..." I eye the elegant, polished table setting and flick my thumb along the edge of a silver fork. "And if I *was* into exhibition?"

I don't dare look at his face, but the sound he makes... Part startled grunt, part amused laugh. I squirrel it away in some far recess of my brain to parse over later.

"In some ways, I wouldn't be surprised," he admits, startling me. "A woman such as yourself, always in the public eye, always watched and whispered about. How did you put it? *'I want to give them something to stare at.'*"

"So fine, you got me. I want to writhe naked in front of a bunch of strangers." How I said that without laughing, I will never understand. "But *you* don't. You strike me as a private man, Mr. Villa. One who doesn't enjoy sharing his experiences."

"There are ways to satisfy both of our requirements," he says softly. "If that is what you desire."

"How so?" I ask instead. "You throw me to the wolves, letting your male 'entertainers' screw me while you sit back and watch?"

What I intended as a joke lands more like a grenade.

"No." He sits straighter, and were his eyes whole, I'd imagine them flashing. "I apologize if I was not clear before. No one will ever touch you but me." His voice is so thick that I feel it in my fucking bones. Crackling tension robs every ounce of air from my lungs—but a second later, his posture relaxes and I can breathe again. "At least until our arrangement is over. *Sí*, that is one boundary of mine I will never bend."

"So how—"

"I need to know if this is truly what you want. You need to be sure, no doubts or second-guessing. Once I finalize the arrangements, there is no going back."

Even considering what he's offering should be ludicrous. One might argue it could easily be written off as driven by extreme emotional distress, at the very least. Deep down, I know it's not. I have no excuse of mental frailty to fall back on. The same impulse driving me now is the same one that drew me to his art in the first place, I suppose.

Curiosity. Discontentment. Enthrallment. Jealousy.

"*Dulce niña*, how about I tell you?" he murmurs before I can reply. "You may correct me if I am wrong, *¿sí?* But as much as you may try to deny it, you want to be like them. You want to know what it's like to be on fucking display—but on your own terms for once. You want—no, need—to let the world see you as you are, in a way they can't mock or deride or scrutinize. It's why you wanted me to paint you in the first place, is it not? This desire you feel… It is more than lying naked on a pedestal on a rebellious whim—because you've already stripped yourself bare, robbing them of any ammunition to use against you."

His words reflect an assessment that goes far beyond this moment. He's amassing everything he learned during his unknown months of surveilling me.

"There is a hesitation in you," he adds as if to prove as much. "A fear I doubt you are even aware of. Something that makes you unafraid to bare your skin yet causes you to flinch when I touch you, even as you moan. I believe it is deeply rooted in why you've remained alone for so long. One of the reasons I asked for your trust was in the hopes that we can both learn what is really troubling you."

Something more than the past, he seems to imply.

"We can discuss it further after you eat," he adds, gesturing to the doorway.

A waiter appears as if on cue, carrying the caliber of fare I've come to expect from a man with his taste: an entrée of expertly seared steak on a bed of fresh greens paired with a serving of wine to wash it all down.

I sample everything, tasting nothing. Eventually, I find myself watching Damien more than anything else. He manipulates a fork and a knife, mechanically chewing every now and again, but I'm not fooled by his air of indifference. I sense that his full attention is on me. Listening to every scrape of my utensils over my plate, tracking how much I consume.

He's studying me, compiling a dossier of my behavior that I bet contains far more secrets than the one I discovered in my father's office.

"All right." Sighing, I finally set my fork aside. "So, what if I lied before?" I try my damn hardest to sound nonchalant. Like these words don't matter—when, in reality, they symbolize everything. "About why I'm still a virgin. What if Simon *does* have everything to do with it?"

"*¿Sí?*" He copies me and carefully dabs at his mouth with the tip of an ivory napkin. "Then I would be assured that my skills of deduction haven't drastically degraded within the span of twenty-four hours," he says. "Tell me the truth *por favor*."

"It's childish," I admit. "But...I've never stopped seeing his shadow everywhere I look. And I've always thought, even though I know it's ridiculous..." Tears sting my eyes and I frantically blink them back. "I-I can't stop..."

"Go on," Damien encourages.

"I've always felt that if I let anyone else in... One day, they'll leave and it may prove him right. All along, I wasn't worth it. Leslie should have lived, not me." I choke out a watery laugh, but I know even he can sense the tears I can't keep from falling. "My virginity, as stupid as it sounds, was one of the few fucking things that was always *mine*. No one else's. My parents, my innocence, my friend—I've lost everything else. I can't lose any more. Not to him."

"I'm sorry." Damien pushes back from the table. "Perhaps I did miscalculate. I am not the man you should surrender such trust to—"

"But you're wrong."

He stiffens and slowly lowers himself onto the chair.

"Is it pathetic that you're one of the few people in my life to *ask* me who I am? What I want? I don't think you understand how much that affects me," I concede. "Being asked a question and having someone actually care about the answer. If you're worried about hurting me, then don't be. Love isn't what I need from people. I've had it. Have it. I know I could easily find someone out there to cherish me. A man who would coddle me and keep me on a leash just like Heyworth has. But it's not what I want. Not what I need. I need...challenge. Someone who will shove me into a room stocked only with blank canvas and dare me to strip."

His jaw twitches as though he's recalling that very memory.

"A man who tests my limits and preys on my fears," I continue. "I'm sorry if this is making you uncomfortable—"

"No. Never." He shakes his head. "Far from it. But I am not sure if I am quite the man you think I am. I could disappoint you."

"And I think that's part of the thrill," I confess. "You could. You could be the worst kind of monster under all this suave polish. But for some reason, I still want to play your twisted little game a little longer."

Unlike Simon, at least he's given me a choice.

"So, now what?" I ask, pushing my plate aside. "More stalling?"

"Oh, no, Ms. Thorne." His devilish laugh stiffens every hair on the back of my neck. "Now, I'll take you up on your proposal. We will play my twisted game. May the best man win."

"Or woman."

"*Sí, sí.*" He chuckles even more deeply. "Or woman."

Six

e arrive at his club well past the hour when other establishments would be closing. I vaguely recognize the gilded hallway marking his private entrance, but this time, we stop short of the hall leading toward the viewing booths.

There's a peculiar tension I sense in the air even before he speaks.

"I'll allow you a minute to rethink your request," he warns, his hand on mine, imparting heat. "You say the word and we'll leave. I'll take you home and you can rest—because I'm partly sure delirium may be fueling your newfound lust to experience the forbidden."

I have to laugh at that. "No," I say, shaking my head—for my own benefit, not his. "I…I'll play your game, Mr. Villa. I *want* to."

"Then play you shall." He lowers his mouth near my ear. "You will star alone tonight," he says, dropping all pretense. No more word games. This is real. "Just you in front of a full audience— but I want you blindfolded. I'll let you wonder as to their faces. Their identities. Their reactions. Because none of them matter to you, do you understand? This performance is for *me*. Show me who the sheltered girl is behind her mask. Reveal to me what she needs. In a sea of these pretentious fucking people, you listen for *me*."

He draws back as his words ripple down my spine.

"Daphne will assist you from here," he calls to me while advancing toward the viewing rooms. "I look forward to your performance, Ms. Thorne. I do suggest that you follow *all* of her instructions. *Adios*."

"Hello." Daphne is a smiling blond in a slimming black dress who appears as if conjured. "Follow me, Ms. Thorne," she says before heading in the direction opposite Damien. "Mr. Villa has made all of the arrangements."

I don't know what I expect to discover when she finally ushers me into a small room. An elegant vanity and a wooden wardrobe would be far down on my list. It's an intimate, surprisingly tasteful setting adorned with a ruby color scheme similar to the theater-like atrium I viewed the last time he brought me here.

"You can undress," Daphne says. Then she crosses the room and points out a door opposite from the one we entered through. "You can leave through here when you are ready," she explains. "It opens to the stage."

"Is that where…where I'll be blindfolded?" I ask.

Daphne shakes her head. "No. Once you are ready, I'll be waiting on the other side." She nods to the door again. "There, I'll blindfold you as well as relay Mr. Villa's final instructions. There is a robe you can put on until then," she adds as if sensing the nerves crawling up my throat, robbing me of my voice. "Whenever you are ready."

She slips through the door, leaving me alone, and I eye my reflection in the vanity's mirror.

I look so young. So tired. Purplish bruises encircle my eyes, and my ratty hair is in dire need of a deep condition and a brush.

No wonder Damien changed his mind so suddenly on indulging my impulsive request. As I look now, few men would desire me.

Once I strip my coat, my beautiful dress enhances my appearance, but only by a little. I'm a dull, plain shadow overall. The kind of woman who may be whispered about and hounded but only because she makes for such an easy target.

A haunted, hollow doll.

My fingers shake as I reach around to my back, searching for the zipper of the dress. When it's loosened, the fabric easily falls, revealing more pale, unremarkable skin.

In a horrible way, I'm relieved Damien is blind. He can't see the gaunt, rail-thin body I do. Or the scars on my thigh. Or the fear in my eyes.

Yet he somehow sees beyond it all, peering beneath the flesh to the parts of me I can't disguise. Now, I think I know exactly why he changed his mind; this is a test, designed for me more so than him.

Can I truly trust him despite all the people who may be watching? Whispering? Judging?

Am I that fragile doll Heyworth coddled or an opponent worthy of playing the monster's game?

The answer terrifies me as I step out of my shoes and approach the closed door, knocking once.

I don't know.

But I want to find out.

*D*aphne stays true to her promise. At my knocking, she opens the door, a slender strip of black silk dangling from her opposite hand. Without a word, I turn, allowing her to secure the blindfold over my eyes. It's soft against my skin but impenetrable—a sheet of endless dark.

"There is one more thing Mr. Villa insisted upon," she murmurs.

I jump as a cold, hard surface brushes my ear and settles against the lobe. Solid. Slightly heavy. My thoughts spin, desperately trying to put a name to the object.

"This way," Daphne says without giving an explanation herself.

Taking my hand, she leads me forward and I can almost feel the atmosphere shift from the stale, close air of the hall to the wider, echoing theater. My first thought is to assume it's empty —Damien Villa wouldn't dare share his new doll with the world.

He's merely toying with me.

But faint murmurs and whispers nibble at my ears to spite my pathetic assumption. People—more than one.

"You can lie here," Daphne suggests, stopping short.

I tentatively reach out, alarmed as my fingers brush a silken surface that gives slightly when I apply pressure. A mattress? I lower myself onto it, and soft footsteps betray Daphne's retreat. Barring the audience, I'm alone in this arena now. Thin fabric forms a fragile base beneath me as unseen eyes take in more of me than anyone has ever seen. The blindfold obscuring my vision serves as my lone piece of armor.

And I don't even know how many spectators are present. Ten? Twenty? Hundreds? Their murmured voices echo in a constant hum: an ocean of rejection, or scrutiny, or judgment.

Panic sets in. My hands twitch upward to cover myself as my heart hammers a silent command against the inside of my rib cage: *run.*

I can't do this. I can't…

Wait. That low, rumbling clearing of a throat rises above all other noise. I'm insane—there's no way I could pick him out so easily. So definitively. It's another man I'm straining my ears to catch. A stranger, whose voice drips directly into by ear, fed by the object nestled there. An earpiece, I realize.

"Sweet *dulce niña.* Did you think I'd let you have full rein for your little performance?" His deep, raspy laugh twists my stomach into knots. "I warned you: This performance is for me."

"Oh?" I gasp, unsure if he can even hear me through the device.

But he can—another grated chuckle proves it, laced with faint hints of static.

"I thought you were supposed to be teaching me control?" I whisper—but even the faint sound isn't loud enough to drown out the persistent hints of the others in attendance. I can smell them. Perfume. Cologne. Cigar smoke. An amalgam of strangers watching me. Waiting.

They demand entertainment.

"This is mine," Damien declares as casually as if commenting on the color of the sky. "Lie back. Do not hide. Place your hand on your belly. Now breathe deeply. Like that."

I obey, letting the sound of my breathing and the blood humming through my veins drown out all other noise.

"Keep it there and let your other hand sweep along your hip. Feel the softness of your skin. Like silk, ¿sí?"

I don't know if it's his voice or the warm sensation of my fingertips gliding over me that hypnotizes me. First my throat, then skimming down the sides of my breasts, across my stomach. Back up.

"Now…spread your legs, sweet girl. Let them see what they will never have."

I stiffen. Refusing is my first reaction. I almost can't bite it down. "I can't—"

"Sí," Damien growls. "You will. Nice and wide, sweet girl." God. A moan edges his voice so unexpected in that grated tone.

My body jerks, my thighs parting as if of their own accord.

"You've done it," he hisses as if spitting the words through clenched teeth. "I can hear them gasping. So beautiful. So pink—"

Heat floods my cheeks and I almost stop listening. Shut down. Ignore.

But he's right. I can hear a distinctive shift in the room: a change presented in a sudden hush the farther my legs drift apart.

"Touch yourself," Damien commands, his voice so damn thick. Each word is drenched in his accent, barely recognizable as English. "Just once. Mierda." He hisses as I slip my hand between my legs. "Good girl. I can hear your breathing change. Again por favor."

My finger grazes a sensitive ball of nerves and a cry rips from my throat. Nerves prickle and twitch, unsure of how to process each hesitant touch. With pleasure? Shame? Both? My quivering thighs battle to close together. Hide. Retreat. God, who knows who could be watching. What they see. How I look.

And the more my brain runs through every frantic fear and scenario, the less they seem to matter.

"Stop," Damien snarls, jarring me back to the present. "I said *once*, sweet girl. I doubt these bastards deserve more—*mierda!*" he grunts as my finger slips, which draws another gasp from my lips. "You're disobeying, Juliana." A hoarseness laces the warning—he sounds anything but upset. "Don't stop there, then. Add another finger, sweet girl."

A part of me shies from the dare. But another, bolder impulse seizes control of my limbs. Two fingers stroke my flesh in tandem. It's lightning. My back arches, my throat contracting around another strangled cry.

"Imagine I'm there with you," Damien murmurs. "Remember what it was like when you were at my mercy."

I stiffen at the memory, the images almost too sinful to imagine —but my brain produces them anyway. Him kneeling in front of me. His heat on me. Inside…

"Yes," he grates. "You're touching yourself again. I can tell. I can practically taste you, even from here." He curses. "Stop. Too much—"

But I can't. Forsaking his order, I perform solely for me, letting my fingers twist and stroke of their own accord. Harder. Faster. Deeper.

"This is what I wanted for you," he growls heatedly. "Selfishness. Greed. They all want you, sweet girl. But you're mine, aren't you? Can you sense them?"

I can. They're staring. Focused only on the image I'm displaying. Only what I want them to see.

A million people may be in this room, but he's inside my head. Listening. Studying the slick sound of every stroke of my finger. Imagining himself touching me instead. I bet he can sense the moisture growing the longer this moment extends. The world may be watching, but none are sensing the same things he is. Smelling me with flared nostrils. Tasting me in the air.

I picture him interpreting every little sound I make, imagining their cause.

He wanted to know my limits. My wants. My desires.

Perhaps they're pathetically simple? I need him to see me—to explore me in a way no one else would dare. Deeper than any other man could. Harder and more intimately than anyone else has the right to.

I want him.

I want him.

I want him to want me just as insanely.

I'm on the verge of something soul-shatteringly destructive when I catch that low, tortured growl again. It's a promise, ringing true even as my sharp gasp drowns it out.

He'll give it to me, those dangerous things I desire.

Whether I'm ready or not.

SEVEN

$\mathcal{S}$omehow, I manage to stand on jellied legs and return to the dressing room. Daphne helps me into my dress, but when I finally reenter the lobby, Julio is the one waiting for me. Damien is nowhere to be seen. Not even as we exit the building and enter the car idling out front.

He isn't in his suite, either. The stale air lacks his trademark scent as Julio ushers me inside while remaining in the hall. In fact, all I smell is my own sweat, and nervousness rises like a slap, erasing the thrill from the club.

As childish as it fucking sounds, did I do it wrong? Did I upset him somehow, even though I followed his damn instructions to the T? I listened for him. Performed for him. Bared myself to him.

And the bastard can't even pat me on the back for a job well done.

Damn it. I hate what uncertainty does to me when it comes to him. It nibbles, chewing at my nerves in a way disappointing Heyworth never did. Wearing a mask for my father was a superficial game—this one has gone deeper. Too deep.

My cheeks sear as I linger in the foyer, debating whether or not to even stay. Could I face him? Let him laugh: *Silly Juliana, it was all a game. You gave me plenty of fodder to sell to the tabloids, however. Gracias.*

I turn for the door and brace my hand on the doorknob—but I don't know what makes me release it in the end. Maybe pride. I won't give him the satisfaction of running this time. I'll meet him head-on. Because even if this was some cruel, sick form of humiliation…

I don't regret it.

The thought gives me the strength to march into my room, my head held high like the bastard's watching. Maybe he is—listening anyway. He can hear me laugh in defiance of his goddamn mind games. He can hear me…

Gasp as I leave the monotone color scheme of his suite and enter a world of roses. Beautiful, swollen budding roses in more colors than I have considered possible. Natural. They cover nearly every available surface, spilling from vases or in petals scattered over the bed and the floor. In the midst of it all is a silver box perched on one of the pillows. An ivory card lies beside it.

I pick up the card first with trembling fingers. All it contains is a slash of elegantly penned script: *You were exquisite.*

Not quite the reaction one would expect when paired with cold, disappearing silence.

Intrigued, I set the card aside and turn my attention to the silver box. It's thin, delicately crafted, and when I lift the lid to reveal what's inside it, it takes every muscle I possess to keep from dropping it.

Lying on a bed of red silk is a thin silver chain suspending a single perfectly round pearl.

And I know before I even run my finger along the edge of it that it's *the* pearl.

Our pearl.

I put it on, shivering as it settles between my breasts. So delicate…

And yet so dangerous.

So damning.

*A*fter everything I've been through, it should be impossible to sleep. Impossible. Yet I wind up blinking my eyes open to pale light flooding the room of Damien's suite. My nostrils flare, swollen with floral scents. Sighing, I roll onto my side and scan the room, observing the forest of roses in the different lighting—and they are still here.

But I'm sure I closed the door last night before stripping my clothing and climbing beneath the sheets. It's open now, and in the shadows of the hall, something draws me from the bed for a better look.

A potted arrangement blocks my path—one that I'm sure wasn't there last night. Carefully nestled in an ivory vase, an array of orchids and lilies in varying shades of white clamor for sunlight. So beautiful and—in a way—so wasteful.

Breathtaking gesture aside, it's a fact that all of these flowers will be dead within days.

As I finger the pearl hanging from my throat, I have to wonder if that's his point. Beauty decays. Natural freshness withers. A true artist would seek what he could from such fragility and then move on from the rotting husk. Does he look at me the same way? A beautiful bloom to be plucked at just the right moment. I'll make for a lovely diversion for a while, but eventually, he'll have to toss me aside and find another bud to corrupt.

It's the natural order of things.

Noise from the other room draws my attention and I rake my hands through my hair, clearing the morbid thoughts as I follow the hall.

I find Damien waiting for me in the living room of the penthouse, seated on the leather chaise. Damn. Despite his penchant for disappearing, the man can cut a figure when he wants to. An ebony suit enhances his broad shoulders and a blood-red tie creates a startling contrast of color.

My fingers twitch, still caressing his pearl. For a second, I consider creeping toward him, potentially catching him off guard. Perhaps I'd run my fingers along his skin, tracing the stern line of his jaw he hides so well around me. But the second I cross the threshold of the room, he stiffens.

"I apologize for last night."

"Huh?" I clear my throat to disguise my surprise. Odd. It's not quite what I was expecting: a genuine apology uttered in a guttural baritone. "Don't tell me, Mr. Villa," I start, feigning nonchalance as I linger in the doorway. "You didn't want an encore?"

"Far from it," he counters, shifting to face me.

Damn. My inner thighs clench as his tongue dances along his lower lip.

"I had to sleep in my studio in fact, to ensure I didn't insist on that very scenario."

My heart lurches in my chest. "Oh?"

"*Sí.* The intricacies of your little performances never cease to intrigue me," he admits, sounding even raspier. His hands are braced over his knees, the knuckles damn near white in comparison to the rest of his skin. "I can only imagine how much you enjoy thwarting my expectations at every turn."

He makes it sound criminal: thwarting him. Confusing him. Surprising him.

I suppose I should feel smug. Instead...

"Thank you," I croak, turning away as my cheeks heat. "I mean it. I...I didn't know how much I needed a diversion until—"

"I understand," he says, only unnerving me further. "But you did ask me for one other favor, and before we discuss last night, I owe it to you to report what I've found."

"Did you find her?" Hope bubbles up, distorting my voice before I can choke it back. "The other victim? Is she—"

"I did," he says carefully. "But it's bad news, I'm afraid. Lynn McKelvy died several years ago."

The stress he put on that terrible word sends my brain spinning with a million possible reasons. "How?"

"An overdose," he says.

"You mean she killed herself." I cross my arms over my chest—they're trembling. "Didn't she?"

His solemn nod is all the confirmation I need.

"That's awful." I stagger forward and wind up sitting beside him, my face pressed to my palm. My head is spinning. God, I can't think. The weight of everything comes bearing down, a torrent of conflicting emotions. Guilt. Pain. Rage.

"Awful," Damien agrees. "But what happened to her is not your fault—"

"Isn't it?" I counter bitterly. "All this pain and my father knew. How could someone be so selfish? How?"

Though I could ask myself the same question. I haven't looked at my cell phone since last night for a reason. Dread of what I might find? Fear of what I might not?

I don't even know if him being alive or dead terrifies me more.

"How could he lie to me?" The kind, lovely man who comforted me all those years ago. Who snuck candy into my hospital room. The doting yet stern figure who bought me a puppy for my ninth birthday and rented out the entire zoo for my enjoyment. No matter how hard I try, I can't reconcile that man with the monster all facts point to him being. "How could he—"

"If it is any consolation, there may be one way for you to find some ounce of closure." He slips a hand into the pocket of his coat and withdraws, of all things, a slim, pink book. Stickers coat the cover in a mockingly colorful collage given the morbid topic of conversation—and something tells me it's not his. It looks old and well worn, swollen with crinkled, written-on pages. "Lynn McKelvy kept a journal that her sister salvaged from her belongings. At my request, she's loaned it to me. Do you want it?"

I force my fingers to uncurl, gripping the end of it. Overall, it's barely the width of my palm, yet it feels so weighty in my grasp. Balanced on my lap, I don't know if it's a gift.

Or a curse.

"Thank you—"

"I would caution you not to. At least not yet." He stands, finding his cane. "But I hope it brings you some measure of comfort."

"Have you read it? I mean, had Julio read it to you?"

A muscle in his jaw lurches and I marvel at that. Not smugness for once. Unease? "No," he says.

"Why not?"

Men like him don't relinquish knowledge so easily. Lynn could have written about the menial ins and outs of her daily life—or Simon.

Yet he's given it to me first.

"Thank you."

"I have business I need to attend to," he says, heading for the door, his cane in hand. "I'll return later."

"I should go home anyway," I say, standing as well. "I appreciate you letting me stay here—"

"Oh, that is right. We never did clarify this one, small matter." He inclines his head, displaying that dangerously charming smile. "I will continue to uphold my end of our bargain, but in return, you fulfill one daily task for me, ¿sí?"

A shiver runs down my spine as I force myself to reply. "Oh? Like what?" It's chilling how quickly he can turn the tables. I never know what to expect from one minute to the next. Charming Damien? Mocking Damien? Disarmingly gentle Damien?

"You sleep here for as long as this arrangement persists. Though I will remind you that you've already agreed to do so."

"W-What? But I—"

"I'll see you later tonight," he says, but this time, it sounds less reassuring. More like a dare. Or a threat.

"I suppose you'll pay for my things to be brought here?" I inquire, placing my hands on my hips. "I mean, your clothes are lovely, but I would prefer my own. If I'm to stay here for any period of time, at least."

There. I *almost* sound confident, but if he's caught off guard, his posture doesn't reveal it.

His back is to me as he continues his slow, lazy pace to the door —but his laugh resonates in my belly. "Of course. I'll make the necessary arrangements."

"And," I add, waiting until he pauses near the entrance to the foyer, "no listening devices. If I want you to hear me, you'll hear me. If not, you accept that." The seriousness in my tone negates the playful nonchalance I wish to convey. But it's like he said: He wants me to trust him.

And I can't if he treats me like an enemy one second and a plaything the next.

"I mean that," I insist as seconds pass without a response. "Please."

"As you wish. *Adios.*" The door opens and his footsteps drift into the hall. "We will have dinner tonight," he adds before leaving entirely. "I'm afraid pizza, however, will not be on the menu."

In a telling display of leverage, he doesn't give me the chance to refuse before the door closes after him.

Touché.

Alone, I hunch into myself. I'm shaking, twisting that goddamn journal over and over until I finally gather up the nerve to open it. The first entry is dated over four years ago. In surprisingly neat script, Lynn McKelvy recorded her day-to-day thoughts. She had a boyfriend named Tim. A sister named Sarah. Wonderful, attentive parents.

And…she hated her birthday. Dreaded it in fact. That single looming date dominates nearly every passage. In the same sentence where she bemoaned boring chores or a shitty day at work, she prefaced it with a single foreboding statement: *It's a month until my birthday. A week. A day.*

Until the date finally came and went. Afterward, the entries become sparser. Less coherent. The last scribbled statements chill me to my core,

It didn't happen. No card. No present. He didn't come.

And I should be relieved…

But I'm not.

EIGHT

*L*ynn McKelvy feared her birthday—not the day itself, but what it meant. Midnight ushered in a series of disturbing events that had become a ritual of sorts. They seemed so benign on paper: receiving a card from an unwanted well-wisher. A few carefully curated presents, all from *him*.

A reminder of the hell she barely survived as a child.

But four years ago, in her case, they seemingly stopped coming.

And rather than relish that fact, it terrified her.

As I finish the last page of the journal, there's only one method I can think of to salvage what I can from the smoldering wreckage of my sanity.

Step one: ignore reality—starting with shoving Lynn McKelvy's diary beneath the pillow in my room and pretending it doesn't exist. It's foolish. Childish, but I'll worry about the consequences later.

Now, it seems far more vital to wallow in a scalding-hot shower and attempt to erase Damien Villa from my skin. Scrubbing and soap are no match; he stains my flesh like oil paint, highlighting the glaring flaws I'm used to suppressing. In the end, I scuttle into a robe in defeat.

My hollow gaze watches me from the mirror's surface, noticing the subtle ways he's tainted me. The skin on my neck flushes pink as if remembering his touch. Even the usual fear surging through my veins feels different now. Electric, capable of sowing more damage upon my psyche than a few memories.

Like those of my own hated birthdays.

Simon's never missed a single one. Those three tortuous days always play out in chilling predictability. First, the wine—merely a card when I was younger—followed by a wrapped newspaper clipping from the day I went missing, then the doll, a replica of Leslie's. Then a rose.

And finally…

I rack my brain for the image required to fill in the blank. Every single year, it came on the third day without fail, but this year…

Bile congeals into a creeping creature, crawling up my throat. *No…* I rake my fingers through my hair as if searching for that one terrible memory. But I can't find it. How ironic that over a week of chaos has allowed me to forget. *This* year, on the third day, my final present never came.

Logic escapes my brain as I throw my coat on and lunge for the front door of the suite, ripping it open. I hear someone call my name as I race to the elevator and ride it to the lower floor, but I can't stop. Panting, I tear onto the street and flag down the first cab I can, taking it straight to the Lariat.

"Hey!" the driver snaps as I shove the door open and climb out without bothering to hear the fare. "You owe me, lady!"

But he'll just have to get in line.

My once familiar, if cold home is a labyrinth now. A few nights away have warped the gilded hallways, transforming luxury into a foreboding maze. My front door is the portal to a nightmare world and every nerve urges me to run as I open the door and step inside.

On the surface, it looks as I left it last. No avalanche of flowers. No lurking Damien Villa.

No final, haunting warning from Simon.

Though perhaps he decided to deliver it in person?

A shadow flickers on the fringes of my entryway—near the kitchen. A stranger. A man. Panic paralyzes me. It takes a heart-stopping second before I notice the uniform the intruder is wearing, the navy blue of a police officer.

"Can I help you?" I blurt in a rush.

"Ms. Thorne," he says, stepping from behind my counters, his hands elevated. "Sorry to bother you, but Chief Harrison wanted me to secure—"

"Secure?" I croak. "Just because my father's in the hospital, that doesn't mean you get to do his bidding. Not without a warrant or whatever it is you need."

He raises an eyebrow. "Ma'am, I was sent by the chief. For your safety. Apparently, there's an investigation into—"

"I'm sorry." My chest heaves as those dangerous keywords land on the overwhelming pile on my psyche like drops of gasoline. "Just please g-get out!" I point a trembling finger toward the door. "Now! Get out!"

"Of course." The man lurches past me and respectfully inclines his head. "Sorry to startle you."

The full extent of just how badly he has doesn't sink in until the door finally closes after him. My knees tremble, knocking together. I have to stagger forward and brace my hands over the counter just to stay upright. My poor, abandoned pot of oleander wilts nearby: a few naked stalks amid a swath of fallen petals.

I brush my finger along the rim of the tiny pot, remembering its original intent: to terrify me. One morbid present accounted for —though not one of Simon's.

Pushing myself upright, I remove my coat before I leave the kitchen in search of my fourth gift.

And I rip the entire suite apart looking for it. His usual spot would be the bathroom, taped to the mirror, my final reminder of why we play his twisted game.

But it's not there.

Or in the hall.

Or in my bedroom.

I give up somewhere in the middle of searching the walk-in closet. Around me, I sense the world continuing, the day elongating. Shadows loom and deepen across the floor, but I can't move. It's selfish in retrospect. My father could be dying. Damien could be moving on to his next conquest.

Or Simon could be waiting to finish me off once and for all.

When heavy footsteps intrude into my suite, I'm convinced it's him—ha, not even a police presence would deter him. My old tormentor has come to finish me off for good. Is that what really happened to Lynn McKelvy?

I should feel terror building with every slow, approaching step.

But I don't.

All I can do is tilt my head to watch a figure appear in the threshold of my room, bathed in indigo twilight.

"I did offer to retrieve your things," Damien announces before advancing a step. "Though I will admit your method seems more…lively." He tentatively nudges a wad of clothing strewn across his path with his foot, but his clenched jaw betrays just how unsure he is. One of his hands feels out in front of him to maintain his balance, a rare sign of instability.

"Wait!" I lurch upright and kick any nearby objects out of his way. "I'm sorry, I—"

"You're crying." He grabs my wrist with uncanny insight, pulling me toward him. His cocked head warns that he's tracking every hitch in my voice. There's no point in trying to disguise it. "I know packing can be overwhelming for some, but I suspect that is not the case in this instance."

"Lynn McKelvy was attacked by Simon," I croak in a rush. "I know it was him. He haunted her on her birthday too. Every year. But then one year, he stopped…and she died—"

"Slow down," Damien urges. His hand sinks into my hair, parting the thick strands. Subtly applied pressure urges me closer to him until my face is resting against his chest. "Breathe."

"She died," I stammer, fisting my hands in the front of his coat. "And I don't—what if he killed her? What if he's planning to finally kill me? My last present never came." Tears stream down my cheeks, heedless of the fingers I deploy to combat them.

"Easy. Easy, sweet, girl." Damien shifts, fully engulfing me in his arms. "Talk to me."

"It never came," I insist, between gasping sobs. "He always sends it on the third day, always."

"What?" he demands, but his voice is tenser. Brittle. "Talk to me, sweet girl. What didn't come?"

"A picture," I confess. I can see it: the same sick image used to torment me every single year since I was eight years old. Squeezing my eyes shut doesn't erase it. "My class picture from second grade."

Scrawled across it would be the same mocking phrase, year after year: *Was she worth it?*

Was my life worth Leslie's?

The answer resonates in my soul, just as true now as it was then: *No.*

"What if he kills me too? What if…what if he hurt my father?" I can't even imagine the prospect, and my fingers tighten over the luxurious fabric in their grasp. "People connected to your brother's case have wound up dead lately. What if—"

"No one will harm you," Damien says as though it's as solid a fact as the sky being blue. We breathe air. He'll protect me. "Though I can't say the same for myself…" His pained tone draws my attention down to my hands. I'm clutching his arms, nails drawn.

"S-Sorry!" I loosen my grip, but he captures my hand before I can pull away completely.

"You don't ever need to apologize to me."

"Not even for suspecting you of the unthinkable?" I counter. "I can't lie and say I haven't considered it, that you could be the reason my father is in the hospital. What if you wanted to hurt him that badly?"

He's gone as far as sending me poisonous shrubs and bugging my apartment for over four years. Would it be much of a stretch to assume that he's capable of far worse?

"I despise Heyworth Thorne," he admits. At the same time, he slips one of his hands around to my lower back as if to ensure I can't run from such a confession. "I loathe what he stands for—but the justice I seek can't be found if he's dead. Trust that I have no interest in hurting him physically."

"You just want to destroy his reputation," I surmise. "But why? I know about your brother, but there has to be more to it than that—"

"I will tell you," he swears. "But not like this, when you are panicked and hysterical." He brushes his hand along my forearm as if to use my trembling as evidence against me. "You need rest. I am going to take you back to my suite and tie you to the bed if I have to. You may even enjoy it, ¿sí?"

"I can't…" An exhausted sigh nearly robs me of balance. I sway as he tightens his grip, steering me against his chest. For the first time, I notice the real world beyond him. Rain is lashing at the windows and a streak of lightning lances across his face, illuminating the tension in his jaw. "I can't sleep," I croak. "I can't think. I'm so damn tired."

"Fine. But staying here is obviously distressing to you." Through gritted teeth, he proposes, "So let me take you somewhere else—"

"No. What if—"

"Away from here," he continues to insist. "Look at me." He cups my cheek against his palm as thunder resonates through the walls. "You shouldn't be here alone. Not during a storm." Ironic, considering that his heat feels more destructive than anything lightning could inflict. "Let me take you somewhere else. Anywhere else."

"Why?" My voice lacks the taunt it should have. "It's not just the storms I'm afraid of. I'll never escape him. I'll never—"

"Enough." He lunges, but the act his lips inflict isn't a kiss. It's a kill shot. Swift and decisive, designed to shut me up. Distract.

Disorient.

And it works. Shock strips me of everything—thoughts, fears, common sense. All that remains is searing fire.

And I want to burn in it.

His touch is an inferno I eagerly throw myself into. Grunting, he captures my waist in both hands, igniting me through the thin silk of my robe. His tongue invades, his mouth conquers, and there's nothing I can do to withstand the onslaught but breathe.

So I do, inhaling all I can of Damien Villa. It's a dangerous game to play. With every frantic gasp of air, my chest meets his, causing my nipples to harden beneath the friction.

"Wait," he breathes, pulling back. "Just wait—"

"Please." I slide my hands down to his hips.

"*Mierda*." His teeth nip the tip of my tongue in response, sending a jolt of alarm through my entire body. A warning. *Submit, Juliana.* Let him regain control and this won't go any further.

My brain is more than willing to comply. My body, however, rebels.

"Please." I flex my fingers, sending each nail into the material of his shirt. In retaliation, he jerks me closer. Our mouths collide again, grappling for the upper hand.

No one wins. We wind up panting, openmouthed, in a standoff he decides to break by sweeping his thumb around to the tie of my robe.

"Interesting outfit choice, Ms. Thorne," he growls against my tongue as I curl my fingers into the waistband of his trousers. "Can't say I'm not impressed. But *easy*, sweet girl." He finds my fingers and gently moves them from his zipper. With a practiced twist of his fingers, he undoes the fastening himself. "Let me take care of you, ¿sí? Close your eyes."

I obey, shutting out everything but him. The ragged sound of his breathing, the rasp of his heated skin over mine…

"That's it," he all but groans as my fingers brush his abdomen. "I'm not going anywhere."

God, the hoarse sound building in his throat resonates in my bones, so much more alarming than thunder. It's concession.

"I propose another bargain." He cups my chin, recapturing my mouth while his other hand fists itself into my hair, holding me captive for every searing, searching thrust of his tongue. Against my parted lips, he breathes, "You give me tonight. All those fears, your pain…it's all mine."

His deft fingers yank the material of my robe from my shoulders as he guides me back step by step. When my knees finally brush the edge of my mattress, he eases me down and my eyes flutter open just enough to take him in. A mixture of neon streetlights and lightning paints him in varying degrees of blues and yellows. He's abstract artwork too beautiful to ever own.

My fingers smooth down his torso anyway, sliding beneath his suit jacket to study him thoroughly. Rapid heartbeat. Formidable chest that vibrates as he snarls something into my open mouth.

He tenses the lower I go. Lower. Lower. *Jackpot.*

"Easy, *dulce niña.*" A warning exhale blows from his nostrils as my fingers find what I assume is a tailored pair of boxer briefs and… There's no mistaking what's beneath my palm. Heat. Fabric. Pulsing. Danger.

A knot in my belly tightens as I peel the cotton down bit by bit —but he was right. Watching him isn't enough. I make myself blind again, flicking my tongue along his jaw. God, it's like I can taste in his skin the things my eyes alone would never reveal. The spicy hint of excitement. The bitter tinge of irritation for not having complete control.

He is a toxin more potent than my dying oleander.

His fingers, dangerously soft, smooth over my hips, positioning me against him. The width of his knee starts to nudge my thighs apart and shock pierces through the fog in my brain.

"Easy, sweet girl." Before I can even tense, his mouth teases a moist trail from my jaw to my ear, nipping all the way. "Tell me to stop and I will," he murmurs against my earlobe.

His body advances where his mind shows restraint, however. Grasping hands drift between my legs, stroking a searing path along my inner thigh. When he slides his thumb along my core, air escapes my lungs in pitiful gasps. I writhe, drawing my knees together, easing them apart. I'm exposed to him like this, with no blindfold or distance to hide behind.

I have a first-row seat to how his nostrils twitch. My parted lips capture the hiss escaping his clenched teeth as his fingers find me slick and ready. The next kiss holds no mercy. No sanity. He gives. Takes. Bites.

"Mine," he growls, cupping my waist, urging me against him. "I knew you'd feel... *Mine*."

With my eyes closed, I find his ear again, brushing my lips against the lobe. Words escape between pants. "Please —Please—"

He's gone. I blink, finding him on his knees, wrestling with the front of his trousers, tugging them off completely. My eyes go directly to the part of him I've only felt until now.

My lips part in awe. He's beautiful. He's terrible. A thickened ridge of flesh jutting to attention. Pulsing. For me. I reach out, curling my fingers around the swollen tip—but nothing could prepare me for how he feels: silk over steel.

"Lie back." With harsh, unsteady motions, he fishes a square silver package from his pocket. "Something told me to always be prepared when it comes to you," he says as if in answer to my questioning look. Upon bringing the wrapper to his teeth, he tears it open and slides the sheath along his length. Then he cups my ass in both hands and drags me to him.

My nails pierce the flesh of his shoulders and he sinks into me with the fervor of someone ripping open their collector toy, forsaking its value.

I cry out, flinching at the unexpected burning pressure as I'm spread open around him, forced to accept every inch. All of Damien Villa.

He's in my head, shutting out the world, and the storm, and memories, and everything but this. I'm in his skin, defacing him with hairline scratches and finger-shaped bruises.

His thumb finds the bundle of nerves above where we're joined and rubs. Fire. Sparks. Pleasure gradually replaces the discomfort and he silences my gasp with heated words of Spanish, his lips fluttering over mine, coaxing them apart.

I let him in and he lunges, matching each thrust of his hips with one of his tongue. Pinching pain quickly ebbs, giving way to a toe-curling sensation I can't name. Something too raw. Too sharp. Too burning. Too *much*.

My body grips him like a vise, my knees locking around his hips, guiding every move he makes. He only goes as deep as I let him.

As fast as I need him to. It's a terrible, torturous courtesy, because I don't know what I want.

All I can do is move. And shudder. And whimper. And break.

Suddenly, he rips his mouth from mine and sinks his teeth along my jaw. "*Mierda*," he snarls, followed by a rush of grated nonsense. Promises. Threats. Dark things he wishes to do to me. Things he swears I'll *let* him do.

When he rears back for one last thrust, my hips arch to meet him, driving him so deep that I'm not sure where he ends and I begin.

Everything inside me tightens and releases like a rubber band snapping. My back bows. My eyes widen. Limp in the aftermath, I lie breathless as sanity returns in slow, fleeting snatches. I'm drenched in sweat. He has me pinned between cotton and flesh. The storm still rages around us, but his arms hold me tight, cocooning me from the rest of the world.

"Sweet...sweet girl." He's still panting. Startlingly hot fingers trace my cheek, demanding my attention. "Don't presume that this negates our agreement."

He grips me even tighter. Captured. The same way someone might lock his doll away for safekeeping until he decided to play with her again. A rumble of thunder partially obscures what he murmurs to me next. Something that should haunt whatever nightmares I dare to have.

"Exquisite. Too exquisite, sweet girl. In fact, I think I shall keep you after all..."

NINE

$\mathcal{M}$y Egyptian cotton duvet is worth fifteen hundred dollars and it doesn't compare to the comfort of being held. Heat, sweat, and Damien combined is a sensation that can't be packaged and sold. What a shame. A pleasant ache lingers in my muscles as I stretch my naked limbs, but I should feel guilt, I suppose. Disgust. Maybe those emotions would distract from the grim realization that has me opening my eyes to a dreary view of an overcast sky from beyond my windows.

I'm alone again.

A carefully folded note waits on my bedside table, but I don't bother reading it until I finally find the strength to stand.

The message is simple: *Had some business to attend to. Will return shortly.* At the bottom of the page, he painstakingly added, *PS: I have access to your medical records. I will have mine delivered.*

I swallow hard, uneasy at the implication. Not only has the bastard penetrated my life further, but he…

Well, he got what he wanted. Didn't he?

Thoughts of medical records aside, I drag myself into the shower and dress in the plainest clothing I can find: a black sweater and pants. After ripping my bedsheets from the mattress and tossing them into the hamper, I make my usual cup of coffee. Then I slam my fist into the counter so hard that I wind up crying out and clutching the damn thing to my chest.

What the hell have I done?

Why, I had sex with Damien Villa, of course. Sex with my father's archenemy while he's lying near death in a hospital bed. To put it even blunter: I gave him exactly what he wanted.

Perhaps he'll move on to the next bored, pathetic socialite? Instead of flowers today, I'll receive a calling card or two reminding me of his hate for my father outside my door.

Instead, I find a small ivory box on my welcome mat.

Inside it lies a delicate strip of pink silk covered in tiny, seemingly hand-painted roses. My fingers shake as I hold it upright. A beautiful custom blindfold sufficient enough to use in whatever game Damien may have in store for me next. I carry it and the box inside and place it somewhere within sight, remembering his promise to have my things brought to his place.

When a sharp, shrill tone cuts the silence, I barely recognize it as my cell phone. I answer it absently, but the voice on the other end snaps me from my daze.

"He's awake," Diane says through smothered sobs. "Juliana… He's finally awake."

I enter my father's hospital room unsure of what to expect. From my position near the doorway, I can tell he's still in bed. But one obvious change is impossible to miss. His eyes are open…

Only the expression in them doesn't belong to the charming, witty man I know. Dark-blue eyes sit like marbles in his skull, devoid of their usual sparkle. Instead, they're blank. Staring. Empty.

"Daddy?" I croak, inching closer.

"Juliana…" Diane rises from her vigil beside him and surreptitiously swipes at her bloodshot eyes with the sleeve of her sweater. "You came." The second I'm close enough, she throws her arms around me. "He doesn't respond much," she whispers near my ear. "He doesn't talk, but he may be able to hear you. The doctors aren't sure how long it may last… But it's progress." She smiles tearfully as if trying to convince herself of that fact. Progress.

"Daddy?" I circle around to his bed.

One of his frail, pale hands is resting over his chest, perched atop the blankets. I grab it, but he doesn't even look in my direction. Heyworth Thorne is gone, replaced by a shell.

Or the worst kind of villain: a helpless one. It's as if his goddamn soul is determined to withhold answers from me. Or punish me.

"I know this isn't the right moment," Diane says, lifting something from the bedside table: a stack of documents. "But just in case… You should be prepared. It's his will," she explains, holding the documents out to me. "Thank God we finalized it before—" She breaks off, clearing her throat. "I want you to look it over so that you aren't surprised if the worst comes to fruition."

"S-Surprised?" I scan the document, steeling myself for the worst scenarios my paranoia can dream up. Plenty. Perhaps he cut me out. He never intended to leave me a dime, not that the money matters in the grand scheme. If anything, a legal, binding document will prove that I was always his daughter merely for show. But as I scan the first lines, I shake my head. "This can't be right."

"It is," Diane insists, her eyes welling with tears. "We discussed it beforehand. It's what he wanted. But I think, all things considered, you should have access to some items now. I've already cleared it with the lawyer. They're highlighted there. A safety deposit box he had. I'm not sure what's in it, but you should have access to it."

I blink, fighting to resist how my eyes are burning. "I don't know what to say."

"There's something else." Diane grabs my arm.

For the first time, I sense how her fingers are shaking. Her distress takes on a new connotation; perhaps the tears aren't solely related to my father's condition.

"There might be tighter security when you come back. Family only. The police have opened an investigation. After the doctors ran more tests, they think the stroke may have been exacerbated by something."

"Exacerbated? Like..." I parse the clinical term and can only come up with one comparable to it. "He was poisoned?"

Her lips purse, her face pale. "I don't know. With all of the other reports... I'm terrified, Juliana. I know your father wanted extra security on you before he—"

"I'll be fine." I squeeze her hand reassuringly. "And I'll be back. I just..."

Need to breakdown, alone in a back stairwell, where no one can hear me sob openly into my palm. I thought Heyworth Thorne's death would be the hardest reality to face—but this is worse. So much worse. He's still here, his face the familiar one of my childhood hero. But in those blank, soulless eyes, all I saw was my reflection. My face. My guilt. This is all my fault.

He's gone because of me.

And a part of me still hates him for it.

TEN

*W*ith the city in turmoil over my father's recent scandal and subsequent health issues, there is only one place I can escape to find some semblance of peace.

I try not to feel guilty for invading it. As long as I inhale deeply, relishing the scent of hundreds of blooming flowers, it's surprisingly easy to. Peace seems attainable here—as long as I ignore the fact that I'm an intruder in this unique parallel universe. Its owner may make an exception for me though—for a price.

"I never allow anyone in here," he declares as he advances through the greenhouse, toward the section I'm standing in, sandwiched between nightshade and oleander. "And Julio usually abides by that rule. He must like you to risk upsetting me."

"Or he could just pity me. I'm crying," I say casually before he can deduce as much himself. "I'm upset. I'm...I'm a mess—"

"Because your father is awake."

It's pointless to ask how he knows that. Where my family is concerned, he seems to know everything.

"He is awake. If you can call it that." I finger the very edge of a petal of oleander, comparing the fresh bloom to the dying one in my apartment. The contrast is a stark parallel to my father's health: vitality vs. decay. "He couldn't even look at me. He can't speak. The doctors don't know if he'll ever fully recover. In fact, they're prepared for the worst." I rustle the documents clutched in my opposite fist. "Diane even gave me his will, just in case."

"I'm sorry," Damien says. His steps continue their slow, steady advance and I hate how my heart lurches at his presence. It's dangerous to grow attached to him. To need him. To crave the touch he runs along my lower back in quiet reassurance. "You may have full access to my legal team should you need their assistance."

"You don't understand. He left me everything." I can barely get the words out. "Everything. The house. His money. I don't understand. Did he love me or not? Was I his daughter or a trophy?"

Damien doesn't answer.

"The police think he may have been poisoned," I add. "Targeted by the same bad luck affecting every high-profile official who worked on your brother's case. They were even at my suite yesterday. Invading my privacy in the name of safety—"

"If this is an accusation..." He trails his thumb up to my neck, following the path of my throat. "It is a rather polite one, I must say. As far as cold-blooded murder is concerned, I've been accused of far worse with much less tact."

"Please." I squeeze my eyes shut, sensing every smooth, silken dip in the pad of his finger. "Don't lie to me," I beg. "You said you wanted honesty from me—but I need it from you."

"*Sí*," he agrees. "But first I must ask you directly: Do you really think that I would resort to murdering Heyworth Thorne, knowing how much he means to you still?"

It's a dangerous question and I loathe the way he asked it: in a strained, cautious tone. Like my answer matters to him more than anything else.

Even revenge.

"You hate him," I explain. "Maybe you have a good reason to. But if you care about me, even a fraction, you'd know…he's all I have." Fresh tears well in my eyes and spill down my cheeks, impossible to stop. "He's all I have. I can't lose him. I can't—"

"He had a reputation on the bench, especially back then," Damien says gruffly. "For being fair. Just. A judge who would hear all facts and rule with honesty."

I force myself to nod. *That* is the Heyworth Thorne I grew up with—a man admired in his interpretation of the law.

"But as I sat in that courtroom, with Mathias' life at stake, I saw a different man," Damien confesses, his tone level. The deliberate lack of anger somehow makes his words cut deeper. "A reckless tyrant too interested in bold headlines to actually listen. To fucking see. *Sí*, I saw a fraud too prideful to make the judgment the facts demanded."

"The jury convicted him," I point out. "My father would have upheld it. He wouldn't overrule a guilty verdict."

"I have the case files," he says. "I'll let you read them."

And in some ways, it's a more terrifying prospect than having him try to convince me on his own. More words. More exposed lies. Can I handle them?

"But not tonight. I've humored you enough. You need to eat. I'm taking you to dinner."

"Oh?" I incline my head to view him from over my shoulder. "Is that a command?"

"No." His lips twitch, fighting a smile. "Think of it as more of a request. A stern request in the interest of your welfare. And some selfishness as well. We need to discuss what happened last night."

"Hmm?" I feign ignorance. "About the storm?"

He smiles for real, but there's no warmth in it. An intensity wafts from him instead, more unnerving than his polished, suave charm. "I'd prefer to discuss the sex, if you don't mind."

I cough, clearing my throat. "I—"

"I would like to extend our arrangement as well," he says over me. "In case you thought I desired only your virginity."

"You don't?" I ask hoarsely. "I mean…you didn't?"

"*Sí.*" He frowns, stroking his chin with the tip of his thumb. "It seems I desire more when it comes to you than initially anticipated."

"Like what?"

"Well…" He circles my position, allowing one of his hands to molest a budding flower as he goes. "I'd very much like to feel my cock inside of you again, for one."

"Oh?" I squeak as fire sears my cheeks. "How bold of you to say, Mr. Villa."

"*Sí.*" He takes another step in my direction. "Bold. As is the fact that I know you enjoyed feeling said cock inside of you. In fact…" He's close enough now to cup my cheek with his palm, tilting my face into his touch. "I believe I've discovered a more enticing conquest than your innocence."

A second's pause is my cue to reply.

"W-What?"

"Your fear of the dark." His nostrils flare as if chasing that elusive prize. "Oh, *sí*, I want to take it," he tells me. "Own it. Shape it. You will never hear another thunderstorm without thinking of me."

I close my eyes as the full extent of his promise resonates. No more fear. No night terrors. No Simon.

"And if I refuse?" I wonder, daring to open my eyes again. He's still here, alarmingly intent. This isn't a dream. Painfully real, his heat assaults my skin, awakening parts of me I've felt stir only at his touch. His whim.

"I don't think you will," he says, confident. "In fact, I think you might enjoy this conquest more than the first."

I draw in a ragged breath at the memory. The slickness of his skin. The friction between us. The way the world faded, reduced to him alone.

"I should have you sussed by now. In fact, sex should have concluded my interest in you," he adds, the grit in his tone drawing me from my thoughts. "And yet, at every damn turn, you…confound me."

Confound? I bite my lip against a retort. I'm sure he has no trouble sensing my emotions regardless. My chest is heaving against the barely-there barrier of my clothing, my breaths fanning the air.

"I'm reckless with you," he adds as warm breath nudges my throat, alluding to just how close he is now. "You make me… impulsive when I should have a steadying hand. And you know damn well what I mean."

He stills right when another gained inch would press him against me—yet he's near enough for me to inhale his scent and exhale resolve.

"Do I?"

"*Sí.*" Rare tension sows ripples through his polished baritone. "I expected you quivering and fearful beneath me. Maybe then I could draw the real woman lurking behind the polished façade. I'd make her talk to me."

His hands smooth up my spine from behind, locking me into place. With only a thin bit of fabric as a shield, my body is his plaything. Trembling. Alight. Ignoring my commands to run.

"I'm tired of being afraid, Mr. Villa," I say.

"As if you ever were. Last night, I realized the truth."

I stiffen as his lips ghost the side of my throat, beneath my ratty hair.

"I've been sending you the wrong flower, Ms. Thorne. You're no rose—you're a vine. You grow there in the midst of the weeds, your stem slightly crooked, your petals lacking the uniform nature of all the other flowers. At a glance, you look like the rest. But if someone were to feel…"

He performs that very action as the words leave his throat, sliding his hands up my back, cinching the thin material of my dress beneath his fingers. "They'd realize the truth. Your thorns are sharper. Your petals are softer. Your smell is different." His fingers shake. Grasping. Pulling.

Focusing on his words is hard enough, let alone keeping my balance. I sway.

"I could spend years painting you and never learn more than I did last night just by being inside of you."

Does that infuriate him? Yes. I can hear the scowl in his voice. Damien Villa, the artist so used to deciphering his subjects and throwing them away. I confound him.

But he mystifies me.

"I may even rethink my boundary when it comes to the club," he adds, his voice lowering, just for me to hear. "I could fuck you in front of them all. Let them see: I'm the only man who will know how it feels to have you come on his cock. Like heaven." His palm flexes against my cheek as the thumb of his opposite hand grazes my lower lip. "Exquisite."

I'm too breathless to question. Speak. Inhale. All I can do is savor the sensation of his heat on my skin. His breath mingling with mine. The growl he bites down as I step into him, letting him feel every inch I can press into his flesh.

"Beautiful girl," he praises, his lips grazing my ear before drifting lower. "Beautiful, sweet…*mine.*" With a predatory intent, he finds the exposed flesh, raking with his teeth. Grasping with his nails.

A moan slips from my lips, my head falling back.

It's like he's aware of every sordid thought before I even think it. His mouth finds mine easily. As if he memorized the distance. He exhales at the taste of me, slipping his tongue between my lips. Drinking me in. One word grated against my mouth reveals his impression.

"Maddening. The way you sound… It's sinful. I can tell from one note if you are in pain. Pleasure. Ecstasy. No one else has such range."

As if to prove it, his hand finds my breast, stroking the aching peak through chafing cotton.

"I knew from the moment I heard your voice—really heard it— that I was going to count the many ways I could make you scream."

Another kiss drowns me in him. His scent. His touch. He steers me back until I'm trapped between him and a wall of glass, his to devour. Consume.

"And your smell," he breathes as his hand travels lower, dancing down my belly, hunting for the hem of my dress. "It's so damn easy to tell when you're aroused."

He succeeds in lifting my skirt, finding my thigh without preamble. Featherlight caresses track his progress upward, nearing the space between my legs. I stiffen. He pounces, plunging a finger beneath the gusset of my panties.

"*Sí*," he croaks, inhaling the air while curling his finger in the same cruel motion. "It's like you were designed for me. To entice me. To challenge me. To humble me... You've punished me, haven't you?" He practically hisses the words. "Every sin. Every transgression. You've made me repent."

His thumb roughly encircles me—my only warning before he plunges the tip between my folds. My sharp cry almost drowns out his next words.

"*Dulce niña.*" He slides his hand around to my back and the faint hum of a zipper sounds as the fabric of my dress loosens. Falls. Exposes.

Trembling knees threaten to collapse beneath me. I grab his shoulders tighter, marveling at the ease with which he supports me. One hand braced against my ass allows him to steady me while guiding my hips against his at the same time.

A gasp rips from my throat at the dangerous pressure kicking against my belly. He returns his attention to exploring my body, his touch bolder. He spreads my legs apart, tracing soft, nonsensical patterns into my inner thigh. The gentleness with which he does so sends my already drifting thoughts scattering further. There's reverence in his touch and I have an uncomfortable inkling why so many women have been willing to strip naked for him in the first place.

Someone else could never offer this level of intimacy. A vulnerability found only by having a stranger peer beneath your skin with every stroke.

I close my eyes, savoring the small nuances he can't disguise. The low grunts interspersed with his breaths. The pulsing heat. The thick fingers tangling in my hair, making knots and chaos in the strands. Eyesight would only be a hindrance to him—because without it, he has no trouble sensing the secrets within I've hidden from myself. Sex extends to more than physical pleasure where he is concerned.

It's knowledge.

It's power.

It's primal.

"You wanted to be kept, and I've decided…that I'm keeping you." He slips an arm around my waist, wrenching me even closer.

My legs part as he muscles in between them. My knees capture his waist, holding tight—and I've surrendered to his strength completely.

"Maybe I would have played your game before," he admits before grinding his lips into mine, marking them. "Perhaps. I'd let you go. Let you taunt me like you have. I could withstand it."

"And now?" I'm copying him, grazing my lips along his jaw in return, sensing the barest hint of stubble.

"Too late." He sounds almost as if he pities me. "I want too much, so I'll take all of you."

"By spying on me again?" How I've formed a coherent reply, I'll never know.

"I won't have to."

Oh? A morbidly amusing thought comes to mind, even as my thoughts dissipate as he slides his fingers along my core and mutters something that makes my cheeks flame. Something about *wet*, mingled with broken words in Spanish. "Will you tie a bell around me?"

He laughs. "Maddening woman with maddening ideas."

He finds my panties again and tugs them aside. Every slow, deliberate stroke he inflicts reminds me of a musician playing an instrument only he bothered to learn how to tune.

And I'm pathetic enough to beg for more. "Damien." My lips seek out his earlobe. "Please…"

His breath stutters. The hum of a zipper pierces the air and then he's inside me. Sharp, sweet pleasure instantly displaces any pain. God, he feels so raw from this angle. There's nothing between us but sweat and skin. I can feel his heartbeat hammering a melody mine has no choice but to match.

Thump.

Stutter.

Thump.

He goes more slowly than any man has the right to, sensing every curve and ridge of my body, learning me inside and out. Too thoroughly. It's a violation I never in a million years thought I'd crave.

Teeth gritted, thighs clenched, I let him explore, thrust after deliberate thrust.

Far too soon, he loses his polish, gripping me hard enough to leave marks. Bruises. Brands.

Hissed words of Spanish meet their doom in the crook of my shoulder as his body tenses, slamming into mine and knocking the air from my lungs. God, the friction…

I'm ashes beneath the onslaught. Fire. Heat. Sin.

My world is a collage of sensation of blinding white.

Then silence and a slow descent back to reality.

"Damn," he grates between panting breaths as my senses reassemble. "That's not quite how I imagined the second time we met like this would unfold, Ms. Thorne."

My heart flutters, walking that dangerous line between dread and excitement. "What…what do you mean?"

He laughs, and any doubts are shattered. "I'd thought for sure we'd at least make it to the goddamn bed."

"*I* should be taken out and shot," Damien growls as his fingers dance along the flat of my belly. As if supplying accompanying percussion, a series of garbled, protesting noises rumble from it. "You're starving." He sighs against the back of my throat. "Perhaps I should have insisted on dinner first after all?"

I echo his sigh and lean further into him, relishing the feel of his chest against the curves of my back. Given the warm temperature of the greenhouse, his heat should be an unwelcome addition— but I shift closer, aching to extend the burn of his flesh on mine. Even the floor, slightly damp from the humidity, feels more comfortable than it has any right to.

"I don't want to move," I admit, cringing from the idea of putting my dress on and reentering the real world. Or pretending that what just happened didn't. "I want to lie here naked and never get up again."

"Never?" he wonders in a throaty chuckle. "May I propose a compromise?"

More like an ultimatum, it seems as he pulls away. I turn to watch him sit upright in a graceful arrangement of limbs. Seemingly from nowhere, he withdraws a headset from the tangled mass of clothing beside us.

"Julio," he says into the device. Spanish deepens the distance between us as he dishes out what I assume are a multitude of commands. Then he sets the headset aside and reaches toward our clothing again. "You do not have to move," he says, "But I would like you covered *por favor*."

He feels through the fabric and retrieves not my crumpled dress but his tailored suit jacket. Sitting up, I shudder as he drapes me in the fabric, easily maneuvering my arms into the sleeves.

He doesn't extend the same modesty to himself, however, not even as Julio calls from the door minutes later.

"Sir?"

"Yes," Damien replies. "The atrium, if you please."

Heavy footsteps advance across the far end of the greenhouse, but I never see the faithful bodyguard enter this section at least. A few moments later, the steps retreat.

"All done, sir."

"Thank you, Julio." Once he's sure his servant is gone, Damien stands and extends his hand toward me. "Slight movement, I'm afraid," he admits. "But I promise it will be well worth the effort."

I grasp his hand and allow him to pull me to my feet. Showing no concern for our discarded clothing, he starts forward, fearlessly navigating the aisles of flowers. I notice his hand feeling along the various stands, orienting himself, I suspect. But there's an unmistakable familiarity that makes me envision him spending so much time in here that he's memorized every inch.

"How is this for compromise?" he wonders as we reach the threshold of a large, open space beyond the main greenhouse. The same area he brought me the first time we had dinner here. Then, it served as a makeshift pizza parlor—and a chilling backdrop to a lurid conversation revolving around my virginity and his insane brother Mateo.

Now, the place reads Damien Villa down to the black tablecloth draped over a wooden table, laden with steaming plates.

"Five-star French restaurant to go?" I inquire, eyeing the pastries and extravagant cuisine.

He laughs and advances toward the table, angling one of the chairs toward me.

Once we're seated, we eat in relative silence, him unabashedly naked still. Observing him now reveals more than ever before. He lazily munches on the end of a croissant, but his true focus is tracing the veins on the back of the hand I have braced on the table.

"You are so beautiful," he murmurs heatedly. "*Hermosa niña—*"

"How can you tell?" I blurt, only to realize how rude it sounds. "I mean… Are you merely aiming to flatter me, Mr. Villa?"

"No." His tone dips an octave, suddenly serious. He captures my hand entirely, lifting it for his physical inspection. His thumb grazes the flat of my palm as if the divots and swirls there can tell him all he needs to know. "Your body is a masterpiece. One I hope to explore in full."

"You do still owe me a painting," I point out.

He laughs. "Yes." He lifts his head in my direction. "And answers. You can demand them from me now, if you want."

"No," I say, surprising myself. "Not now. Tomorrow. Just let me have a few more hours of pretending if it's not too much trouble."

"Trouble?" He brings my hand to his lips, pressing them along my knuckles. "Never."

"Let's just hope we aren't interrupted this time," I say. The way his jaw twitches is the only clue I need to know I've said the wrong thing. "I'm sorry—"

"Don't be." A heart-stopping grimace twists his lips, part frown, part...smile? "Mateo is, let's just say slow to warm to new people. He was always that way. But there is no malice in his hostility." He shrugs, his jaw softening a fraction. "In some aspects, he is like a child. Painfully demanding, but affectionate to those who earn it. Though it seems he is more of the former around me lately."

"He made you trade him something to stay away from me," I surmise, licking my lips. "Didn't he?"

His head shoots up, cocked to the side. "It seems I didn't give him enough."

"Did you?" I press.

"Perhaps." A muscle in his neck flutters, and he shakes his head. "Fine. I gave him control over a facet of our mutual business arrangements. Let's leave it at that."

I look down, eyeing the table as an uncomfortable sensation floods my belly. Gratitude? "You didn't have to—"

"You don't know Mateo," he says over me. "It appears we both have complicated relationships with our family members, ¿sí?"

"That sounds…relatable," I admit, fighting to sound cordial.

"Pardon the cliché, but I would blame our upbringing," Damien admits. "Our father was not an easy man to live with. Mateo learned that more than most."

"Oh?"

"What is a polite way to say… He favored corporal punishment."

"I'm sorry."

"Again, you do not have to be. It wasn't a terrible life in a sense. I'm grateful for it."

"H-How did you leave?"

A thoughtful grunt catches in his throat. "Our mother was American. So my brothers and I had dual citizenship through her —making us technically citizens, not immigrants. The media tends to skew some facts." His cold, quick smile takes my breath away. A heartbeat later, it's gone, smothered into a flattened line.

"You grew up in Colombia though," I point out, recalling what my father mentioned. "Supposedly, Mr. Villa, you are linked to the drug trade."

"*Sí*, supposedly," he admits. "My father owned a ranch of sorts. We tended the fields. He grew an array of unusual crops. Only later did I realize that the plants we grew supplied a criminal enterprise. Allegedly, of course."

Like his supposed links to cocaine.

"I'm sure you did what you had to do to survive," I say carefully. "I know what that's like."

"Oh?" He chuckles. "Maybe I've lost that ruthless drive. After all, I've just alluded to illegal activity in front of the daughter of an ex-judge."

He expertly mingles fact with the veiled threat. Though a part of me suspects it's more of a test. He's deliberately spoon-feeding me key bits of information that, if leaked to the press, don't confirm or deny the rumors. Smart man. Perhaps too smart.

"I think you're calculating, Mr. Villa," I tell him truthfully, still tracing an invisible path over the back of his hand. "You wouldn't let anything compromising slip around a potential threat, no matter how much you may enjoy getting her naked."

"Ah, but that's where you're wrong, Ms. Thorne. It seems I repeatedly find myself saying things around you that I shouldn't."

"Like?"

"For instance, would you believe that I have never mentioned my past to anyone?" His tone lowers in an accusatory fashion. Like I'm to blame for his slip of the tongue. "Even in such admittedly sparse detail."

"You mean you've never told your past women"—I deliberately pick three names at random—"Christina, Babina, and Martina, about your childhood?"

"No." He slides his hand from beneath mine only to capture my fingers entirely. As I watch, he runs his thumb along my palm. "I haven't. They never held my interest beyond what I sought to learn from them."

Learn. A nice way of phrasing sex. "And what about me? Do I hold your interest?"

He frowns as if hating his answer before it even leaves his mouth. "I'm afraid to admit that you have my full attention."

"For now," I say coyly. "But who knows how long that may last? Maybe as long as one of your pretty roses?"

"I'm afraid not." His grip tightens. "If only it were that simple, Ms. Thorne." He stands.

I balk. His free hand brushes the table for guidance as he circles it toward me, and a tug on my wrist urges me to my feet. One ruthless yank pulls me close and his lips flutter over mine. Once. Twice. On the third brush, mine fall open by accident, letting him in. Urging him deeper. My fingers are in his hair before I can help myself. God, it's softer than his skin. Like silk. Vaguely, I'm aware of the edge of the table striking my hip as he steers me to face him. Before I realize it, I'm sliding back onto the ledge.

"Wait." I break the kiss, panting for air. "S-Stop."

He does, his breath feathering my throat in heavy, unsteady bursts as I curl my fingers around his biceps, intending to shove him off. Clear my head. Think. He muscles in closer instead. Silverware scatters, sliding dangerously close to the table's edge.

"I'm merely following your rules, Ms. Thorne," he says into my throat. "You desire to be kept—as well as distracted. I aim to oblige."

ELEVEN

I wake up twisted within the silk sheets of that infamous red room. As my eyes open, the mirror on the ceiling paints my appearance in stark relief: swollen, bitten lips, a nest of hair, and a hollow, sallow face.

My phone is ringing. It has been almost nonstop for the past five minutes, but I can't seem to move to grab it. At least not until the millionth ring when I finally crawl off the mattress.

"Juliana," Diane says when I answer, her voice strained. "We… Can you come to the hospital? We need to talk."

"What's happened?" Fear rides a wave of nausea threatening to escape from my throat. "Is he—"

"No, no, your father is fine," she says quickly. "It's just… There are some arrangements we need to go over. Just come down when you can."

After hanging up, I shower and then dress in the plainest items of clothing to be found in Damien's mocking wardrobe: a white shirt and beige slacks. As I enter the foyer, I don't find him lounging on the leather chaise or lurking in the corners.

But on a table near the door, someone left a gray folder with a single rose draped across it. Printed in ominous black font are the words *Borgetta Murder Case*. Swallowing hard, I tuck the file beneath my arm and slip the rose behind my ear.

Ten minutes later, I'm racing down the hall outside my father's hospital room, my stomach in knots. Inside, Diane is sitting beside Daddy's bed, his hand in hers. He lies motionless, his eyes open and unseeing—but standing nearby is a tall, mustached man I don't recognize.

At least not until Diane says, "This is Chief Harrison, Juliana. A good friend of your father's." Her strained, uneasy smile makes me force one in return.

"Hello, chief." I step forward, vaguely pairing the man's stern features with a face I've only seen in the papers or on the periphery of Daddy's lavish political gatherings throughout the years.

He has a relatively prominent family from what I recall. His son is a promising lawyer, his wife a defense attorney. Dressed formally, he certainly matches his job title. A brown trench coat hangs open to reveal the badge pinned to his crisp white dress shirt, and the faint hint of cigar smoke tinges his imposing frame. My nostrils wrinkle and I can't shake a chilling sense of déjà vu. Maybe I'm forgetting a more recent meeting?

"Juliana." He extends his hand for mine and shakes it before I can ponder my memories further. "I'm so sorry to hear about what happened. My men and I are doing all we can to help."

"The police would like your permission to secure your apartment, darling," Diane says, cutting to the chase. "They've already been at the house. For our safety."

"S-Safety?" I raise an eyebrow.

"Yes." Chief Harrison steps back, his eyes downcast. "I'm sorry to be the one to tell you this, Juliana, but your father's physicians believe that his stroke may have been caused by something he could have ingested—they aren't sure what yet. But I want to assure you that we are doing our best to get to the bottom of it."

"The tests haven't come back yet," Diane explains as we turn to daddy in unison. "But your father would want you safe."

"That's why your officers were at my suite the other day?" I ask, fighting to keep the suspicion from my tone. "For my safety?"

"I apologize if their presence alarmed you," the chief says. "But given your recent association with Damien Villa, I know your father would want your security to be of the utmost priority."

I swallow hard and struggle to keep my tone cordial. "My association?" Judging from the barely concealed hostility in his tone, this man shares the same view of Damien that my father did. *Does.* "Is he a suspect?"

"I didn't mean to insult you," Chief Harrison says, but his expression doesn't reveal an ounce of contrition. His eyes rake over me, lingering near my throat and the pearl hanging there. "I know your father tended to shelter you. You can't be blamed for not understanding just how dangerous such a man may be. Even I am forced to mingle with him on occasion."

"Because of rumors?" I innocently question.

He smiles. "Tell me. Have you ever heard of *La Muerte*?"

I shake my head. "No, I haven't."

"As you wouldn't. You're a smart woman, but I doubt you've spent much time researching Colombian gangs. It means the order of the death," he says. "One of the more dangerous outfits to operate below the border. In fact, one of its former leaders was rumored to have run something of a cult—killed a few years ago."

"Interesting," I manage to croak.

"Very," Harrison agrees. "Even more interesting is the fact that some of the rumors state that the Villa boys are none other than that man's sons, continuing their legacy so to speak. And if that rumor has any merit to it at all, you have no idea what such a family may be capable of."

But maybe he's wrong. Damien himself alluded to that very possibility: *Maybe I've lost that ruthless drive.*

"This is all a precaution, Juliana," Diane insists. "Just in case."

"I should be going anyway." Chief Harrison nods toward Diane and extends his hand in my direction. "I'll keep in touch, Juliana. I hope to see you at the gala as well." His grip tightens harder than I expect as he swiftly shakes my hand and then releases it. "Best of luck."

I watch him go, rubbing the hand he touched against my pants. It's throbbing.

"Gala?" I ask, looking back at Diane.

"That's what I wanted to talk to you about," she admits, wringing her slim fingers together. "Chief Harrison offered to stand in, but I think you should. You should represent your father at the annual Wellington benefit gala."

The Wellington family has a long history in the city's political landscape. I think one of them was a presidential candidate, and several have served as senators or prominent businessmen. The last one to make a mark is the youngest son of their last influential patriarch: a man more inclined to dole out money to politicians than mingle among them. He died a few years back of a heart attack, but Daddy still attended every year, kissing up to the executors of his estate.

"I've never been," I say thickly. "He never took me."

"It's tomorrow night," Diane says. "Your father was a headliner. He planned to secure donations—" She breaks off, swallowing hard. "Please. *You* should represent him. It's what he—no, it's what I want. Please, Juliana."

I've never seen her like this, her eyes bloodshot, her hands trembling.

"All right." I step forward and carefully throw my arms around her, hugging her tight. "I'll go. Don't worry."

She squeezes me in return. "Thank you. Thank you. I know he'd... Thank you. And"—she pulls back and swipes a wayward lock of hair away from my face—"I hope whatever your father left for you gave you some ounce of closure."

I lower my gaze to my purse, remembering the documents tucked inside it. "I haven't gone yet," I admit. "But I will."

*J*ulio is waiting for me at the hospital's private entrance, standing beside the car. Without complaint, I enter the back seat, but as the faithful bodyguard takes the wheel, I clear my throat.

"Damien put you in charge of my security," I start, settling my hands primly on my lap.

"*Sí.*" The man shoots me a wary glance from the corner of his eye. "Can I help you with anything, Ms. Thorne?"

"I want to take a detour," I propose. "A detour without getting approval from your boss first. A *personal* detour that I'm informing you about rather than running off on my own."

"So, if I may ask, why are you?" Amusement laces Julio's otherwise professional tone.

A smile tugs on my mouth as well—at least until I mull over his question. "Because I'm scared," I admit, turning to stare out the window as the city streets pass in a blur. "I'm terrified, enough that I would rather not shun one of the few people capable of protecting me."

"So where to, Ms. Thorne?"

I bite back a sigh of relief. Will he really keep this quiet? I have no choice but to take the risk. "A bank," I say, fishing a stack of documents from my purse. "Here is the address."

He nods, and moments later, we arrive in front of an upscale establishment in the heart of the city. When I approach a woman at the front desk, she eyes me warily until I say what must be the magic words.

"I'm Juliana Thorne. My father has a security deposit box here?"

"Oh, yes! Your mother called the other day." She rummages through a desk drawer and withdraws a small silver key, which she places within my reach. "They're in the alcove just past the security guard. The number is on the key."

I follow her instructions, my heart racing as I wonder what could be inside the harmless structure. Each security deposit box is small, built into the wall, and no larger than a shoebox. Nearby, other people hunch over their private sections, rummaging through their belongings before locking them away.

When I finally gather the nerve to open my father's box, I don't find a glaring item labeled *Evidence of Simon*. In fact, the only items here to discover are a genuine diamond necklace belonging to his first wife, Bethany, who died when I was nine, and legal documents that look like they pertain to the ownership of the house and other properties. Frowning, I strain on tiptoe and slide my hand over the inside of the box. Just when I start to withdraw it, my fingers strike something soft and crinkly—a single piece of paper.

It's a handwritten note, but one penned hastily on official letterhead. It's old and weathered, but I can make out the barely legible font of the city's precinct underneath a logo. *J. Mirangas*, someone wrote. *Age 8. Morrison, PA. 10/28.*

A wave of nausea washes over me and I have to brace my hand against the wall and close my eyes to steel myself against the onslaught. The page is a crumpled mass in my fist, but I can't loosen my grip. I can't even breathe.

My name. Someone from this police department—in another state, let alone jurisdiction from my old hometown—gave Heyworth information on my case. Supposedly, he was asked to consult by the Morrison police chief. So why would another official from a city hours away have written my name down on a paper destined to collect dust in Heyworth Thorne's private bank?

"Miss?" The security guard outside of the alcove stands in the doorway, watching me. "Are you okay?"

"I'm fine." Forcing a smile, I return everything to the deposit box and lock it. "Can I keep the key?" I ask the girl at the front desk, who nods.

"Sure! Access to the alcove is available twenty-four-seven," she chirps. "Just present your ID to the guard."

"Any more detours, Ms. Thorne?" Julio inquires as I meet him beside the car.

"Not at the moment," I say while climbing into the back seat. I wait for him to reclaim the wheel before I add, "But can I trust you to keep this little trip between us?"

Even more so now. Not because I don't trust Damien with what little information I learned, but I don't think I can say it out loud and parse its meaning. Not now. I don't even have the energy to flip through the file he left for me, either; it's still lying untouched on the seat.

"We might have an agreement," Julio says, surprising me. "But in return, I will need a favor from you."

"Oh?" I bite my lip, curious about what someone seemingly so loyal could want in return for deceiving his boss.

"You may have noticed that it is...easy to forget Mr. Villa's physical limitations," he says. "¿*Sí*?"

I nod. "He does seem fairly capable."

"And in some ways, it is easy to forget that he is not invincible. Human. I think even he has forgotten that at times."

I picture the suave, confident artist and find myself agreeing.

"Being around you is good for him," Julio admits. "He's had several women he's strung along—but you are the only one who talks to him like he is a man. The only one who punishes him when he upsets you and makes him seek your forgiveness. You challenge him, and I think he needs that more than anything. Friction. Resistance. Challenge. It makes him remember how to interact."

"Because he's used to getting his way," I surmise, recalling Chief Harrison's not-so-subtle insinuation.

"You see a different side of him," he admits. "A side I'd almost forgotten existed. The other Mr. Villa..." He makes a low sound in his throat and shakes his head. "Trust me, he is a man you have not seen, and you do not want to."

But maybe I have. A man who sent me oleander as a warning and broke into my apartment when he assumed I'd insulted him by merely buying his painting.

"He can be dangerous," I say thickly. "Can't he?"

"Can't we all?" He shrugs. "I like to think of him as not cruel, but transactional. So many people demand so much of him…he's come to see the world as a game, where he must be on his guard at all times."

"Demand," I echo. "Like who? His brother?" It's a stab in the dark. One that seems to hit a bull's-eye.

"Mateo," he hisses. "You'd do best to never interact with him."

So he isn't aware of Mateo's impromptu meeting after all.

"Mateo is dangerous," he adds. "In this world, he only sees himself. No one else."

"Why are you telling me this?" I feel my eyebrows furrow. "As secretive as Damien is, I doubt he'd approve of his loyal bodyguard spilling even a hint of his personal life."

Which means that this is about more than a petty bribe for his silence.

"Because I want you to understand," Julio says, proving as much. "If he hurts you—Mr. Villa—and he may—don't forgive him easily, if you decide to at all. Make him earn it. Make him feel it. I fear that may be the only way for him to learn, *sí.*"

"Learn what?"

He cocks his head to look back at me, forsaking the road. "The risk," he says before turning away. "The risk that comes with losing something you value due to your own actions—when no amount of money in the world can salvage the damage. The only way to fix it is to open your heart."

"And you think he might hurt me?" I question.

"*Sí.* He will—*mierda!*" He slams his fists onto the horn as a car cuts in front of us. Growling through his teeth, he adds, "But he will not mean to, that I am sure of. I doubt he will even realize it."

It's an ominous warning. One that resonates as I watch the cityscape pass in a collage of flashing streetlights and oblivious people.

A warning that, oddly enough, doesn't make me feel threatened. More like…

Resigned. Because deep down, maybe a part of me has known all along that whatever exists between me and Damien was doomed from the start. Even his brother felt obligated to warn me.

And perhaps there is a twisted peace in that.

TWELVE

*J*ulio escorts me to the penthouse suite and ushers me inside. There, Damien is sitting in the living room, on a leather chaise positioned near the windows. If I didn't know better, I'd assume his pensive posture was due to appreciation of the amazing view of the city bathed in amber sunlight.

"How do you feel?" he wonders without moving from his relaxed position: legs outstretched, arms sprawled out beside him. It's such a contrast to his usual poised rigidity that I'd smile if his expression weren't so stern.

"I'm fine," I lie, placing his untouched file back where I found it this morning. Shadow drapes the cover, adding an ominous aura to the truths it may contain.

"Your father's condition is stable," he says, deploying his uncanny knowledge of my every move.

Intentionally? A hard swallow can't displace my unease. Does Julio really intend to keep our little secret? Something I sensed in his tone holds the paranoia at bay—concern. Damien may be his employer, but he cares about him.

"The doctors seem convinced he may recover with little complications," Damien adds.

"For now," I agree, crossing the room to join him. The moment I sit, his hand finds mine, placing it on the ridge of his knee. "But there is an open investigation. They think...he may have been poisoned."

It feels so strange to say it out loud. So surreal. For all of my father's obsessive paranoia, I never truly believed something like this could happen. That someone could want him dead.

How ironic that a prime suspect might be seated beside me.

Damien's grip tightens as if he's sensing my thoughts. "You can accuse me, if it helps," he suggests, admitting as much. "But trust me when I say I did not harm your father. Not in this instance."

I raise an eyebrow. "This instance?"

A muscle in his jaw lurches as he turns my hand so the palm is upright. "I may have attempted to persuade his donors away from supporting him," he confesses. "I may have mounted an ad campaign to thwart his chances at reelection. And I *may* be funding his opposition..."

"But?" I prompt, sensing one.

A sudden tightness hardens his expression. "But I would never kill him."

And I want to believe that, more than I have the right to.

"You did not read the file," he adds, catching me off guard.

"I..."

"I'm not insulted," he says. "It's funny. Something told me you wouldn't."

"Because I need to hear it from you." I shift, gently detangling my hand from his. In the same motion, I run my fingers along his jaw, amazed at just how welcoming he can feel. Beneath the cold, sometimes ominous demeanor, he's silk under my fingertips, a wealth of contradictions. "So tell me. What happened to Mathias?"

"We should start with Emily Borgetta," he suggests, tilting his chin into my touch. "A beautiful, if flirtatious, young girl with a wealth of besotted suitors at her disposal. Heirs to various fortunes, diplomats, the son of a police chief, even. As the daughter of a prominent businessman, the world was at her disposal. At least until the day she was found murdered in her apartment, possibly raped. Nothing was stolen, therefore making the crime far more heinous: personal in nature."

"Your brother was the only suspect," I say, scouring what few shreds of information I know about the case. "They were dating."

"He wasn't the only suspect." As if settling in for a long story, Damien rearranges himself, leaning back into the cushions of the chaise. His hand finds mine again, gripping tighter in a subtle way that warns I won't break free easily. "She had other suitors. Other men in her life who were questioned. But *Mathias* was the only one arrested, the poor *malparido* immigrant—at least that's what the reporters crowed. Even if he was a citizen as much as the rest. Even if there was no DNA linking him to the crime. No real conclusive *evidence*. Out of the rich, white suspects, he had the brownest skin."

"But there was enough there that a jury found him guilty," I point out.

"Guilty," he agrees. "But tell me why the expert witness who could testify as to the validity of the lack of DNA was barred from testifying? Why evidence of Emily Borgetta's phone records and a list of her prior lovers weren't allowed into evidence? Why the fact that Mathias had been questioned for nearly forty-eight hours straight in a nonstop barrage by the police department was not allowed to be presented in front of the jury?" He pauses, letting every bitter accusation sink in.

"Why not?" I ask, hating a part of me that already knows the answer.

"Every decision in that aspect was up to one person who consistently ruled against the interest of Mathias: Heyworth Thorne. His reasons are difficult to parse, but I believe that it was for personal gain. Someone powerful had an interest in closing the murder case quickly. Mathias was an easy scapegoat and Heyworth Thorne the willing pawn."

"I want to deny that, but…" I swallow hard, eyeing the city beyond this room. "But I think I'm starting to wonder if my adoption was more than a merciful whim on his part. What if he picked me because…" God I can't even say it. My fingers tremble in his grip, and I rake my free hand through my hair, twisting the strands. "What if he's the reason Simon was always able to find me on my birthday? What if he gave him access to me? What if all this time—"

"You're upsetting yourself," Damien warns. His thumb traces my cheek, capturing the tears he shouldn't be able to sense.

I'm not sobbing openly for once. I'm just…numb.

"Diane wants me to fill in for him at a benefit gala," I croak. "She wants me to smile, and pretend, and reassure his donors in his absence. She wants me to lie for him, but I'm not sure if I can."

"The Wellington gala?" he wonders, unsurprisingly correct. "Ironic in a way. Gerald Wellington was nothing more than an odd recluse who had an obsession with 'purity.' He seemed to think that there was no such thing as innocence. That even the most sheltered and pure harbored dark intentions. One merely need magnify them."

"I haven't heard that assessment," I admit. Racking my brain, I don't think I ever met the man in person. Just watched my father attend every gala. "He never made me attend that particular event though. Maybe he knew the irony as well?" I try to laugh, but the sound trickles out far too softly.

"Would it help if I were there?"

He makes it sound so simple. So casual.

"How would it look?" I wonder—without refusing outright. "If I show up with my father's archenemy? I might as well be dancing on his grave."

"We don't have to appear together, then," he suggests. "But I will be there. We both may have our own aims, but I will still be there. For you."

"Thank you—"

"Don't." He laughs in that dangerous way that churns my stomach. "Because I would like to request something in return *por favor*."

"Oh?"

He lifts our clasped hands and brushes his mouth against the back of mine. There, he murmurs, "I want you to sleep here tonight."

"More sex?" I quirk my lips. "Isn't that already part of our arrangement?"

"You don't understand." He laughs, shaking his head, his thumb still stroking my palm. "I want you to sleep with me tonight. In my bed. I don't require sex, but…"

His deepening tone invokes a shiver I'm sure he senses.

"I want you naked," he admits. "Beneath my sheets. I want to be able to touch you. Hold you. All to better assess your fear of the dark, of course."

"And own it," I say, referring to his newest conquest. "Do you really think you're up to the task, Mr. Villa?"

There's a storm building on the horizon, evident in purplish clouds swarming the skyline.

"I'm willing to employ my...resources to attempt such an endeavor," he warns. "Though I have some work that must be done this afternoon."

"Work," I parrot. Disappointment unfurls in my chest before I can help it, erasing the tendrils of fire sowed by his words. "After all this time, I still don't know exactly what it is you do."

"*Sí.*" He releases my hand, bracing his on his knees. "Though I'm sure your father told you all about my career path."

"But I want to hear it from you." I reach for his hand again. It twitches as if he has to fight not to pull away. "I'm sure there's more to you than supposedly running a criminal empire and using art for money laundering purposes."

"Is there?" He tugs his hand free and stands, grabbing his cane propped against the end of the chaise. "I need to leave earlier than expected, it seems. I'll be back—"

"I've offended you." Even if I have no idea how. "I'm sorry if I did."

His footsteps slow and then increase as he approaches the door. "I'll return later tonight if you decide to humor my offer. *Adios.*"

I listen to the door close after him, unwilling to move from my slumped position. Already, the sunlight is fading, surrendering to a darkening skyline.

The muted color scheme of my surroundings works to enhance the ominous aura tainting the atmosphere. Alone again with my thoughts, I find it harder to ignore the most dangerous ones teasing the edges of my psyche.

My father.

He's dying.

He's lying.

And without him, I have no one. Damien Villa may be a fitting diversion now, but for how long will he stay? How long until I bore him? How long before I can no longer take the secrets evident between us even as all other boundaries fall?

How long before I break under the pressure of it all?

I shower and linger naked in the bathroom of my private suite. To Mr. Villa's credit, the décor is complementary to the scarlet and ebony hues of the bedroom itself. A large sunken tub with golden features and black marble flooring create a dark, luxurious oasis.

And a lonely one.

When I finally return to my room, I grab a robe and then creep into the hallway, inching toward that dangerous barrier that divides his half from mine. If one were to describe my assigned rooms, they might as a mocking array of posh socialite meets repressed exhibitionist—but his...

The hallway extends, opening onto a large, spacious room stocked only with an easel and a stool. Simplistic at first glance, but the atmosphere feels different in here than at his other studio. Dark walls and onyx stone flooring lend to a quieter space.

Calmer. I imagine him painting something far different from the average nude muse while in here. A hint of what such subject may be reveals itself the farther I roam into the suite.

The next room contains a relatively simple bed draped in black sheets. But the walls...

Painted canvas covers nearly every inch of them. So many scenes are depicted that I wander aimlessly, observing every one.

They transport me. Into amber fields. Ochre skies. A riverbank. A sea of growing crops. Each scene is frozen in painstaking detail, creating a parallel universe fit to rival that of his greenhouse. Flowers are a tangible escape.

But in this room, he created one from memory.

Enthralled, I find myself sitting on the end of his mattress, lost in the clashing views. It's a strange thing to be inside someone's mind. To see the world how they do, even if it's via snippets. Fragments. Damien Villa may be blind now, but he hoarded his recollection of the sky. The various hues of blue. The golden kiss of sunlight. How many secrets lurk behind his blindfold?

Hours must pass as I try to ponder that very question. Eventually, I feel tired enough to risk lying down—but my eyes have barely closed when I hear it. Thunder shattering the silence. Lightning flashes, illuminating the room and throwing every shadow into stark relief.

I find myself lurching upright and pacing circles until I wind up retreating to the scarlet room, drawn by a faint, musical melody. My cell phone. It rings again as I fish it from my purse, battling another monstrous roar of thunder. I reach for it and find a call from an unknown number. Only God knows who it could be. I shouldn't answer, given the hell of this past week.

But when lightning strikes, my finger slips.

"Hello?"

"While I have kept your room free of surveillance, I feel it is only fair if I am allowed to monitor *my* private space." An amused voice, slightly accented, drips into my ear like liquid sin and a breath I didn't realize I was holding escapes in a gasp. "You were in my bed," he adds, lingering over the possessive term. "I'm disappointed you chose not to stay there."

"I…" I grit my teeth to keep from gasping again. "I thought you were in the middle of business, Mr. Villa—"

"I am," he says. In the background, I hear men's voices, discussing some unknown topic. "But when more important matters come across my radar, I must give them my full attention. I sincerely hope you enjoyed the comfort of the mattress. I fully intend to ensure you experience it thoroughly."

"If only you weren't so damn busy." I feign a strained sigh as thunder rumbles, sounding fainter compared to the tenor of his voice. More lightning flashes as if fighting for my attention. "I'm sure you'll be tied up for most of the night."

"Unfortunately, yes…" He sounds wary. Oh my, I wonder why.

"That's too bad," I exhale, distantly aware of rain lashing at the window. "If you were here, I'd let you help me experience the comfort of your bed firsthand."

"Oh?" His tone falls flat, suddenly cold. Maybe the change in demeanor has something to do with how heavily I'm breathing into the receiver? I'll hate myself for this later. I know I will.

But when he speaks, he's louder than thunder. Even whispered and hushed, his voice outlasts the rain. I'll take it over silence, and later, I'll lament over how pathetic that makes me.

"Yes. I'm sure we could give your precious mattress a thorough 'testing.' Maybe I'd even let you taste what I know you can't stop thinking about since the other night." God, did those words come from me? Apparently so.

Harsh, heavy breaths fan into the speaker, distorting all other noise. "Is that so?"

"*Sí.*" I try to mimic the sultry tones of his accent—a low grunt from his end is my reward. I roll onto my back, ignoring what my free hand does as I let it drift along my thigh—but my body's reaction betrays me. My breathing falters. Then quickens to match the suddenly rapid rate of his. "Very much so." My fingers make contact with sensitive flesh, which draws a moan from me that isn't faked. Isn't part of the game.

"Damn." His teeth clip the word. "I'm giving your proposal serious consideration."

"If only you were here…" Another brush of my finger over heated skin elicits another moan voiced into the speaker. Thunder. Flashing. Darkness. All of it threatens to ruin the facade even the illusion of his presence wraps me in. "I need you here—"

"Gentlemen." It takes my brain a second to realize that he's no longer speaking to me. "I'm terribly sorry. We'll have to reconvene at another date."

I hear muttered voices and shuffling of what sounds like furniture. Then his voice returns, aimed only toward me.

"You got your wish," he warns, sounding more as though he's promising my doom. "I'm on my way to collect in full what I'm owed."

I gasp. "You're joking—"

"Far from it, Ms. Thorne," he growls.

Which means he really just ended what sounded like a meeting for me. Because of sex. Even so, he doesn't hang up right away. I can tell he's moving. Quickly.

"I suggest you hurry, Mr. Villa." I'm not playing fair, but I'm beyond caring.

I'm warm instead of frozen for once. On fire instead of shivering. Thunder rumbles, but I feel damn near invincible instead of fearful. Lightning crackles, but I barely even hear it. Just the promise conveyed in every curse he mutters under his breath as my fingers stroke and my breaths quicken in response. It's unfair that he can do this to me.

"I can't stop thinking of how you felt inside me—"

"Son of a bitch." Rapid breathing stutters through the receiver. Is he running? The blaring sounds of traffic flood the background before I can be sure. Then the sound of a door opening. Slamming.

"I want you inside me like I've never needed anything else."

"Maddening woman." More cursing diminishes his usual polished persona. He sounds harsher now. Vulgar. "You don't know what you're—"

"I can't stop imagining how your tongue would feel on me."

Utter silence comes from his end and I know I've crossed a line from which there is no turning back.

I bite my own tongue, but it's no use. It's like he said. I'm fucking mad. "Tell me how it would feel."

He groans. "Like heaven, sweet girl. I'll show you."

My heart stutters at the promise. Hopeful. God, I'm going insane.

"I'll show you how badly I've craved your taste. And there... you're already moist for me, I bet. *Dios mío,* woman. I'll show you."

He doesn't whisper. His driver must hear him. And he doesn't care.

With every grated word, fingers stroke the tiny bundle of nerves that has me seeing stars. One. Two. A galaxy of them. "And then what?"

"*Mierda,*" he swears, his voice rasping. "I'll have you on your knees, *dulce niña.* You'll regret this little game."

But therein lies the joke. For the first time in so long, I'm not playing someone's game. The rules have been forgotten. I'm on an island unto myself. And with every uttered word, the further I remove myself from any hope of redemption.

"Damien," I whisper, dropping the pretense. My voice shakes and I squeeze my eyes shut against another startling flash of lightning. "I...need...you...here *now.*"

He bellows something, presumably to the driver amid a smattering of honking horns. Another door slams followed quickly by the delicate chime that sounds like that of an elevator arriving.

He never stops speaking to me. Harsh words too filthy to process—but the twisted promises aren't what makes my heartbeat stutter. All that matters is his tone. Thick. Gritty. Desperate.

Even the world's best actor couldn't fake the tremor in his voice.

Finally, I hear the door to the suite itself open and slam. I lurch upright, straining my ears to track the surge of footsteps marching toward my room.

Seconds later, a monster appears at the foot of my bed, dripping rainwater onto the floor. His hair fell out of its usual ponytail, his blindfold slightly askew.

"You don't even understand how important the meeting you derailed was." He laughs while shedding his coat, leaving it at his feet. "It will take months to rebuild those connections. Perhaps even years. And yet…I'm here—and not for sex," he clarifies, inching a step closer. "I could hear the tremor in your voice. I knew you were afraid—"

"No," I start to argue. "That's not why I wanted you—"

"I know." He nods, shrugging off the concern. "But I'm still here regardless."

And even he doesn't seem to know why.

Neither do I.

"You could always leave," I pitch halfheartedly, hating the hitch in my voice. "I'd hate to think I interrupted some massive criminal undertaking—"

"Come here." He crooks a single finger, beckoning me closer.

I shed the silken sheets and rise to my knees. Even from the slight distance, I see his nostrils flare, his tongue tracing his lower lip.

"*Dios mío,* I can smell you already," he growls, inviting with a crooked finger. "Now, sweet girl. Tonight, you show me firsthand how to touch you."

Heart hammering, I inch closer and he extends his hand, heavy palm upright. A tremor racks my spine as I lie back and guide him between my legs. I'm groaning before I even feel him. He cups me roughly and the friction negates the softness of his skin.

"Spread your legs for me. Wider—*sí*, like that." With every word, he flexes his hips, rubbing himself against me—but never inside. So close to what he promised.

It's torture. It's sin. I moan against him without a damn given for anyone who could overhear. Still, I let him set the pace. I let him control the intensity of sensation, barely fucking enough.

It's raw fire against tender flesh and all I can do is bite my tongue against the onslaught.

"No," he growls, easily maneuvering above me. "You let me hear you. You moan when I touch you." His thumb slips inside me, triggering an echo of what he craves. "And when I fuck you, sweet girl…you scream."

His knee nudges my legs farther apart, and he grips my hips, positioning me. The rasp of his undone zipper teases the air before I feel him. Taunting at first, sliding a pulsing ridge of flesh between my legs. Sinful, raw friction next. Nowhere near enough. Then, without warning, he thrusts hard. Deep. Strangled noise rips from my throat.

"Like that," he groans, rocking his hips to almost draw free before slamming back in. "*Mierda*, like that."

He bucks, thrusting deeper. Unhurried. Air thickens. The world fades. My hands clutch his shoulders. My knee curls, fighting for leverage against his thigh. His nearness triggers every memory from the other night. The soreness. The pleasure.

My brain is reduced to a senseless thought on an infinite loop: *Need more.*

He's trapping me in this memory, more vibrant than any painting hanging on his walls. I'll never forget the taste of him on my tongue. The words he growls into my ear as my breaths quicken and the tension building inside me overflows.

Afterward, I don't know how long we lie still, his arms around me, his mouth at the base of my throat. Clarity returns only as he shifts easing back as a disappointed pang shoots through my belly.

"I won't go far, sweet girl," he says thickly. Sure enough, he only snatches up one of the sheets kicked toward the bottom of the bed. "I may require your assistance," he says, a wry smile tilting his mouth, visible even in the dark.

I help him unfurl the blanket and he draws it around us both, resuming his previous position of holding me.

"You're shaking," he says, running his hand along my arm.

"It could be shock," I playfully counter. "I think I'm relaxed for once."

Despite everything. All I feel is his heat sheltering me from another storm raging beyond the confines of the suite.

"One day, I will take you south," he murmurs as his fingers creep up to my hair, sinking into the strands of it. "The storms there are fiercer, but the sound… Here, it's just loud, aimless noise, but there? Out in the country, it's like a symphony when it rains. The animals howl. The trees creak. You would never feel alone, of that I am sure."

A tired laugh escapes me, sinking into the sheets. "It sounds beautiful. Do you miss it there?"

"Sometimes…" He stops stroking me, but his arm tightens, drawing me farther against his chest. "Maybe in some ways I've stopped myself from going back—at least alone. Not because I fear the memories, but…"

"But?" I retaliate for the intimate way he's touching me by sliding one of my hands back to rest on his hip.

A low sound rumbles from his throat. "But I don't want to become the person I was when I lived there," he admits. "He was violent. Cold. He could do unspeakable things without hesitation. There was no poise…no patience. I've left that man behind and I've taken great pains to become someone else. Even if that someone is a reformed *'criminal mastermind who uses his paintings for money laundering.'*"

My lazy smile falls flat. "Tell me about it. I…I won't judge you," I add in a rush.

"It's not a part of my life I like to relive," he admits. A hitch disrupts his deep baritone—a rare, fleeting slip in his façade.

"But you know about my past," I say softly. "I want to know about yours."

"Fair enough." His heavy sigh bastes my skin in warm breath.

I inhale it, feeling that one wrong move may shatter the fragile trust he's willing to extend my way. "Start with where you grew up," I suggest.

"*Sí.* As I mentioned before, I was born in a small village in southern Colombia. My mother was an American missionary who came to the country on a mission trip, where she met my father. He was a farmer who seemed kind and respectable, at least at first."

"And then?" I prompt when he's fallen silent.

Muscles flex beneath his skin and I wince; he's holding me even tighter. "She quickly learned that he was not the man she thought he was. And that was the reality my brothers and I were born into."

"I'm sorry," I whisper.

He laughs. "Don't be. In some ways, I had a wonderful childhood. Children, after all, tend to be oblivious of such things. Violence becomes a rare, fleeting event in a world filled with lazy days running through the fields or swimming in the rivers. A bit like a thunderstorm, if you don't mind the comparison."

"It fits," I admit. "So why did you really leave?"

His lips flutter over my shoulder and I arch into the contact. Only now does he give me more.

"We grew up," he says simply. "And our father…he became worse. His usual methods of tyranny before then had been the average daily outburst. Striking my mother, or myself, or one of the others. But as we grew older, something in him changed. One night, he cornered our mother and accused her of eyeing another man. She hadn't, of course, but the truth didn't matter to him. In his madness, he decided that the only way to punish her was to ensure that her eyes could never stray again."

"No—" I stiffen, my breath caught in my throat. Admittedly, I haven't thought too much about his blindness—just the one snippet of information he's revealed before now: that he blinded himself.

"*Sí, dulce niña*," he murmurs into my skin, once again deploying his uncanny skill for reading my mind. "I confronted him, and he chose to punish me instead."

I close my eyes, imagining the horror of it. "And that's why you left?"

"Part of it," he admits. "I can tell from the dread in your voice what you're thinking—but don't. Do not pity me. In some ways, my…injury made me stronger. I don't take the beauty in life for granted. I capture it. Enhance it—or corrupt."

More specifically, he hordes it, trapping what entices him in paint and canvas. Even if he can't see them, he can relive what he lost in the act of painting. After all, I experienced firsthand how passionate he can be when it comes to his art.

"What happened next?"

"Despite my…sacrifice, my mother died not long after," he says. "I knew that, without her, my brothers and I needed to come to America—any way we could."

I fill in what the rumors about him claim. "Even via the drug trade."

He makes a low sound in his throat. Part laugh. Part groan. "Perhaps. Those desperate boys may have built a life using whatever skills they could. Pardon my evasiveness, but I am not used to baring my secrets in front of the daughter of a judge."

"You can trust me." I'm surprised by how earnest I sound. "I have my own share of secrets."

"Oh?" His fingers still over my hip.

"I told you that Diane gave me my father's will?"

He nods, leaning into me with every motion of his head. "*Sí.*"

"She wanted me to find whatever he left for me in a safety deposit box. I went alone."

"And?" If he's angry about the deception, I can't tell.

"I found an old note written from someone in the city's police department."

"Really?"

I stiffen at the sudden grit in his tone. Maybe he is angry after all.

"What did it say?"

"It doesn't really matter," I whisper. "The point is: It just proved something I didn't want to face."

"And what was that?" His tone softens just enough for the tension to leave my limbs.

In his arms, I feel brave enough to admit the truth I haven't faced. "When I read it, I...I hated him. Just for a second, but I felt it." Tears spill down my cheeks, but I don't bother to brush them away. "I hated him. Do you remember how Diane begged me to represent him at a benefit gala?"

He nods.

"Well, I haven't even picked out a dress or made arrangements. I'm not sure I can show my face to those people and pretend that everything is fine."

"And you don't have to. Trust your emotions. Do only what feels right."

"That's the problem," I admit. "I don't know what's real or not. I don't know what I should do—"

"I will tell you," Damien says, sweeping his hand along my thigh. "All you need to do now is sleep. In the morning, if you change your mind, I'll be there for you."

"Thank you," I whisper. "I mean it. Lately...it's like I can't feel anything anymore."

"Oh?" His fingers slip to graze my inner thigh. "I'm insulted, Ms. Thorne. You must be a damn good actress if you are incapable of feeling *anything.*"

My moan betrays me as a liar, and then I inhale, fighting for clarity. "Outside of bed," I blurt. "Outside… Away from you."

He goes rigid. Just as doubt creeps in, he molds against me, cradling me in muscle and heat. "I am content to make you feel," he concedes. "For now."

"Oh?"

"One day, I will demand more. But we can save that discussion for another time. Just sleep for now, sweet girl. I don't want to tire you out too soon. Sleep."

And I find it easy to within his arms.

Even as the storm continues to rage around us.

THIRTEEN

ddly enough, I don't feel abandoned or insulted by the empty bed I've woken up to. Especially not when I roll over and find a bouquet of black roses where Damien last slept. I finger a single stalk and lower my nose to the petals flooding the air with their crisp perfume.

A smile lingers on my lips as I shower and get dressed in a plain gray dress—the closest thing to black in my wardrobe. While I brush my hair, I make a mental note to remind Damien to have my things brought over. Though it seems he's decided to ignore my wishes for now. Instead, I find a white box placed tauntingly in front of my door. It's wrapped in a bright-pink bow, dangerously inviting.

My fingers shake as I open it. Inside, I find yards of tulle and lace —a dress made of the thinnest beige lace imaginable. A skirt of tulle billows from the waist, but the only form of coverage the wearer might hope to find comes in the form of delicate silk appliqués sewn around the garment.

Flowers. Thousands of them, presumably affixed by hand, spanning nearly every color of bloom imaginable.

Score one Damien Villa. I can concede defeat in this round. I don't even know whether to add the dress to my closet or plant it.

I briefly consider trying it on before I finally notice the envelope tucked inside the box.

Heyworth Thorne could only pray for such a representative, someone wrote in elegant script.

A kind, if bracing reminder of reality.

Returning to my room, I reach for my phone but find no new messages from Diane. By the time I arrive at the hospital, that familiar weight of dread returns, dragging on my limbs like a lead ball and chain.

I hesitate near the door for at least an hour, wringing my fingers to the point of pain. Finally, I step inside, steeling myself for whatever I might find.

"No change," Diane says tiredly as I approach.

Daddy's eyes are open, staring blankly even as she strokes her hand along his cheek.

"I'm going to go get some lunch, darling." She smothers a yawn into her palm and forces a smile. "Want anything?"

I shake my head and settle into the other chair pulled up to his bedside. For what feels like hours, I stroke the back of his hand, searching his empty eyes for any hint of life. God, there are so many questions I need to ask, but when I finally gather the nerve to voice one, all I can think to say is, "Why?" My finger shakes, tracing the path of his cheek to no response. "Why, Daddy? Were you sent to find me for a reason? Was this all just some twisted game—just tell me why!"

"Is everything all right?"

I look over to find a nurse at the door, an eyebrow raised.

"I'm fine," I say, swiping at the tears welling in my eyes. "We're fine." Once she's gone, I admit, "I went to the safety deposit box," directing the words at my lifeless father. "I saw the page you had hidden there. But why? What is it you couldn't tell me?"

I wait—a folly that doesn't sink in until one of the machines monitoring his vitals shrieks, sounding an alarm. The nurse returns to fix it. Leaves again. And I laugh, shaking my head.

"I'm crazy." Sighing, I withdraw my hand and start to stand. "I'm going crazy—"

"Dead." The raspy voice echoes like a gunshot.

I jump, scanning the room for an intruder, but all I find is shadow. Shadow and...

A pale hand that lurches toward me, grasping mine so tightly that I gasp.

"D-Daddy?"

His cold, blue eyes turn to me, blinking. "Dead," he croaks again. "He's dead...he's dead. He's dead!"

More alarms go off from various machines and an army of nurses races into the room, scrambling to quiet them.

"I'm going to ask you to step outside, dear," one of them says, guiding me to the door.

Even in the hallway, I can hear him. Shouting. Screaming in an eerie refrain.

"He's dead!"

"*M*s. Thorne?"

I jump as a woman in a lab coat appears at the mouth of the private lobby near the ICU. "Yes?" I scramble up from a couch, smoothing my hands along my rumpled dress. "How is he?"

"Stable for now," the woman says with a strained smile. "He's asking to see you. I would ask you try to limit tiring him out too soon, but you're free to see him."

I follow her into the hall, my heart in my throat. Before I even enter the room, I can sense a shift in the atmosphere. The air isn't so heavy. Someone opened a window, allowing in a fresh breeze, as well as turned on the main light in the room. Bathed in the yellow glow, Daddy is lying in bed, propped up by a wall of pillows. His frail hands settle together over his lap, but his eyes…

They tiredly focus on me as I approach.

I falter and brace my hand over my chest. "D-Daddy?"

"Sweet pea." His thin, frail voice barely rises above a whisper—but my heart throbs at the sound. I never thought I'd hear it again.

"How are you feeling?" I take up a chair beside his bed and grasp one of his hands.

He squeezes once reassuringly, and despite everything, a smile tugs on my lips. Though I can't prevent a tear from escaping, sliding down my cheek.

"I've been better," he says with a weak laugh.

"I was worried about you," I admit, swiping at my face with the back of my hand. "We *all* were. Diane should be here soon. She got stuck in traffic—"

"I'm sorry, Juliana." He brushes his other hand along my cheek. "I'm so, so sorry."

"We don't have to talk about that now." I force a smile and fiddle with his blankets, smoothing them. "We just need to focus on your health—"

"I've lied to you." His reedy, broken voice sounds nothing like the confident man I know, and a panicked part of me isn't ready to have that image of him I've held for so long tarnished.

"Daddy, please. We don't need to talk about that now—"

"I've lied to you," he insists, his eyes watering. "All this time... I'm so sorry."

"Then just... Just tell me why."

It's strange. I've never begged him for anything before. Not the most coveted Christmas presents, or the chance to stay up even a minute past my bedtime. I accepted his rules and cherished whatever he desired to give me. Based on that simple trust, I love him more than I've ever loved anyone.

Or so I thought.

The same way I thought he loved me. That my adoption had been the whim of a kindhearted soul and not an act of greed. God, I need to believe those lies more than ever. But they're slipping away from me like tabloid fodder printed on cheap paper.

"You have every right to hate me." His fingers flex in mine as he stares into my eyes. They're bloodshot and hurt to keep open for too long. Or maybe it's his face that stings my vision and makes my eyelids lower. "I don't blame you, sweet pea. In some ways, I hate myself for what I've done. There is no excuse."

"You knew who he was," I say thickly. "The man who attacked me. All this time and you knew."

"Juliana…" His face pales. Artificial light enhances the wrinkles and he ages decades in seconds, becoming a wizened old man I barely recognize. "I refuse to lie to you again." He releases my hand as if burned. "It's true."

I wince as that hollow feeling inside of my chest festers and spreads like cancer. *Truth*…that twenty years ago, Heyworth Thorne defended a man accused of murder before he ever sat on a judge's bench.

And the man in question?

"Who?" My words run together, slurred with tears and pain. "Just tell me who he is please!"

All those years of therapy after Leslie's death. The grim insinuation that maybe I had something to do with her murder. The agonizing years the Matodas have gone without closure.

All of it congeals into a painful ball weighing on my chest.

"Is that why you adopted me?" I add hoarsely when he hasn't replied. "Guilt?"

"Perhaps," he admits. "Or greed. I knew I'd been used. I wanted to right that wrong—any way I could. Even if it meant using a little girl by taking guardianship over her so that if the moment came…I could give authority for her to testify."

"That's why you adopted me?"

He doesn't deny it. The man I've thought of as my father simply lowers his head, his features agonized. "I knew what I'd done. And I thought if I could get you to the right officer who could ask the right questions, we could bring him down for good. But then I met you. This sweet, innocent girl… Call me whatever you want, Juliana, but don't you doubt for a second that I love you. Too much, some might say. And they *have* said." He blinks, sending moisture dripping down his cheeks. "In the end, I couldn't bear to put you on the stand. I knew what that would do to you—"

"Don't use me as your excuse." I replay those early days over and over in my mind. All those birthdays of playing cat-and-mouse with Simon. All those nights wasted fearing my unseen boogeyman. Another terror takes hold, impossible to swat aside this time. "Did you give him access to me?" I can't even look at him.

"Never," he swears in a tone I've never heard him use before. "I would never let that monster near you! I made sure, even when I —" He breaks off, coughing.

"Daddy?" I draw back, lurching to my feet. "You need rest. I should go—"

"No!" He grabs my hand with a strength that contradicts his frail appearance. I doubt I could pull away if I tried, so I sit. "Everything I've done has always been to protect you. Maybe not as well as I should have," he admits. "But at least you'll never have to worry about that monster again."

Twisted hope and dread form an anvil that crushes my lungs. Gasping, I choke out, "Who is he?"

"I can't tell you his name. I think it would confuse you more and I need to explain." Pain distorts his pale features. "Just trust me when I tell you that he's dead. Has been for four years now. He will never hurt you again."

I recoil, frowning. "Dead? N-No. That's wrong—"

"He's dead," my father insists. "I saw the bastard lowered into his grave myself. I spent so damn long watching him. Waiting for one shred of—"

"Heyworth!" Diane appears breathless in the doorway, one of her hands braced against her chest. "Heyworth!"

They scan each other, their eyes brimming with tears, and I don't have the heart to ruin the moment by dredging up the past. Not now, when I can barely form a coherent thought. *Four years.* My mind keeps replaying those words over and over.

"I'll leave you two alone," I croak, standing.

"I know the gala is tonight darling," Diane starts, "but I may be late—"

"Stay here."

"I'm sorry, sweet pea," Daddy calls after me, his voice broken and hoarse. "I'm so, so sorry."

Because he's lying to me, I decide as I race into the hall. He has to be. Because if Simon died four years ago…

Only one man in the world has the means and knowledge to replace him.

Someone worse than a monster.

FOURTEEN

I don't know how I've made it back to Damien's without breaking apart. Screaming. Instead, I'm dead silent during the ascent to his suite. Numb. With my thoughts in turmoil, I enter the foyer and find a note waiting for me on the end table instead of the man himself.

I'll meet you there tonight, it reads. *Do wear the dress.*

His dress: a beautiful, mocking confection of a betrayal too cruel to fathom. A strangled sound creeps from my throat and I'm on my knees, my eyes streaming. Somehow, I manage to smother any sound against my palm and stand. On trembling legs, I enter my scarlet room. Here, I pull my new dress on, but I don't even recognize the stranger staring back at me from the mirror's surface.

Her hollow eyes stare blankly ahead, no less soulless than one of Sampson's eerie paintings. All I need is a sea of flowers to drown in and the irony would be complete.

When I enter the hall hours later, Julio is there to usher me into a waiting car, and I arrive at the gala to find a crowd hounding the few patrons brave enough to enter the building through the throng.

"We can go around, miss," Julio suggests, but I shake my head and push the door on my end open.

Every year, the Wellington family throws the event at the same mansion on the outskirts of the city. The modern design serves as the perfect backdrop to the mixture of old money and hopeful delegates arriving by the carful.

It's the perfect setting to face my past.

A perfect setting to accept the truth: I was only ever of use to anyone as one thing.

A token. A pawn. A piece in a game.

"Juliana!" a reporter shouts, startling me back to the present. "Is it true that your father's health is in stable condition?"

"Allow me," a man cuts in.

I turn and find someone looming behind me, cutting a striking figure in a tailored black suit.

"May I?" He takes my arm and guides me forward.

Despite the crush of reporters, we enter the venue unmolested. In the foyer, Harrison helps me out of my coat and tosses it to a nearby attendant.

"I'm surprised you came," he says, raking his gaze over me. "Rumor has it that you weren't particularly fond of your father's return to politics in the first place. And this event... Gerald Wellington was a man even your father despised, though he was more than willing to take his money."

"I've always supported my father publicly," I croak. "Always."

"I heard he's awake." Stepping forward, he leads me past an army of valets laden with trays of wine ready to be served to the partygoers. "One might presume you'd be with him."

"He wanted me here." God, I hate how my voice keeps breaking. Maybe the will didn't cement it, but just being here does. I am Heyworth Thorne's daughter for better or for worse. He lied to me; there's no erasing that. But at the end of the day, he still trusts me with his most important possession of all: his name. "I'm doing this for *him*."

"Well, perhaps you may be interested in lending his support in the form of an endorsement?"

"An endorsement?" I raise an eyebrow, scanning the ballroom for a familiar face in a sea of beautiful strangers. A few weeks of self-imposed exile and I barely recognize the polished upper crust of society anymore. I'm a tainted doll now with visible cracks, drawing eyes everywhere I go.

"Yes. In light of Heyworth's unfortunate health concerns, my son Kyle has decided to run for mayor in his stead." He nods toward a man standing near a corner of the room, surrounded by fawning guests. At a glance, a slight resemblance is obvious in their confident stature and dark-brown hair. "An endorsement from you in your father's place would be a fitting show of solidarity."

"I appreciate the offer," I say, forcing a smile. "But I should discuss it with him first."

"He's talking?" His head swivels in my direction, his eyebrows furrowed. "His condition has improved that much?"

"It's better than expected," I admit, blinking tears back. "But still touch and go."

"I see." He lowers his head, his eyes downcast. "I'm sorry to hear the old son of a bitch still isn't at his full health. Maybe I should schedule another visit? See if he knows anything about what may have caused his condition?"

"Maybe…" I trail off as a figure near the back of the room catches my attention.

A man standing tall, his eyes shielded by a blindfold. Whether he realizes it or not, women flock to him, casting him searching glances.

From them, he might choose his next willing muse.

His next victim to destroy.

"Excuse me, Juliana," Harrison says, releasing my arm. "I'm sorry to abandon you, but I think I see a colleague."

Abandon. The word stings more than the context—turning into agony the more I observe the blindfolded figure across the room. His head is cocked and I imagine him intently listening to every bit of conversation around him, discerning more through observation than I figure most could ever see at one time.

Like the fact that I'm the center of attention. Several pairs of eyes dart in my direction, scanning the daring cut of my gown. I copy them, eyeing the dress as if for the first time. As odd as it feels to suspect, I can't shake the feeling that he created this. Designed it, maybe. It's too damn intricate. A risqué play on fashion only a true artist would dare attempt. Jaw-droppingly sheer fabric and strategically placed appliqués to shield my nipples and waistline from view. At the same time, it's matronly in shape, with a high neckline and a formfitting bodice. I catch several photographers pointing their camera in my direction, and I suspect I'll make tomorrow's society pages.

"I was wrong," someone murmurs heatedly into my ear.

I look over at the corner; the secluded figure has vanished.

"I knew the dress would look stunning on you," the man in question admits into my ear, sliding his hand over my lower back.

"But given the reaction tonight, *mierda*… I almost wish I could see it myself."

The world seems to think so. As if on cue, I catch several murmured compliments directed my way.

You look beautiful.

You look marvelous.

What a stunning dress.

Pretty statements that merely skim the surface. How I look, never how I feel. To them, I'm just the same old Juliana with a different coat of paint. But therein lies the real question. Who is the woman they've known all along?

And who is the man by my side?

"I need to talk to you," I croak.

"*Sí.* And I need to talk to you." He extends his cane, deploying it like a sensor to ensure he doesn't come close to anyone else. "Though, as promised, I will ensure we aren't seen together for long. When you are ready, head to the restroom, *¿sí?*"

He pulls away and I watch him go, my heart in my throat. There's nothing left to do but simper, and smile, and mingle.

It's nearly an hour before I escape into the bathroom, but Damien isn't lurking inside the stalls. Shaking, I claim a sink for myself and splash cold water on my face. Looking at my reflection, I try to see the same woman everyone else is. But I don't. I see a fraud in a dress that fits her too perfectly. Silk roses cup her breasts but threaten to expose her with the slightest shift of fabric. The entire construction is an elaborate dance between elegant and obscene.

Looking at myself, I settle my suspicion once and for all: He designed this. Only a madman could taunt me in the form of couture. Only Damien Villa could design a trap in the form of a dress.

And only he would be cunning enough to masquerade as a monster.

When Damien doesn't appear, I exit the restroom.

"Excuse me. Ms. Thorne?"

I turn and find a man approaching me. Tall and imposing, he cuts a striking figure almost as chilling as Damien. A name comes to mind as I meet his gaze. Kyle Harrison. He shares the same, piercing gaze as his father, honed like a laser.

"I hope my father spoke to you," he says while reaching for my hand. I shiver as he grasps my fingers, lifting them to his mouth, "I would love an endorsement from your father, even with his... current issues."

He smiles.

I cringe. "I appreciate the sentiment, but I'm not sure if—"

"Think on it," he urges, releasing me. "I would hate to see his legacy end in ruin."

I watch him go, so lost in thought that I nearly collide with someone walking past me. A giggling woman who staggers to regain her balance. Not that she seems to mind. "Are you Juliana?" she asks, her voice breathy.

When I nod, she steers the train of her navy-blue gown with one hand while offering me a white envelope in the other.

"A man asked me to give this to you." Her raised eyebrow indicates curiosity, but the wine on her breath leads me to believe she won't remember enough of this encounter to gossip about it later.

"Thank you." I take the note and watch her stumble into the restroom. Then I rip it open and read while hunched against the wall.

Come to the east wing.

The sender didn't even bother to sign it—not that he needed to. I can smell him. Sin and malice embedded within the paper itself.

Heart in my throat, I head further down the hall and slip from the ballroom altogether. The east wing is a simple trip across the foyer, but a man is standing guard near the archway leading toward it. My footsteps slow as I approach him, but he merely nods, allowing me to pass unaccosted.

It's dark. The winding hallway is illuminated only by the moonlight drifting in through beautiful antique windows that display a view of a private garden. Once I reach the ballroom, I have a crystal-clear view of the man responsible for this game of hide-and-seek. He's near a window, and bathed solely in the glow of moonlight, he's breathtaking.

"How do you like the dress?" he wonders, his voice easily reaching me.

I flinch. I'll never understand how he can make me feel more exposed than I did in a room with hundreds of people watching my every move. He doesn't just skim the surface. He has his head cocked so that his ears are in the prime position to capture every slow, unsteady breath I take. My deliberate footsteps.

"It's lovely," I say robotically, stopping short.

"Only for you... Is something wrong?"

I can't remember how to move until he beckons me with a crook of his finger and a challenging tilt of his chin.

"You're awfully quiet tonight."

The moment I'm close enough, he reaches out to decipher me through heated fingertips. Tasting me with a slow flick of his tongue along his lower lip. He breathes me in, analyzing my every action, and I stand there until he delivers his assessment.

"I designed this damn thing with you in mind," he admits, his voice quickly losing its polished cadence. He sounds guttural. Raw. Too damn honest. "I knew you'd wear it—"

"I feel overdressed," I counter, fighting to breathe.

"Oh?" He's scowling now. "It appears as though you're the talk of the ball. I could hear those bastards simpering from here. Though it seems none of them have noticed that, beneath this"—he swipes a teasing handful of fabric—"you're wearing nothing at all. How scandalous, Ms. Thorne."

I wrench away from him and cross my arms over my chest. One touch and he senses what a room full of people overlook. "Sometimes it feels like you know me better than I know myself," I whisper, my eyes burning. "*Too* well…"

"Oh?" His steps cease their slow advance. "I'm sensing that isn't a compliment."

I close my eyes, remembering the first time I saw his artwork at his gallery. That room where all those paintings of other women watched me. Now, their dead, blank stares take on a taunting aura, their gazes smug. *You fell for it,* they tell me. *Stupid, foolish bitch.*

"Have you been lying to me all this time?" I whisper brokenly. "About my father? …Simon?"

"Juliana." His voice is deeper than before. Like he already knows damn well what I'm thinking. That he won't deny it. That he can't. "Talk to me," he commands. "What did you learn that is making you ask this?"

What did I learn? "The truth. That *you* were Simon."

It sounds insane out loud. Four years. Four years of torment. Of misery. Of lies, and pain, and memories…

But the more I relive every tortured moment, the more it makes sense. Only a man with such an intimate grip on my life could utterly control it.

And only an artist would relish in my misery.

"The real man has been dead for four years, according to my father. But you… You studied me," I say brokenly. "You studied *him*, and for four years, you've played his game."

"It's not what you think." He takes a step toward me, but I flinch back.

"Isn't it?" I force a callous laugh, but pretending doesn't help me now. Nothing. Turns. Off. The. Pain.

If anything, it grows, swelling into an agonizing lump in the pit of my stomach. Without giving a damn for decency, I double over. A gag racks my throat and vomit spills onto the floor. Noisily. Messily. I let him hear what the truth does to me. It destroys me. I'm brought to my knees by the force of it, robbed of even the voice to scream.

"I won't deny it," he says like it matters, still paces away. "But I won't hide the rest from you, either. You deserve to know the full truth."

More?

"I didn't leave the gifts for you to find—but," he adds before hope can even take root in my chest, "I know who did, at least vaguely though not a true identity. In some ways, I facilitated their actions, if only out of curiosity. I knew they upset you. I didn't know why—but upsetting you was enough."

"Because you had leverage," I whisper, seeing things how someone like him would: through a lens of hate and revenge. "Over my father. Over me."

That's how his world works, a muted landscape of give and take. Of death and decay. He doesn't admire flowers for their beauty— it's for their fragility, a reminder of the cruel balance he lives by.

"Why would I intervene in the life of the daughter of a monster like Heyworth Thorne?" he wonders. "It was more advantageous to me if I sat back and watched. I gathered what information I could use to my benefit, but your safety was not of my concern. I will admit that."

"So who is he?" I demand, swiping at my mouth. "Will you tell me that much?" But I'm not even surprised when he shakes his head.

If anything, he knows how to inflict pain with ruthless precision. "I have my suspicions, but the perpetrator is more powerful than I gave them credit for. They never used the same thug to plant your gifts." He pauses, waiting for that revelation to land.

And it does. Like a gut-punch.

"W-What do you mean?"

"They used hired experts, but never the same one twice. When questioned, the men couldn't name who hired them—and trust me, I was very *persuasive* in my questioning. The one night I finally did try to intercede, they ceased their little façade entirely."

"That's why I never got the fourth present," I say, ignoring the rest of his statement.

"There's more. I think whoever is responsible sent the attacker after you. The man with the knife."

My hand flies to my shoulder, tracing a healed wound through the fabric of my clothing. "The man who cut me at the hotel? And you never said anything?" I rasp. "Why?

"I had a hunch who it might be, but they are proving harder to nail down, just like your 'Simon.' Perhaps they are one and the same? But the more evidence I could use against them, the easier it would be to assert my influence when I finally unmask them."

"Even if they killed me?" I remember the fear. The isolation. The desperation. "You didn't help me. You let him…"

The world spins and I stagger to the wall, bracing my hands over it. It takes everything I have just to stay upright. To breathe.

"You let him hurt me," I choke out. "You left me alone—"

"I didn't know in advance or I would have stopped it," he swears. "But I won't make excuses. I should have told you." His tone is so different from the man who has comforted me during thunderstorms. This time, he doesn't smooth my hair or comfort me. He doesn't lend his presence like an anchor against the darkness clawing its way into my mind. He's the lightning rod for despair, incapable of understanding human suffering. So he merely watches me break. "I know nothing I can say could earn your forgiveness—"

"Forgiveness?" A broken laugh trickles out of me as I put the remaining pieces together.

Simon's sudden absence. The roses. *Roses are not your flower,* he said to me during our first true conversation. That was because he'd stolen it. He'd corrupted it.

Feeling sick, I tear at my neck, ripping his necklace from it. When the delicate pearl strikes the wall, I feel no satisfaction. Just pain. Maybe in his own twisted logic, he tried to tell me the truth all along. Oleander and roses. Poison and Simon's favorite gift.

"I…I thought I could trust you—no." I close my eyes and confess in a rush, "I did trust you. I *trusted* you."

It sounds so pathetic now. Trust a man so incapable of simple human emotion.

"I didn't want you to learn this way," he says, toying with me yet again. "Come with me. I can explain—"

"No!" I use the wall for leverage to steady myself. Then I run, stumbling for balance on jellied knees.

He doesn't try to stop me.

He doesn't spout any more lies about trust.

He lets me go without a word, and I leave a trail of tears like blood.

FIFTEEN

a stern-faced driver chauffeurs me to the hospital, but something feels different even before I step foot onto my father's floor, still wearing Damien's elegant creation.

"Miss?" A uniformed officer blocks my path as the elevator doors part. The gun prominent on his hip catches my notice first, his strained expression second. "I'm going to need to see some identification," he demands, extending his hand.

I fish through my purse for my ID. Eyeing it, the man deepens his frown. "Ms. Thorne? I'm going to need you to come with me."

"Is something wrong?" I ask. Alarm lances down my spine as I notice other officers clustered in the portion of the hall near my father's room. From here, the staticky noise issuing from their handsets creates an ominous hum.

"This way," the officer in front of me urges, but rather than lead me to my father's room, he takes me inside a small sitting room instead. "I'm going to ask you to sit, Ms. Thorne."

My heart lurches to my throat as I comply. "Please tell me what's going on."

"Your father is in serious condition," the officer says. "It seems as if there may have been foul play involved—"

"Foul play?" Panic sends sweat drenching my palms. "Like how?"

The man frowns and fishes something from his pocket. A notebook. Flipping it open to the first page, he says, "Have you ever heard of a shrub called oleander? Do you know anyone who might keep it potted or grow it?"

Grow...

It's like my brain disconnects from my body. I can see the world drift in and out of focus, but I have no control over my limbs. Trembling legs rob me of balance, and the man has to grab my arm, grunting in concern.

"Ms. Thorne?" When I don't answer, he adds, "We have reason to believe your father may have been poisoned. If you have any information, we request that you make a formal statement..."

He says something else, but the words meld into a frantic hum, drowned out by my heartbeat. I can't even see him anymore, just white flowers tucked carefully within a small pot, proudly displayed on my kitchen counter.

God, it's like I can hear him.

Dulce niña, did you really believe I wanted more than the obvious?

You meant nothing to me...

Just a means to an end.

And I always get what I want from those with something I desire.

"Juliana?"

I groan at the insistent voice—so distant yet so close, murmured inches from my ear. At least I think so...

My brain is a sluggish collection of thoughts, barely discernible. Groaning again, I try to make sense of anything. My body. My sanity. Gradually, I remember how to force my eyes open and the world comes into focus via blurred, broken snippets glimpsed from behind heavy eyelids.

A room. White walls. A haggard, worried face wearing an expression so pained that it makes my heart throb.

"Juliana," the woman says, her blond hair framing her angular face and her sunken cheeks. Diane. "Darling, can you hear me?"

I try and fail to nod, but my attempt must come across anyway, because she sighs, raking her trembling hands through her hair.

"Thank God. I was so worried. They had to sedate you, sweetheart."

"S-Sedate," I echo in a rasp. The word triggers an avalanche of memories.

Screaming. Crying. A nurse shoving a needle into my arm, her voice resolutely calm.

"You need to calm down, Ms. Thorne."

What a cruel dare. One I have no hope of obeying.

Because my father was nearly murdered—at least twice. And the man responsible used me to do so.

Even worse? He's taunted me with the murder weapon all along.

How long? I wonder, closing my eyes again as moisture seeps from them regardless. *How long was he watching? Waiting?*

"Where am I?" I ask if only to keep from sinking into the myriad of paranoid suspicions.

"Safe, darling." Diane smooths her hands along my hair, brushing strands from my face. "A private sitting room. Here."

Something cool brushes my lips, urging them to part. When I do, cool liquid drips between them. Water.

"Any better?" she asks.

I open my eyes again, this time taking in the narrow space surrounding us. Small. White walls and simplistic furniture. The kind of room dramas and sitcoms have made synonymous with stern doctors issuing bad news.

"Is he dead?" I whisper. God, I can't even look at her. My eyes burn, blurring and unfocused. Bile rises in my throat, blocking any other sound I could make. I can't stop seeing his face. Those eyes. His voice.

I love you, Juliana…

"He's stable," Diane says, her fingers stilling against my forehead. "Chief Harrison has personally overseen his case. He will find out who did this."

But I know who. My lips freeze, refusing to say it out loud. Almost as if that simple denial can prevent the fact from being final.

"Can I see him? My father?"

"Not yet, darling," Diane says. Her reddened eyes brim with tears even as she forces a smile. "He's still in the ICU—" She breaks off, staring beyond me, her lips clenched tight. "I'm so scared, honey. I'm so, so scared."

"Me too." I grab her hand, squeezing with reassurance.

Together, we sit in silence, separated from the chaos of the hall.

The smell draws me awake. Sharp and crisp. Familiar? My nostrils flare, identifying the traces of a masculine scent—but a different breed from the rich aroma tainting Damien. Cigar smoke. I swear I've smelled it before. It's harsh, evoking images of a stuffy bar or enclosed space. Secretive. The footsteps approaching me are heavier than Mr. Villa's as well, but in a way that conveys something more potent than mere confidence. It's arrogance.

Before I even open my eyes, a face appears in my thoughts and I name the figure out loud. "Chief Harrison."

"Morning, Juliana," he replies, his tone soft—for Diane's benefit, I realize. She's snoring, slumped onto the couch beside me. "I hope you don't mind if I ask you some questions?"

I stand, smoothing a hand over my wrinkled, stale dress. It's a gray one of Diane's, borrowed in place of the ball gown lying crumpled in a corner. "Of course."

"This way, then." He inclines his head.

I follow him into the hall. It's quiet, presumably early in the morning. Apart from a few scattered doctors and nurses, the main occupants of the hallway are wearing matching blue uniforms and sporting guns on their hips. His officers.

"I'm sure you've already heard what the doctors believe may be the cause of Heyworth's decline," Harrison starts, casting a glance toward my slightly sore arm. "I'm afraid to admit that we don't currently have any suspects. I have to ask… Do you have any idea where your father could come across something like oleander?"

A hard swallow contracts my throat as I find myself eyeing a section of wall across from us, cluttered with cheerful signs and reminders of hygiene. One sign in particular catches my interest: a bright-blue one urging any visitor to avoid visiting while experiencing a list of symptoms. Coughing. Sneezing. Fever. Pain.

The human body is apparently unoriginal in expressing when something is wrong. Right now, my throat is on fire, my lungs burning, my muscles throbbing. I lick my lips, ready to say it out loud, that terrible, horrible thing. It should be easy too. My only suspicion.

The obvious suspicion.

"No," I hear myself rasp. "I don't think they even grew the shrub at the house."

"Interesting." Harrison cocks his head, his dark eyes unreadable. They trace the contours of my face, settling over my trembling lips. They give me away, betraying all the things I can't seem to voice. Like the fact that I'm lying. "And you can think of no one with access to something like that? Someone who may want to hurt him?"

Pain lances through my heart as remnants of an accented voice whisper across my brain. *Do you really think I would hurt him, knowing how much he means to you?*

"N-No." I shake my head. "I'm sorry. I can't think of anything."

Harrison frowns, running his fingers along his jaw. "I'm disappointed, Juliana. If anyone could give insight into your father's health, I thought it might be you. You two were so close."

I flinch. Any other moment, I'd write off the pointed grit in his tone as paranoia. Exhaustion. Emotional distress. Taking a step back, I observe the man again. There's nothing untoward in his posture. Even his expression conveys concern. Too much concern.

"Let me give you my card," he says, reaching into his breast pocket for one. He extends it to me, meeting my gaze directly. "If you can think of anything at all, please don't hesitate—"

"If you had a suspect, would it even matter what I thought?" I ask, running my tongue along my dry, cracked lips. "You probably have the evidence—"

"Witness testimony *is* key evidence," Harrison corrects. "Sometimes in cases like this, it's the eye-witness account that clenches a verdict more than any piece of evidence. In fact, your father knew that better than anyone."

"K-Knew?" I echo. "Diane said his condition is stable. He should recover. Unless you've heard differently—"

"Of course." The man sighs and stares in the opposite direction. His hand captures his jaw as his thumb strokes the stubble growing there. "But in cases like this, who knows how quickly things may change? After all, as long as your father's attacker is still out there, he could try again."

"That's what your men are here for," I surmise cautiously. "To prevent that from happening."

"Of course." He nods and inclines his head. "But I will let you in on a secret, one that isn't very PC. My men are diligent, but they are human, and your father has some powerful enemies. Who knows what methods of deception they are capable of using if killing Heyworth Thorne is the ultimate goal?"

It feels like too pointed a statement to serve as general advice. Paranoia, I tell myself for the second time.

"I would hate for his condition to worsen," Harrison reiterates. "Which is why it is imperative that you tell me of any information that can help. Anything at all."

"I…" Motion catches my eye before I can finish the statement: another officer walking by, slim and pale. Familiar. The man who canvassed my apartment the other day.

"I have my men on him around the clock," Harrison explains as the man marches past my father's room. "Don't worry. He's in good hands."

"You've known him for a while, my father," I say. "Do you know anything about my case?"

He strokes his chin with the pad of his thumb. "The Borgetta case?"

"No." I shake my head while watching his reaction for any subtle shift. "*My* case. Leslie Matoda's case?"

And in some ways, Heyworth Thorne's case.

"My knowledge is a bit rusty on that front," he admits, shrugging. "I know they never caught the guy. He must have been quite the powerful man to avoid detection for so long. Or perhaps one with very powerful friends." He laughs, but there is no warmth in it. "I admire your strength to have survived such an ordeal. Even with your scars."

His gaze darts to my hip and I subconsciously run my fingers over my thigh, my cheeks heating. Did Daddy mention my old injuries to him?

"I'm sorry if discussing this upsets you," he says. "I know it was never closed."

"He wasn't caught," I admit thickly. "But… Hypothetically speaking, what if there was no real evidence? Just the word of a traumatized little girl. A girl in the crosshairs of a powerful monster."

A girl who someone in *his* department put on Heyworth Thorne's radar decades ago.

He sighs. "Some might say nothing would matter without hard evidence." Despite his blank expression, his tone hardens, a muscle in his jaw twitching. "Others…might suggest that a little girl's testimony, no matter how fragmented, could have an impact on a jury's ultimate decision. That, all discussions of her trauma aside, she would have to testify."

"And if she couldn't?"

"Couldn't?" A harsh sound escapes his throat. "Pardon my bluntness, Juliana, but what would matter more? The police doing their duty by putting a monster behind bars or one little girl's psyche?"

The answer is obvious. Painfully so, even. But one man may have seen it differently.

He may have felt so protective of one little girl, so involved in her trauma, that the mere hope of putting a monster away might not outweigh the damage of forcing her to stand alone. Forcing her to relive the same night over and over. Forcing her to face that man without true certainty her words would matter.

Such a man might grow overly protective of said little girl. Not because she was a pawn to use at his disposal, but because he loved her more than anything. Even his cherished version of justice.

"I'm sorry, Juliana." Harrison waves something white beneath my nose. A handkerchief. "I didn't mean to upset you."

"You haven't," I insist. But I accept the handkerchief regardless, swiping at my eyes with the delicate fabric. "It's been a stressful few days. That's all."

"I can imagine," he agrees. "Your father was awake. It would be rude of me to pry, but I can only assume that he didn't mention anything that may help to track down his attacker?"

"No," I say. "He... He just told me to be careful of who I trust. In this world, who can you really?"

"So cynical," Harrison scolds. "Your father was always a cautious man. Cautious, pragmatic, but sometimes to his detriment."

Something in how he said that phrase resonates in my bones, lingering even as he steps away from me, heading in the direction of his men.

"I'll let you rest in peace," he says. "But I'll be waiting for a call from you. Oh, and, Juliana?" He pauses, his head tilted expectantly, demanding a reply.

"Yes?"

"Heyworth and I may have had our differences, but I'm sure there is one point we both would agree upon: your safety." Again, he waits, almost as if daring me to question.

"My safety?"

"Yes. I've taken the liberty of stationing my men near your suite at the Lariat as well as here at the hospital. Any visitors will be logged and searched, and any move you make, even if it's a quick trip to the bathroom, you will be accompanied by one of my men. I want you to feel protected—"

"That's not necessary," I start to say, but he raises his hand, cutting me off.

"Oh, I believe it is entirely necessary. After all, you are Heyworth's most prized possession. I'd like him to know, if and when he recovers, that your life was in my hands. Have a good day, Juliana."

"Miss?" Another officer appears by my side. "Chief Harrison requests that you stay close by. We'll be positioned just outside if you need anything. Just ask."

"Thank you," I say, forcing a smile. The moment I slip inside the sitting room, my shoulders slump. Ice sinks into my spine, solidifying it as an uneasy dread builds in my belly. Paranoia, I tell myself over and over. Reckless paranoia.

Or perhaps, amid all his lies, Damien Villa uttered one semblance of the truth: *Trust your emotions.*

***

*I*t's nearly the evening when another officer pokes his head through the doorway of the sitting room. "Good evening, ma'am. Can I get you anything?"

The question sounds harmless enough on its face. If only the man weren't wearing a uniform obviously a size too big. A Spanish accent colors his words as well—not particularly unusual for the city PD—but his eyes convey anything but the stern professionalism of Harrison's men. They shift, darting pointedly to the doorway.

"Is everything all right?" Diane murmurs sleepily, stirring beside me.

"Yes. Go back to sleep." I reassuringly run my finger along her back before standing, creeping toward the doorway for reasons I can't explain. Has life with Damien Villa corrupted me so thoroughly that I see deception and subterfuge no matter where I go? I'm almost convinced, until the officer leans in the moment I draw close enough.

"Vending machines are that way," he tells me, nodding down the length of the hall. This time of night, fewer officers linger, positioned at random intervals—but their mere presence reinforces Harrison's subtle boast. My "safety" is in his hands.

"Ms. Thorne?" The officer indicates in his chosen direction more strongly, gesturing with a wave.

I follow warily. When I reach the curve in the corridor, I don't find a vending machine. Just a hand reaching from nowhere to clench my arm and drag me into a vacant room.

"Easy," someone murmurs near my ear, their accent familiar. "Mr. Villa sent me. I'm a neutral party, merely here to see if you are all right."

"Neutral?" I whisper, turning to face the hulking figure behind me.

Julio. He's wearing his typical dark, nondescript suit and standing near the doorway of this empty hospital room.

Seeing him brings it all back like a punch to the gut.

"Do you know what he did to me?" Tears burn my eyes, forcing me to blink to keep them at bay. "No?" I ask as his jaw clenches without him offering up an answer. "For four years, he watched someone pretend to be my worst nightmare. Why?" I laugh when he remains silent. "Because this was always just a game to him. I was always a pawn."

"*Sí*," Julio says, but there's a flatness to his tone, neither confirming nor denying my statement. "But, though he sent me, I am not here for Mr. Villa. I'm here for you."

I bite my lip, unsure of whether or not to believe him. He could be lying, participating in another elaborate scheme.

But it's not like I have any other options.

"Chief Harrison has put an unofficial security detail on me," I blurt.

"*Sí*." He scowls, cutting his gaze to the doorway. "The bastards are especially…vigilant. Just getting to you was challenging."

"I don't trust him," I admit. "But I don't trust you, either. I can't trust anyone." I rip my hands through my hair, squeezing my eyes shut against the hopelessness building in my chest. "I can't—"

"I know," Julio says, his voice eerily level. "But I will confess that, while Mr. Villa sent me here, I came on my own. I wouldn't have otherwise," he adds. "But know that, for now, I am yours to command. Just say the word."

I frown. It's too tempting to consider. A trap?

Or a reprieve?

I only have a split second to decide. So I close my eyes and whisper, "Get me out of here."

"As you wish." His hand brushes mine, tugging me forward. I open my eyes as he drapes his coat over my shoulders and pulls the hood over my head. "Stay close."

SIXTEEN

*J*ulio could be lying to me—but there is no mistaking his skill. When we exit the hospital minutes later without arousing suspicion, I have a clear idea of why Damien keeps him so close.

"How do I know you aren't planning to hand-deliver me to him?" I ask as the man ushers me into the back seat of a black car. But it's different from the model I'm used to. Key differences stick out: the tinted windows and smaller blueprint. Not one of Damien's.

"I could be," Julio says as he climbs into the driver's seat. "But I think you and I both know that Mr. Villa is a bit more…direct than this method."

He has a point.

"Chief Harrison says my father was poisoned by oleander," I say. "Do you think D-Damien… Could he have done it?"

"Never," Julio says without a shred of hesitation. "If Mr. Villa were to kill someone, there would be no question that he was the culprit. None. If anything, he would have to call me in to clean up the mess."

I have to consciously keep my mouth from dropping open. "You make it seem like he's done as much before."

He doesn't answer, staring resolutely through the windshield instead. His silence conveys more than any words could, however. A quiet reinforcement of his earlier warning: *The other Mr. Villa. He is a man you have not met, and you do not want to.*

"Where are you taking me?" I ask.

"Someplace safe. Neither Chief Harrison nor Mr. Villa will be able to find you, unless you desire to be found."

It sounds too good to be true. A mythical concept so beyond my current circumstances. I'm skeptical when Julio navigates us through a district in the heart of the city, finally stopping in front of a nondescript brownstone townhouse.

"If you make a list of your things, I can procure them for you," he explains while exiting the car and circling to my end. As he opens the door, he adds, "In the meantime, make yourself comfortable."

A suggestion made all too easy by the home's simple-but-clean layout. It's a step back from the luxury of Damien's suite, but a welcome change all things considered. The small living room contains just a modest array of brown leather furniture centered around a TV.

"I wonder if it's made the news?" I find myself blurting.

Julio quickly grabs a remote from an end table and flips the television on.

Sure enough, the blazing headline sports a grim update as to my father's status, but the main footage features a vaguely familiar man standing in front of a podium instead of a shot of the hospital. It must have been filmed hours earlier, because the sun is shining behind him, casting an aura of authority my father could have only dreamed of staging for himself.

Leaning toward the screen, I struggle to catch the words of his speech.

"…honored to have the family's blessing to continue on in my campaign," he says, his lips contorted in a charming grin. "I hope to make Heyworth and the rest of the Thornes proud. I do not accept this lightly."

"Our blessing?" As I speak, my thoughts clear and I'm finally able to put a name to the face. *Kyle Harrison.*

"The chief's son," Julio says with a familiarity that makes me suspect he's delved into the man's background more than I can imagine. "Political aspirations have shaped that boy since his days in prep school. Judging from your expression, I doubt your family has thrown their weight behind his endorsement, however."

"No," I croak. "I never gave him an answer."

"It seems they took that as confirmation," he says as the news coverage cuts back to the anchors seated in a newsroom. "Should I look into it?"

"Yes," I say without thinking through the consequences—such as potentially involving Damien even further into my life. "Something feels…wrong."

"*Sí.*" He nods. "I'm on it."

He heads for the door, but I follow him.

"One other thing?"

"*¿Sí?*"

"Damien… Did he ever look into my case, truly? Or was it all just a lie?" My brain jumps to a terrifying conclusion before I can help it. "What if he knew Simon's true identity all along? Birds of a feather…"

"I admit that I am not sure," Julio says. "If he was involved, he did not utilize my skills."

"And if I wanted to confront him?" I ask, jutting my chin into the air. "Would you take me there?"

He frowns, seeming to mull it over. "Considering that I have pledged to be of use to you, it seems I wouldn't be able to refuse."

"Good." I start forward to the door. Paces away, I turn and sit on the couch instead. "Then keep him away from me. And keep me away from him."

*D*amien promised me that all of his resources would be at my disposal to aid in hunting down Simon's true identity. Now? I have only my phone, a paper towel serving as a makeshift notepad, and a pen sporting the logo of a hotel I found on the coffee table.

My scribbled notes are scattered—just pieces of information I subconsciously know I have no hope of piecing together on my own. Still, I force myself to put them into perspective.

Simon has been dead for four years according to my father.

Damien claimed he wasn't behind the continued presents, but someone else—someone powerful enough to hire skilled men every time to break into my apartment.

Men who scoured through my personal belongings and crept through my personal spaces. For years, leaving behind the ominous stench of cologne that I'd always linked to Simon…

And all along, Damien had watched.

"Don't get sidetracked," I scold myself. Drawing my knees up to my chin, I huddle against the back of the couch and continue to read, straining my eyes through the low light. The house is small, but I got some sleep in a small bedroom upstairs. When I awoke, I discovered an oversized shirt and pair of jeans Julio must have left for me, my makeshift detective uniform.

After tapping the pen on the paper, I start off with the easiest facts to comprehend: Chief Harrison claimed my father had been poisoned with oleander.

But Harrison's son is publicly claiming my father's endorsement.

Harrison also had access to my apartment.

But Harrison was also an acquaintance of my father's. I'm not sure if they were particularly close, but close enough that the man was a vague, though regular fixture at my father's events throughout the years. Could... Could he have been the one all those years ago to scribble my name onto a piece of paper that is now resting in Heyworth's security deposit box?

My temples throb, protesting the conflicting bits of information.

Then there's the matter of Lynn McKelvy. Her presents stopped when the real Simon died.

My tormentor didn't choose to continue haunting her. But why?

I'm making myself dizzy, pouring over the possibilities until my eyes burn—but reading is the only distraction I have from the low, rumbling noise gnawing at the edge of my awareness.

It's darker now. A blueish glow taints the room despite it being early in the afternoon. As I look up, a flash of white illuminates everything for a split second. And I freeze—the perfect victim for the thunder barreling through the quiet a heartbeat later.

I jump up, slamming my hands over my ears. But it's no use. I hear him anyway, no less real than he was twenty years ago.

Come out, come out, Juliana.

I see him: a shadow, lunging from the corners of the room, chasing me. Hunting me. I scream and turn to run. Escape. Clumsy limps hinder me. I'm not quick enough to avoid the edge of the end table. The glass catches my calf, sending me sideways, and I land hard, biting my tongue. A booming crash doesn't belong in my forest memories—neither does the icy pain dripping through my veins, concentrated over my right arm. But I can't move.

I can't breathe.

I just wait for the inevitable.

And, like clockwork, he comes for me.

"Juliana!" Grasping fingers clench my wrist, trying to pull me upright. "Ms. Thorne? *Mierda!* You're bleeding…" I know that voice. I think. That person…

No. He's not really here.

I'm not here.

I'm there.

I'm *there.*

Alone. I'm always alone…

"Shhh." A man's voice drips into my ear as if to directly challenge the thought—but it's not Simon's. Not Julio's, either. "Easy, *dulce niña.* I've got you."

He pulls me upright—lifting me from the floor, I realize. As I blink, the forest disappears, and I'm back in Julio's safe house.

Rain lashes at the windows, goaded by another roar of thunder so strong it rattles the walls.

I flinch, fighting to cover my ears or my eyes—anything. But someone stronger pins me tight, smoothing their hands through my hair.

"I've got you," he murmurs. "I'm going to put you down." Somehow, he manages to navigate to the couch and pivots to lower me onto it. "*Mierda!* I need to assess your arm. I think you're still bleeding, sweet girl."

Still? My eyes fixate over a swath of glittering objects scattered over the floor. They gleam, illuminated by another flash of lightning: jagged pieces of glass. Part of the coffee table is shattered. By me. Numb, I look down at my arm, unsurprised by the dark-red substance coating my skin from forearm to fingertip.

"It feels deep," Damien hisses, probing the edge of the wound with his finger. "We need to apply pressure. Here." He sheds his tailored coat and uses touch to wad the sleeve of it against the worst of the bleeding.

"Don't," I croak as he cinches my forearm in a single fist. "Let go of me. Don't touch me!"

"*¡Detener!* I'm not leaving you alone like this."

I've never heard his tone so deep. Iron.

"You're in shock," he adds a fraction softer. The fingers of his opposite hand find the inside of my wrist, pressing along the tendon. "Your pulse is weak. You feel so damn cold—"

"Like you care." I want to shrug him off, but I'm too tired. I lean back against the cushions of the couch, my eyelids fluttering. "You're a liar. So is Julio—"

"He cares for you more than you realize," Damien growls, sounding gruffer once more. His grip tightens and I hiss, feeling the faintest tendrils of pain. "I had to beg him to tell me where you were. Me. *Beg*." He scoffs at the absurdity, and through my blurred vision, I see his mouth twist into a frown. "I was worried about you."

"Leave me alone." My eyes drift shut again, blocking out his face. But not the pain. It's centered in my chest rather than my arm, however. Pulsing. Pinching. Burning. "I'll call the police—"

"You're too weak to move," Damien snarls. He pulls me in closer as if to prove it.

I can't fight him off. His heat is a vise, encasing me from all sides, squeezing out the numbing chill. This close to him, I feel everything. His hammering heartbeat radiating through his chest. His rapid breaths betraying how quickly he raced to me. His fear, pungent in the scent of his sweat.

My thoughts splinter, becoming too sharp. Too much.

"Let me go—"

"I never beg," he says into my ear, returning to that confession. "Never. I never pace my fucking suite in a frenzy. *¡Maldito sea!* I've never torn through the city like a madman looking for a woman who hides from me. I've never threatened to kill Julio with my bare fucking hands if he didn't reveal where she was. I wouldn't harm him," he says, almost as if to reassure himself of that fact. "But I still said it. Maybe in that moment, both of us believed it." His grip tightens even as he maintains the pressure on my injured arm. His breath scalds the side of my throat, his voice a low, insistent hum I can't ignore even if I wanted to. "I threatened him, *dulce niña*. All I could think about was you in this storm. A part of me hoped I'd find you standing here with a knife, ready to ward me off with violence. Unaffected. I would have left if I found you so."

Not panicked. And terrified. And weak.

"But you are only human," he tells me, his voice hoarse. "Human, and strong, and few could survive what you have. I forget that sometimes… The strength it takes. A weaker person— a weaker man—might turn off all emotion after such a betrayal. He might become bitter, and cold, and able to order murder in the same breath as he might order a meal. But you…" His lips nudge my skin, keeping me tethered despite another slamming roll of thunder. "You still love Heyworth Thorne, even after all he's done to you. You're strong enough to hold a vigil over his sickbed and defend him in public. You still fight to see the good. You believe in him, even as he hurt you."

"*You* hurt me," I rasp into his shoulder, too exhausted to pull away. "My father…he loves me. You don't—"

"Do you know when I realized, sweet girl? That I was a fool?" His voice relentlessly overpowers mine until I finally trail off. "It was when I found you in the woods. Even in your voice, I could hear it. Shock that I came for you. Gratitude. In that moment, all you wanted was someone. Me. You wanted me there. Not because of money or the many things you could extort. You were alone and you *needed* me. *Sí*, sweet girl. Such an innocent little request, and it shattered me to my goddamn core."

He nuzzles my shoulder, hesitating as I stiffen.

"I was wrong," he continues. "I was a bastard. Selfish. I don't deserve to be near you, let alone touch you like this." He slides his hand up and down my lower back anyway, gripping his fingers against the shape of me. "So you can feel no guilt or shame for using me. I'm here. Use me as your barrier against the storm. I can suffer that for you. When it's over, you will hate me again. You hate me still. I know… But I will stay anyway. I will comfort you anyway. I'll shoulder the burden so that you can protect your heart, sweet girl. Mine is already forfeit…"

I stiffen and peel my eyes open to an unfamiliar bed in an unfamiliar room. The simplistic color scheme recalls the memory of Julio's safe house. Sure enough, the view from the nearest window looks out on the same view of the residential area of the city. Safe. Quiet.

Far from the realm of my father or Damien—at least in theory.

I may be alone now, but another person left clues of their presence scattered around me, impossible to ignore. Like the blankets drawn carefully over me. As I kick them aside, I'm faced with the fact that someone removed my socks and shirt, making it easier for them—or a doctor—to access my right forearm. A crisp white bandage covers stitches, I assume. Vague images of watching someone maneuver a needle through my rent flesh reinforces that suspicion.

Someone also left a cup of coffee on the nightstand, now cold, as well as my abandoned cell phone—which could serve as a tracking device should they decide to utilize it. I grab it, intending to smash it, only to read the smattering of text messages flashing across the screen.

Diane: Stable condition. Doctors expect full recovery.

Sighing, I fall back against a mound of pillows. I should be relieved, full of naïve hopes of reconciliation and my father's health restored.

But I'm not.

Damien's words are in my head. *You love him. You forgive. Your strength.*

Love. All this time, I considered Simon's motives as hate. Hate for me. Sadistic glee at watching me suffer. A joy at causing pain—and maybe those emotions *had* driven his initial attack.

But his replacement? What would drive a man to torment a woman for years? In a way, Damien has never shied away from his reasoning: the love that he claimed kept me from becoming someone like him. Love for his brother that drove him to despise my father. Love that became pain.

And maybe the true imposter-Simon had the same motivations guiding him? Love for someone, the way my father loves me.

The theory haunts me as I climb off the mattress only to find a pair of clothing folded neatly at the foot of the bed. Reluctantly, I change into the clean sweater and pants, and then I find a bathroom down the hall to wash up in.

I look awful. A haunted shadow of the beautiful Juliana Thorne I spent years striving to be. Anything to make Heyworth Thorne proud. Anything to prove that I was worth living the life that should have been Leslie's.

Anything to hide from the trauma no one else could see.

My phone is in my grip, I realize as I return to the hall. Damien could be using it already, listening in on my indecision. Tracking my every move.

I bring the device to my ear, but it doesn't ring. I have to dial the number myself and wait for an answer from the other end.

"Juliana…" Damien sounds wary this morning. A raw note of exhaustion betrays his lack of sleep.

How long did he linger after having his private doctor stitch me up? How long did he lie in bed beside me to the point where I could still smell him when I woke up? How long has he kept his own phone close, hoping I'd call? Knowing I would?

"I can have the police there in minutes if you would like to report my actions as assault."

There's no mocking humor tainting his accent. I can't tell if he's serious or taunting. Maybe that's the point. Dealing with him is a game, pushing my heart to its limits. Knowing at any second he might caress it with the tip of a paintbrush or stab a blade through it.

"I think I know who's behind the attacks," I admit. "I think he's going to try killing my father again. Then…I think he's going to kill me."

"¿*Sí*?" A fierceness makes him sound more intimidating than ever.

"It could be you," I admit. "The one killing everyone involved in your brother's case. The real culprit behind the attack on me. You really were behind the Simon imposter. This is all your game…"

"*Sí*," he admits. "It could be me. I won't insult your intelligence by proclaiming my innocence. You have no reason to believe me."

But he's wrong. And that's the terrifying part.

"It could be Mateo," I add. "He's angry. No one would believe he wasn't capable."

"*Sí*," Damien admits. "Even I, at times, am not sure of what he's capable of."

"But I don't think he is. He's too angry. Too driven by rage. He would be sloppy."

But this killer is clean. Precise. His goal isn't to sow pain and fear —it's more calculated than that. In his view, maybe even pure.

"I think you can help me draw the real killer out into the open," I say cautiously. "But you'd risk exposing yourself and sending your empire crashing down around you. You'd have to risk lowering your precious mask and letting the world see the monster underneath. And you'd have to do so knowing that, even then, I still can't forgive you."

His silence ratchets the tension building in my chest, squeezing every ounce of blood from my heart. I'm dizzy, swaying in time with my surging pulse.

"Could you?" I croak, finally demanding an answer.

"Tell me what you need," he says. "Tell me. And I will do it."

SEVENTEEN

*A*fter I hang up with Damien and venture downstairs, I find Julio waiting for me in the living room. He stands near the now missing coffee table, sweeping what seems to be small shards of glass into a dustpan. As I approach, he sets his broom aside and faces me, swiping his hands over the front of his professional suit.

"Morning, Ms. Thorne."

"Thank you," I say, forcing the words past my thickened throat. "I'm sorry if I caused any trouble between you and your employer."

"*No hay problema.*" He waves me off and returns to his broom. "I'll clean up this mess and I have Mr. Villa's permission to move you to another location. One that he does not know of and will never discover without your permission."

I don't even need to see his face to know it's the truth.

"Why would you do this for me?"

"In some ways, it's selfish, Ms. Thorne," he admits, meeting my gaze directly. "I'm doing this for him. We had our bargain, after all."

Make Damien earn my forgiveness—not if but *when* he hurts me.

"I need a favor," I say, changing the subject.

"*¿Sí?*" Instantly, he stands to his full height, crossing his hands over his front. "Say the word."

"I can explain on the way there." I head to the door. "The first favor, though, may test your skills…"

"Oh?" He follows, raising an eyebrow. "How so, if I may ask?"

I look him over, biting my lower lip. "Well, I'll need you to pretend to be my publicist, for one."

Standing in front of a sea of reporters, I can't escape an overwhelming sense of irony. It's the world my father cherished. The world I thought he'd forsaken me for. A world of glitz, and glamor, and deception.

Despite being hastily compiled, my "news conference" has attracted enough reporters to ensure broadcast coverage—yet, in some ways, I feel no different than I did lying naked in front of a theater of strangers at Damien's discretion.

On display, yet…

In control.

"Good morning," I say, speaking into a microphone affixed to a small podium. The ballroom of the Lariat looms behind me, a perfect gilded backdrop. "My father and I would like to thank the well-wishers and those who have kept us in your prayers during this difficult time. I admit that, in the chaos, my family has been quiet, and I thank the media for respecting our privacy. However…" I clear my throat as doubt creeps in.

I could be wrong. With Daddy's life on the line, I could be placing him in more danger. I could be gambling everything with nothing at all to gain.

"After much reflection, my father and I have decided that we welcome all inquiry into the Borgetta case. There was evidence that admittedly wasn't allowed to be presented to the jury. Other suspects that deserve to be questioned. This terrible ordeal has helped my family to realize that Mathias Villa also deserves justice, no matter where its harsh light may shine. In that event, on behalf of my father, I suspend his campaign for mayor—as well as withdraw any endorsements that may have been granted on our behalf."

An audible gasp rises from the crowd.

"My father's record may not be perfect," I add, forcing myself to keep going. "We thought he was a hero, but he is only human. Therefore, I'm calling for an inquiry into all his past cases, extending to his time as a defense attorney. I think it was his intention before his health failed. The truth must come out into the open, no matter who it may touch. My father may be human, but some men become monsters. Thank you."

I turn away as the throng of reporters erupts, issuing a barrage of questions. It should be harder than it is to ignore them. Luckily, Julio serves as an effective barrier, falling into step behind me as I escape via the residential wing and enter my suite.

"I'll be out front, Ms. Thorne," he warns before retreating to his chosen end of the hall.

I enter my suite and shrug my coat off, tossing it aside. Sighing, I move to the couch, observing the view. From here Damien's painting is a chilling distraction from even the breathtaking landscape of the city stretched beyond it. The woman eyes me warily, her empty gaze a warning. *This is what he could do to you.*

Hollow.

But wait... Her irises are darker, swollen, her lips bitten red. Long, dark hair cascades down her shoulders as she writhes upon a bed of tiny white flowers. Oleander.

The painter exposed her entire body in microscopic focus. Her breasts. Her hips. The jagged scar along her thigh. Vulnerability exudes from her, matching the rigid posture of his previous muses. But there's a strength to this woman that sets her apart. A stubborn tilt to her chin. A sternness in her mouth. The artist tried desperately to capture as much of her soul as he could—but it was only a fraction. She holds on to her secrets, daring him to capture what little he could. Daring him to crave more.

It's so beautiful. So raw...

I don't realize I'm not alone until it's too late. Footsteps rush toward me as pain rips through my throat—the result of a hand clenching tight from behind.

"You little bitch." Chief Harrison sounds more amused than angry—but fury leeches into his fingertips. They dig into my skin so hard that the world goes black for a second. Gurgling noises die in my throat as I claw at his grip. I succeed in loosening it only a fraction, peeling one of his fingers from my windpipe. "How long have you known?" he wonders, eerily calm even as I resist. "How much did that spineless little bastard tell you?"

His grip loosens enough for me to croak, "My father?"

He laughs. "How did he spin it?" he wonders, shoving me forward, toward the glass doors leading to my balcony. "Him, the wonderful, doting father. You, the naïve innocent he had to protect from herself. When, in reality, he was a fucking coward."

"You told him about me," I say hoarsely. "You gave him my name—"

"I gave him a chance at redemption." He tightens his grip, drawing tears from my eyes. "A chance to bring a monster to justice. The man who killed your little friend... Heyworth represented him. Took his money and then helped him walk. And he went right across state lines and did it again."

"So you gave Thorne my name," I say, standing on tiptoe—the only position that loosens the pressure on my throat enough to breathe. "Why?"

"So he could find the abandoned little victim," Harrison says coldly. "Pump her damaged brain for information. Feed her what she needed to know, enough to form convincing testimony. Then get her into a foster home where the parents could be easily 'convinced' to force her to testify. If they lived in my jurisdiction, I could claim credit for the collar, and Thorne would have his guilty conscience wiped clean."

I picture the plan as he relays it. That traumatized little girl would have been easily manipulated. But forced to face Simon again, she would have shattered.

"He was too soft," Harrison hisses, following the same thread of logic. "Too weak."

"He adopted me instead," I surmise. "As my guardian, he refused to let me testify without hard evidence."

And in some ways, he's sheltered me ever since. Justice demanded a cruel solution, but he was too selfish. Not out of pride, but because he loved me too much.

"The prick was terrified of Thorne," Harrison says with a chilling laugh. "He taunted his other victims, but never you. Not the precious Juliana. *You* were his special one—"

"Who was he?" I wince as his grip tightens.

"Who?" He laughs again, which raises goosebumps over my skin. "You really are that naïve? Think carefully. Your father whored himself in front of any donor with money, but there was *one* in particular he never paraded you around. Do you remember?"

No… Not at first. Then, suddenly, a name comes to mind like a light flipping on.

"Gerald Wellington," I say hoarsely.

"Yes." Harrison nods. "A sociopathic degenerate with too much money and time on his hands. Rumor has it that he liked to test the innocent. Play little games. Like cornering two weak little girls, perhaps? Then making one of them choose who got to die."

The world transforms for a split second. I'm there again, trapped in the woods, running for my life. Running from Simon.

"Thorne knew who the bastard was from day one," Harrison says, chuckling at the irony. "He made sure Wellington knew as much too. Thorne ensured the man was all but a recluse, but he still played with his victims. He couldn't resist. The ones who weren't you at least."

Like Lynn McKelvy.

"So you reminded me for him," I rasp, horrified. "It was you. All this time, it was you."

The police department supplied my father's security, even during the time he was mayor, giving him unfettered access. To my room. My homes. My life.

"A little reminder in case Thorne ever changed his mind." He laughs, grinding his grip into my windpipe but not hard enough to obscure it entirely. "He may have forgotten, but you never would, Daddy's little princess."

"And the Borgetta murder?" I choke out. "You made my father suppress the evidence that could have acquitted Mathias Villa. Why?"

"Thorne told you that?" He shoves me forward and reaches out with his free hand, unlocking the sliding glass door. Cool air blows the hair from my face and I instinctively stiffen, resisting his grip even though it's futile. I have no chance in hell of overpowering him. "I should pay him another little visit—"

"Kyle killed her, didn't he?" I say in a rush, hoping to keep his attention on this topic. "His name was among the list of suspects. Suspects you refused to have questioned in full. He killed her—"

"Shut up!" He wrenches me around, using his size as leverage to drag me out onto the balcony.

I reach out blindly, grasping the railing before I can fall over the edge.

"I think it was your precious Damien Villa," he declares. "Murdering the key players. Killing your father with oleander. Causing your suicide. In fact, I'll make sure there's enough damage to your skull to obscure the bruising on your throat." He tugs me closer to the railing. Below, my coveted view looms, desolate this time of the morning.

"But it's too late. My father kept the evidence," I say. "I've already had it sent to the news—"

"Hearsay," Harrison says. He lets me go, his lips quirked, his smile chilling. "We both know that, as your father feared, nothing sticks without fucking evidence. So I suggest you jump on your own. It will be more conclusive that way."

"Evidence," I rasp, cradling my throat. "Like a voice recording? Of you confessing like some cartoon villain."

His smug expression slips, his eyebrow raising. "What?"

I nod to the interior of my suite. "You're smart. You've monitored me undetected for over twenty years. But someone else took up your game. He's played it better. My apartment's been bugged for four years. He's captured everything. Every gift. Every henchman you've had break into my suite."

"Villa?" He scoffs. "The bastard isn't untouchable. You think you matter to him? I have enough dirt to bury him *and* his fucking empire. No. I think he'll sit back and watch you die."

And maybe he's right. Maybe this was all another layer of a twisted, sick game?

Damien will get his revenge threefold and no one would ever be the wiser.

I almost believe it…

Until I hear him.

"I don't believe that will be the case, chief." His accent rides the gathering wind, more cutting than ever.

I turn, my heart stopping at the sight of him looming over the threshold of the balcony.

His hands are outstretched on either side of him, a subtle clue that he navigated here without his cane. "Step aside. Your men should be arriving any minute to take you into custody."

Chief Harrison chokes on a sound between a laugh and a growl. "Are you playing the hero now, Villa?" he wonders. His eyes cut to me, his smile dastardly smug. "Did you tell her? How you advertised her little show to the members of your club?"

My thoughts slow, my heart clenching like a fist over any blood flow.

"Oh yes," he murmurs, eyeing me lewdly up and down. "The bastard told everyone who you were. Fucking yourself like a whore—"

"Lies," Damien says simply. "You know I would never betray your trust. Never."

Even though he lied to me. Even though he let a monster creep into my life every single year for so damn long.

"It was quite the show," Harrison says, inching forward a step. "I'll be sure to leak it to the press. I'm sure that's what he wanted. They all know, you little bitch. And if you think this blind bastard can save you…"

He lunges, his hands reaching for my throat.

But they never make contact. A horrible gurgling noise mingles with a crack sharper than any I've heard as Chief Harrison's head jerks. The angle is too odd. Unnatural. His eyes stare blankly ahead, his body slumping…

As if from far away, I hear my own high-pitched whisper, "Oh my god—"

"Breathe," Damien snaps. It's his hands releasing Harrison's throat. His body that captures the massive officer as though he weighs nothing. Even without his sight, he pivots, navigating his way into my living room, the body in tow.

A chill renders me numb as I remember his confession from all those nights ago. *I worked hard to change the man I was.*

A man who moves with a predatory grace as he dumps a dead body beside my coffee table and prods the black device sticking from his ear. "Julio." He says a stream of Spanish. Then he breaks off and turns to me. "Juliana." His soft tone triggers the tears trapped behind my eyes until now.

I blink and they fall, painting my cheeks.

"Sweet, *dulce niña*." He takes a step forward and then hesitates. "I'll take all responsibility," he says. "I will turn myself in to the police. I will reveal my part in Harrison's deception. If that is what you want, I will do it now. Julio is with the police... I will."

He should be lying. It should be so easy to doubt him now. God, I want to. I need to.

"The bastard was lying," he adds, cupping his ear again, ready to dish out another series of commands. "I would never reveal you to them. Never—"

"He was there," I croak, finally placing the odd smell I sensed in the air. Cigar smoke. *Harrison,* lingering somewhere in the atrium during my exhibition. Damien even warned me himself: The chief knew to keep quiet about the club. Perhaps because he was a member all along. "He knew about my scar." And now his pointed mentioning of it makes sense. "He guessed..."

Relief visibly robs Damien's body of tension. Only belatedly does he seem to remember his promise. "Julio," he murmurs into his headset. "Send up the police. Tell them—"

"No." I don't even know where the refusal comes from. It's wrong, going against everything my father taught me about justice. But if I've learned anything at all from recent events, it's that sometimes heroes are the worst kinds of monsters. And sometimes their victims are inherently selfish. Could my father survive his ordeal and then outlast a murder trial with his decades-old secrets at the heart of it? No. "I…I want him to disappear."

"Are you sure?" His posture changes in the blink of an eye.

I'm too exhausted to nod or give some kind of nonverbal agreement. I have to say it. "Yes."

He nods and prods his headset. "Julio. Tell the police Harrison has escaped the suite. Possibly through a back stairwell. Ensure the cameras malfunction and then make the arrangements. You know the ones." He turns back to me, his head cocked, picking up my rapid breathing. "Did he hurt you?"

I can't lie. I can't seem to speak anymore, either. I stand, moisture rolling down my face, my body swaying.

"*Mierda*." He crosses to me, capturing me in his arms before I can fall. "Stay with me, sweet girl." He runs his fingers along my shoulder, inching toward my throat. When his thumb nudges my throbbing windpipe, I wince. "The flesh is inflamed. You're wheezing," he deduces, drawing his hand away. In response, his grip around me only tightens, drawing me into his chest. "If he did lasting damage, I'll resurrect the bastard just to kill him again—"

"Stop," I rasp, too limp to physically fight him off. "Just…"

"I know, sweet girl," he murmurs, bringing his mouth against the crook of my shoulder. "I've frightened you. But I'm not leaving. Not now. Not until I know you're safe."

With him? A man who killed someone in front of me? A man who smells like sin and perfection despite the persistent stench of Harrison's cigar scent permeating the air? A man who tightens his grip even further when my knees buckle and I'm in danger of falling once again?

"Easy." He guides me back and eases me onto the couch. "This is a dream," he tells me, his voice taking on a polished calm. It's colder. Harder. Broken. "I will handle everything. Just sleep, sweet girl. Sleep."

Sunlight streams in through my bedroom window, painting the muted color scheme in a golden glow. It's as if nature itself decided to conspire with the whims of Damien Villa. He told me to forget—but I remember resolutely.

For now, the dark, grisly images are mere snippets, but they linger in my mind as I stagger into my living room. Unsurprisingly, reality contradicts nearly every single one.

There is no dead police chief lying on my carpet. The sliding glass door to my balcony is closed. Every item and piece of furniture is perfectly in place. When I scan the top news stories on my cell phone, only my father's improving status makes the headlines. The only flaw in the design I notice is when I pass the fridge and spot my distorted reflection.

Gasping, I brush my fingers along my throat. The violent, purplish discoloration could be a trick of the light—but the agony I've been ignoring with every breath I take isn't.

A part of me giggles internally as I slump against the counter, my face in my hands. New memories to torment me. A new monster to haunt my nightmares. I brace my hands over the marble in front of me, and by accident, the fingers of my left brush something unfamiliar: a folded piece of paper.

On it, someone scribbled: *Julio is stationed on you twenty-four-seven unless you decide to revoke him. I've taken the liberty of removing your garbage and it has been disposed of. I'll set up meetings with any remaining mutual acquaintances. If you need me, you know where to find me, dulce niña. Otherwise, I will respect whatever boundary you set. Adios, Damien.*

EIGHTEEN

*S*ome claimed that the bigger a man was the harder he fell.

But sometimes he needed to fall. Only then, in the aftermath of the chaos, could he reassemble from the broken pieces the parts of himself that had been lost in the façade. He wasn't perfect. He wasn't a monolith of wisdom, integrity, or stellar judgment.

He was human.

And it took my father nearly a grueling month of intensive recovery to realize that. His smile isn't smug as he faces a throng of reporters waiting beyond the hospital's main doors. He looks tired and older than ever.

But in his exhausted, haggard expression, I see hints of the man who rescued me all those years ago. My old childhood hero.

"Should we face the cavalry?" he wonders as Diane and I flank him on either side, each of us holding a papery hand of his. His security team surrounds us at a respectful distance, but as we step from the shelter of the building, they provide no cover from the avalanche of questions.

"Mr. Thorne! Do you regret withdrawing from public office?"

"Is it true that you plan to publicly renounce your judgment in the Borgetta murder case?"

"Ms. Thorne! Are you still involved with Damien Villa?"

As we finally climb into the waiting limo, the metal frame mutes the noise enough for me to hear my father ask, "You're still coming to dinner, sweet pea?"

"Yes," I rasp. "I just have something to take care of. That's all."

Something that requires that the driver drops me off at the private residential entrance of the Lariat. Leaning toward him, I kiss my father on the cheek. "I'll see you later tonight."

Questions burn in his gaze even as he physically bites them back. "Of course, sweet pea."

I enter the hotel and cross the lobby. My hand slips into the pocket of my coat, withdrawing a slip of paper I'd crumpled and thrown away—only to salvage later—so many times that the font has worn away in places. An invitation to a private gallery held in a more secluded ballroom of the Lariat.

A part of me knows better than to attend. I should have been packing my things, preparing to move in with my parents at their newly purchased family compound on the outskirts of the city. I should have been helping my father prepare his public address on his role in the injustice against Mathias Villa.

Anything but inching down a deserted hallway and entering a closed room.

This showing lacks the pomp and grandeur of Sampson's first splashy outing. Only a few paintings are on display: each one portraying the same woman in excruciating detail.

I move, drawn forward to a painting hanging at the back of the space. It's beautiful, even if grotesquely raw in a way. Pale limbs were on shameless display. Scars. Curves. Pimples.

But her eyes are the most striking—almost impossibly so. Tears brim in them. And anger. And rage. A pain so raw that it takes my breath away.

"My finest work, I think," a man announces, his voice low near my ear. "What are your thoughts?"

My breath catches, and I reach out, unconcerned as my fingers brush the canvas directly. Whirls and divots in the layers of paint reveal a painstaking level of artistry. Devotion to capturing every single strand of hair. Every flaw that could be discerned through touch.

Everything about *me* in stroke after stroke.

"I'm afraid that you keep straining the theory that you are truly blind, Mr. Villa," I rasp.

"Not blind…" Fingers like silk caress the flesh of my shoulder bared by the neckline of my sweater. I flinch, but something won't let me pull away. "No man could risk being so vulnerable around you. He must employ all of his senses, *si*—an arsenal of senses to decipher you. Smell. Touch. Taste."

I shiver as his breath warms the back of my throat, creeping like wildfire.

"I'm sure even this painting portrays only a fraction."

"I shouldn't be here," I admit, blinking. "I should be…"

Furious. Hateful. Bitter.

"I know," he says. "You have no reason to forgive me, and I don't have the right to demand it."

"So why all this?" I gesture to the surrounding space. To the other paintings hanging just beyond my line of sight. "I could still hate you."

"I know," he says. "You have every right to."

"Didn't you get what you wanted? My father is going to publicly renounce his own judgment. Your brother will be vindicated. Though I'm sure you've already gotten your revenge."

According to the news reports issued earlier this morning, Kyle Harrison has vanished from his expensive penthouse home, presumably on the run given new evidence brought to light. I know the truth, however, and Damien grits his teeth, confirming it.

"So why contact me?" I ask.

"Stupidity. Insanity, perhaps," he says. "For a man with my resources, I'm not used to begging for what I want."

My heart lurches, ramming against my rib cage. "And what do you want?"

"To start over," he says simply. "I want to introduce myself to the beautiful woman who visited my exhibition and expressed interest in my work like no one else. I want her to know that I am willing to earn her trust through any means available to me. I want her to know…"

"What?" I croak when he falls silent.

"I want her to know that I will never abandon her. Whether she can forgive me or not."

Tears spill from my eyes, painting my cheeks. "I'm hungry," I blurt.

Another deliberate step brings him closer still. "Oh?"

"Yes. I'm in the mood for pizza." Turning on my heel, I move for the hall, calling back, "You have five minutes before I change my mind."

His laugh brings fluttering butterflies to life in my stomach. "As you wish, Ms. Thorne. I am yours to command."

A WORD FROM THE AUTHOR

Hey there!

Thank you so much for reading! If you enjoyed the story, please leave a review and recommend the book to any friend you think would love this twisted world. You'd have my eternal gratitude. Even a short sentence goes a long way!

Then, come join the rest of us dark romance lovers in my Facebook Group where you can get snippets, sneak peeks of upcoming books and even help vote on aspects of future novels.

Come to the dark side:
https://www.facebook.com/groups/lanasbeautifulmonsters/

WANT MORE STUFF TO READ?
Join my newsletter and get a **free book**! Plus, you get to stay updated with any new releases, random giveaways and exclusive sneak peeks!
https://www.lanaskybooks.com/newsletter

Other Novels: https://lanaskybooks.com/

ABOUT THE AUTHOR

Lana Sky is a reclusive writer in the United States who spends most of her time daydreaming about complex male characters and parenting her Cockapoo Joey. She writes dark, twisted romance across several genres. Her titles include everything from mafia romance to vampires.

facebook.com/AuthorLanaSky

twitter.com/lanasky101

amazon.com/author/lanasky

pinterest.com/lanasky101

goodreads.com/lanasky

instagram.com/lanasky101

bookbub.com/authors/lana-sky

ALSO BY LANA SKY

For more titles by Lana Sky, please visit:

https://www.lanaskybooks.com